The Last Candles of the Night

The Last Candles of the Night

IAN BEDFORD

[Lacuna]
2014

Published in 2014 by Lacuna
  http://www.lacunapublishing.com

Lacuna is an imprint of Golden Orb Creative
PO Box 185, Westgate NSW 2048, Australia
http://www.goldenorbcreative.com

Cover photograph (taken by Kalpana Ram): blackstone sculpture of the dancer Ragini at the Ramappa Siva temple at Palampet, out of Warangal
Cover design, map and text layout by Golden Orb Creative
Typeset in Adobe Caslon Pro (text) and Cochin (titles)

National Library of Australia Cataloguing-in-Publication entry

Bedford, Ian, author.

The last candles of the night / Ian Bedford.

ISBN 9781922198129 (paperback)

ISBN 9781922198136 (ebook)

A823.4

Contents

To Kalpana. To Kavita.

dilam be-dast-e-to murghi ast dar kaff-e tefli
ke na koshad, na gozaarad, na saazadesh qafasi

My heart in your hand is like a bird in the keeping of a child
Who neither kills it, nor cages it, nor sets it free.

—'Ali Sher Nava'i of Herat

Hamen khabr hai ke ham hain chiraagh-e-aakhir-e shab
We have heard that we are the last candles of the night ...
—Zaheer Kashmiri

The Nizam's Dominions, August 1947

BASTAR

Godavari River

Palampet

Warangal

Bidar

Sholapur

Bhongir

HYDERABAD

Nalgonda

Godavari River

Krishna River

Bezwada

Krishna R.

Bay of Bengal

To MADRAS

Part One :

Philip

Chapter One. Incident on the Road

1

Now Philip was home for good, Jenny had to change. She was surprised by how little was needed. He prepared his own meals, but Jenny was always fully dressed when he rose, choosing a sari from the chest. In her forty-nine years in Australia, she had seldom left the house without one. But now she dressed *for* the house. He said nothing, appeared not to notice and no doubt she exploited the occasion, Philip's re-emergence, for her own ends, and not to please him. Did Philip please her? She stood wondering. Wasn't it forced, and strange, their indifference?

She stepped, one low step, over the cement runnel of the verandah into the yard, and followed the runnel to the drain with her pan. Nothing should be poured down the sink. For so long as she made *sambar* for the grandchildren Nora would object to the splashed mess held up by the grate: fragments of *dhal* and onion, nothing to perturb her or, in this house, she would be the first to say so. It was her house. There was no man of the house.

But there were men *in* the house, sojourners, one bright grandson, one, not-so-bright, former husband but if he chose to live with her now, it was his business. She declined to make it her business and Nora, on her visits, was meant to take her cue from her mother though she blamed him, detested him, wholly on her mother's account who – for her part – felt nothing. Let him stay. It was Philip's grandparents' house, his own house, or had been, until he relinquished it: made over the deeds to his Indian wife, which was gracious of him. Her eyes fell on the dog's plate, half-hidden by the nasturtiums. She did not bend but slid it, with her foot, a little deeper into the nasturtiums. There was no longer a dog.

Where would he be now? With Jim. They'd be yarning, that men's word. She'd yarn, too, with Jim, for as long as he liked. But Jim never invited her to yarn, though he roomed here as her guest. He thought she'd produced Philip out of the folds of her garment for his entertainment. She could swear he even thanked her for Philip. A true raconteur, he called him. Events, it seemed, had made Philip a raconteur, though he had nothing to tell when she knew him. So the world had been kind. A fund of good stories, to amuse a grandson, that's what he got for cleaving for fifty-odd years to a few hard posts in a distant country, making what she called dead water, an uninhabited pond of his life.

2

Jim brought his girlfriend home. It was a Friday. But Nora – Jim's mother, and Philip's surviving daughter – chose that and every Friday as a time to visit her own mother.

Not even Jenny had met Rhondda before. But wasn't Philip meeting them all? – the whole family? – as if anew? – every time? It was an ordeal for him. There he sat, on the long side of the table, braving Nora, his eyes fixed on Jenny, who offered no protection. Just the three of them – since Jim, forewarned by Jenny, arrived late, after the meal. But Nora had stayed. Her presence threatened to spoil things.

"I'll go," she said. "Jim, this is your house. You prefer to live with your grandmother, but your mail still comes to me. Two of these notices are for traffic offences. Nice to meet you, Rhondda. Perhaps, one of these days, *I* can entertain you."

But she did not go. As if it were her sole pleasure in life and she would not be torn from it, she sat beadily eying Philip. She saw this redhead had been brought by her son for his grandfather, to grace him on his pedestal. She would say nothing, but, all the more eloquent for saying nothing, she would continue to tax him with the lasting and unforgivable dislocation he had brought on their household.

Jenny directed her former husband: "Take this pair to your room. They've brought wine, drink as much of it as you like but we won't have it here. Try not to make a noise."

Philip led them off, Jim scooping nectarines from the sideboard. An hour later, Nora took her leave. Jenny appeared, once, at the doorway to Philip's room. "I'm glad you all came. Good night."

She lingered in the passage, half-captivated – despite her self-banishment – by the booming of a voice of yore. Not that Philip boomed. The booming was all in her ears. The Nizam, is it? He's dredged *him* from nowhere.

Jenny was as little interested these days in the Nizam of Hyderabad as in any other topic in buried India. She was surprised and entertained, all the same, by her eleventh-hour discovery of how smoothly Jim's calculations had worked. He'd played this beautifully. All Jim had known to begin with – and not from her: even this datum he had prised from Philip! – was that fifty-odd years ago the youthful Army Reservist and BA Honours graduate from Sydney University had woken up headmaster – no less – of a three-teacher pilot school in an outlying district of the Nizam's Dominions. That was all Jim had, to his purpose. For a grandson with his imagination, it was more than enough. Philip, of course, had not stopped with Hyderabad. He had never looked back. For the next forty-odd years he'd climbed rungs. He took all the prized posts in education, including a head-teacher stint at the world-famous Mayo College near Ajmer. By the mid-'60s he had founded a school of his own – with two more yet to be started up. An appointment to the Public Schools Commission, a paid trip to Ghana, a senior advisory role with the Government of India – abruptly terminated in the '90s. That was Philip. He had taught school to poor tribal boys and girls, to the sons of Rajput chiefs and to a generation of trainee administrators and scholar-officials. Except for wrongs done to him, recent wrongs, these achievements of a foreigner in India were all he ever wanted to talk about – though, heaven forbid, not to Jenny. He bored people stiff. But now listen to him. Jim, and his redhead, had him tamely eating out of their hands, neglecting his grand achievements and fuddling on about nawabs and princes, 'vanished supremacies', Razakar diehard militias and his personal exposure to the squalor and violence of the last days of Hyderabad, as if youth would never end.

Jenny tiptoed from the passage. She left the stage to Philip. What she'd have overheard – had she stayed – was Philip's account of the Nizam, based wholly on report, since he had never set eyes on the Nizam. "I once thought I had. It was the week I arrived. I was taken in a motorcar to the palace, for felicitations after my job interview. When I say the palace, the Nizam in fact was hidden away in King Kothi. Quite a plain building, King Kothi, but the palace *I* saw: I can't remember it from the outside, but the rooms were magnificent. Polished wood tables, gilt mirrors to the ceilings, velvet roped curtains; there was an elephant who plodded in circles, so a lift could ascend one floor. I watched this elephant. I stared right into the lift, which was a wardrobe. Stiff tunics and *pajamas* on wood frames. People were everywhere, men with vast beards, mischievous-looking boys who had nothing to do but handle things and, I was told, Abyssinian slaves: they weren't slaves, but they were black as night. Display cases without glass panes: you could reach right in. A room full of sabres. I waited a long time in an ante-room, crowded with bearers, slaves, regimental servants or whatever they were, in my grey wool suit from Lowes. I felt like a shopwalker at David Jones. Then

a stout, formidable man entered the room. His step was so mountainous and
alert, though a trifle slow, that it had to be him. Who else could it be? I was
thoroughly prepared for the Nizam, I was braced for him; but, of course,
this wasn't the Nizam but a person with crossed ribbons over his tunic,
sleeves with gold braid, a turban with a crest or a kind of stiff quill, like
a hoopoe. His boots were tooled leather, like they once made in Queensland for Aboriginal rodeo-riders. There was no doubting the majesty of his
appearance, but, as I say, it wasn't him."

"Who was it?"

"The Vicar al-Umra Bahadur. I bowed to him, but that wasn't protocol."

"Will you show how you bowed, how low you bowed?" said Jim, but
Rhondda reproved him: "Other people know how to bow. You may not."

"The Vicar al-Umra. A distinguished person, but so they all were. He
had nothing to do with me."

"Then why was he there?"

"Why was he there? You're asking me why he was there? He belonged
there. He walked those rooms. The Nizam had his court, all the great
noblemen had their courts. His was one of them."

"Did he speak to you?" said Rhondda. "You must have had dealings with
someone."

"Mainly Englishmen."

Rhondda turned up her nose at Englishmen, but Jim was alert. "Who
were those? Part of the reform team?"

"The reform team. Health, tribal welfare, education. I was education. A
very low-level appointee, but they were glad to have me. There had to be
appointees at all levels. They were honeycombing the State with schools and
schoolteachers. They were running out of time."

"What month was this?"

"The beginning of October. The good weather."

"But already, in August …"

"You're right, August '47. The date of Indian independence. August was
behind us. India had had her independence, but not all the states had signed
up. Hyderabad was the grandest of them – and the last. That's why I say,
they were running out of time."

"You saw what was coming."

"I saw what was coming, but it was a new job."

"Yes, I quite understand new job," said Jim, who had not yet had a job:
he was a final-year undergraduate in architecture at the same university as
his grandfather so long ago. Rhondda, too, studied architecture. When they
were not studying architecture, they studied each other.

When Jim studied Rhondda he sometimes saw the need for a lesson that would take her a little out of herself, help her along. He had proposed his grandfather to Rhondda as this kind of lesson. A twofold lesson: he proposed his grandfather both as a kick-start to the imagination and as a historical prototype of himself, though he was none too sure of the resemblance, of what, besides blood, united them. "Wasn't it rather more than a job?" he said.

"What would you call it?"

"*I* don't know what to call it. I want to know what you call it. Your school in the jungle, your magical observation-post at the heart of events – when all was new. When India was a new country."

"An old country."

"However old it may have been," said Jim, "in 1947 India was a new country. It was brand-new to everyone, not just to you."

"I was in Hyderabad. Hyderabad was an old country, and it was not going anywhere."

"That's what I mean. The perfect location. Inside and outside India at the same time. You stepped into India, and found yourself in Hyderabad. You stepped, as you thought, into a bold new Republic, and found yourself in a feudal state tottering on its last legs. You bowed to the Vicar al-Umra."

"I thought I owed him that courtesy."

"The last Mughal state," enthused Jim. "Like the last unicorn – if it ever existed." Jim laughed, believing he knew how to engage Philip. Have him with his back to the wall, defending something. Of course Hyderabad existed.

"So that's what you think. I was poring over the last Mughal state?"

"No, the state fell apart. You stayed on. You survived that state."

"I was employed there. Where else would I go? Where else in India would I go? The Nizam's Government gave me the job. Nobody else was appointing headmasters my age."

"You stayed on in Hyderabad for the sake of a job!"

This *was* what Philip had said, or appeared to have said, but Jim had sounded the wrong note. Philip was unsmiling. Something about staying on? About the job? It made him seem venal, perhaps? – a time-server? To correct that impression, and to entice Philip to tell more, Jim proceeded to fill in a scenario, the complete breakdown of civil society. "Peasant revolution, invasion by the Indian Army, lifts worked by elephants, always something to see and do up to the last moment – and beyond that moment … You must take us through everything that happened …"

"What's this? Time travel?"

There was nothing indulgent about Philip's retort, and Jim and Rhondda saw at once that by laying it on thick about something, whatever it was, the last Mughal state, they had overlooked a vital ingredient of this proxy journey of theirs into the past. They had neglected the character of the man before them and his stake in his own past. He was Jim's grandfather. In the society of his family he would wonder – was entitled to wonder – what there was to be interested in besides him.

3

Philip was jarred – shaken – by their entwined assault, by the presence of the young woman. When they left, the house was profoundly quiet. Jenny kept to her room. A mantle clock somewhere – an heirloom he could not recall, but it may have been ticking away in the house since his childhood – made itself heard, stumbling eerily as if it were lost.

You stayed on in Hyderabad for the sake of a job!

I stayed because Anand was in trouble, as simple as that. I stayed because Ragini stayed.

I might have responded in a word to Jim, to Rhondda: I stayed on for friends. Friendship. They'd have had to concede. They'd have wanted to know more about these friends.

Why should it matter to them that I stayed? However did I allow them to pull me in? India is a world in itself – more than a world – but why talk about Hyderabad in the first place?

Was it because the boy was so keen? He pictured himself where I was, and he wanted to know more. He'd like to adventure, as every boy should, at his age ... In my day, it was the army, the Second World War. I missed out on active service. Was it because the war ended? I can't recall why. Young Jim would have liked to be me, or so he imagines, he'd have liked to set off. To hell with his studies, says he; but he won't set off, because of the girl. She'll keep him beside her, and I can see, at a glance, just what the temptation is. She's gorgeous.

I was wrong to give in. I must have been addled, or bewitched, to talk about Hyderabad, even to think about Hyderabad, for the first time in God knows how long.

Jim's questions had perturbed him.

In this room near the street, once Philip's grandparents', not even Jim, its last occupant, had improved by much on a layout a hundred years old. There was no longer a queen-size bed with a doll and ornaments in the centre of the room but the wallpaper, the pictures, if not those of Philip's own childhood, were twice Jim's age. What had stayed his hand? Could it have been the window-seat, with its oak carpentry and immovable 'lid'? Or had Jim been one of those children who refrain from inhabiting their room but colonise the rest of the house? That would explain why Jenny, for all her ruthless house-piety, left an unsorted pile of gadgets, pennants and sporting equipment at one end of the verandah, none of them girls' toys. Jim was born here; then he came to live here again, while his sister Vinta, nine years younger, kept to her mother's house. Wasn't that usual? Or was it unusual? Wasn't it a tradition, in this family, to live with the grandparents? Or was that just boys? Philip had had no sister. There were too few children to test it out.

That night, Ragini appeared to him. He had fallen asleep planning his next day's interview which was fixed with a curriculums expert from a church school enterprise, a person trying to get religion on the agenda.

He woke to the impression that someone was in the room, someone was prowling the room – yet not this room! – scanning its properties, the lie of the land, but without touching anything, concealing an interest. He knew as he stared that it was not this intruder who had wakened him but his shame or error in declining to speak of her, to the two who wanted to know everything. Declining to speak of her existence, and of another's existence. He had done nothing wrong but the woe of the omission – like a tune he could not get out of his head – woke him at last in exasperation, not his exasperation but the exasperation of a woe, which had sent its personal messenger.

4

But about Ragini, there was nothing woeful in the least. She roved – still without addressing him – the empty schoolroom, empty of pupils and occupied solely by the teacher, who had mistaken a holiday for a working day.

Ugadi. The day was Ugadi. Amazed at his recall, Philip sat up. The light switch was at arm's length. He flooded the room with light and the wraith vanished.

He again slept. But in less than an hour – perhaps at once – he awoke to the lit room: wine-glasses, tumblers, an ashtray for the nectarine stones, and his day clothes where he had left them, the pants neatly folded. The bachelor, widower or discarded husband entertains in his room.

He resembled all three, but least of all the second – for Jenny was alive.

Had he been willing to move, he'd have tiptoed into the corridor to reassure himself of her presence, her snarled breathing. Jenny would be there.

He lay in the dark. For half a lifetime, he had not encountered that image. He had thought of Ragini, year in, year out, but always, so far as he could, in the abstract and he had never thought of that day, the event of that day, jubilant Ugadi, the first day of the Hindu New Year in Warangal District. The first calendar day of the year, of the impossibly hot month of Chaitra (March–April), a day when nobody went to school. But on this occasion the schoolteacher went to school.

The 76-year-old Philip had a long day ahead of him. He showered and changed, unrested. These assignations he kept were like job interviews. Yet surely job interviews were behind him! He had *completed* his life's sequence of interviews, in India, twenty years ago, always with success. The would-be benefactor he now met in his home suburb of Rockdale was far more of a job applicant than Philip himself. His need was the greater, and Philip saw at once that the scheme he'd cooked up, to interest state schools in Comparative Religion with Philip as the Hindu – but why not a real Hindu? – was doomed to fail because its planner would strike the Education Department as he struck Philip, as far too eager, and – professionally speaking – as pert and small, not powerful enough. Now if it were Hillsong ... But what would Hillsong want with a Hindu? – even a Caucasian Hindu who at sixteen years old had taught Christian catechism at the West Botany Street Methodist Church a mile down the road. Philip's collaborator was a born-again, word-of-flame Protestant evangelical – though an unsuccessful one – who had lost audience, and was obliged to bring other people into his project. He was doing his best to sound ecumenical. "Now let me hear what you think."

"What I think is that two are not enough. We need to involve more religions."

"But that's what they have now. More religions. In a secular programme – which is what they have now – all the religions under the sun are allotted one period a week for religious studies."

"You want more than one period."

"I want this in the Higher School Certificate. I want to make Comparative Religion into a core subject. Is that how you think of Hinduism, one forty-minute period a week?"

This strategist – Keith Ball was his name – was as disappointed in Philip as Philip was in him. But he refused to let him go. He detained him, bid fair to restrain him, he all but implored him – yet without respect. Philip regretted he had no watch. He must travel to Merrylands for his next appointment. He peered around Keith Ball's head. There was the municipal clock on Bryant Street, another old timepiece, once as familiar to him as life itself.

Why had she come? There had been years, time and to spare, for her to come. Why now? He asked this of Ragini as if she were the agent, as if it were her doing. But Ragini was not the agent. The 23-year-old woman he had glimpsed in the early morning dark exploring blackboards and turning over equipment in a schoolroom of 1948 harboured no intentions and was not even a real person. If there was a summons, it was Philip who had summoned Ragini. If anyone was the agent, it was Philip himself – then which part of him? It was no conscious part. Philip, when all was said and done, did not believe in breaking himself into parts.

Keith Ball was recasting his entire project there and then. "I should take a back seat. I should let you draft the submission and, I'm sure you're right, we do need other religions. You decide what they'll be. I'm sure I can squeeze Christianity in there somewhere."

Philip took in none of this, but he sensed an emergency. Keith Ball was in trouble.

Why step into Hyderabad after all those years?

He was conscious of furious paddling on his own part. He remembered that Warangal Ugadi, though not much of it. It was a day he'd outlived. He'd outlived that day; there were others, too, he had outlived, had contrived to forget, fifty years and more without loss. It would be no advantage now to remember them. It was possible still to avert his mind, and he set out, actively, to do so, as if safe distance, a horizon, could be attained once and for all. Then, suddenly, he gave in. He would abandon that tactic. Face it and let it go.

An hour later, Philip was advising a party of Indian undergraduate students in the distant suburb of Merrylands. They had no paid work and were neglecting their studies. He really believed he could be of use here.

5

A holiday. Philip should have known. He was wakened that morning, not by the pre-dawn prayer from the mosque amplifier, but by the Hindu *suprabhatam*, projected at three times the volume of the Muslim prayer and (his watch showed) well before five. Just a bit quieter and he'd have lain peacefully and heard it out. But his peace had ended. He gathered his clothes but did not try to light the lantern in the pitch darkness.

There were people outdoors. The bazaar shutters were down, but a few bare globes dangled from wires in places. Had he had his wits about him Philip would have seen, by their light, what the street traders were selling, and noted the excitement of the children, infesting the street at this hour. But he did not look about him. He had only one goal: to trace the music to its source, and return to bed. When he did return – from as far as the Hanuman temple near the train station – his servant had arrived. Bashir had pumped up the lantern and was brewing tea – tea-dust, Philip called it, but he drank it. On the table, resting on crinkled paper, were two mangoes, glossy and plump, one gold, one red.

"Who are these from? From you?"

"Today spring." The servant, a Muslim, acknowledged the festival with his gift. He did not proclaim it.

Spring, they call it. Already, as Philip rode out, the temperature was climbing. The season was outlandish. How could there be spring flowers in a month hotter than the Australian January? But spring flowers there were. They were mostly cut flowers, strung in garlands or braided in the hair of girls, who were unusually scented in India. Philip dismounted and walked his bike. Women were scouring the house steps and pouring chalk patterns between thumb and forefinger in the dust. A boy on a step had a clutch of chickens, all different colours: red, sky blue, orange. Holidayers everywhere were wearing new clothes.

To persons, including foreigners, who were used to putting two and two together, it should have been plain that today was no ordinary day. If Philip failed to reach that conclusion, it was perhaps because no day in India, to him, was an ordinary day. They were all like this. Every day bore its own sign. There were days of the ritual calendar, days known to history, and all those days when nothing was afoot but something profoundly new to him was bound to occur: he had not yet divined the mystery, nor did he try to, of that boundless succession of unusual days. In December, his third month in Warangal, the few Muslim Shi'a had taken out their *'Ashura* procession with whip scourges, paper tombs and the sight of blood. On a day in February, when the news of Gandhi's assassination reached Warangal, rival groups marched in procession and heads were broken. Weekday and Saturday, holiday or no holiday, the police set up roadblocks and pursued fleeing villagers. Philip was quick to empathise – and not with the police! – but he kept out of the way. He was choosing no sides. He had a school to administer, a task baffling in itself. Warangal claimed to be a town but all this long main road proved to be, as it stretched from Kazipet station, by way of the Thousand Pillar Temple, to the ruined, marvellous 13th-century fort with its stone geese, was a string of rustic hamlets, steel telegraph poles and ponds of standing water. This sequence held the town together. But it varied in character from place to place and so singularly from day to day that even the most tranquil days seemed subtly and wholly unique and at variance with all the others, so nothing could be learned from them. Never the same secret twice.

This might explain why Philip arrived at his schoolhouse without remarking on its unusual desertion, except as an index of the lateness of others. Yet this could not be. Lateness never happened. The pupils, it was true, were often late, those that turned up. And the two assistant teachers had never arrived! But the three kitchen staff – cook, bearer, and kitchen-hand – an accountant from time to time, the peon who sometimes arranged pens and inkstands, and an infinite number of visitors, spectators, local identities, concerned relatives and others who attached themselves to the school, were punctuality itself. They were always to be found in advance of him, perhaps not all of them but enough to make a conference of every schoolday. Philip let himself in with his own key. He threw open the one window in the blackened kitchen and stood relishing the cubicle without its smoke. Then, seated behind the great desk, he surveyed the three rows of desks and forms – without yet knowing himself at a loss.

"I knew I'd find you." It was Ragini. She spoke from the door. She refrained from entering the schoolroom, not out of diffidence but in order to hold him in her sights, in the longest perspective for as long as possible.

"And I knew you'd come."

"You knew I'd come. Why is that, now?"

"I knew you'd want to ask."

"Ask? What about? About Anand? You've gone to him, then?"

"I haven't 'gone' to him." Philip left his desk to be nearer. "I did travel to Hyderabad at the weekend, and of course I saw Anand. In fact he ran *me* down – at Monty's. He'd been combing the town. He had a lot to say."

"Yes, the more he has to say, the less he has to say. I've heard it. Please don't tell me about it." She eluded his approach and stepped into the room, deep into his own territory. "Why was *I* so sure you'd be here? You haven't asked why."

"I'm always here."

"Where are your boys, then?" Ragini was inspecting the wall chart. "Today is Ugadi. It's a public holiday." With a fingernail, unlacquered and a little torn, she tapped the chart. "Since you're teaching them English, why is the alphabet in Urdu?"

"The alphabet is in two languages."

"English and Urdu. There is no need for Urdu. These children speak Telugu. Why are you teaching them two alphabets – neither of which they'll need?"

"I'm teaching them one alphabet. 'A is for apple.' Apple in Urdu is different. It starts with an S, I think," said Philip, who had barely noticed the small Urdu letters in the bottom of every frame.

"Why do you even *know* that?"

Philip decided to instruct his tormentor in some of the realities of his own position. He had gathered by now that he'd come to school on the wrong day. But the way with Ragini was to counter-attack. "I don't choose the equipment, you know. This chart is professional work, it's in three colours. It's published by the Dar ul-Uloom. They write the text-books, which are in Urdu, and I work up the curriculum. If you want Telugu, you can teach Telugu."

"How can I?"

"Because you have so much spare time, and you drop by so often … Some revolutionary! Always in the vicinity …"

"You'd like me to teach in your school."

"Please do. If you want them to read and write Telugu" – there, he had her.

Ragini would have to think hard. "If your offer is sincere …" she began. She had mounted the stair to his desk and he took her in: a beautiful woman, erect and lithe in her marine-blue sari, her delicate features clouded by effort as she turned her thoughts to outwitting him. It was no part of Ragini's condescension to decline a challenge. "If your offer is sincere, I will teach."

"On Fridays. You'll teach every Friday."

"I'll teach when I can. Those children will learn some Telugu, reading and writing. Don't pay me. I'll do this for love, the way I do everything for love."

"You do, do you?"

"Yes, for love. Why, what do *you* think, Philip? Why do I do what I do?"

Instead of overturning her bluster, Philip viewed her with a kind of awe. *Was* it bluster? To Anand, no part of it was bluster: he accepted, or swallowed, all of Ragini, her comings and goings, her insurrectionary boldness, her magical self-image. It was why she gave him no peace. Challenge her self-image – which Anand must have done, without knowing – and you opened a breach which he despaired of closing. To Philip was entrusted the work of repair; but he had no idea how to go about it on his friend's behalf.

"There is a word 'love'," he said, "and I know what I mean by it. Do I know what you mean by it?"

So little concerned was Ragini with what Philip meant by love, or with what he thought she meant by the same word – she had moved on – that she left him beached, pondering her depths. And this was a man who had earned, at the very beginning of their acquaintance, the right, the licence to make fun of all Ragini held dear: a style friendship takes in Australia, which, coming from him, and no other, pleased her very well. He, and no other, could tax her with her sublime indolence as a revolutionary.

Stationed by his desk, she was facing the street door. She glimpsed the distraction before he did. A group of small boys, noting that even on Ugadi there were people inside, had ventured into the schoolroom. The instant Philip turned, they vanished. But soon there were more of them. They clustered undispersed, marking the presentation of something, a gift for the occasion: two dishes of *payasam* from the bazaar.

The head and only teacher was disregarded. She who presided at the desk was approached first. Tugged by three fingers to the doorway and out into the bright sunlight, Ragini exclaimed, "See how your pupils look after you."

"These are not my pupils."

"We'll begin with them. In Telugu. I'll hold my first lesson."

The belt of the road where the school was – a cracked cement building, mystified and dignified by its purpose alone – was a precinct devoted not to schoolbooks and learning, but to cycle and auto machinery in small booths. One shop, in defiance of size, housed a lorry. These were hammering places. The only substantial building was being pulled down. For all the variety of notices in three languages – Brake Linings, Engine Repair, Motor Lubricants – the entire quarter was given over, so far as Philip had observed, to bashing and soldering and fender bending. But today this activity was at pause. It might even have been possible to hold a school lesson without percussion and backfire. The shop grilles – stouter by far than the shop masonry – were sunk by spikes in the earth and padlocked for good measure, a token of holiday intentions. Holiday structures had been wheeled into place: flower stalls, toy stalls, food stalls, an itinerant pile of chairs carried by human legs. From the pile two chairs were subtracted for Philip and Ragini. Ragini was as good as her word. She was about to teach.

How this situation was reversed – how they found themselves, once more, in the dark of the schoolroom – Philip was unable to establish. No one calamity forced their retreat, but a host of small events. As Ragini was addressing the children, a loftier audience – adult men and women – edged nearer. "Schoolteacher!" Philip looked up. All these were wellwishers. They had nothing to do with the school but respected its function and were delighted to interfere in its workings. He could handle Sri Sudhakar Venakataiah – who was always in the street – and, left to himself, he would have seen off an officious woman, unknown to him, who addressed Ragini in English as "Madam" and began to interrogate her, in good old unrivalled fashion which Ragini should have known was harmless. Instead, Ragini fired up. She answered question with question: "You are asking me what? For what purpose? You are a headmistress? At which institution?" The woman replied, "I am not a headmistress. I am not a schoolteacher. I am not a student. I am a person from Warangal, not a person from Bezwada or Madras Presidency. Hear me out. What is your business here? Why are you here? You are studying at which college?" Ragini responded with a flood of Telugu: her victory, or her mistake. While the two sorted things out, making them worse, the class of boys Ragini had assembled heard music in the distance. They were off. A band was playing. The pitch of the instruments – brass and woodwind, by the sound of it – wavered enticingly with the band's approach. This might be the effect either of distance, of an unfamiliar musical scale, or of erratic timing. Philip rose in his chair to have a view of the uniforms. But before he could glimpse them Ragini had seized him by the arm and abruptly steered him back into the shadow and seclusion of his own school.

Once inside, she closed the door. Not the thing, in India, to close doors on onlookers.

"Won't they object?" Philip was conscious, too conscious, of sexual mores.

"Object?" echoed Ragini, on whom this concern was lost. "The infernal woman, she thinks she knows everything about me. Where did she learn that from? – Madras Presidency! Do I look like a foreigner?"

"What did you say to her?"

"Nothing I hadn't heard from you. What's the phrase? I learned it from you. I told her, in English, to pull her head in."

"That's good, you need enemies, all you can get," said Philip. "The *kotwal*, the jagirdars, the Nizam's troops, the forest contractors and the Razakars are not enough for you. You bawl out onlookers on the street. They'll come looking for you."

"They've forgotten me already."

Ragini spoke with a confidence Philip found absurd – and compelling. The woman in the street had known too much. She was right on the ball. Ragini, to be sure, did not hail from Bezwada, a town across the border, in now-independent India. Ragini was a local, raised in this district. But for two years, she had studied medicine at a Madras college. Why she had travelled to Bezwada, Philip could not say – but she had, if only to stay a month. And had abandoned her medical studies. Such was his impression. Something to do with the Andhra Mahasabha. Philip took stock of all he knew, all he'd been told by Ragini of her life. The woman in the street knew too much, though not so much as Philip. She knew nothing of Ragini's sister, of Ragini's village, Narayanaguda, of her home, called Tirumalai, of the illness of her father, and perhaps she believed – wrongly – that the Andhra Mahasabha was a Communist organisation. It was plain she knew nothing about the person herself.

Philip had never before shared a space with Ragini with the door closed, and no-one else in sight. He should pinch himself. He'd be mad not to savour the moment. But what he said was, "You should leave now. At once."

"Please don't know what's best for me, Philip."

"I'm aware you're a will-o'-the-wisp. You can shimmy through road-blocks. But I saw the look on that woman."

"You want me to leave."

"How could I *want* you to leave?"

Ragini threw the door open. Not to depart, but to allay the intolerable heat in the room. The street noises moved in. She drifted along the walls of the room, to the alphabet chart which had claimed her attention in the first place. "A is for apple," she intoned vaguely.

"You can't teach school here, any time. They'd pick you up in no time."

"I *had* had the idea," she continued with her back to him, in a citation voice, as if she were reading it off the charts, "of taking you somewhere for Ugadi, to a place you'd like. That's the Kavi Sammelan, where the poets gather. They read out their verse; it's all in Telugu but what will you care, you'll understand. Poetry is poetry in any language. Will I call for you? – oh, no, I'd forgotten. I'm not to show my face."

"I'll come."

"Shall I arrange someone else for you?"

"No. I'll come with you."

She assented, a motion of the head. Dipping it sideways, in Warangal fashion, the opposite of a nod. It meant a nod. Glorying in his reprieve – he had dismissed her, but she refused to go – Philip returned the favour by addressing her wants, abruptly contriving her release from her ordeal of expectancy. "I did meet with Anand. Just as you hoped."

"Still upset, was he?"

"He takes the blame. He's hard on himself. You know what he's like. He makes no excuses, he accepts his share of the blame, even when …"

"Even when someone else is to blame."

"Did I say that? It's the last thing on Anand's mind, who's to blame. Who's to blame, who said the worst things. He wishes he could unsay his. I don't say yours were the worst things."

"So, your friend caught up with you. At Monty's. I can't say I'm surprised."

"What does that mean?"

"Monty's in Secunderabad. Isn't that where you two forgather? Isn't it an alehouse? – where the British get drunk? Let's not talk about him."

"Of course we'll talk about him." Philip was vexed, by the way she pretended to close down the subject – when Anand could talk of nothing else. "He was looking for me. I'm the one who drinks in an alehouse. I'm the one who hangs out with British cantonment officers."

"They're your people."

"They're not my people. But I do like a beer."

"How many of them are there? The Britishers. Aren't they all gone?"

"Who cares?"

"Of course there is Mr P. Hardcastle, the Director of Public Instruction. Your boss. He likes a drink too. It's all right, I approve of Hardcastle."

"You approve of Hardcastle!"

"You're all trying to help, but at the last moment. All these good people were appointed to help, but at the last moment, to clean up the act – you too."

Philip offered no defence.

But his conjecture was sound. It was Ragini who abandoned the topic of drink and returned to Anand. "If he thinks I insulted his Swami, I'm not interested in his precious Swami. His Swami is in gaol. So why isn't Anand in gaol? It's not hard for a Congress Party worker to find himself in gaol. All these Gandhian tactics are ridiculously easy. All you have to do is appear in public, you offer *satyagraha* as they call it, and the Nizam's police will throw you in gaol. If Anand so believes in his Swami, why isn't he in gaol in Gulbarga along with the rest of them?"

"They can't all be there. Somebody has to stay out of gaol."

"And that somebody is Anand."

"They're chosen. All the *satyagrahis* are chosen. Don't you understand party discipline?"

"Anand runs away. He bolts to Sholapur in India when his fright becomes too much for him. In and out of Hyderabad," said Ragini, who appeared to be enjoying herself; she must have been: for none of this was true. "That's some brave Maratha. He says he's a Maratha, but his hero Shivaji would be ashamed of him."

"Anand's hero is not Shivaji. Anand's hero is Gandhi, who has been assassinated. Anand belongs to a party with inspiring leaders, but with very few rank-and-file workers in Hyderabad. He has always pointed this out – to you too. He's not a leader. He's valued for his time and his work. Anand is not important enough to go to gaol."

"You're so right about 'important'."

"Anand has never turned his back on anyone. He's the most courageous person I know."

"Do you have many courageous people, in Australia?"

"Anand is fighting the Nizam, just as you are."

Anand this, Anand that. In doing his best for Anand, Philip believed he might even be falling into a trap. She was laughing at him. Seeing how far he'd go for Anand. He was about to enlist in the joke, when she placed that interpretation of his firmly out of court. She passed beyond bounds. "I think he's a disdainful person."

"Disdainful? I haven't found him disdainful."

"And why would you? What would he find to say about you? It's me he despises."

"Oh, I hardly think so."

"Let's not talk about him. *If* I'm an enemy of India, let me remain so and Anand can do battle for India. 'To right social wrongs'. And what are these wrongs? So proud he's in Congress. Did you know his Swami met Patel in Delhi? There's the man to right social wrongs. There are all kinds in Congress. I believe it was their own people who got rid of Gandhi."

"It was Hindu communalists. It was Godse."

"And do you believe there are no Hindu communalists in the Congress? Anand doesn't think so, but they'll do for him too – *and* for his Swami."

"He speaks well of you," said Philip. That sounded so mild – but it was true. Ragini should listen.

"So he does. Do you know what he says? That we're comrades, and we should sleep together. I don't mind sleeping together – that's with a comrade. He's heard me say this. But Anand and I are not comrades. You do not say of a comrade that she poses as a friend to her nation but she's really the enemy. That she's working for Moscow – just because he hears me say 'the people'. I should say 'India, India' more often. It would make no difference to what I *do*. That's what he wants of me, this comrade, to mend my tongue."

Philip listened in wonder. He was exercised by 'sleeping together', but there was more to trouble him. "What Anand said to me was ..."

"He says I'm marvellous. I know, he says it to me too. He has all these birds for me, good and bad. When he's not calling me a peacock – the bird with the tail: not a peahen – when he's not telling me I *strut* and show off and glory in a poverty not my own ... that's what he says ... when he's not telling me I'm a spy and instructing me to leave his country and claim exile in Moscow, I'm Anand's forest *kili* – his parrot. You've seen those green parrots? – not the tame ones. I'm Anand's *vanakili*. What does *he* want with a *vanakili*?"

"His 'wild bird'. He calls you this. And he's right."

"Oh, you think so? He's right about one thing. Our compact is off. Whatever he thought was 'on' between us."

"You can't mean that."

"You haven't heard him, Philip. He says I'm the daughter of a landlord. Well, so I am. Does this mean I'm working for the landlords? According to Anand, I must be. That's his logic. He tells me it's Marxist logic. I suppose he thinks: 'isn't *she* the one who's a Marxist? *Here's* sauce for the goose'. I am not a Marxist. I've never read a word of Marx. I'm a poor forest *kili*. Anand himself would not take one step into the thick of the forest, not where I go."

And Ragini lost herself in the wall-charts – for her, the only distraction in the entire room.

Philip, having stood stock-still, now found himself wandering. He corrected the angles of all the chairs behind the boys' desks and surveyed the teacher's desk, on its dais, from the floor. That dais reached the wall and was Ragini's proud eminence, as she scanned the charts – stalling, she must be! He gave her time.

She did not use the time. She stepped down abruptly and crossed, without warning, to the open door. There she turned. Stranded among his pupils' desks, Philip called helplessly – it was all that came to him, "You don't 'strut'. He's wrong."

"Who says I strut? Oh, Anand."

"How can he have got you so wrong?"

She was on her way out, but she lingered. She had sensed nothing odd, though Philip, artless in his admiration, was distinctly aware that he had put his foot in it. What was more, he was unable to stop. "I think you alarm people."

"I what? I alarm people?"

"They misunderstand you."

In the silence that followed, Philip improved on this insight. "People are afraid. Not *of* you, but *for* you. They can't live up to you. And they can't save you. Anand is typical. He knows you're the daughter of a landlord but he sees you vanish into those dark forests, and he asks what it's for. I don't say *I* understand you. I've heard you explain. Injustice. Murder. What's done to village women by the forest contractors. I've seen you armed. That day you stepped into the clearing and you were carrying something heavy, a bolt-action rifle. But the police have Bren guns."

"I was not carrying a rifle."

"We don't know how to call you back."

Even as he spoke, Philip was visited by the notion that he was so far out of his world, and out of his depth, that his grandparents, cousins, classmates and his former girlfriend would not have recognised him. If words of his were somehow to be recorded, and circulated among them, they'd bawl with one voice: this grandchild, apple of our eye, prize student and disloyal lover, is raving. What police, what forests and what Amazons with rifles? Is there such a country? Some woman has swept him off his feet.

Ragini had her question. "Who is this 'we'?"

"Did I say 'we'?"

" 'We don't know how to call you back.' Who is this 'we'? You and Anand?"

"Leave Anand out of it."

"The 'we' is you then. And why would *you* call me back? What business of yours is it? Why detain me?"

"I didn't mean to detain you. As if I'd detain you. I think I meant …" Philip lurched on, "I think I meant to accompany you."

Ragini rubbed her eyes. She touched her forehead. "This heat is bothering me. You'd suppose I'd be used to it, but I'm not."

"You heard me. I said what I said."

"And what was that?"

Philip considered repeating his words over. He was unable.

"If you mean to accompany me, Philip, accompany me to the bus station. I've clipped my cycle to the rack at the bus station. Will that be enough? Or do you mean to accompany me further?"

"Further," croaked Philip.

" 'Into the valley of death', I suppose you mean."

He was in a fix. And had placed Ragini in a fix. Yet the fix he was in was the fix he deserved, whereas in her case, her fix surprised her. It had come out of nowhere, and was evanescent.

"Is there something you believe you can do? Do for me?" she said gently.

"Not really," said Philip humbly. "Just be with you."

"Be? How?"

With her next words, Ragini's tone changed. It held, now, an acid note, a mocking note, which did not seem to be meant for him personally but to outsoar him, leaving him neglected. "Shouldn't you have asked for more?"

6

Asked for more! But he had not asked for more. He had stuck by Anand, stood up for Anand. She had nothing to reproach him with.

Why had she come? After fifty years, why had she come?

Philip lay where he was thrown – at the bottom of a well. He did not flinch or stir. In the house at Gibbes Street, Rockdale, there was no more he could do. At this point his memory – event-perfect, like a recitation – knew its limits and evaporated.

As the slow pieces, the lumbering furniture of the room emerged into view – the bed, the window-seat and the armchair, which had caught fire from a radiator when he was nine and had had to be re-upholstered (he recalled its former pattern) – the schoolroom at Warangal could not have been further away. Yet the past of this room was more distant than the past of the schoolroom. Nothing, to Philip, was more inevitable than this room. It was his grandparents' room. Now Ragini had appeared in this room! He stirred at last, and busied himself. He ransacked the kitchen for the tea-canister and made tea at the stove.

He clung to this safe activity. He warmed the pot. He fetishised the brew. He avoided, and tried to discount, what he had remembered. He was surprised at the fluency of that memory, how surely and easily it had unfolded, haunted by foreknowledge, but withholding its rebuke till the end. *Asked for more*: but he had not asked for more. If that was her rebuke, it was a light one. Was her rebuke all there was? Or would memory plough on? Would the past return, or strive to return? Even if it did not return, would he seek it out? Would he seek to learn more? Was to seek more simple prudence, or an act of defiance, defiance of some power? What power? He did not know what power. There was a kind of foreboding. Nothing too bad, he hoped! Nothing that could not be forgotten – as it had been, for most of a lifetime.

You defer a pain, you might not submit to a memory for a lifetime – but its vigour is intact.

If that were true, there was pain you would never come to know. You would die hoarding it. You would hoard and deny this pain, put it off: you would die happy.

7

Why had she come?

When names aren't asked for – and Jim hadn't asked for names – there can be no denial in refusing to give them. Jim had spotted no denial. But why refuse? Why disown Anand and Ragini? Something in memory would explain this omission. But why should he have to search, to belabour memory? Shouldn't he just know? There *was* a kind of looming awareness – as if of a betrayal. But Philip had betrayed nobody. He had nothing to repent of and what dismayed him in that schoolroom episode – on the surface, at least – was no misdeed of his but the revelation of his insignificance, his absolute insignificance in their lives, in the life of India, and perhaps, definitively, in his own life – though he clung to his life.

His want of importance, his thistledown unimportance and want of stake. The moment this secret was out, the life-force in Philip rallied to disprove it. Ask anyone in India, they'd have shown you a life teeming with accomplishment. It was only as he stood on the brink of a new beginning, a new and perilous beginning in his native country, that the fear of his inconsequence was borne in on him. It was *this* that brought Ragini: the emergency of the hour, his present crisis. He did not like to think of it as a crisis.

As for the schoolroom, the event was over. Why, then, was it *not* over? What of other events?

The image came to him of a road in the Warangal district. By that road Philip was voyaging, from Warangal to Hyderabad, for the first time since his appointment to his new job. It was December 1947 – long before March '48, the event of the schoolroom. A bus, without driver or conductor, stood pulled over on the roadside. He, Anand and the rest of the passengers had been forced off the bus. The midday sun blazed.

Philip and Anand were bareheaded. They stood with the others listening to an endless harangue – in Telugu, foreign to them both. Anand, though born and bred in the Nizam's Dominions, hailed from the districts where Marathi was spoken. But he stood as if weighing every word.

Philip, too, weighed every word. He weighed every pause, every gesture, for signs of a resumption of journey. Had he and Anand moved, inched their way, to the shade which was visible as an outline, a pattern of leaves on the bare ground, they'd have set off some fruitless commotion, endangering the passengers as well as themselves. All their fellow passengers were villagers. None were townsmen. And the party of ambush were villagers, or appeared to be. Philip wondered all the same at the remarkable difference in being, like a difference in human kind, between the two sets of villagers who otherwise resembled each other in every respect: poor, dark, scabby-legged. One party knew what they were up to, and the other did not. The gulf between them seemed all the wider because the gang or *dalam*, who had emerged in ambush from the bushes lining the road, were at such pains to close it. The orator and his free-strolling companions, like the bunched audience, endured the full heat of the sun. They did not seek the shade.

"What's he saying?" Philip contrived to whisper. One of the gang – there were only five – had noticed his tailored pants, his shirt with long sleeves rolled up and, above all, the boots, and was staring at him. Philip did not stare at this individual. The *dalam* appeared to be weaponless, and were far outnumbered; but there could be no thought of taking them on.

Now the passengers were freed to disperse. They were not permitted to rejoin the bus, which was boarded one after another by members of the *dalam*, who may have wished to see for themselves what the interior of a state transport vehicle was like. Rather than move to the shade, the passengers, and the bus-crew as well, entirely to Philip's surprise, trailed along the road. They reached the bend of the road and rounded the bend. They were not prevented. Philip and Anand joined the trek. One of the gang swung from the boarding-step of the bus and followed at a distance, keeping them in sight.

"Why are they letting us go?"

"They're not letting us go. Where would we go?"

Anand knew no more about it than Philip did. Once round the bend they saw, not far away, the booths of a market-village, which appeared to be thriving. "There'll be a grain store," Anand now decided, "and a telegraph office. They *are* taking a risk."

"Will you phone the police?"

"Phone the police? The Nizam's police? I'd as soon phone the Razakars."

"They're harmless, to us, I think," said Philip, referring to the gang, and not to the police or the Razakars.

They walked on. Thin jungle, on both sides of the road, was cleared in places and in one of these clearings a small boy sat alone by a pile of flat stones which could only have been dumped from a lorry. He was beating stone on stone, without much dinting them but with the effect of an intricate rhythm to which he sang – in a formed voice, no infant treble. A kingfisher, a gorgeous green, light-green at the throat and with a bit of russet at the head, darted from a thorn-bush. There must be paddy-fields somewhere, to account for the bird. "They're harmless to us. The only real *harm* they do is to themselves," said Anand, declaring his opinion at last.

"What are they? Communists?"

"If they're Communists, we'll see at the *mandi*. There'll be a hammer-and-sickle on every building. I think they're Communists. The reason they've let us come so far is that they own the village."

"Own the village?"

"They occupy the village. Not all the time, but they depend on these villagers. But they're too near the road. The police will come. They're taking one hell of a chance," said Anand as if he, a rival in politics, would take no such chances. "I've seen them like this outside Warangal: standing around, unconcerned, in broad daylight, as if they were immortal – I don't understand it. I don't understand this way of fighting."

"So your people don't just stand around, they offer *satyagraha*. The gaols are full of them. How many Congress workers are in gaol as we speak?"

"Swamiji may call it off. He's beginning to think it's the wrong tactic."

"And where is Swamiji? Isn't *he* in gaol?"

For a newcomer and outsider, who knew nothing about right and wrong tactics, and least of all in Hyderabad, where both the Congress and the Communists were banned, Philip – in Anand's company – found much to say. He expressed his views, poked fun and made light of matters. And this was encouraged in him, for the sake of friendship! Philip had discovered a friend like his friends in Australia: one rather better informed, entrusted with weightier responsibilities for his tender years, but alike! – and at times perplexingly different. The marvel of it all was that Anand, from their first chance meeting, had gravitated to Philip like a snake to an anthill. They entered the market square. At one stall the bus passengers had gathered and at another were the driver, the conductor, and the driver's companion, a fixture on these buses. Companions were a part of the scene in India, whoever you went looking for and whoever helped you look. The doorman, the mechanic, the doctor, even the cycle-rickshaw driver had his companion. For every incumbency, its shadow. Both Anand and Philip would have liked to confer with the bus crew about what they thought was going on – but they did not have the Telugu language. Anand tried in Urdu and was met with a single word: *badmash*.

"If they're *badmash*, then why aren't we dead? All those words wasted," said Anand. "That speaker of theirs poured his heart out, but to the conductor they're still *badmash*."

"They're *badmash* to me."

"The passengers were the real audience. I wonder what they think."

The fare at these stalls, to Philip, was not very appetising. Wherever something looked appetising – a basket of moist dates – the flies buzzed. But he did like the square, the bare earth pounded by generations of bare feet, the procession of trees with shaped leaves, like the trees in watercolour miniatures at the old British Residency in Hyderabad – he must learn trees' names. A handful of people, not enough in the market at this hour of the day for real haggling. Sun-dazed, the entire spectacle. But there, parked under the trees at the very margin of the scene – beyond the whitewashed storehouses, all inscribed with the hammer-and-sickle and with messages in two scripts, Urdu and Telugu – was a vehicle, a bus like their own, the sight of which, before he knew why, lured him. Anand placed a hand on his arm. "Not there. Don't go there. Aren't you thirsty?" – and Philip *was* thirsty, thirsty enough to accept and drain a soft-drink, unrefrigerated, from a dubious bottle. And then another. Wasn't that an all-woman bus?

Philip disregarded the warning and approached the bus. How cheering, the cluster of rural women surrounding the bus in their bright *cholis*, red, green, matched with the subdued colours of the saris draped over their shoulders, their brown midriffs bare, legs swathed to the ankles, arms stacked to the elbow with coloured bangles, the flash of jewelled nose-rings and toe-rings, the beauty of their features which were all of a kind, that aquiline beauty he had inspected in the miniatures from Golconda in the Residency collection. Telengana women. They were happy to greet him – what was Anand's warning about? Then he saw. At the open windows of the bus, not at one window but at successive windows, like a frieze of nodding flowers, heavenly enticements, a sight appalling in its majesty and beauty: he turned away. A vision no man should contemplate – except in his imagination. Anand consoled Philip on his return. "Don't be put out. You're an Englishman. I don't mean Englishman, you know what I mean. A kind of blundering fool. You can get away with it."

"*We* call that 'peeping tom'."

"What a good word for it." As Anand hustled him still further away, a lorry, its carrier space filled to bursting with sashed and turbanned figures bristling with weaponry, bounced at speed along the unevenly tarred road that bordered the square and vanished in the Warangal direction, rounding the bend. Anand affected to take no notice. "Where there are women, there are babies," he said. "They all need feeding, or they set up a wail. Don't be ashamed. That was mortifying, but we need people like you. Let me tell you why we need such people."

But Philip had ceased to listen. "Who *was* that? Police, or ..."

"Or Razakars? That was the police. The Razakars have much better uniforms."

Philip was blinded by an after-image, not of the police lorry, but of the windows of the all-woman bus: a confusion of naked breasts, of gaping or feeding infants. With their placid, silent dream-countenances, these mothers were nothing like the mothers he knew. The mothers he knew did not chew betel or expose their breasts. He felt that it was somehow his duty to reappear at those windows and explain something, explain himself, to this universe of women.

"Expensive, too," said Anand, still referring to the Razakar uniforms.

"We don't know who pays for them. Perhaps, where you're situated, you can find out."

"Where I'm situated? At the school?"

"Let me tell you why we need people like you. We need the kind of foreigners in India," said Anand, "who won't be put off, people who butt in and out wherever they like out of sheer ignorance. People who will always be forgiven."

"Who needs such people?"

"They're needed by the nationalist movement. They're needed for their access to government."

Was he speaking in jest or earnest? Philip could not be sure. "Who pays for the Razakar uniforms, is that the question? You want me to find out in Hyderabad. You want me to spy for you!"

"I don't mean spy on the Nizam, the Nizam is nothing. The Nizam is too stingy to pay for uniforms, even his own. I mean Laiq Ali, or his Cabinet, or a Cabinet Secretary. You must know someone."

"I know Englishmen. I don't know any Cabinet Secretary."

"Englishmen! We're back where we started!" But just as Philip was sure that his leg was being pulled, that this was not a serious request, Anand changed his mind for him. "We do have very poor intelligence where government is concerned. We don't know what they'll do next. We were sure the Nizam would sign the Standstill Agreement. But he took weeks. What were the obstacles? What happened? They're unpredictable. But they know all about *us*! Congress decision-making in Delhi is splashed all over the Urdu newspapers."

"I'll hear what I'll hear. I won't go looking for it. You've heard my objections."

"Objections? It's a cruel and murderous administration. Do you think of that?"

"It's not all cruel and murderous."

Anand gave up for now. He bowed faintly over his matched hands, to show he despaired of Philip. A shallow explosion, a burst tyre or motor exhaust noise, reached them from a distance. Then came a second; then two more. His few weeks in India had made Philip all but impervious to auto sounds. But Anand was alert. "Those were shots."

Already the square was shaken up. The stall-keepers and stall patrons stood their ground, but the bus passengers were scurrying on the spot like disturbed ants. The crew, alarmed for their vehicle, had taken off in the direction of the shots. "We'll all go. Or shall we stay here?" Philip darted a swift glance at the women's bus. The same still faces. The mid-afternoon stillness reigned as before, with one difference: a puny gramophone, whose turntable had been revolving unnoticed in a stall, was now audible. Someone had had the patience to rig a loudspeaker.

"You go." Anand mimed his own fixity, his face and hands motionless, his feet planted. Philip inferred that neither Anand, nor anybody in his right mind in this part of the world, would go where police were. Unless, of course, they had a bus to retrieve. It might have been sensible for Philip, too, to remain where he was, yet, for reasons unclear, to set out in the wake of the bus crew seemed right to him. It was somehow a test of him. He might do some good.

8

Anand let him go. With Philip occupied, he retrieved full authority over his person. He slipped the leash of Philip's imagination, and thought and acted as himself.

Philip would come to no harm. No-one would shoot Philip, not because he was an Englishman (he was not) but simply by the law of averages. Anand watched him to the bend of the road. The moment he vanished, Anand sought the company of his male fellow passengers and began to speak with them, not in their native Telugu but in the language, Urdu, of which even villagers in the Nizam's Dominions had a smattering, Anand less than most. He often corrected Philip's Urdu, so had not wanted to expose his weak skills to Philip. Yet he was desperate to converse, to learn something.

He had barely got started when Philip reappeared. He arrived at the double, with an out-of-breath, badly shaken colleague whom Anand identified as a fourth member of the bus crew, who had stayed with the bus. Philip did not approach, but waved. The two vanished into a shop on the near side of the square and emerged soon after carrying a not-so-light object, a charpoy, kept aloft over their heads by arm-muscle power. This load had already descended on the head of the exhausted messenger.

They started back the way they had come. "A man is dead," suggested one of the passengers, but Anand heard himself correcting him. "Perhaps he's alive. Perhaps he is only hurt. Leave it to the bus-crew. We have no reason to stir from this place."

"If it is a *baghi*," said another passenger, speaking in Urdu for Anand's benefit, "they will let us go. We will reach Hyderabad by evening. If it is police …"

"Better a *baghi* shot than the police," said Anand, profaning his own opinion. These men were not sure. Not knowing who Anand was, they would not show their hand. So it had been for him through the whole of Telengana.

"At least we will soon have India," he said. His statement was received in perfect silence.

But these people were Hindus. They couldn't want the Nizam. Was it the *baghi* they wanted? Anand's gaze slid along the walls, from slogan to slogan. He read, in Urdu, *jumhuriyat*, 'democracy'. What did the word mean, to them? The word was accompanied, everywhere, by the hammer-and-sickle. It could not mean what his mentor, Swami Ramananda Tirtha, or the Congress high command thought of as democracy. Who would want this *jumhuriyat*? A few commissars. This answer, which might do for Russia, was perhaps not adequate for the Communist Party in Telengana. Anand was out of his zone. There were few, or no, Communists in the Marathi-speaking districts, from which he came. But all over Telengana the villagers scrawled, or allowed to be scrawled, fierce messages on their walls. These dirt-poor villagers looked forward, or appeared to look forward, to their *jumhuriyat*, and perhaps they knew, better than he did, what they would make of it.

When Anand, at his party's request, visited the badlands, he dropped by Philip's school. He had met Philip, not in Warangal, but in Hyderabad. Because Philip was an absolute stranger to India he had accepted a job, out of sheer ignorance, which he would never have been offered in his own country. He did not know the half of it. Not knowing the half of it, his role, as Philip saw his role, was a benign one. It was amazing to find such a school, in such a place, run by such a person. Who went to it? Who sent their sons (there were no daughters) to Philip's school? Philip of course had no idea. The question had not occurred to him. Anand looked in at the school and sat down on a form. He did so as Philip's guest. But if Philip came to Marathwada, would Anand receive him as a guest? He would not. Not because his family was poor, and not because Anand, the only son, was a graduate and his mother doted on him, and Anand lapped it up. Friends were one thing, family quite another. He did not want Philip to meet his father and had not the least intention of introducing him to his unmarried sisters.

The afternoon wore on. Those male passengers who had straggled were reabsorbed, by a collapse of will, into their bunched family groups. Anand toured the stalls, gulping soda-water out of bottles, all with a curious glass-marble stopper, and relieved himself under a distant tamarind where a goat was tied. In this market were carpentered booths and brick grain-storehouses, but no 'shops'. He could not find where paints were sold. The idea had crossed his mind – though it would be folly – to replace some of the wall messages. So great was his frustration, and a kind of dejection, that he'd have started a bonfire if he thought the blaze would bring India any closer. Far loftier to be thrown in gaol, as a *satyagrahi,* than to tour these alien districts as a Congress 'observer' – only to court criminal arrest with a paint-brush in his hand.

Reprieve at last. The bus appeared, two figures leaning from the pole at the boarding-steps. One was the boarding-team assistant and the other was Philip. The families climbed aboard. Philip now vanished down the bus, saving a seat for Anand. His rushed forays into the aisle, his lively expression, his impatient bodily attitudes were enough to convince Anand, boarding slowly behind a family redistributing its luggage, that he had a tale to tell. Unlike an infant, Philip did not bawl it all out at once. He crafted his story. He led Anand through the chain of events, his return visit to the market to snatch a bed, his pounding his way – unable to communicate with his fellow Samaritan – back to that hold-up point in the road. Philip had anticipated a body, but the scene was all chaos and action, the police with their service rifles diving into the bush and emerging without a prisoner or trophy of any kind unless, thought Philip, they had someone in the cabin of their lorry. He tried to peer in, but his companion took fright and prevented him. The bus crew reclaimed their bus. The police posse was called in from the bush. They sped off in the direction of Warangal. It was only then that Philip thought he spied blood on the ground. "Either they wounded some-body – and he got away, or he did not get away …"

"We'll suppose he did," said Anand, to put an end to the matter.

The bus was in motion. Philip would not be hushed. He implored Anand to inquire of the bus crew, but what good would that do? The crew, too, had been late on the scene. Their only witness, the assistant who had run for the charpoy, spoke nothing but Telugu and had slumped over a luggage rack in exhaustion.

"I know I saw blood. I do hope they escaped, but who were they? Pulling over a bus in broad daylight. I call that foolhardy."

A voice chimed in. "Listen who's talking!"

A woman's voice. Philip whirled round. He could see nobody.

Anand located the speaker, seated so plainly on the seat behind them.

She was a young Hindu woman, a little bedraggled in her green cotton sari but so absurdly beautiful that Anand forgot to draw breath.

"Philip, you're surprised it's me."

"Ragini. *You're* here. How did you join the bus?"

"I was always on the bus."

This could not be true. The bus had been emptied out by the *dalam*. But Philip – who had looked the wrong way, who was still gaping in mid-air, as if she flitted there – did not correct her. It was not where she had sprung from, nor when, but the fact of her being there that so impressed him, that impressed both of them.

Anand was the next to speak. "You're Ragini."

It was not for such a magnificent creature to own to herself. Philip rose to the occasion. "Anand, this is Ragini. You two have to meet each other. She comes to the school."

Ragini, hearing Anand's name, did not seek to confirm it of him. "But why aren't *you* at the school?" she asked Philip. "You should be. It's term-time."

"Term-time or not, I've shut down till next week. I have to make my report."

"Your report, to whom?"

Philip knew this to be a dangerous question. "The usual people. The same people as usual," he said vaguely.

"And those are?"

Heartened and entertained by this line of questioning, Anand again found his voice. "*You* try talking him out of it," he said. "The Nizam's people. He shouldn't be teaching school, not for them."

"But he's a born teacher."

Philip, the object of dispute, looked from one to the other.

"I've sat in on one of his lessons," Ragini declared.

"Do you really think these lessons will continue," said Anand, like a batter returning the shuttlecock, "once the Nizam's Government is out of the way?"

"The Nizam's Government. You hope it will fall."

"I'm working to that end."

"Anand is working to that end for the cause of India," said Philip, so completing the introduction on both sides. "But he's found it hard going in certain districts. I don't believe too many people are listening to him."

"I'll listen to him. What's this about India?"

"India is the name of our country. India is our nation," said Anand, thrilled by his new audience though none too pleased with Philip's brief digest of his adversities. "In places where this truth isn't known – there are still a few places; Hyderabad is one of the biggest ..."

"*The* biggest," said Ragini.

"I'm a Congress worker. I tour the districts for the Indian National Congress." Anand broke off. He had not meant to come to the point quite so soon. As in cricket, for a demon bowler, a short wind-up was necessary. But what most wrong-footed Anand – and Ragini, who perceived it – was a change in the motion of the bus. It was slowing down. After barely two miles, they were being pulled over yet again.

"More police," said Philip. This time no lorry. But a van, uniforms. A senior officer, judging by his braid, and his constable climbed aboard. They spoke not a word, not even to the driver. They glanced without close inspection at the row of seats, and left morosely and abruptly, like men deceived. The journey was resumed.

Enduring this interval, Philip observed a detail in Ragini. Not just her agitation, as a lone Hindu woman, which she did well to disguise, but a surprising detail. "Have I seen you wear jewellery before?"

Ragini pointed to her nose-stud. That she always wore.

"No, no. Are those your best clothes?" He thought not. "Then why the jewellery? It makes you look ..."

Anand would dearly have loved to supply the missing epithet. There was absolutely nothing wrong with the clothes, with the *choli* and sari, which were colour-matched: well-worn, but, of course, she'd been travelling. Nor could he object to the earrings. These dangled, resplendent, like something from a trousseau. Anand wondered, a trifle anxiously, if Ragini was married. She wore the *pottu*, the dot on her forehead, like all Hindu women except for widows. He was shocked by Philip, who acted as if he divined something. How did he come to be so free with her?

"Now you must admire these." Ragini, to Philip, held out her wrists and forearms. "Normally it's just two bangles, the chunky ones. Now see how many."

"I like them."

"They're not for you to like or dislike. They're not for anyone."

"For the police, perhaps?"

"They're to fool the police. You're right. The earrings to show I'm a respectable person. The bangles to show I'm an authentic person. You do see why."

"I can guess."

Ragini switched her attention to Anand. "Because I'm a woman, I'm dangerous to the police. All women are dangerous, but not all women have to appear dangerous. You see these *ammalu*, on the bus, with their families. All these women are wearing jewellery."

"The worse for them," said Philip, "if the Razakars come."

She ignored him. Her rebuff was intended. Ragini was afraid of his speaking out of turn. She did not want Anand to know the first thing about her.

Philip saw this, and held his tongue. Yet even if he blabbed, there was little enough he could tell. From the day Ragini appeared in his classroom (he had first thought – heaven help him – as his teaching assistant!) she had had the air of knowing him only too well. They could speak, directly, of whatever popped into their heads. But except for father and sister, and despite her infrequent tales of the medical college at Madras and of the two nursing hospitals, in Madras and Warangal – one outside and one inside the Nizam's Dominions – he had learned nothing confidential, since she rarely confided. She belonged to the Andhra Mahasabha, a revolutionary organisation. She rode a green bicycle, she told lively stories of her forest rides, she came and went. He sensed her relief on her visits, an abatement of watchfulness – as if she assigned to Philip a recreational value.

Ragini, "always on the bus", had not been on the bus at Warangal and had not been on the bus when it was intercepted. This left one place where she could have climbed on the bus.

"Are you a student?" she asked Anand.

"Do I look like a student?"

"No, answer me. Are you a student?"

"I am a graduate," said Anand shortly.

"Graduate already. So you must be high up in the Congress Party."

"I am not high up." And it was not as a graduate that he meant to appear. Anand felt the initiative had been taken from him. For Ragini he described his posts, of which Warangal district was only one. In the Kannada-speaking districts, he watched Bidar airfield, from time to time, on the trail of the Cotton brothers. Anand's account of himself was more halting than usual. He was all but tongue-tied. And yet he was feted for his eloquence in a number of places. His mother and sisters thought of him as a marvel, but they were not all. As a follower of the Swami, he was credited, in Hyderabad Congress circles, with a silver tongue. Two silver tongues – one speaking English, and one Marathi. Yet far from moving Ragini with his pro-India, pro-Congress oratory, he seemed only to awaken her skepticism, and – could it be? – her boredom, though she plied him with questions. The listener with whom he struck a chord was Philip. Philip was amazed to hear that the Cotton brothers – two of them? three of them? – sometimes landing at Bidar airfield, and widely supposed to be flying in arms and supplies for the Nizam's besieged government, were Australians. "Don't you go near them," warned Anand.

"Go near them? I'd never heard of them. No-one has seen them. Have you seen them?"

"No."

"Have you seen their plane?"

"Hobnob with the Nizam all you like," said Anand, knowing full well that Philip was as far from the Nizam as he, on his airfield vigils, was from the Cotton brothers. His voice held a stoniness, a displeasure, which was as little lost on Ragini as on Philip. Yet neither attributed it to its true source. Ragini's ease with Philip, her reluctance to accord to Anand even a fragment of the esteem he owed to himself, as a Congress worker, was enough to deprive Anand of his dexterity as a social being. It was he – not Philip – who was made to look a foreigner in the land of his birth. 'Student' in India should be a thrilling word. Instead she treated him like a minor. Anand talked too much and risked making a bad impression on Ragini: while she, who spoke little, sublime in her silence, made on this freedom fighter an enormous and ever-growing impression.

9

A further police roadblock emptied the bus. One of the passengers, exasperated now beyond measure, quarrelled with a scared-looking constable in ragged uniform. *All* these police looked scared. Such an intimidated-looking corpus of armed men was rarely to be found and the three companions relished the sight, one with irony, one with his usual bafflement, and the third (Anand) with contempt. These were policemen? The dissident passenger, released from questioning and allowed to rejoin his family, relayed in a loud voice all he had been told, or had managed to infer.

Towering over them was a granite monolith, ghost-pale in the advancing twilight. The rock of Bhongir. "How can they be looking for Razakars?" said Anand. "No Razakar would dare to show his face in this *ashram*. Not even the police have the courage. I'm surprised they're here!"

"Only by day," said Ragini.

As if to confirm her view, the police were dismantling their dusk roadblock in extreme haste. They threw trestles and markers in the back of their lorry – which was, at least, freshly painted, with a legend in Urdu – and sped away. But a new setback followed. A bus tyre had to be replaced.

Philip knew of Bhongir. On his outward journey, from Hyderabad to Warangal along this road – in a sedan car carrying four English-speaking appointees of the Nizam's Government – the mystique of the place had been impressed on his imagination. The town of Bhongir was only an hour's drive from Hyderabad and was patrolled by armed police in the daylight hours. But at night they fled. 'Fled' was the word used to Philip without reflection by a Deputy Officer of the Advanced Education Unit and, as Philip now saw for himself, it could not be bettered. A prominent landholder of this region had distributed his lands to his tenants and dependent small-holders, in the Communist cause. Now these tenants, too, were Communists, without ceasing to work their lands. They were faithful till death. Not even firepower could dislodge them.

"Their arsenal should be around here," said Anand, approaching the rock on foot, as the bus was made roadworthy. "The police raid houses, but it would take them a year to comb all the crevices of the rock. It's not even defended."

The approach was littered with boulders. A dense thicket was cleared in one place, allowing an easy climb. Stairs were cut in the rock, leading to a fort which, said Anand, the patrols occupied till dusk, and to no avail.

"Do the peasants keep guns?"

"Rifles. Like hidden treasure. But only they can find them."

It seemed to Philip that Anand exaggerated the resourcefulness of the peasants, who could hardly be supposed to hide guns in an acropolis trampled by the police from dawn to dusk. Anand might well mock the abilities of the armed bands – the Communists – but he seemed to revere peasants. Was it because they kept to one place, tilling the soil and so constituting 'the people'? But 'the people' was Communist propaganda. "Were there peasants in your family?"

Anand did not answer. The rock glimmered, suspended by the long twilight in the sky near at hand, almost in touching distance. Stately birds – the size of quail – waddled briskly and efficiently to cover under their very noses. They heard the crying, clicking and whirring without being able to detect which bird was responsible for which sound.

"We'll go back." Anand led the way.

The bus motor started up. "Where is she?" he exclaimed, as they stood in the headlamps.

"Climb on. She'll be there."

They had cut it fine. The bus tyre had been swiftly changed. The crew were in a hurry, and would have left without them.

"Someone is in our old seats." Instead of dropping into an available seat and allowing Ragini to find them, as she'd done in the first place, Anand pushed his way down the corridor, stumbling over baskets and legs and peering into faces.

He appealed to a family to lend him its battery-torch. He shone it round
the interior, and even – forlornly – on the side of the road.

He slumped beside his friend. Philip's thoughts were beginning to run on
the encounters in store for him. He was not sure where he'd spend the night:
he was depending on people to meet the bus, but it would arrive late. Hardcastle would be there, but the quarters Hardcastle had at last found for him
on his earliest visit were at Rock-Hill Palace, that is, at a distant outpost in a
stony hinterland at three in the morning, with the doors locked and no-one
about but a rabid dog on a chain. Hardcastle had seemed so sure of this
place, where, he said, he knew the nawab. But there was no nawab. He had
installed Philip on a chair on the verandah, patting down an already limp
cushion as a token of comfort, and had welcomed him to Hyderabad with
the gift of a half-bottle of Pondicherry brandy which he seemed disposed to
investigate there and then. Philip recoiled in his seat at the memory of that
awful night vigil which – never mind Hardcastle, whom his driver at last
whisked away – was at that point only beginning.

Anand was meek and quiet. Philip made no bid to console him. In the
dark, the bus lost speed. Again! The co-driver was fumbling at a loop of
rope, which was all that held the door closed: but even he could not stave
off the inevitable. Now the vehicle was quite still. Voices rang out. Could
this be happening again? Someone boarded. Might it be a single, female
passenger? No such luck. Dark shapes crowded into the aisle, rasping in
hoarse voices, in Urdu. These men meant business. The foremost snatched
the torch from Anand's lap. He had failed to return it to its owner, or to
switch it off. The intruders moved down the aisle which cleared for them
at once.

Every face was scrutinised – so intently, thought Philip, as to make of it
not so much a face as an artifact, a portrait. These men could distinguish
a Rembrandt from a fake Rembrandt. They felt women's ears, for gems or
gold. But they issued no challenge. They left the bus: Razakars. Muslim
vigilantes, banded like fugitives for the showdown. That showdown was
yet some way off. When the Indian Army came – as it must – the Razakars
would fight. In the meantime, they terrorised the districts. Their links
with government were obscure, but certain. The passengers – a bus full of
Hindus – had been lucky to escape them.

Anand's silence was truly unnerving. It was he who had said even the
Razakars would steer clear of Bhongir. They were two miles from Bhongir!
Instead of apologising for his doomed insights, he was scribbling in a note-
book, with the aid of the pocket-torch, which had been restored to him.
Philip saw two possibilities. He could ask Anand what he was writing or,

alternatively, he could remind him that the torch had been borrowed. He refrained from both.

The jolting of the bus on a bad road was not conducive to writing. But Anand persevered. "I wonder who those *goondas* were looking for?" said Philip, after a time, striving for philosophic distance.

"Well – she got away."

To the mind of Anand, it appeared that he and the Razakars – shining their torches on the faces in the bus – had an errand in common. Both sought their Ragini, their all-in-all.

Here and there, as the bus travelled, unpredicted lights – lanterns in kitchens and workplaces, or on desolate hills – further mystified the darkness. Up front one of the crew, the assistant's assistant, the poorest and most negligible person on the bus – but it was he who had run for the charpoy – broke for some reason into an arcane melody, in a voice as limpid and beautiful as Philip had ever heard. This lad was cheering them up, after all the inconveniences they had suffered.

"What does the song say, Anand?"

Anand broke off to listen. "Something about God."

He resumed writing. He had filled the first couple of pages of a brand-new exercise book bought in Warangal to be a journal of record. Philip, who had found him the stationery shop and approved the binding, was surprised when Anand tore out the pages in a single swoop and handed them to him.

"What are these for?"

"Promise you won't read them."

"I won't read them. What are they for? They're for Ragini, is that it?"

"You know where to find her."

"You're wrong. I don't know where to find her. She finds me."

"Then the next time *she* finds *you*," said Anand – he was far from reconciled to his friend's privileged access to Ragini, though he quite believed in it. He did not bother to finish the sentence. Philip accepted the pages. Poor Anand. He did not know his idol. She eluded them, of course she eluded them. She was elusive. She was not one to wait around on a bus for Razakars. She left as she chose. Philip could cite half a dozen of her disappearances but, beyond those instances, he had little more to reveal to Anand.

10

Where Ragini went when she vanished, by the rock of Bhongir – that, to Philip, was unimportant. He would meet her again.

But where, in all Hyderabad, did Anand go? Philip knew of one place. He knew there was a curious 'hostel' in the Old City, somewhere in Lal Darwaza. A place glimpsed by night. There Anand went from the bus station. The bus arrived late ...

And Philip? Where did he go? Lying, now, fully awake in his bed in Gibbes Street, Philip knew no more of that night. The night had served its purpose, brought a man and a woman together. Nothing depended on where he went.

So many of his memories of Hyderabad, the ones he retrieved, were like that. Not that they were obscure, night-obscure. Some were flooded with light. But they were non-successive. No one thing led to another. He would find himself where he was, but with no idea, no idea in memory, of how he got there. Except for the night he arrived, at that terrible 'palace' with the mad dog, he could remember now *no place in Hyderabad* – and there had been many – where he laid down his head to sleep.

This practice of remembering was so novel to Philip that at first he had expected whole scenarios to unfurl around him, for as long as he stayed on deck. Sometimes this happened. More often, the past, like dough, like the surface of the waters, would close, leaving no sign it had ever been troubled.

Now he was remembering in earnest, the gaps daunted him. It seemed he had plunged, as swimmer, into Black Lagoon. A kind of peril lurked just out of his mind's reach.

The night's journey was over. He was walking, it appeared, by the river – but in broad daylight. Had he curled up all night at the bus station? Was this some different occasion? Gazing at the south bank of the Musi – as anyone must, who walked the north side – over the emerald-green flats to the battlemented walls of the Nizam's city, he refrained from crossing the bridge. Like a wise child at Christmas, who reserves the best present for last, Philip in those early days had resolved not to set foot in the Old City, south of the bridges. He would do so in his own good time: when he was invited. For Philip was not a tourist. He was an office-holder in the Nizam's administration. The Nizam, it was true, did not observe this capital distinction between the north and south sides. He resided on the north side, at King Kothi.

The Musi was prone to flood. But when it was not in flood, its bed afforded a tract of prime land, the most bountiful for yield in all the districts. Who owned this land? Whoever the owners were, they were nowhere in sight. An army of labourers, with huts and byres and animals, swarmed for miles along the ribbon of bright green – rice paddy, or lucerne – until the waters swept down on them without warning. As he turned away from the river, towards Sultan Bazaar, Philip heard a dull roar – not a wall of water but a primal force, all the same, or so it appeared at a distance. A few steps nearer and the roar began to disintegrate into ragged particulars, yells, clashes of metal, what sounded like gunshots as someone fired, presumably into thin air.

A Razakar rally. Dispersed voices blended into one rhythmic shout of a few syllables, repeated over and over.

Philip stood aside. Even as he did, the scene in memory changed into something else. Monsoon cloud filled the south and east. The streets now were patchily lit against the dusk. Every depression on the ground glittered with a month's accumulation of rainwater. Advancing on him from the direction of the British Residency, a new procession took up the width of the street to Rain Bazaar. The procession showed in the twilight as if it were beamed from somewhere, a level shaft of uniform black heads and white garments. Policemen in their diagonally-belted tunics and diagonally-striped, paper-boat turbans strove to clear a way for traffic. The marchers, weirdly inoffensive and gawky, banners aloft, trudged beside their bicycles. No menace lurked in this procession. These marchers would burn nothing down. Could it be a Congress rally? Were these timid processionists, hustled by their cheerleaders – one with a stumpy leg – Anand's constituency?

Fifty-three years had passed. Philip could not tell who the marchers had been. The Congress then was banned. Were they trade-unionists? Had the Nizam's Railway – a not-for-profit institution (as it ought to be) – fallen behind in payments to its workers? Philip was baffled by the procession. It should have been easy, for him – it was a 'modern' procession. The 'modern' speaks for itself, even – or especially – among the sights and sounds of the decay of the old order. The 'modern' is most intelligible when it predicts ruin. But nothing, in Hyderabad, was intelligible in the usual sense. Hyderabad was a folly. It was, of course, destined for ruin. This did not make it more intelligible. All swept away now. How could it count, to anyone, if he were to recover those meanings, which no longer 'meant'? What was the purpose of all those undisputed errands and unblinking procedures, the bazaars, the obscure crafts, the bewildering pageantry of holidays that arrived out of nowhere, the Abyssinian guard, the troupes of musicians in livery, the female armed warriors whom he had watched, in all their regalia but never on parade, lounging like ordinary shoppers on the stone benches of the Moazzam Jahi vegetable market? Why was a quarter of the population in triumphal dress? Was this the deceit of memory? How, if it was, could he correct a mistaken impression? And why should he care? History had pronounced its verdict on the Nizam. Wasted effort. An unjust social order. That order had vanished, like water-vapour, and nobody in India regretted it for one moment.

11

Philip, the Nizam's office-holder, and world record headmaster for youth – he was twenty-three! – had others to report to, senior officiators whose jobs were no more secure than his own. They assembled in various places. Philip would appear at the most recent address – a pavilion, say, in the Residency gardens – to find that the venue had shifted. This time – this time? the time he returned on the bus with Anand? – he was directed to Osmania University, on rocky ground several miles to the north-east. Osmania University had been founded twenty-five years ago by the present Nizam, and was famed throughout India – so Philip had been told, and this was true – for its choice of language of instruction. Throughout India, university classes were held in English. But here, they were in Urdu. The textbooks were all translated. To some, this enterprise was quixotic, but in Philip's small circle, everyone approved. Lessons were taught here in the mother tongue. Well, in *a* mother tongue. Osmania University, moreover, knew scholarship and, even in the estimate of the English, had housed famous persons. Besides local persons, a cast of international investigators had been enlisted by the new-leaf Nizam for his social reforms. Osmania had made a home a while back for the anthropology Professor C.H. von Furer-Haimendorf of London University. What a precursor.

The reform educationists took to these temporary lodgings with mixed feelings. They were far from the centres of intrigue. But they relished the place. They were housed now in the Arabic department. The Arabist scholars had been drafted en masse, it appeared, to duties of state elsewhere. Philip had never entered such a fine building. All was grey granite: high, elegant windows carved out of granite, granite staircases, a granite floor so fastidiously levelled and polished with hand-tools that you could see your face in it. You could read your expression. You could at least infer your expression. The melody of rote learning from the classrooms was a distraction: so too was the smell from the toilets, which was wind-borne, as there was sometimes a wind and the toilet doors stood open. But the work party were content.

"I enjoy that buzz, that hum," said Hardcastle. "It shows they're working at their lessons. No more flag business."

Smart saw it differently. "The ones who hum are not the ones who ran up the flag."

"Did anyone look up this morning?" All eyes were on Philip, the last to arrive. "Was the flag aloft?"

"The flag?"

"The flag of India."

"The flag of the Union: white, orange and green," said Smart in a mock-Irish accent, "except for the *chakra* in the middle. What's that for? Can anyone suggest to me what the *chakra* is doing? In India, it's true, they may have spun their way to freedom. But now they'll need Five-Year Plans." He mistook the imperial *chakra* for the Gandhian *charka* or spinning-wheel.

Philip was intrigued. "The students ran up the Indian flag?"

"To the top of the building. They ran it up on Wednesday. Laiq Ali came over in person, to see it brought down. We had students from everywhere: five thousand in the grounds surrounding the entrance, including four busloads from Nizam College. The police hung back, Government brought in reinforcements. Whoever put up that flag must have scaled a sheer wall, like a gecko. I don't know how it was done."

"There are footholds," Middleton suggested.

"You show me the footholds. No-one can climb that wall. The crack engineers, the team from the Irrigation Department, couldn't bring it down. They lost face. They had to shoot it down – with ropes and arrows. There are still a few rags fluttering."

"Were there arrests?" said Philip.

"None. All for show. The gaols are full." That was Smart's opinion, but Middleton corrected him: "The gaols are empty. Laiq Ali has just released all the *satyagrahis*. It's whistle-as-you-work, pretend-it's-a-natural-calamity, offend-nobody. A few *lathi*-beatings, that was the worst of it."

"You see, where we are," said Hardcastle gravely, to Philip, "we're transcendent observers. We watched the whole *tamasha* from the Arts College portico. And what do we know? Nothing. We know nothing and we're entitled to know nothing. So let's get on with the job."

The job that morning consisted of reports on schools. No official from the Nizam's Government was present. Before the signing of the Standstill Agreement in November (Philip was told) the Education Office had kept a close watch on proceedings and, up till August 15, the date of the calamity of Indian independence, the Nizam himself had been interested in schools. Now all but the core functions of government had fallen away. The core functions no longer included education. New schools had opened, thanks to earlier decisions, and budgets were approved for these; but some had no

teachers, and there was no consolidated record of the enrolment of pupils.
"We're the only ones counting," Hardcastle said.

"There's a teacher problem. Old, bearded moulvis are putting up their
hands wherever we look, but they're not what we want. We can't get Hindus
to apply."

"Why *would* they apply?" said Smart.

"They'd apply for the money. Double pay, we're offering, in some
districts," said Middleton, but Hardcastle shook his head. "We've ruled that
out."

"If we've ruled it out, I don't see how we can manage."

"We'll manage till the heavens do fall. When the heavens do fall,"
said Hardcastle, "we'll have Muslim *and* Hindu teachers staffing the best
English-language schools in the subcontinent. We won't offer double pay.
Double pay is for foreigners."

"Meaning me," said Philip.

"Son, you're a headmaster. You're on triple pay."

Philip was mortified. This was news to him. He'd been quoted a salary
in Australia, but – triple pay! in local terms, a fortune – and unmerited!

"We'll find you an assistant to train. We'll find you a Hindu. That should
be possible, Sukku, don't you think? – in a town like Warangal?"

All eyes were on Sukku – "Doctor", as they sometimes called him, a
Ph.D. in History from Madras University. Dr Sukhanandam was never
absent, but seldom entirely present at these scheduled meetings. As Philip
had explained to Rhondda, his associates in the reform project were mostly
Englishmen. This fact had not lessened their commitment to primary
education in the schools of Hyderabad. While the Nizam's state faltered,
they alone had the time for it.

"What do you say, Doctor?"

Sukhanandam did not appear to be listening. Yet his very abstractedness
conferred on him a kind of mystique. He had not yet been known to fail a
question, or to ask for its substance to be repeated. His voice was faint, yet
his answer rang as clear as a bell. "No Hindu will teach."

Hardcastle and the others repaired to the Secunderabad club. But Philip
took Sukku to Monty's. His guest, a teetotaller, accepted the gift of a vegetable samosa on a plate and surveyed, without energy – he was not energetic
– but with tolerant curiosity, the threadbare appointments of this unusual
place. Montgomery's Club had no bar, two or three bearers and a kitchen.
A screen at one end of the room blocked a few select tables, and the lights
were dimmed. There were no posters, mirrors, paintings of gods or framed
messages from the Qur'an, or indeed ornaments of any kind but for a wall

clock of the kind you would find on a railway platform. The polished-wood, square tables, each with four upright chairs (lounging was not encouraged), aptly communicated the sober business ethos at Monty's. Yet this was not a sober place.

In all Secunderabad and Hyderabad, Monty's was the one establishment where Philip felt at home. Yet even here he glanced round him with precaution before selecting a table. Others besides him felt a similar affection for the place. On his very first visit to Monty's, Philip had encountered a desperately out-of-pocket Australian who, finding himself in India, had wandered off the beaten track. He did not want to team up with such another.

The clock showed seven minutes past three, as it always did. Philip ordered, for himself, his first bottle of beer in a month, and plain water for Dr Sukhanandam. The bearers at Monty's did not mind whether you drank big or small. You could stick to your post all day, for the little they cared. Round the room, table by solitary table, sat red-eyed garage mechanics and rickshaw drivers who had acquired the habit of drinking brandy at Monty's rather than arrack in low-beamed, lantern-lit dens with their boisterous peers. So glad was Philip to have a glass in his hand that his spirit embraced theirs with emotion. "Anand should be here."

Dr Sukhanandam was surprised. "Does Anand take alcohol?"

"Not much. But he'd sit here beside me, just as you do. We've had some of our best talks here."

Sukku took this in. Though not himself a participant in 'best talks', it was he who had led Philip to Anand. Philip's nocturnal glimpse of the outside of Anand's hostel had been in his company. By a means all his own, without ever appearing to be at the centre of anything (or even to be paying attention) Sukku contrived a sort of access to widely dissimilar cliques and individuals, ranging from a priest at the Jain temple to Congress plotters and planners, as well as a nawab or two. He was neither an enthusiast nor a teacher: what then was his function in the reform group? He put people in touch with people.

"I have seen very little of Anand," he said. "He is always touring."

"He came to Warangal."

"What kind of a bold spirit!" muttered Sukku, disturbed by the thought. To Philip he said, "You are another such person. You venture everywhere."

"I don't venture anywhere. I did venture to Bastar, when I first arrived. I go where I'm sent."

"Always to villages."

"Warangal is not a village."

Sukku passed over this distinction. "I would not leave Hyderabad. I am called a socialist and a humanitarian, but the illiterate people of our villages, they are disturbing to me. I cannot go among them. Your British and Danish missionaries associate with such people – but no educated Hindu can do it. We are unlike Muslims and Christians, we have nothing that binds us together. You can't conceive of the strength of our pollution feelings: it is not just uncleanness, but the disdain we feel!" – his temperate features were distorted by a sudden horror. "Sick. We become sick. We should not be so, but there is nothing in our culture to prepare us to confront these people. Some European scholars come, and they say, 'This is India, just India. There is no reason to be ashamed of caste.' Do you believe this? There is no reason to be ashamed of caste?"

"How can *I* be ashamed of caste?" said Philip, taking the question personally. Sukku's expression in return showed him the insufficiency of this answer. But what could he say? How could he presume? A key was missing, and he strove to supply it. "I am not a Hindu, so I have no stake."

"You accept caste?"

"No, of course I don't accept it."

"But you are not ashamed of it?"

"How can *I* be ashamed of it?"

Sukku had difficulty in fathoming this outlook. He paused for further explanation. When none was offered, he struck out on another path. "In India we are rich in variety. We are rich in variety, in this one thing. So many castes we have in India, so many faiths, so many languages, so many gods and goddesses, so many crafts, so many ways of life. So this is how I should regard my country? As a full-to-bursting museum? I have nothing in common with such people. They simply distress me. I like to associate only with educated people. But, what is the good of these?"

Philip was lost. "The good of educated people ... ?"

"What is the good of all these castes?"

"There is no good. There is no good," said Philip, a trifle impatiently, having to exceed limits to declare himself.

"We should do away with caste. I myself *believe*," said Sukku, with dangerous irony, but the irony was all in Philip's head, "that we should do away with caste. I am a bit educated. This is not the common opinion. But the poor Hindu, the villager, he must live in the dust through necessity. He has no chance to form an opinion."

"I'm sure he has one."

"He has no chance to communicate an opinion."

It was a time of afternoon when the angle of the sun's rays caught the tinted-glass windows high over the capstone of the arched entry portal at Monty's, briefly inflaming the room. You would think the *kotwal* would close this place down. Perhaps the authorities kept it on, allowed it to thrive, as an admonition to Hindu and Muslim alike, a kind of hell. Yet it struck Philip as a desirable place. The patrons of Monty's caused no trouble. Comparing it with Sydney, with the pubs of Sydney, it was an improvement, at least pictorially. Only Sukku, with his tumbler of water, betrayed a discomfiture he owed to his thoughts, not to his surroundings. Philip resolved to cure him of it. "Think of the poor Khan Bahadur," he said, "who must live in his *palace* through necessity – with its forty rooms. Isn't a *haveli* a palace?"

"That *haveli* is a palace. The Khan Bahadur, why are you interested in him?"

"Can you guess?"

"You would like to meet him. Meet his wife."

"As a fellow Australian ... What did you say her name was?"

"You will find she is not so Australian," said Sukku, withholding the name. "She has lived in Hyderabad too long."

"But she's young, isn't she?"

"Young. She is young. She is junior. A second wife."

" 'Junior' does not sound young, it sounds infantile."

"You are making a request. This may take time. I have many friends among the Kayasthas. They can bring you to the Khan Bahadur. But to ask him to dispose of his wife ..."

"Dispose of her?" exclaimed Philip. He searched in vain for a hint of devilry in his friend's features. All he intended was to meet the woman.

Just drop the matter. If Sukku would help, he would help. He had done so in the past. He had produced Anand, though with no thought of doing Philip a favour. He knew people, and to make this known he would produce people – where the case was relevant. This thought set Philip wondering about his own relevance. There were, in India, two people, Ragini and Anand, for whom he cared a lot. And he mattered to *them*. Philip could not have said why, but he did. But should these two matter to one another: or should one come to matter to the other, since one was enough ... what would become of Philip? A go-between! There and then, he renounced all sociable designs on the nawab's wife, and relieved Sukku of his obligation. Even so, to make sure it was there, he groped for Anand's missive to Ragini, in his back pocket. Philip, a moral person, with strengths where you least expected them, would not read the letter. He would deliver the letter ... It was gone. He had lost it, that wretched scrap of paper, and without even meaning to. All was saved. His spirits soared, until he remembered the other pocket.

Chapter Two. The Fort at Warangal

1

When Philip emerged from the back bedroom in Rockdale – this could be at any time of the morning – he would stand for a moment in the passage, striving to gauge by ear what was in store for him in the further rooms. 'Back' and 'front' were reversed in this house. The room he now occupied in fact looked over the street. There was a street door, but only tradesmen ever knocked at that door. Ever since Philip was a child, growing up in this house, so much of the daily action was concentrated in the 'table' room, the kitchen, the yard and the walled verandah (not to speak of the 'geyser' or bathroom which opened off the kitchen) that he had never doubted where the 'front' lay and would retain this orientation for all houses till his dying day, warped for life. Jenny, when she was brought to the house, having escaped this conditioning, did not make the same mistake. The two sometimes quarrelled about it.

Once he had learned, by overhearing, what to expect, Philip advanced from the passage through a dark room, which in his childhood had professed only two functions: 'listening to the cricket', pre-War, when the Ashes tests were on, and home entertainment on Saturday evenings. The men (and a cricket-mad aunt, the closest Philip had to a parent) retreated here for their dedicated purpose in summer, the only time this room was ever in use in daylight. When it all became too much for them they would adjoin to the yard, aunt included, to bat and bowl. His grandfather bowled slow lobs; he could leg-break a tennis ball. This room had contained armchairs, a radio and an upright piano. Every member of the household, Philip too, played and sang at the piano. They did so by family custom. His mother, who died with his father in a car-crash when Philip was two, was said to have been a gifted musician. Philip had nothing of that. He had taken lessons, but could not remember 'practising' the piano in this house.

His bedroom gave onto the passage. Two more, Jenny's and a third, opened off the darkened room. The boy Philip had slept in the third –

sharing it some of the time with an unmarried uncle. That room had held tall, glass-paned bookcases with his mother's books. Now it was 'Jim's room'.

Philip proceeded to the 'front' area of the house. His hand rested on the doorknob. He was listening – one last precaution – for his daughter Nora's voice. Some days she arrived early. When he could be sure the coast was clear, he turned the knob slowly and advanced into the room.

Jenny was seated at the polished-wood, hexagonal table with her back to him. Her visitors looked up before she did. What she now occupied was his grandfather's place, not that she knew it – for the old, deal table was gone – facing the yard. Today's circle of friends were 'hospital'. Jenny was in no sense a hostess or home entertainer, but friends dropped in on her – often in the mornings, to avoid family, to avoid Nora, whose demands on her mother were exclusive. Here were her former workmates at the Kogarah Bay public hospital: the beloved former head nurse, and two much younger than Jenny, a nurse and an administrator who still worked there. In her mid-thirties, Jenny had been appointed Deputy Registrar at a wing of the hospital, and she became Registrar. For want of medical training she rose no higher, but she toured the wards, and became a facilitator to nurses, canny in her knowledge of trifles of unspent funds and unused equipment, willing to beard specialists and senior doctors. It was said of Jenny in admiration that to make herself more useful, she took Nursing as a TAFE course. This was untrue. But to cast her as useful was profoundly true.

The women greeted Philip sincerely, though without exuberance. He was, to them, a well-mannered, rather distinguished-looking man of seventy-six, still a husband – for Jenny had never spoken of any divorce. Jenny, in fact, had barely spoken to them at all about Philip. Here he was: not fully a member of the household, as they all knew. But they knew it had been his house. They smiled and looked up.

"Kate's returning to work," said Jenny. "She can't stand to be retired. They've had the retirement party, now it's the back-to-work party."

"All finger-food, Monte Carlos and instant coffee," said the retired head nurse.

"No, we won't hold it at the hospital. We'll hold it at the Sailing Club. Dance music."

"And men," said the younger nurse, who could not have been more than thirty. No-one laughed, no-one cheered. There was a silence, which allowed Philip to put in, "I'm sure men would turn up." His wife stared lightly over the yard where Patch, the fox-terrier, had once dug for bones.

"Too true. Good for men. I'm not agin men," said the retired head nurse, in her level tones. "Men would be all the rage, along with the biscuits, at a back-to-work party."

2

Another occasion. Again the passage door opened, and Philip emerged from within the house. Jenny looked up. He did not know these people, and she wanted him to learn how things stood.

"Philip" – no mention of 'husband' – "this is Father Mercer. Father Mercer, Philip. Deirdre, this is Philip. Philip, Deirdre. Milo, Philip. Philip, Milo. Milo is the church organist. Deirdre looks after the children's services."

He won't remember them, so I'll stop at that. Jenny left several people unintroduced. There were too many for the hexagonal table, and no chair for Philip.

She watched him intently, willing him to be on his way. Philip scrutinised the faces for kindness – eight altogether. He decided on Milo. "You're the organist."

"Yes, I am."

"What do you play? Hymns, mostly?"

"Hymns. Interludes. Processionals – for the service."

Jenny said brightly, "But your window is safe," and Father Mercer spoke up, on cue, "It's a fine window. We had to take it down, but it's stored on a shelf of its own, in the lumber room. When we negotiated for the building, we forged an understanding with the Uniting Church that nothing would happen to your grandparents' window. That's not in writing, but we'll keep to it."

"You took it down," said Philip. "Why was that? Was it theologically inappropriate?" He spoke with a levity which freed them to pass on to other topics. Philip stayed. He fetched an armchair from inside – which meant a struggle – and propped it in the doorway he had just opened. Ignoring Father Mercer, he befriended Deirdre, then relapsed into silence.

Jenny cleared the tea things to the kitchen, signalling that she required no help. In her mind she composed a fierce eulogy to the Catholic Church, and to the people who took her in without attempting (except at the beginning) to convert her to their faith, to their sense of their faith. She was, and remained, a Hindu, as anyone could see (though no-one did see) who penetrated the house to her bedroom and beheld the shrine to the goddess Parvati in one corner of the room. Not Jim, not Vinta, not her daughter, followed Jenny to her own bedroom. Her attachment was secret. In the 'table' room, where they sat, there were no holy pictures or calendars, Hindu or Catholic, no bleeding hearts, meek and mild Jesuses or plump baby Krishnas – she set no store by such things. That must be why she had taken so readily, forty-odd years ago, to the Uniting Church. Were Philip to enter Jenny's room (as if that could happen!) he would find, all the same, something of upper-caste India: a formal, well-dusted room with too many elaborate wood chairs, wall furniture and the shrine, of course. Her Parvati would surprise him, but so would the chairs.

3

The passage door opened and Philip emerged, gradual as always. He found Jenny alone. The room was empty of callers. The indelibly stained tablecloth was back in place, the carpet was worn and the sideboard within reach. Jenny this time was more wary and vigilant than her former husband, scooping flyers and booklets from the table-top and burying them in a drawer. Her composure was breached.

Philip prepared his breakfast under her eyes. He had bought wrapped *parathas* from the Fijian Indian store in Merrylands. He greased two pans in the kitchen, frying the *parathas* in one and an egg in the other. "Was Jim here?"

"You've spent a long night in your room. If you'd come through earlier, you could have talked with him."

"I'll talk with you."

"Hasn't it all been said?" Jenny sat without moving at the queen table in the house that was hers. Let him talk – not any old talk, but talk that meant something. Home for good. What did that mean?

"Fresh start, today," he said. "New people, new suburbs. Sydney is all new suburbs. Or new suburbs is where the Indians live."

"More Indians. Didn't you leave India to escape them?"

"I find one right here."

"Is Indian what I am? That does me some credit. After all these years in Australia," she said, "if I'm still an Indian, I'm a very determined one."

"After all those years in India," countered Philip, "I'm still an Australian, which is why I came home."

This, precisely this, kind of thing, she meant to discourage. Words that spoke themselves. Home, home in Australia, because I'm an Australian. Home because of the whistle-y-bob. That would make as much sense. Her roving eye had fallen on one object from Philip's era that remained in the house, not because Philip prized it but because the girls, who grew up in the house, had prized it, and her grandchildren knew it for what it was: the whistle-y-bob. When callers remarked on this strange, festive object, a kind of wire cage padded with wool (long since discoloured) and dangling strips of cotton, Jenny would say, without further explanation, "That's the whistle-y-bob."

Using the egg-slice for both pans, Philip assembled his meal, took the first bite standing up, in the kitchen, then, like a delinquent facing the music, carried his plate to Jenny's table. He repeated the journey there and back, returning with a glazed scenic table-mat of cows in a field. She watched him eat. "You talk with Jim a lot. All about India, I suppose."

"What makes you think so?"

"Which days in India?"

"Early days."

"Why them?"

"Jim's twenty-three," said Philip at once, "and I was twenty-three. It's all his doing. I keep a lot back. There was Hyderabad and, right at the beginning, there was Bastar. I don't believe I've told you about Bastar."

"Once you did."

"No, I don't think I did." When Philip had eaten he washed up plate, pans and cutlery, drying them and replacing them in the wrong cupboards. Jenny merely watched. "I'll shower, and be gone," he said. "In a month, I'll be out of your hair. I won't stay in the house forever."

"Stay as long as you like."

"As soon as I find work, paid work – I'll be off. I'll still visit, of course."

"Paid work, what does 'paid' matter to you? Paid or unpaid. That's not the point, is it? You'll just have to get used to Nora."

"She comes every day."

"I can't stop her coming, she's my daughter. And I can't stop ..." *I can't stop you staying.* Jenny broke off. And Philip contrived not to notice. He had that gift.

Philip tinkered with the shower in the bathroom. The gas mechanism was antique, but he handled it like the native to the house he was. The water had to run first. When he had the jet lighted but not pointed, he emerged, still fully clothed, from the bathroom. "Who do you think she blames me for – you, or Tilly?"

"Nobody blames you for Tilly. If ever there was a girl who went her own way ..."

"I was in Nagpur. Five hundred miles away."

"And I was here. What does it matter where you were, or I was? What's come over you? You don't blame yourself, do you?"

"*I* don't. I wondered if Nora ..."

"One thing about Nora. She'll let you know. If Nora blamed you for Tilly's death, you'd have been told twenty years ago. What *does* she tell you? She wanted a father. She tells you you abandoned her here, and you abandoned me here. If Nora had been anything like Tilly, she'd have gone looking for you. But Nora is a homebody. She's straight as a die. Things to her are black, or they're white. Now you, and I, see all shades of charcoal and grey, but that young woman, who has never known a moment's doubt ..."

"A moment's doubt would help," said Philip, reflecting that his second daughter was not all that young a woman.

That autumn afternoon, about the time Nora was expected, Jenny lingered in the yard for warmth. *I'll soon be replacing the plum tree. No, Philip can replace it.* There was no real garden, except for the fernery down one side, and the nasturtiums round the drain; but two trees, an apple and a plum, had stood without change, bare of fruit, lopped every year, since the boy Philip climbed in his climbing breeches. The trees put out leaves. Eternity. Let the tree stand. Why replace things? No change in the appointments for Master Philip. He'd told her of Mrs Conrick's Jacko. When she ventured to water the ferns, she seemed to glimpse Jacko the clipped-wing magpie, stalking like a demon on the other side of the paling fence. He pecked through the fence. "Couldn't fly," Philip had explained, in exoneration of the malice of that long-dead creature.

Not only the yard but the entire nation was consecrated these days to the absence of change, to the 'as before'. Its leader, John Howard, seemed resolved to push it back even further, to an era when change was undreamt of. But was there such an era? Jenny believed this was the first such era. The nation itself, the white nation, what people meant by the nation, was a hundred years old this year, 2001. Add the hundred years' colonial rule before that. At the time Australia was 'discovered', as they liked to put it, Tipu Sultan, in South India, was incorporating the French Revolution into the colours of his turban. The Bengal Renaissance was under way, and the Mughal Empire, whose capital at Delhi was the seventh in a long line of dynastic capitals, all on adjacent sites, each grander than the other, was perceived to be moribund. The Marathas were at the gates, while on the faraway Kaveri the Prince of Renouncers was a child, declaiming his anthems to Lord Rama in his father's village.

Diagonally across the mowed lawn in this backyard ran a cement path which ended at the door of his grandfather's workshop. Along that strip cricket had been played sixty years before – with the door as backstop – and behind that door were a bench and a wood-turning lathe, which Jenny had left as they were. Sixty-year-old woodshavings: perhaps not, but there lingered the carpenter's odour and ambience of planks and glue. Jenny kept gardening tools, a tarpaulin and an old wardrobe in that shed. Philip had poked his head in there – once – had seen things were much 'as before', and had emerged content, but he had no plans for it.

All these years in his house. Jenny had never, for one moment, been thrilled by the house: just as she had never enthused about Australia. Yet, for her, house and nation had worn fairly well. 'As before' wore well, for a none-too-heterogeneous people (*that* was changing) in a vast land, with their sound institutions and their fair, though not clamorous, sense of justice. She was inclining to count her blessings – the blessings of this land – when she heard the side gate creak. That would be Nora. But instead of Nora, Nora's daughter Vinta, Jenny's fourteen-year-old granddaughter, came hurtling down the path, oblivious to the shade of Jacko. She stopped like an angel on a pinpoint and began dancing on that point. "*Avva*, we won, we won. *Amma* won the bid, *amma* won the bid. She's taking the choir to Newcastle."

"To Newcastle!" Jenny embraced her granddaughter, whose excitement was tuned in an instant, by magic of girlhood and family relation, to her quiet, absorbed surrender to the long embrace. Nora appeared and stood by. An embrace was hers, too, if she wanted it. But she kissed her mother, with due affection, on the unroughened side of her face, which Jenny turned to her.

"It's not that bad, *amma*."

"What's not bad?"

"Your face. It's clearing. Have you been using the ointment?"

"Old age," said Jenny. "No ointment is good enough."

She led them indoors. A store-bought cinnamon tea-cake stood on the table. "Put it away," said Nora, "for your church people. I've made *payasam*. It's not up to your standard, but you never make it. Help me with the fridge now" – she had marched to the fridge door with her offering, a dish in greased paper. But before Nora, swift and determined in her allocations, had crammed the broccolini on the jar of yoghurt to make room on the shelves, a storm of piano music burst on them from within the house. Vinta had rushed to the stool and was performing a Beethoven sonata movement with all the attack the genius composer would have wanted. Jenny left the kitchen and stood at the inner door to watch. This kind of music. Not hers! too loud! – but she adored the sight of her vigorous, elfin granddaughter pounding at the keys, her eyes gleaming and her brown face exultant. If she struck wrong notes, Jenny did not discern them. To her mind, all the notes were wrong. Vinta's musicianship was the talk of their small family and of her competitors at Rockdale Town Hall, where she had been placed first in a championship for all ages. She finished the sonata movement. Jenny applauded freely and Vinta, darting her a fierce look, would have proceeded to the second movement had Nora not intervened from the kitchen. "Enough of that, now. We know you're good."

"*Avva* doesn't know I'm good."

"You should come with me more often. That bung piano ... How often do you have it tuned, *amma*?"

"I've never had it tuned. Philip will have it tuned."

Jenny had been brought up on a different music, but that was in India. How she had loved that music.

"Bring your piano books next time," called Nora in the dry, proud tones of a mother who reproves excellence. To Jenny she confided, "She refuses to sight-read. She'll glimpse the page, once – maybe twice – then it's all in her head." This was untrue, but Nora exaggerated to meet her mother Jenny's conviction, acquired in India, that musical proficiency of any kind, though it ran in families, and depended on practice, was displayed in public as a spontaneous gift.

"What's this about Newcastle?" said Jenny, at table. Vinta had polished off her *payasam* and was playing the piano quietly, upon that instruction, as the women 'caught up' – as they did, in person or by phone, every day of the year.

"I'm taking the choir. It's like Vinta said, we put in from the St George district and we were chosen, above Mortdale I'm glad to say. That's the state-wide festival in November."

"Now is May. Will you have time to prepare?"

"Who has time? All the same, it's an honour. I've spoken to Jim. He'll come. Win or lose, the entire family can have a holiday at Port Stephens for a week. You can close up the house."

"Philip will keep the house open."

"Philip will be here? In this house? In November? I hardly think so."

"Wherever he is – I'll ask him to move back. I'll accompany you to Newcastle, but I'm not leaving the house empty for a week. What time in November?"

"Has he found a job yet?"

"There's work, yes."

"I don't mean work. Is he bringing money into the house? His pension's tied up in India, that's a lot of help."

"He'll bring it here. For now, he has money. Nora, don't make me have to defend him."

"What *is* this 'work'?" said Nora, who had flushed a bright red. "The refugees these days are in detention centres. Let him teach at Villawood, if he's teaching English. What is it Australia needs that he's got?"

4

Philip had no car. He drove a car in India, but in Australia – which lacked water buffalos, street cows, hand-carts and cycle-rickshaws, three-wheeler auto-rickshaws which turned on the spot, and laden wagons wending from the canefields or the cotton-ginning yards – the traffic was too fast for him. Nora should have seen him now, seated on a bench on a harbour ferry, patiently examining his copious printouts and handwritten pages on schools, universities and halls of residence, curricula, fee structures and bursary entitlements.

All these he'd sorted into folders. To Nora, he'd have appeared to be lazing, out here amid the weekday pleasure-craft and the seagulls, but he was hard at work. The dry-as-dust reading matter was not entrancing. It was a means to an end. Allowing his gaze to drift over the low, mutinous bush of the headland, a rest to the eyes after his pages, a rest to the eyes after the foreshore-hugging brick walls, aluminium-frame windows and red-tile roofs, the palatial residences and stingy 'private hotels' of the domestic harbourside across the water as you left Circular Quay, Philip recalled what that end was. He was an educationist. He knew – he addressed – young minds. He addressed young Indian minds. He had addressed young minds in India for half a century, to thunderous (though waning) applause. Such was his vocation in India. Out here he had wanted something different. It was not to be. One role awaited him. His old skills – unremunerated – were back in use.

Young Indians were entering Australia in droves. Neither they, nor their families home in the Punjab, were quite prepared for this experience. On his first trip to out-of-the-way Merrylands – the day he abandoned Keith Ball – Philip was dismayed by what he found. These Indians had come to Sydney for an education. But they had formed no idea of where to look. Not all, he learned, planned on returning to India when they finished their degrees. Yet they all wanted degrees. They insisted on degrees and, since the universities were closed to them, many had enrolled, at substantial cost, in unheard-of institutions operated by sharks of the deepest water. This was the fault of their ignorance, which Philip aimed to rectify. Their ignorance was not just educational. None had foreseen the malevolent duplicity of agents – Australian agents in India, and Indian agents in India and Australia. A pox on these agents – not all of whom realised they were duplicitous agents. Some thought they were helping. Perhaps he was another such agent.

At some time in Philip's long absence – punctuated by his short visits home – government in Australia had repented of universities, as if in atonement for a capital sin. Funds and subsidies were curtailed, and into the breach plunged any number of baneful enterprises. Unlike agribusinesses in agriculture, these businesses offered not even economies of scale. Well under way on Philip's return was a part-open, part-clandestine traffic in foreign students, many from rich families (for there were few scholarships), and many from poor, but saving, families. Wealth, or the willingness to pay, was a qualification, in some ways a dangerous qualification. The wealth of aspiring students from China and India was precisely what beauty must have been for Russian, Ukrainian and Romanian waitresses and debutantes enticed to Europe after the fall of the Soviet Union. Such wealth was the only sound reason for cash-strapped entrepreneurs with no conscience or background to hone their abiding interest in these forlorn castaways.

Philip could not be too reproachful of these pitiless maggots. He, too, had glimpsed his opportunity in a brand of distress. He wanted to be of use. He thought he could help. But *was* he helping, or *who* was he helping? The three girls at Merrylands were his only success. He had found them a programme, in the nick of time – it was May – to prepare them for the mid-year intake at one of the rural universities. Their documents were in: he had hounded them. Victory to Philip! – he had had a card printed, out of the euphoria of that result, with the title 'Educational Consultant' and an abbreviated list of his achievements in India. (Notable shysters had similar cards.) The girls at Merrylands would soon be part of a Universities Admissions Programme. Philip believed they would complete that programme, yet he also knew or guessed that these girls, who were close companions, who had lived half their lives in Australia, who had matriculated (just) at Australian schools with Australian-born friends, and were polishing up their results for better things – these girls would not leave Merrylands or the city of Parramatta to study in a country town university when the time came. Philip had had a glimpse of their world, as they of his, and although he had infected them in one sitting with a taste for the glamour of higher learning, they for their part had uncovered to him the whirl of their world of film-song and film-clip video stores, Punjabi-fare emporia and imported Punjabi designer *churidar* and mirrored-blouse boutiques in one stroll along Wigram Street, Harris Park. He could hold out no hope to these imperfect students of a big-city university enrolment; and they would not abandon their world yet. Any disconsolacy of theirs as immigrants he failed to detect and the help he offered would lead to nothing.

Philip suffered and squirmed at the memory of his two visits to Sydney Airport, to apprehend Indian youngsters travelling alone. These kids, raised in India, had seen touts before, and knew how touts forgather at airports.

Philip was outnumbered and quite outclassed by his rivals: the sharpest, who turned up both times, carried a placard for a business college which (Philip knew) had not yet made the down payment on its mid-city premises and was recruiting for staff in the strangest places. Because he spurned placards, Philip had approached his airport quarry in a confidential manner, which made things worse. Rocked now by the swell from the Heads, which transformed the forty-minute zoo crossing briefly, though fiercely, into an ocean voyage, he contemplated the drift of his plans. He had expected to be taken on in a government programme. His future, he had thought, was in Australian education. He had finished with India. But it seemed he had not finished with Indians. He had need now of some government accreditation to place these kids. Not a chance of it. No accreditation for Philip. Perhaps 'families' would be different.

What Philip meant by families was an institution within which one or more adults would instruct a minor in what was best for her or him. This meant he could advertise. Parents read *Indian Link, India Down Under* and the Fijian and Sri Lankan Indian papers. His new approach bore fruit at once. But it meant refocusing his attention on school leaving-age candidates, or misfit teenagers who were unhappy with their school, or whose parents were unhappy with their school. Now the second such interview lay before him. The first had gone badly. Philip had not allowed himself proper time. He blamed ambience entirely. The session had unravelled in a Serbian souvlakia restaurant in Hurstville where Indian vegetarian parents were not at home. Why he had chosen that place he would never know. Why had he resisted the family invitation of a home visit? A parasite on a payroll, who would not know an Indian from a Red Indian, would have avoided that mistake.

The ferry berthed at Taronga Park wharf and Philip, ignoring the waiting bus – he was always a walker – climbed the steep hill to the Aquarium entrance. There they were: a jovial father; a handsome boy, not sullen at all; another grown male, perhaps an uncle; and besides these, attached to their party, an agreeable-looking Chinese boy and *his* father. Philip, from a distance, was surprised by their number, and rather hoped the companions would fall away. If not, he would make the best of it.

He did make the best of it. Midway through the afternoon, the party of six had bonded together, were enjoying the animals, enjoying each other's company and talking education. The Indian boy, Ashwin, from Ludhiana, lingered long in the platypus enclosure while the Chinese boy, Terry, could not get enough of the elks, Barbary goats and other ruminants. Philip was pleased to find that Ashwin was as charming as he appeared and was not warring with his father, a lab manager in a medical tests facility. The uncle was a doctor, with his own practice. He had lived many years in Australia and it was this, rather than his profession as such, that commended him to his younger brother who, as a new arrival, deferred to his foolish opinions as a matter of course. The Chinese father said nothing, being there to accompany his son, Ashwin's greatest friend. These two were year-eleven students at a government school, Fort Street. What did they imagine was wrong with Fort Street? Philip was afraid that both parents, goaded by the uncle, intended to shoehorn their sons into a private school, at cost, for no educational reason.

This uncle was proving a bugbear. At one time Philip found himself conducted on a personal tour of the zoo, harangued by the uncle, who even lectured them on the Floral Clock. That was not all. Success in Australia had turned him into an Indian chauvinist. He found the Australian birds 'raucous', the kangaroos 'ratty' and it was he who ordered Ashwin to stop hunting for the platypus in its tank of weed – "there's nothing there" – when in fact Ashwin had been contemplating its movements for some time. He said the tiger was from Bengal, though it was Sumatran, and complained it was impounded in too small a cage (this was true), in contempt of its fiery nature. Philip said at once, "No worse than torturing the animal."

"I call *this* torturing the animal."

"No worse than beating it with sticks through the bars. I've seen that happen in India. In Hyderabad Zoo I watched a visitor lobbing one-rupee coins to the otter. It couldn't resist catching them. It sank to the bottom of the pool."

"One-rupee coins. When were you in India? There are no one-rupee coins in India." But Philip was relating an incident of fifty-one years before.

"Was the otter dead?" asked Terry. He was glared at, not by his own father, but by the uncle.

They toured the cages in silence. Philip took no pride in his intervention, but he had silenced the uncle. The boys turned to Philip with a new respect. Ashwin's father, deeply conflicted, passed some way ahead and was the first to glimpse the lyrebird.

"You should see the village boys near Ludhiana," related Ashwin – himself a town boy – "teasing the monkeys."

Terry recalled a host of zoo incidents in Malaysia.

They bought buns and Pepsi and picnicked on a slope away from the kiosk. Lapped by the fronds of the cycads, towered over by the eucalypts, they identified free cockatoos, parrots and rosellas and basked in the vision of the harbour framed by the leaves of the paperbarks and the smooth, rosy limbs of the angaphoras. Things were so perfect that Philip was reminded of his own chauvinism, his Australian chauvinism, which he had forgotten he had. But tasks were imminent. His folders were in his hand. Straws in the wind, pointers in their conversation, had disposed him to address three topics: matriculation subjects for the boys for next year, choices in tertiary education, and things to do with themselves besides studying. With a wary eye on the uncle – who had lapsed, however, into no-man's-land – he had begun thumbing through his documents when the Chinese father gave utterance for the first time: "What will you charge?"

"Nothing for you," said Philip, surprised at the question. The man was superfluous to their party, though Philip was glad of the boon companionship of Terry and Ashwin. "I won't charge anything, you should charge me. It's been a pleasure for me too."

"No, no," muttered the father. The boys looked away. On cue, they discovered a cage they hadn't investigated down a pathway and took themselves off. The four grown men, as if orphaned, were left to fend with one another. Ashwin's uncle came superbly to life. "I'm sure you have a schedule of fees," he said. "By the week, by the hour …"

"By the hour," Philip repeated. "By what hour?" It was dawning on him slowly.

"Terry is good at mathematics," said Terry's father. "He will not need coaching in mathematics. But I think you are an English teacher."

"I am not a coach or a teacher." It seemed to Philip that the verdant scene was too brightly lit and that this was fire, fire curling each leaf as his venture turned ashen. How could Ashwin's father – to whom everything had been explained – have made this mistake? *After* a twenty-minute phone conversation, and exchange of emails! "I am not a teacher," he repeated, still softly, but without explaining, without being able to explain what he was. An 'educationist'? What was an 'educationist' if not a teacher?

The men gaped at him.

5

"We should talk in the house."

"Why the house?"

"*Avva* would like to hear us," said Jenny's grandson – and it did seem pointed, neglectful, their leaving the house to walk two streets, Gibbes Street and Bryant Street, to the park. Rockdale Park, as Philip told Jim, had been landscaped out of recognition. The cricket pitches on which he'd played as a boy, hard concrete with matting, the tall pavilion, with its cat – Kipling was right about the cat – and the flying razzle-dazzles, which would bear a child parallel to the ground – all these were gone. In their place: flowers and shrubs. It was not bleak, but there was far less in it for a boy. Bleakness was imposed elsewhere, and in mammoth proportions, by the elevated road freeway that cut through the suburb. "She may like to join in," Jim said.

"She can if she likes."

"No, best if she could listen. She's becoming suspicious of you and me."

"What makes you think so?"

"She is. She asks what we talk about."

"And what do you say?"

"I tell her."

"Then tell her. You know what to leave out. Leave out the zoo and the Indian parents. Already she supposes I can do nothing right."

"It's not your fault. These are new ways. We're all learning."

"Chinese, too. Now Chinese are coming into the picture. They're perfectly at home in I.T., with their computer skills. They need language."

"Then sock it to them."

"I'm not a coach. In India, I never coached the boys. I stood up in front of them in the classroom. I made sure they understood what they were doing before I left the room."

Said Jim, out of nowhere, "Why don't you try the Labor Party?"

"I'm a consultant, not a coach," Philip insisted. "Force-feeding is what it amounts to."

"The Labor Party," said Jim – decisively, and not for the first time. "I don't mean State government. Labor is a circus in New South Wales. I mean Federal Labor. Labor swept Queensland, in January. They cut the Liberals down to three seats. They'll soon be in power federally. Now is the time *to strike* – while they're out of power. Get yourself known. Help them prepare. They're the party of education. They'll want education. And you take a global perspective."

"You think very highly of them."

"Not highly. I'm a branch member. I'll take you along to the branch."

"I know branch meetings."

"Yes, of course, there is nothing like branch meetings. My branch is run by a faction, and it's all I can do to get a word in edgeways. That's democracy these days. My proposition for you is not branch democracy. Would you like to know my proposition for you?"

"Join the party. And once I'm a member of the party, go to the top. Take my proposals to the top, isn't that what you say?"

"Not here. Go to Canberra. Go while they're out of power. You'll have till December."

Jim had had little experience of age, of aged persons. There was his grand-mother – but Jenny was, to him, a known quantity. He had run to her, clambered all over her, depended on Jenny all his life. She was not so much old as there. But here was a new aged person, intimately related, who bristled at the first approach but whom, Jim had discovered, you could pat down.

Philip was energetic. He was seldom still. He had a lifetime bottled up in there, but unlike his estranged wife Jenny – who also had a lifetime bottled up – he wanted to talk, talk it all out; there was only one condition to all this talk. He talked about interesting things – his achievements in India, other people's achievements, careers in education in India. But he would not talk about the *most* interesting things. In Philip's view India, where he had spent nearly all his adult life, should be represented in principle as a normal place, a place like any other.

They had reached the park but, by tacit decision, they continued walking, across West Botany Street and then, by a swerve, down Bay Street which could lead only to the Botany Bay foreshores. The terrain was flat, and their pace was swift. For once, Philip appeared to read Jim's thoughts. "Teaching, teaching. You must think it's all I know. All I've ever done."

"I'd like you to tell me much more."

"More, you say. Well, there *is* more."

"I knew it," said Jim mildly.

"But, of course, what *you* want to hear about … you being a rash youth …"

"From the start," Jim insisted, not quarrelling with this view of himself. "You were in India so long. Something grabbed you, grabbed you from the start. I like to know everything from the start, particularly in your case."

"In my case? It happened so fast. If you mean Hyderabad, it vanished in the blink of an eye. Is that all you mean? I should tell you about Hyderabad in the 'forties? I've done so."

"I know you think you've done so." *Try harder:* Jim framed this command in his head.

He went further, he framed a question, without moving his lips, or failing in his stride, a thought he might one day speak aloud. Why did you marry an inexperienced young woman – in the 1950s – transport her from India to Australia, and abandon her here? Why did you return to India?

6

At Brighton-le-Sands, at the site of the demolished saltwater baths, where they sank, wearied at last, on a seat missing a plank looking over a strip of sand to the bay and Kurnell headland, where Captain Cook landed, Philip did his best to explain Hyderabad, the state and its world. He had first mistaken it for a part of India. And so it was. Yet India was no *container*. Its *parts* were wholes. Each *part* constituted a world in itself. This was true of parts all over India, and was true of the Nizam's Dominions. Philip did his best to evoke and describe the Nizam's Dominions. The earthen plain, the jumbly palatial city ... He explained Hyderabad to Jim while their eyes rested on the Kurnell headland at Botany Bay. He explained irrigation, the system of 'tanks' – *cheruvu*, in the regional language. Some tanks dated from the thirteenth century. He described their crumbling green parapets, overbrimmed by green, silent water and surmounted in places by stone-carved and eroded figures whose authority had vanished, absently patrolling a surface that stretched to the horizon. The past appeared to Philip, fished from the water. He lost sight of its image, hauled from a depth which was not the depth of memory but the depth of water, the glimmer of the surface that stood for that depth. How could you retrieve what was lost, in that weed-green element? Philip had Jim picturing Hyderabad as a lost dimension, neither space nor time, with its own properties. If you pictured it as time it would vanish. Well, people had pictured it as time, and it *had* vanished. The world was enlaced, was haunted, with such lost dimensions.

"The state would fall. Everyone knew that in advance. The British had allowed it to stand, as well you know, a replica of the old Mughal empire. They had nothing more to fear from the Mughals. The Mughal capital was in Delhi. The British, in the nineteenth century, had destroyed that empire and transformed Delhi. But Hyderabad lingered on, with the old protocols."

"Protocols," said Jim. "It was drained of life."

"It was not drained of life. It was emphatically not drained of life. It was drained of all reason, it was drained of justice, and perhaps it was drained of wisdom, but not of life. I'd never seen such an abundance of life."

"You knew it would fall, and so," said Jim, "that gave it abundance of life – like a school playground on break-up day."

But that was not the case, said Philip. "You know I had friends there."

"Well, it's so long ago now," said Jim, who was tiring of the subject, not for all time, but for that afternoon. He had something in the here and now to discuss with his grandfather. "You've met Rhondda," he began, unsurely. It was, he confessed, his first relationship, was sexual to the core, and had been going for a long time.

Back in Gibbes Street Philip found Nora and so was deflected out of the house, towards the shops and the railway. He watched football on pub tele-vision. He thought of Jenny. She never referred to her health, but he knew she visited the hospital – too often, he thought. Perhaps just on social visits. After all, she'd worked there for years. Philip typically dined out but this evening he returned before dark, with flowers from the florist. Nora took one look at the flowers and darted him such a glance that instead of placing them in water he carried them to his own room, to be presented later.

7

There were public dates.

August 15, 1947, the Independence of India. Hyderabad held out.

November 29, the Standstill Agreement. India then refrained from invasion.

January 30, 1948, in Delhi, the assassination of Gandhi.

September 20, the invasion of Hyderabad by the Indian Army, miscalled in India the 'Police Action'. Philip by then had lived in India for a year.

There were dates all his own. That Ugadi, 1948, with Ragini. The first meeting, three months before, of Ragini and Anand on the bus journey. These events had appeared to him out of their linear order. He should strive for a linear order. No leaps or ambushes. Keep them in line.

The next date in line. Soon after Ugadi: was it March or April? The schoolroom, with its two overhead fans for the nine pupils (never more than six at one time) and its desk-fan for the teacher-headmaster, was perhaps the most comfortable place in all Warangal to see out the hot weather. The parents of children certainly thought so: in these days there were more parents than children, looming in the provisional darkness between the street door and the entry-way to the kitchen at the rear of the class. Mohan, the cook, whose kitchen was always stifling and who, in good weather, stayed mostly in the street, hobnobbed with the parents in the cool of this select gallery. Philip instructed the children and rebuked the parents. There was too much noise, he said, for those who wanted to learn.

This headmaster taught in English to a mixture of ages. All the pupils were boys. The younger boys caught on while the two or three adolescent boys were distracted and baffled – but continued to attend. Philip had refined his message, pitching it to the youngest. He taught letters, numbers and native animals. He taught some non-native animals (such as the platypus), world history (the downfall of Hitler), but no Indian history. The Prophet Muhammad, the family of the Prophet, the four Rightly Guided Caliphs and the usurpation of Mu'awiya were all on the syllabus, but Philip did not teach them. He knew very little about them. His pupils were Hindus.

The Muslims had their *maktab* schools but the Hindus had nothing. The syllabus was in Philip's hands and he kept his audience, and managed to impart something, by sticking to what he knew.

All through his classes the street door opened and closed, on noiseless hinges but to blinding effect as a sliver of light continued to catch, then to elude, the one unbroken glass panel of the books cabinet. A kind of heliograph was at work. Philip contrived to ignore it which is why he at first missed Ragini who *was* signalling. She would not cross the room. When he saw her he bounded to the door in four strides.

They stood in the street.

"Is he there?"

Philip said he was there.

"It will have to be now, right now. I can't roam about at night. Anand has the key, hasn't he?"

"I made him one."

"Are you sure he'll be there? I can't linger outside the house."

"Take my key." Philip drew it from his pocket.

"But there's a servant …"

"Bashir. He's all right."

"'All right.' What's 'all right'?"

As she turned to go, Philip detained her by the arm. "You be sure *you're* there," he warned.

"I'll be there. And you come home. When your work finishes."

He returned to his desk. In the classroom, the intruder parents were agog. Some had followed him into the street.

The boys, too, were agog – to the sentence in English, which they'd copied from the blackboard. A dutiful class. A good teacher, too: he would have them explain what it meant, and spell out the words.

Philip's lodgings were far from the school. He cycled for thirty minutes down a long street, the one street of Warangal. By the time he reached home, he had wheeled through several hamlets. Philip was pleased with where he lived. His house was no different from the others in its line, with nothing to proclaim 'foreigner', except for blank spaces at the doorstep and kerb. There one adornment was missing. His street door, opening flush on the street like all the others, was new-washed at the base, with a yellow distemper, and daubed with white spots. Bashir had made sure to fix tamarind leaves over the door. The teacher of world history had baulked at the swastika, though it stood – in India – for good luck. He refused the swastika, but would dearly have loved someone to draw, to sow, a *kolam* out of rice flour in the kerbside dust before his house: a coloured one, if possible.

The skill belonged to women. Bashir couldn't do it. These beautiful and intricate designs were renewed by true housewives at the neighbouring housefronts every morning. By afternoon they were trampled, but that was all in the way of good things. They sprang forth, resplendent, with the morning light. Philip searched for his key, which he had forgotten he'd lent Ragini. She beat him to it. She opened from the inside.

What was this? Her face *fell* when she saw Philip. Before his eyes her energy, radiance and extravagance dimmed, like a light-bulb cooling.

He walked in. After all, it was his house. He found nothing to say but, "Home at last."

Where was Anand?

That was what Ragini wanted to know. "There's been no sign of him. Four hours I've waited."

"This is wrong. We had an agreement. He's to stay in the house. He's not to show his face."

"It's appalling." Her voice was severe, but her body was trembling. He had never seen her like this.

"I can't think where he's gone. He's quite disregarded all I said."

"I'm afraid he's been taken."

"Taken?"

All the cares of her world were on her slim shoulders.

Congress workers, like Anand, were in danger should they appear: but in these districts, they so seldom appeared. The anti-Nizam forces in Telengana nearly all belonged to the Andhra Mahasabha, an umbrella organisation with two kinds of branches: open branches and secret branches; some said, Communist branches. If Ragini was secretive, this was not just because the Mahasabha was secretive. She coddled mysteries of her own. Never mind. Anand was Congress, and made of it no secret.

Yet even Anand was unlikely to be rambling at large with a ticket of identity pinned to his shirtfront. Nobody in Warangal had heard of him but all the same, he should be wearing a *dhoti*. Pants, such as Anand wore, were rare. Philip had this, and more, to convey to Ragini when suddenly the man himself strolled through the doorway, like the true proprietor of these rooms.

"So many here. It's like a water-boatmen's convention."

Philip alone knew what he meant. 'Water-boatmen' were not in fact boatmen, but beetles. On his first sojourn down the coast – the coast of Madras, before ever proceeding to Hyderabad – Philip had been vexed by the multitude of soggy, gigantic beetles which in Pondicherry infested the streets, buildings, and even the hotel wash-basin. Water-boatmen beetles.

Months later, he had told Anand of his dismay. The effect was seasonal, Anand declared: it was a water-boatmen's convention.

Ragini was deaf to his words. Water-boatmen was nothing. Anand might have said anything. He might have compared the two of them to poisonous toads: he'd have been none the worse off, she'd not have heard. "So you weren't expecting me," she said coldly.

"I was. Yes, I was. I was expecting you today. At about this moment." He began to see something was wrong.

"Anand, she's been waiting for hours." Philip did not (as he was inclined to) berate Anand for flouting his instructions. He dwelt entirely on Ragini's disappointment, which Anand too would share when at last it dawned on him that he had been deprived of her company *in solitude* for the past four hours. Now dusk was approaching. She would not stay the night. For how could Ragini stay the night?

"I work hard all day. For one short day, I put my entire house at your disposal."

Philip spoke these words, and the same Philip – seventy-six years old, in his bedroom in Gibbes Street, Australia – remembered speaking them. He remembered. What glued him, re-glued him to such events? What was he up to? He was touring his memories as if to disarm them, as if to ensure, come what may, that he would never again suffer the *intrusion* of memory.

Philip had done wrong. He had concealed mention of his friends – never mind from Jim: from himself! – by stealth and long habit. Nicked at last. Ragini had walked in on him in this bedroom! *Now* he remembered them. That being the case, let them spare him! He wanted nothing to 'come to light'. To ensure nothing would 'come to light', he appeared to be stalking through his memories like a ragpicker. What was there in this ragpile to discover alive? He would find, stupefy and brand it first. Hovering in alarm at a distance, he did not know what was 'in' there.

In the house at Warangal, Ragini was beginning to thaw. She was not willing to be approached by Anand or to touch him, in Philip's presence, but she would listen. Anand pitched his tale to her ears. He had been exploring nearby. Philip knew well, and Anand knew he knew, that the Thousand Pillar Temple at Hanumkonda, which was many centuries old and a wonder of stone mortising, had been closed all year for repairs. It was out of worship. Only the Nandi could be glimpsed from the road. Ragini herself knew this but was willing to forget, to be entertained by a wholly spurious account of her hero's visit to the famous temple. At least he had read the billboard outside the temple. He described for her this beautiful and revered structure. "How many thousand years," he enthused, perhaps confusing the number of pillars with the years, "this temple has stood perpendicular, built of stones, hand-fitted, without use of lime or cement. The genius of the Hindu nation."

This description was proffered ironically. Anand was seeking enhanced common ground with Ragini, by reminding her that even under Muslim occupation, fear-inspiring of late, neither she nor he had become Hindu chauvinists.

"So you found the temple. Philip will have shown you the fort, I'm sure."

"The sublime Hindu fort," said Anand, overdoing it a little. "Most ancient forts of India are Muslim forts, but this is a matchless construction."

"So you'll claim it for India."

"We are standing in India, as I speak. There will be an India, even in Warangal district."

"Where else were you today?"

Anand saw the trap. "I haven't been trespassing in 'your' country. I haven't been trespassing in Communist country, you must believe that."

"Trespass where you like. If there has to be a Congress spy, in 'Communist country', I'd like it to be you."

"I did not come to Warangal to organise. I came to find you."

"Oh, you came to organise. *And* you found me."

"A cat can look at a king," said Philip. Reminded of his existence, the two broke off. "Or a queen," Philip added.

"Yes, Ragini is a queen," said Anand, at last – like one persuaded against his interest. He feigned negligence, but could not keep it up. After all, he had ground to recover, and apology was not his style. Admiration was more his style. "She may not be a queen," he said in a lowered voice, "but this Ragini you see is the most beautiful woman I have ever set eyes on. I've been dreaming of her day and night."

" 'Beautiful'?" queried Ragini, as if beauty was beneath her.

Anand might have carried it off, but Philip believed his intervention was called for. "The two of you may not have noticed," he said, "that what I'm carrying under my arm – is a bottle of beer. The label has fallen off, but it's still beer. And this is …" He laid down the bottle, in its disguise wrapping, and dug from his pocket a meagre, unwrapped object. He stood it on the table.

"A teacup?"

"A teacup, and it's not the first. I have, in this house, two other teacups."

As he whipped off the cap – Philip had a bottle-opener as well – he told how he'd bought the beer, with no personal identification, on the evidence solely of his white skin. He knew the shop. He'd staked it for some time.

"No ice, no refrigerator. So we'll drink it at once, it's warm."

"Before I went out, your Bashir called by," said Anand. "I know you gave him his *rukhsat*, two days you said, but he still drops in. He's been today. Can't keep away."

"Well, how can he? He buys everything. Milk, cooking oil, *vanaspati* ..."

Drinking warm beer, the three savoured their delinquency – petty, and safe. There should be more delinquency like that. Philip had taken a chipped teacup, and Ragini the new one. "How will you get away from here?" said Anand. "Isn't it harder after nightfall?"

"I'll take my chance."

"There are police everywhere. They're in battle fatigues, just strolling about. Shopping for the eggs, like Bashir."

"That's the army. What you've mistaken for police is one section of the army, called the forest unit. Don't you have them in Marathwada?"

"And the ones with berets?"

"The ones with berets are the same as the ones with turbans. Try to keep out of their way."

"Are they particularly stupid?"

"Not that I've heard."

"Then how do you manage?"

Philip had reflected on this problem. "She thinks she's invulnerable," he said, "so of course she is. Forever riding her bicycle: you can pick it a mile off. With green and red spots."

"Lady's bicycle. Because I'm a lady."

"What are they up to, these Communist *dalams*? Is it some kind of a picnic out there? The police wave you through? 'This one is a lady.' Or is it your personal magic, some kind of spell?" said Anand. "You were born in the forest. You were raised in the forest. The birds and the beasts call you by name. The tribals adore you. You dress as a Hindu, but you're really a Gond shamaness with a headdress of hide and bone and worked metal, like Philip describes for Bastar."

"I describe nothing of the kind," said Philip.

"What are you, Ragini?"

Philip too awaited an answer. Anand always got Ragini wrong but he was curious to see how far along with it *she* went. She was resourceful enough, without Anand's turning her into wonder worker and invisible woman. The headdress he'd seen in Bastar – whither he'd been dispatched on an errand of state, four days after coming to Hyderabad – was a bison male headdress worn for display by a young and virile Maria Gond, nothing to do with a 'shamaness'.

"You ask me what I am? Well what do you know, Anand, I'm a town girl! A medical student. I'm as lost in the forest as you would be."

"I can't believe that."

"You think I was suckled by a tiger in the leaves?"

"You're a birdcatcher."

"No, I do not catch birds. There are people who do. There are people who know and use every shrub and flower that grows in the forest, but I'm not one of them. I have to be cared for out there. I have to watch what I eat. That's why I'd be so glad – Philip – of a little home cooking, even Australian home cooking if that's what you do. I see you have a kerosene stove. You can boil rice, can't you?"

"I can boil rice. Probably not up to your standard. If Bashir was here, he'd run to the bazaar, he'd throw everything together and he'd make you a *thali*."

"Then send for him."

"Don't you send for him," Anand commanded. "Let's see what's here. You have flour and ghee. Saucepans. I think there's a griddle plate some-where. I can make *parathas*."

"*Parathas* would be fine," said Ragini.

Anand did make *parathas*. The room was soon filled with cooking aromas. Bashir had stocked the cupboard with eggplant, tomatoes, and a bitter gourd Philip had come to depend on. Onions, a few red chillis, and mustard seeds in profusion. Philip was choking but the others, sound of wind and dry of eye, were wholly in their element. Anand chopped this and that and succeeded in getting it right.

"So you know how to do this. Were there no women in your family?" Ragini inquired.

Anand gazed at her – with affection and amazement. "I'm beginning to understand. You can't cook, can you?"

"Of course not. It's just as you suppose, I was the apple of my father's eye and my sister did everything around the house. I studied medicine. Before that, Ramayana and music. They were so proud of me."

"Of course they were proud. You've told me all I need to know."

Philip was silent. So she'd told him all he needed to know, was that right? Was he any the wiser? Ragini – Anand failed to see – had the relish to impose on others any impression of herself she liked to give. Philip did not know whether Ragini could cook or not. Anand must wait to find out. She was not the artless landed-caste daughter, beset by police cohorts and Razakar paramilitary gangs, with whom upright Anand had fallen in love on the spot. You'd think he'd have learned from the bus ride. But he had learned nothing. Everything came as a surprise to Anand. He'd been conducted by Ragini, all in good time, on the grand tour of their political differences, at heart-breaking cost and with profound misgiving, but had barely yet acknowledged, except in jest, that Ragini bivouacked with the *dalams*. She was a Communist on her own admission! Now look where he was! It was Ragini – not Congress business – that lured him to the heart of the 'red' district. In four months since December, this was his fourth visit. Anand kept coming. He would keep coming for so long as his India was suspended, for so long as there was a Nizam in Hyderabad.

And then what?

"Which sister is the one," Philip asked of her, "– you've told me her name – who would travel to Madras once a fortnight to pay your dues at the medical hostel?"

"Wasn't that a waste of good money?" said Anand.

Their meal was over. It became dark. Ragini had not left. She wheeled out her bike – propped in the house, for concealment – thought better of it, and wheeled it in again. To depart at once – while the two were probing the mystery of her medical studies – would have seemed like running from something. She listened to their chatter. Had she more than one sister? Had she ever enrolled in medicine? Had she spent even one night in a hostel? Why ever had she been credited with an exam pass in February?

"Family influence," said Anand.

Ragini volunteered nothing. Instead, she turned the tables on Anand. What about his own family? "Somebody was in gaol, right?"

"You know damn well somebody was in gaol. My father and my brother are *satyagrahis*, and my brother was in gaol. No medical scholarships in our family."

"They sound quite a family. Warriors for justice, who have themselves imprisoned on purpose."

"Warriors for what? Who said anything about justice? They are warring for India. Justice will follow."

"Justice will not follow for my people."

"Ragini, I wonder how you dare. How do you dare to call them your people? You're a student from Andhra or somewhere, a porpoise of the delta, you don't even belong in their forest. You've admitted it yourself. The only thing in common between the forest people and *your* own people is ..."

"Is what?"

"Is that you're Indians. You're an Indian, these forest people are Indians, and your own Bezwada people are Indians, all the same way."

"I am not from Bezwada."

"There's no glory in fighting for a Communist state."

There, he'd said it. Anand acknowledged that much, though he was quite wrong about Bezwada. Ragini, Philip knew, was a local. Born and bred ... Philip dropped out of the argument. He supposed this was how it was for them. The two were at daggers drawn, they had to be. No-one, for the good of them both, could impose a truce. No-one could say: 'Let's leave politics out of it.' And what politics! Anand, in his hearing, depicted Ragini as the puppet of Stalin. To Ragini, Tuka, Anand's brother, had had himself thrown in gaol out of sheer fatigue. All she could commend in Anand was that he'd stayed out of gaol. Slippery to the core, he had avoided that fate. Their lightness, their laughter was a kind of thunder. Things were becoming really nasty. Yet, somehow, the danger was dispersed. All the vexation died away: though nothing, to Philip's ears, had been unsaid. In all of five minutes, these dire insults were forgotten. Was it a game? Weren't they serious? The house had one lantern. Philip pumped it while the two fell silent. The linen bag caught fire, flared, and dwindled to a safe glow. He carried the lantern to the inner room and dragged in the armchair and the two kitchen chairs. Philip took one chair, the second was vacant, and Ragini subsided, as was her right, into the armchair. There was a pause for suspense, as Anand decided where he would settle.

He chose the floor, crouching at her feet. The one kitchen chair, not to mention the narrow bed, were unoccupied.

"Who was Nathuram Godse?" said Ragini, almost at once. "Did you meet him?" She was referring to the assassin of Gandhi.

"Godse came to Hyderabad. I never saw him – no, perhaps I saw him. He once demonstrated against the Nizam."

"So many people did." Her voice was soft. It was clear what she meant to say: that it was no moral qualification to have demonstrated against the Nizam, since the same was true even of Godse. His crime was stupendous. For all the violence of these years, of the Partition of India, the birth of Pakistan, it was hard to believe that the Mahatma's life had been taken.

That was the end of it. No more India, no more Communist state, not for tonight. The desertion of these topics was, to Philip, a cue for sleep – he had had a long day – but he did not know *where* to sleep. To hog the bed seemed unsociable. But what was sociable? The only society at this hour was the society of two. They continued to converse in low voices. Philip had so placed the lantern that he could not make out what Ragini was doing in her armchair. His own gaunt frame was illuminated. For some time yet he predicted that Ragini might make a bolt for it in the pitch dark: but why would she do that? She was so clearly where she wanted to be.

8

His guests' voices carried to Philip from the dark corner of the room. The lantern's shine was on him. But to redirect it might make matters worse.

He slipped from his chair and from the room. His movements are recalled by Philip after fifty-three years, from his bed in Gibbes Street. In the interest of a story, to accompany Philip from the house might be less enticing than to stay with the lovers in the room. But the story so far is not that kind of story, but the tale of a recall. Who is there but Philip to recall?

He closed the street door behind him. This was the arterial road. It was darker than he'd thought. Not even the railway station at Kazipet, half a mile away, showed a glimmer of light. Philip began walking fast, in the opposite direction, as if repeating, on foot, the day journey to his school. There were few street lights and no camber to the road, so although he bore along the road's centre he kept stumbling into the holes he avoided by daylight. The moon was folded on its dark wing. The street was empty to the eye, but – to the ear – there were signs of life. People had wirelesses and from the darkened houses a thin static emerged, like the buzz of trapped flies along a wire sweetened to allure them. Now and again, as he strode, snatches of intelligible music broke through the noise.

He passed the dark temple – supposed to have been investigated by Anand – at Hanumkonda. He passed the dark grids and piers of the electricity substation. That prerequisite of V.I. Lenin – electrification – had long been met in the Nizam's Dominions, but to small public effect. Workmen or maintenance staff were grouped around a single lantern. From a dark street, Philip heard a living voice. A voice in song, without tremolo, clear and melodious. A boy was approaching the main road up a slope, from the direction of what Philip knew to be the Devi temple. As he gained the road, a vehicle with weak headlights, bereft of glass, appeared on the road, screeched past Philip and intercepted the boy. Two or more pairs of arms bundled him in. The car sped a short way towards Kazipet, then stopped dead. Either it had stalled, or some interrogation was in progress.

Philip raced back. Who were they? Police? A landlord's gang? Brothel-keepers? (He thought of that.) Muslim diehard militias? He had all but reached the car when it drew away from him, slowly, as if merely to elude him, with the boy inside. What was his crime? Singing too audibly, too beautifully, on a dark night?

Philip was so much a citizen of his peaceable country, so little in awe (since nothing ever happened to him) of the forces of order and disorder in a distant land, that he ran without hesitation to the car, thumped the boot, outpaced the car and briefly confronted the headlights before swerving for safety to one side. It was as much as he could do. But his effort paid off. A door flew open. A body was pushed from the slow-moving car and rolled. Philip ran but, fast as he was, before he reached him the boy had stumbled to his feet, darted away and was lost in a maze of paths between the houses. He had no idea his saviour was after him.

Philip gave up the chase. He walked on. He was not fatigued. His pace had increased a little. The incident, far from unnerving him, had elated him – since the boy got away. He pounded in a storm of emotion. What he had witnessed was an abduction. Yet here he was, enthused by his deed, buoyed by his elation, proclaiming in the teeth of *an abduction* that the road was safe! Ragini might have left at nightfall! – or so he proclaimed. There were no *police* about. She knew the road. For her, all its perils were of the daytime. Yet Ragini was still in his house. She had stayed for Anand! His legs knew this, his commotion at heart testified to the truth of his legs, yet now he acknowledged it as a thought, the thought amazed him. She had stayed for Anand. How could he have compared himself to Anand? By once voicing his claim to Ragini, he'd deserved her pity and boosted the authority of his rival … There he went again! *He* was not the rival of anyone. Philip was a guileless headmaster (the only one who would accept the job) toiling for his boys but in fact for the credit of the Nizam. Anand knew this. Ragini knew this. Philip leapt as he ran, punching the air. He was good for nobody. He stood for nothing. Or you tell me what he stood for. He did not even *aspire* to stand.

Good for nobody, stood for nothing. In the room at Gibbes Street, Philip was ambushed by this truth. But was this the same truth, this truth that had seized him on the road at Warangal? – the truth that had prompted him to leap in the road, to punch the air? Was he in fact remembering? Or was this so-called memory of his the work of this moment, the projection of the thought of this room, of his *present* dismay, onto events so distant they had been forgotten?

Without turning to his present dismay, whatever that was – for Philip was not one to feel sorry for himself, or not for long – he inspected the past. It could not be his present dismay that so startled him, but something in the past. Something that was truly a memory, something *at home* in the past that was trying to ruffle him. Something that would not give up. Philip suspected a purpose – as if there were some kindly power, working for his redemption, as in a novel. He did not mean the ghost of Ragini but a superior power, some kind of super-listener who thought Philip was important enough to tune in. He did not think of Beatrice and her Dante, but as a lapsed Protestant he could not help thinking of a Heavenly Father: Forgive me, Heavenly Father. Why are you showing me these things? Philip was an infant. He could sometimes believe that the grace of a visitation, and his own labour of recollection, bespoke a purpose, and, steering that purpose, an occult power – kindly or unkindly.

He returned to the road – staring the night to its conclusion. A long night. He tramped a long way. His school hove into sight, but he ignored it. He reached the fort. The old fort of Warangal was in ruins. But in places the granite walls endured. A gate was intact and through that he passed. There were people about: more people inside this wall than on the streets of the town. None were in touching distance and none approached him. Little colonies of people, crouching, standing, assembled into groups, family groups disposed to sleep. Low voices carried to him. For want of a moon there were lanterns, even a fire here and there. The darkness between the points of light was unbridged. The expanse seemed limitless. Grass was underfoot. He found a spot, leaning against a smooth boulder, and there, at last, his mind and body were at one and he fell asleep.

Something brushed his cheek. A hand. In Australia he'd have been shaken awake, but this touch was gentle. He recovered his senses in enough light to find himself inspected by children, two boys, kneeling to his dwarfed height. The boys were exploring, to see what he became when he woke. Now that was partly known they backed off. They stood admiring him. More boys ran up. Philip's bones creaked. He had been sleeping in the dew against a hard stone. He rose with difficulty. The dawn light was in the sky and the families were busying themselves. He smelled cooking: rice or milk-tea in pans over low fires. He tried to walk, and stumbled against his boulder.

This was no boulder but a carved being. The protrusion that had drilled his spine was a beak or an eye. Something puffin- or parrot-like now surveyed him with the very organ he'd slept on, its appalling eye. Philip stared back. Then, as the boys had done, he ran his hands over this extravagant object.

The mist was clearing for a new day. He saw the place was strewn with such objects, toppled from the walls or from standing-places along the walls. In whichever attitude it had come to lie, each carved object retained its inquisitive personality.

Philip, watched by the boys, stalked back and forth as his limbs acquired warmth. His back straightened. The boys led him to a physical challenge. They began to climb the steps, the flight of steps at a structure inside the gate. These steps were high. Philip was a tall youth but his legs wobbled at the distance from ledge to ledge, stepping like a monarch's legs, while the boys scrambled and outsped him. He gazed from the top over hillocked land, a landscape of ancient mounds, crumbled plinths and pavilions overspread by a thornbush with straggly branches. Smoke rose from makeshift huts. He stood, he saw, on a kind of triumphal dais which the years had spared. Six hundred, seven hundred years. In time to come, he would learn who the raja was, who had stood, crestfallen, at this height. From the bed at Gibbes Street, he strove to suppress after-knowledge. Present concerns, slow-building consequences, after-knowledge. Keep your knowledge at bay, preserve true memory. He fled from his height, without knowing what prompted him: after-knowledge? – or the bedevilling image of Ragini and Anand, alone in his house? The boys were encouraged by this burst of energy. They streamed out the gate with him. Philip pelted ten miles on little sleep. Shop shutters were up, the sun was high and the street thronged with people who seemed to infest his way, like the crowd at an Olympic marathon thoughtlessly impeding the competitor running last. His house door was bolted. From the outside, that was strange: the lock dangling but not snipped to. He hadn't left it that way. Where were they? Chair, armchair and bed were empty, the bed not slept in. Anand, who'd boarded for one night, had taken his belongings and Ragini's bike was gone. Was there a note? Here was the note. 'Philip, you are so good, thanks for having us.' Having *us*? Ragini's scrawl. Not a word from Anand.

Chapter Three. A Nawab's Palace

1

"All this, only to fix a date."

By 'all this', Jenny referred to the presence of her entire family: Nora in her smart clothes – the heeled shoes premising a major excursion; Jim as Jim was; and Vinta as Vinta was, orderly in bearing but unable to keep the scamper out of her eye. They stood in a bunched group in an awkward space, the vehicle entry portal between the lobby and the road at Kogarah Bay hospital. "Home we go, then," said Jenny. "That's all there is for us."

"No, *avva*, no, *avva*, not home," Vinta pleaded. "We've come too far."

"Far? One station down the line?" Jenny was amused. " 'Far' is the moon these days."

"I want to eat out."

"And not in the hospital cafeteria, either," Jim added.

"I tell you what," said Nora. "We *will* eat out. I'll drive us to Tom Ugly's." That would be festive. But as Jenny's wilted stance reminded them, there was nothing to be festive about – nor truly despondent, for that matter. They had come to the hospital expecting a ready appointment, but Jenny had been met with a date – which could easily have been negotiated over the phone.

Tom Ugly's was the name long given to the point of land, some way south, where a bridge crossed the George's River. These days, like most places, it was suburb, but when Jenny was a new immigrant Philip had taken her to Tom Ugly's for the seafood restaurants. The point and the bridge had retained that association, not only for Jenny, but for her daughter and grandchildren. They would find nothing there. The seafood restaurants were gone. They would have to make do with somewhere else, but the prospect enthused them all. Their cohort began to unscramble and to work its way along the pavement to Nora's car.

"There he is. Look."

"What's he doing here?"

Formally garbed in suit and waistcoat, Philip was distractedly crossing the road, yarning with a companion, behind him, who could not quite keep up. Philip placed his trust in the speeding cars to afford him safe passage. "How it's done in India," murmured Jim. But Jenny corrected him.

"Here or in India, your grandfather always crosses roads the same way."

"Chap there escaped with his life," said Jim. "He's off." The two men, after a handshake, had parted. Philip was now alone on their side of the road.

"Climb in," said Nora. "Before he sees us."

But her own daughter had skipped to Philip. She returned with him, beaming. Philip too was beaming. He seemed overjoyed to find them, Jenny in particular. He kissed her cheek.

Try that with me, Nora's stance warned.

"All here together?" questioned Philip.

Jim greeted him. "You're a sly one. Kogarah branch, is it? Or Rockdale? Wheeling and dealing?"

"I am not here to join the Labor Party."

"Then what's afoot?" said Jim gaily.

Philip explained to Jim's grandmother. "You remember, I went to school here. There are still people who know me."

"Was that Paul Best?" said Jenny. "Then you *have* joined the Labor Party. Paul Best is in the Labor Party."

Philip was amazed. "How do you know Paul Best?"

"*You* went to primary school in Rockdale. But, after that, *I* came to Rockdale, and I've lived here for forty-nine years."

"In your house!" said Jim, applauding his grandmother's counter-stroke.

Philip gladly surrendered to his former wife. "To think you know Paul Best. You'll be telling me next you know Alfred Cooligan."

"Is that a made-up name?"

Jim eyed the pair of them as if they were Beatrice and Benedict in person. Not that Philip had shown much dexterity. But he was in fine humour.

"It's the right time to join the A.L.P.," said Jim, "if that's what you've done. They'll soon be livening up the branches with all your old friends. Swept the polls in Queensland."

"So you've told me. So Paul told me."

"Roll on the federal election," said Jim.

"I don't expect to win anything."

"Play to win. 2001 is a winning year."

"It's more the companionship."

"You'll have all the companionship you want. Stirring pots of glue, folding leaflets, hand-writing the addresses on envelopes so people will open them. They'll fit you up with intelligent young women on doorknocks. It will be one hell of a party come December."

Nora said witheringly, "He's too smart."

"Philip is too smart?"

"Not Philip. The Prime Minister. Howard is too smart to let you win."

"Why, what can he do about it? We're streets ahead."

Nora's keys were out. She fumbled at the car door. "Jim, ride in the back for now. *Amma* prefers the front seat."

"The back will do very well for me," said Jenny, "if Philip can come."

"He can't come. I won't have him with us."

"I invite him to come."

"Slip in, then," said Nora offhandedly, to Philip, without glancing at him. "Vinta will sit on your lap."

"I'll welcome Vinta on my lap," said Philip. "Where are we going?"

"Never mind. You have your invitation."

Philip looked to Jenny. Her lips were firmly compressed. Just to have him along she was using, he saw, her quantum of family authority – while he had none.

"We'll be off, then!" he said. "To an unknown destination."

They struggled, five persons into the five-seater, as if they were one person too many. Nora drove a manual, with clutch and gears. The car hiccupped on starting, and failed completely as they paused at the first intersection. The lights changed, the next wave of traffic powered by, but the car was motionless. Nora was motionless.

At last she took off, only to pull in to the kerb. She said in level tones, facing the steering wheel, "I won't have him with us. He neglected us all. He was no father to me, and he treated my mother abominably."

Jim said, after a moment, "So we've all heard."

"It's her choice," said Jenny, in a low, though imperfectly chastised, voice. "Philip, will you help me out? If you're walking home, Jim will walk with you. Jim, when you arrive at the house, your car is there. Bring Philip to Tom Ugly's in your own car."

To her it was all about the car. Or so she contrived to have it seem. Jim climbed out. "Mum could take us all, if she'd snap out of it."

He was readier to disobey his mother than to flout Jenny. This made Nora's defiance all the plainer. Jim, taking Philip's arm, which he would never have tried to do if his wits were about him, guided him back along the highway in the direction they'd come. He looked behind, wielding his grandfather, to see if Nora had changed her mind. But the car was gone.

2

Confused and sad as he was bundled off – he had framed no goodbye to Jenny – Philip strove to regain some autonomy of movement. Jim had his arm grasped tight. He tugged it free. "Why were you there? Why were you all at the hospital?"

"It's *avva*'s old haunt. Her place of work."

"Is she ill?"

"She's fine. You saw that."

Philip made a mental note: Jenny was unwell. Jim, for some reason, would not share his information. They were walking at their usual fast pace in a direction neither had chosen. Jim had a sudden idea. He wheeled. "I'll show you where St George play."

"In my day it was Hurstville Oval."

"You're a half-century out of date."

Philip let himself be led, out of respect for the St George clubs. So this was where they played now, the elect of the famed sporting region, dominant in cricket and football, with eleven straight Rugby League premierships between 1956 and 1966. Philip's 'day' had been earlier. He had trailed behind Arthur Morris and Ray Lindwall, the great Test cricketers, into the changing-shed at Hurstville Oval, soon after the war ended – and had emerged with his bat signed. A decade earlier, and he'd have pestered Bradman. When Philip watched his last game of Rugby League at Hurstville Oval, St George v Balmain, Matt McCoy was the star centre and Jack 'Dutchy' Holland played in the forwards.

"Kogarah Jubilee Oval," said his grandson. "It's closed now. Midweek, of course."

They viewed the grassed oval, the grandstand and the wooden forms with a kind of reverence.

"I'll bring you here one Sunday," said Jim. It was winter, the football season. "Rhondda likes the game. More than I do, in fact."

The perfumed name of Rhondda now lingered in the air for Jim, who had something to confide. Much to confide. It was to be a long walk. Philip bethought himself, in haste, of a matter of his own to confide – and he found it.

"You did ask me once – do you recall? – why I stayed on in Hyderabad."

"I don't think I did. I asked why you stayed on *in India*, when your wife was in Sydney."

Jim was mistaken. He had asked the Hyderabad question. He had brooded on the India question, but had never voiced it. It slipped out now.

Philip, if he noticed the gaffe, gave no sign. He was rallying his thoughts, in no ideal mood for confession. But it was either his confession, or Jim's confession. "I told you then I stayed for the job."

"And why not?"

"I stayed on in Warangal – where my school was – for about fifteen months from September 1948: the month the Indian Army beat down the Nizam. The Indians had waited a year. There were all kinds of negotiations. Standstill Agreements, draft understandings of this and that, breaches of covenant on both sides. The Nizam put his case to the United Nations, at the last moment. He was under blockade. He'd been stockpiling contraband for months. Did you know an Australian pilot, Sidney Cotton, flew into the airfields at night, time after time, with a planeload of weapons?"

"Did he now? Did you meet him?" said Jim, feigning an interest. His interest at this moment was slight.

"No; I'll tell you one thing."

One thing. But he'd told Jim 'friends'. Not names. He baulked at names. Why trouble Jim, why confess to Jim at all? What was this about? A forgotten, a half-forgotten young woman had intruded on his life, but had offered no further provocation. He pictured her as a wraith in a dream, yet her intrusion was real. Nothing more real had happened to him since he returned to Australia.

"I won't make it a long story," he said. "The British left India in 1947. But this was September, 1948. A long wait for the Nizam. The Congress ruled India. They had a branch in Hyderabad, and this branch the Nizam had closed down. The branch was illegal. You know *satyagraha*, non-violent resistance? *Satyagraha* was Gandhi's tactic. His tactic in India, for the freedom struggle. That was in India, but here, in Hyderabad, *within* the Congress, there were furious disagreements over tactics."

"Shall we cross the highway at the lights, or cross here?"

"Some just waited for the Indian Army to move in. But for others, patience was not enough. The north-eastern districts, the Telengana districts, were in the midst of a peasant revolution. You didn't much see it – unless you took to the roads – but it was all around you. Warangal was one of the heartlands. It was safe enough in the town but the villages were a battlefield. And so was the forest, on both sides of the Godavari River. Landlords and moneylenders fled to the towns, to the police posts in towns. The Nizam couldn't help them. The Razakars would fight, but they would not fight for landlords, for Hindu landlords. And the Hyderabad Congress leaders told their members to wait. Wait for the army. But the young men in Congress, the 'impatient' Congress, the ones moreover with a social conscience, the

ones who owed nothing to the landlords – I'll call them the 'firebrands',
though they weren't all firebrands: studious young men, those I met …"

"What's he on about?" railed Jim under his breath.

"Their leader was a Hindu *sanyasin*, in an ochre robe. Swami Ramananda
Tirtha. For most of 1948, he was in gaol. But the gaols were like sieves.
Information flowed in and out. The Swami was aware, and his followers
were aware, that before the army moved in, Communist revolutionaries
would win a base in India. There they would be, the Communists: occu-
pying the land, righting social wrongs and handing over the fields, tanks
and granaries to the villages. The 'impatient' Congress *also* wanted to right
wrongs. They did not want their party to be imposed on that part of India
by the Army, with jagirdars and landlords riding home to their villages
shooting at peasants in *dhotis* and fluttering national flags in Army trucks."

"And you?" said Jim, wanting out. "You stayed. To protect your school?
Just to watch?"

By now they were in Rockdale and were storming past the Lebanese
pastry-shops, the 'Bombay' Chinese restaurant – which set the bland
Cantonese food on fire – the Greek *zakharaplasteikon* and all those shops
and enterprises, undreamed of in Philip's 'day', which proclaimed multi-
cultural Australia. They turned at the red-brick Town Hall on the Bestic
Street corner.

"I think I've told you why I stayed. For friends."

"For friends. What became of them? Who were they?"

"I had two friends. One was Anand. I would like you to know, it was
because of Anand that I stayed on … This is not an easy memory …"

"Anand meant a lot to you."

"I have not had such friends before or since."

"And the other?" said Jim.

"The other was Ragini."

"Ragini. My grandmother's name. That was my grandmother's name,
before she was Jenny. Ragini was *avva*'s name."

"Ragini is a word from music. It's the same name."

"And what is Anand?"

"Anand is 'happy'."

"And that describes him?"

"Well enough. Not particularly. Why should it describe him?"

" 'Music' and 'happiness'. Your two friends. And 'music' is *avva*'s name."
Jim reflected briefly, but nothing occurred to him. "That's a sweet name
for her. But it's no wonder at all she changed her name. Where's the music?
There is nothing very musical about *avva*. A grandson would know."

3

There was nothing very musical about Philip either. That aspect of Ragini had escaped him. Either he missed it, or Ragini forbore to show him. She tried him on poetry. She tried him on the Telugu language, quoted him Sri Sri and all the revolutionary verses she had by heart. She may even have sung them, but only to portray to her friend what the revolutionary people were up to.

Music. On the last day of April, Philip and Anand met at Charminar. To get there, to Hyderabad, Philip had had to wait for the ten-day vacation. But then, how he raced! The bus journey stretched to fourteen hours, thanks to the road-blocks and a motor breakdown. All the while he sat, his feet were in motion. It was the dry season. The bus bumped into the Hyderabad depot at dead of night. The raddled pavements beside the Musi were mud-hard, but Philip, not pausing for a rickshaw, stamped his way across the bridge to Anand's hostel. Anand was not home. A co-tenant said he was in Aurangabad. He would return the next day. Philip left a note. He fixed an appointment for Charminar, and Anand kept it.

For the first half-hour – as they watched the street through the grille of an Iranian café somewhere between the monument and the river – not a word was said about events. Philip nursed his grievance. Through some quirk of comradeship, the closer that grievance edged – though still unspoken – the sunnier his behaviour. Nothing yet about Ragini, misused hospitality, the flown coop and the absence in her note of any clue to her whereabouts. It was Anand who rebuked Philip for his own misconduct. He had heard (from Sukku) that Philip now sought the acquaintance of the Khan Bahadur. This could only be for one reason. It was not to drink whisky on a Kashan carpet under a multi-piece chandelier between columns of Italian marble, watching the dust drift and the walls crumble. Anand well conjured up a vision of the Khan's palace, though he had never been inside it – or indeed inside any *haveli*.

At last Philip had had enough. He put it to Anand that he had deceived him. His accomplice and he had made a clean getaway. They must have been cock-a-hoop.

"No, no," said Anand, looking mystified. He moved on, to another topic. He quite had the measure of Philip. To obtain satisfaction from Anand, Philip would have to repeat the dose.

"If Laiq Ali knew what he was doing," Anand said – referring to the Prime Minister of Hyderabad serving the Nizam – "he'd spare his troops a battle they can't win, and train all his firepower on the Razakars. Better disarm them now – himself! – not leave it to the Indian Army."

"When their time comes," said Philip.

"When their time comes? Their time will come! India will invade. An agreement has been broken. The Nizam must be counting the days. All deals are off."

"I know your Army will invade. They'll slice through the Hyderabad Army like a knife through butter. That part will be easy."

"Which part won't be easy?"

Philip replied in a distanced voice. He could not believe he was saying this; he sounded like a hurt schoolboy, in the days of inane schoolyard crushes, long before women and their wiles were dreamt of. "You should ask your friend."

"My 'friend' is … ?"

"Ask Ragini. Ask *her* which part will be easy. Will the peasants be easy? Will the peasants be waving in the Army, with Congress streamers in their hands? I don't think so."

"You don't think so. And what do you know?"

"I know what any damn fool can tell you."

"Ragini and I may disagree," said Anand agreeably. Philip had rattled him a little. "But you'll find we are working for the same thing."

"Not from what I hear."

"And where do you hear what you hear? From the Khan Bahadur? From his Australian wife? *Those* are people, are they, with their ears to the ground?"

"I hear from the school. From Sri Srinivasan in the street. From the tiffin-shop owner. From the quarry guy at the workshop. From domestic staff. From Bashir. How ever did you stave off Bashir? He arrives every day before cock-crow. I thought you'd at least have left a note by Bashir. 'Thank you old pal, Philip, for the gift of a beer, and the hospitality of a bed.' "

"We never touched your bed."

"For the armchair."

Philip was never to learn what came next. He'd left them snuggled in the armchair, and hared straight as a die for the chill stones and immemorial perspectives of the fort of Warangal. But he did hear one detail that left him too furious to speak.

That detail was not explicit. It came, a mere mention, when the two had all but made their peace. Anand and Philip walked, uphill from the Musi, to the radial point, Charminar: a pierced granite monument the colour of old lace. Philip had once climbed Charminar. He had more than once feasted his eyes on the granite honeycombing along the top lintel, wondering at the clock-with-hands nestled between the columns. To his eyes, this twentieth-century adjunct spoiled the effect. He was more impressed by the nearby *haveli* at Chowk Maidan Khan, which sported an elegant *naubat* pavilion facing the entrance. There drummers and shahnai players stood daily, to proclaim the comings and goings of the master of that house, a rival hidalgo to the Khan Bahadur – who had nothing of the kind.

The bazaar shutters were lowered in the heat of mid-afternoon. Philip could not help wondering if the Khan's Australian wife – whom he soon would meet – would be pleased with a gift from the bangle or cosmetics stalls, which she must know by heart. Better for her a packet of assorted biscuits from Arnotts in Sydney! He had all but overruled his grievance, a glad respite for him, but by now Anand was remembering Ragini. "Such a gracious, even-tempered person", that kind of thing – nothing Philip could recognise. Anand, of course, would have been wiser to stay off the topic but Philip, protective of his calm, was barely listening. Suddenly he was all ears.

"Which forest? Which part of the forest?"

"Did I say forest? I said temple."

"You said 'forest temple', the Siva temple. How did you get to Palampet?"

"To Palampet?"

"There is only one temple of that description. She took you there!"

"The Siva forest temple," mused Anand, who could feign surprise but was a bad liar. It was his own revelation. Yet he spoke as if the conjunction of those three words beggared belief.

Philip was struggling to give voice. "She took you to Palampet!"

"If that's what it's called. She did." Anand was not one to be reproved. He harangued Philip. "I know, and I thank God for it, that you met Ragini before I did. You and she have some special understanding. I even know why: she drops in on you at the school, and she enjoys your company. She's told me all that." He hung fire. Philip fought for breath.

"You suppose you know a great deal about Ragini," Anand went on. "At times I've been glad of your advice."

What was coming? From a none-too-ceremonious friend like Anand, this was silken courtesy.

"You *are* the guided-tour expert on Ragini. We'll leave out politics. Politics is easily misunderstood, especially by a person from a foreign country, a person whose heart is in the right place, but could not direct a soul in India to where that place is. Ragini is a bold and sincere person. Don't you agree? We both agree. And that is where your knowledge of her begins and ends."

"You have better knowledge!" Philip got out.

"Listen, Philip. One question about Ragini. Have you heard her sing?"

"Of course I've heard her sing."

"No. Sing. Like a bird in the forest, since you're so keen on forests. I don't think you have heard her sing, because I'm told, by Ragini, that whenever she's tried, you've interrupted her. Always chattering about something else. It's not that you're tone-deaf, says Ragini. But it just doesn't register. You have all the time in the world for *her*, but you have no time for music."

"What does music have to do with it?"

"If only you could withdraw that question. You've proved all I've said. 'What does music have to do with it?' "

Philip was more frenzied than bewildered, but he was bewildered all the same. His silence, as they continued to walk, was a more glowering rejoinder than words could be.

"Stop. Philip. No, stop. Listen. Tell me what you hear."

Philip heard various noises.

"You must stand stock still."

"I am still. You asked me to stop. 'Stock still' yourself."

"Don't look. Listen."

Philip did listen. His mind, white-hot, radiated energy but took in nothing.

They were standing outside the Mecca Masjid on the straight yellow road south of Charminar. The year was 1600. The sun beat on the lime-washed flagstones of the mosque forecourt where half a dozen solitary persons were stretched at their ease, basking in the sun, in God's shade. These scenes of dizzying calm in the heat of the day were always accompanied in India by some weird sound or other. At Philip's school it was the hooter of a flour-mill he had never set eyes on. Anand, if he wanted noise, must mean noise from the mosque, yet never in his life had Philip known a more slumbrous place. Not a sound, not a murmur. Nobody was worshipping aloud, giving thanks or remonstrating with God. All he heard were incidental sounds, carried from a distance.

"Now you're listening," said Anand. "We'll walk on."

Philip obeyed. He walked on. What music? His friend was more angered, more relentless, and certainly far more pedagogical than he had ever imagined him to be. Anand not only heard music where there was none to be heard; Anand was not merely a combatant, on the side of the angels, in the Hyderabad freedom movement, while Philip fought for nothing – other than the occasional train ticket at crowded Secunderabad station on the Nizam's Railway – but he, Anand, had befriended Philip's one other friend, had stolen his girl (the same person, but the offence was different), had decamped with her to her temple, her secret place, and was now instructing

Philip to 'listen', since all he did was 'look'. Had Philip learned to 'listen', he would not only have become a better person but he might have earned Ragini's respect – her love! – instead of her amused toleration. This was Anand's message.

There *was* something to be heard. There was a rhythm. Furtive, bottom-less, unmistakable. People were chipping away in the little dark booths where life went on all day. Deprived of Anand, Philip would have found this out eventually. He'd have peered into workshops to see what was going on. But to 'look' like this was not what he was asked to do. Quite against his will, Philip was flummoxed by an oddness, an incompleteness to the rhythm – as if some mobile object, a kind of vehicle, was trying to run on its own wheels but could not get it right. That unstable object, which lived wholly in the realm of sound, was striving to gather its parts around it to proceed in an orderly direction. Philip headed towards the workshops but Anand detained him. Bouts of light hammering of an unusual timbre, skewed, overlapping and intersecting, made up a pattern of beats which, Philip could tell now, was random: the work of many hands. What, then, did Anand want of him? To esteem this as 'music'? To make a whole biscuit of this crumbled event?

He slipped Anand's guard, asserting the rule of eyesight and his power of free movement. In one silversmith's workshop after another, craftsmen were hammering with wooden mallets at thick envelopes, slid and backslid with a flat palm and outstretched thumb along a worn slab of steel. One of the men broke off. The moment he did so, the rhythm was simplified, faintly. He extracted from his envelope an unbound volume of purple cloth, of what Philip took to be vellum, between whose pages gleamed pools of battered silver. He identified the process at once. His colleague, Hard-castle, had described it to him. These shallow pools, infinitesimal silver, were to become the foil covering of the best quality sweets or *pan*. Music? A sub-trade of the confectionery industry! Forsaking Anand, Philip marched briskly along the road until that sound was no longer in his ears. In the next line of shops, fine-tooth combs were being sawed at sight, with a blade on a handle, out of roughly trimmed chunks of horn. Then came the bicycle shops, a surprise (this was 1600): solder, fire, bellows and an infinitude of fine metal parts. Philip hailed the workmen, who returned his greeting. Anand caught up.

"A fine detective you make." He mistook Philip's show of visual alertness for a dumb search for clues.

The entire lesson was wasted on Philip. Much later that day, in the evening, he found himself listening to real music, in an ample drawing-room with curtains and marble fixtures. The performers, *designated* musicians, were a harmonium player, a *tabla* player and a vocalist. Philip was not much diverted and thought sadly of Ragini, supposed to take pleasure in this kind of thing. The woman in his sights – an Australian like himself – was listening far more intently than he was.

4

Anand's reproaches were well-founded. Philip had not yet glimpsed the wife, but the appointment was made. Although he was no more than a schoolmaster, Philip had already been welcomed, in private audience, in his own palace, by the Khan Bahadur.

That, said Sukku, was not his real title. It was a standard honorific, under cover of which, by grace of the Nizam, individual noblemen, in distinct spheres (so they would not be bumping into each other), lived off their estates, performed duties, and circulated in the capital. These days, the last days of Hyderabad, took a lot out of people. Pride and self-consequence were twisted into new shapes. Trappings, entitlements and the rules of precedence were in some ways more closely regulated than ever before. Access to the Nizam had never been more difficult. But in circles far removed from the *darbar*, some noblemen had abandoned their share in ceremonial distance and had opened their palaces and *havelis* to a discerning public. Poets and *sarangi* players, *khatib*s and *rawza-khans*, Hindu *vakil*s and agents and administrators like Sukku who had formerly been stuck in the ante-rooms, now found themselves guests at table. The Khan Bahadur, with his new, foreign wife, became something of a byword.

Sukku accompanied him on his first visit. By the afternoon of the concert, two days later, Philip had taken full stock of the Khan Bahadur and his host of him. What the host saw was a young man, affable and inoffensive, a fellow-countryman of his new wife and also (the nobleman believed) a rising force in the new order, which was staffed by Englishmen. The notion of an Indian new order eluded him. He was all for reform, and saw that ideal in Philip.

What Philip saw in him, or what interested him in what he saw, was a man of note willing to appear in company with his wife. Most *begums* were kept out of sight, but not this *begum*. Yet Philip would have to wait for the *begum*. On his first visit, no woman showed her face, not so much as a slave girl.

On that first visit Sukku and Philip, who arrived on foot, had mounted a flight of steps to a deep *varanda* under a pediment supported by a row of columns. Elegant roofed windows, and false entrances to the height of a door, pricked the façade. They smelled new plaster. The *haveli* rose to only one storey but its glistening floor fanned and multiplied into an interminable sequence of empty rooms, flanked down one side by a corridor which served as a picture gallery. There was no inner courtyard but a clipped lawn, with ornamental trees, surrounded the entire complex like the grounds of an Italian villa.

Their guide was the Khan in person. The trio sped through the rooms. All Philip remembered of them now, after fifty years, was the enormous size of the wardrobes and linen cupboards, which were rooms in themselves. They loitered in the picture gallery. Barefoot retainers lined the walls. The Khan offered no description of the photographs, watercolours and engravings but stood helplessly before each one. His guests probed for information, but it soon became clear that the Khan hadn't much idea of his ancestors. "*Is* this the Khan?" thought Philip, wondering if the true Khan hadn't been eliminated in a palace revolution (since this was a palace). The garb of this dignified companion – pinstripe suit, waistcoat and tie – hid the impostor.

But there was no mistake. You had only to look. The patrimonial physiognomy, at home in every portrait, was faithfully reproduced in the Khan himself. A high forehead, round face, snub nose, hair parted in the middle and, in the eyes, a subdued twinkle, hinting at better things. They paused before a hunt scene. The Khan in the picture had bagged a tiger. Nothing was said. Two gaped, the third stood impassive. At long last a trim, vigorous old man in a turban, a long light cloak open down the front, like a Persian mullah's, and a cotton *pajama* appeared, out of breath, and began to recite historical and biographical details. This old Shi'a family, so it proved, which had arrived in the Deccan in the sixteenth century and had frequented all the courts, from Gulbarga, Bijapur and Bidar to Hyderabad, was one of the premier Muslim service families in India. Philip gleaned so much sense from this old curator, librarian and custodian of the dynastic silverware and glassware that he looked around for him next evening, at the dining table, imagining his tongue-tied employer couldn't do without him. But he was never to set eyes on him again.

Philip was seated – the evening of the day he met Anand – at a long table with twenty guests. Sukku, if only he were there, could have explained. Was this a grand occasion, or a very ordinary occasion? Philip had no way of telling. The Khan's Australian wife, along with her husband and an aged woman, perhaps his mother, entered the room late. Two chairs were drawn for the women, several places down on the same side. He caught only a fleeting glimpse of them. Opposite him, directly, sat the Khan Bahadur.

The man was transformed. A grey-green frock-coat of a pile brushed in one direction, with an erect collar, and buttoned all the way down the front, made a new man of him. He had worn his stand-alone turban to the table and there handed it to an attendant, who accepted it gratefully. His hair-part was the same. Once he sat, service was immediate. Lids were lifted, in an instant motion, from three iron tureens in the centre of the table. Waiters in *kamarbands*, on bare, noiseless feet plied the plates, but before Philip could switch knife and fork (he was left-handed) the Khan Bahadur addressed him. The entire room paid notice. The Khan's words had to be repeated. Their pitch was intimate, low, faintly musical, as if the hereditary proprietor of a 19th-century *haveli* with thirty-seven rooms, each with its polished-wood furnishings of one kind or another and its cut-glass chandelier, were crooning at Philip.

"I recall your school is in Warangal." A simple statement, once repeated.

"It is. Yes. That is where it is."

The Khan Bahadur raised his voice to include everyone. "I would like you all to meet this gentleman, who is one of a new breed of scholars and experts who will bring Hyderabad to international notice. He is serving the Nizam in a remote district. He is a schoolteacher."

That was all. It sounded, to Philip, both too much and too little. The word 'schoolteacher', in Australia, meant a species of professional who was underpaid. Compared with radio announcers and the like, he was unworthy of notice. Why not 'headmaster'? Yet perhaps even the Khan Bahadur, who weighed his words, would have seen that that title was overdone.

Philip, now, was placed on the spot. Just as his plate was heaped, and his nostrils assailed by the most delicate aromas he had met with in all his born days, he was embraced by a silence he was called on to resolve. All eyes were on him. The utmost he could do was to parrot the last communication that had entered his head.

"I thank the Khan Bahadur. I am glad to be here. I am glad to be serving the Nizam in a remote district. In Warangal," he supplied, and for those who knew Warangal, "It is not so hard to get to."

A diner responded. "You are the schoolteacher appointed by the Nizam?"

"Yes, I am."

"And you teach in Urdu? The lessons are in Urdu?"

Something told Philip that this intervention was not well-meaning. To reply would be unsafe. The speaker (somewhat to his left hand) was invisible, but since all the faces he could see were encouraging, buoying him in his work as schoolteacher, Philip took heart. He directed his eyes to his plate and the question was lost.

In the hour or more devoted to eating – eating more purposeful than in Australia, with far less talk – the guests were served in their places. They did not approach the side-tables, where the meats and *dhals* stood, nor did they help themselves from the great tureens, which held three kinds of *biryani*. Their plates were heaped with delicacies of all kinds, lamb kebabs, goat's meat with spinach, a beef dish with a rich *masala*, an eggplant dish with an even richer *masala*, fried and stuffed peppers, patties with a dozen ingredients, a pomegranate salad, heavily spiced lentils and beans: but the wonder to Philip had been communicated to him long before he ate. Just as a traveller senses, from the mist and the cold, that he has grazed the invisible presence of a great mountain, so Philip surrendered to the enveloping odour, the steam-borne savour, sentiment or micro-climate of a kind of heavenly animal whose body was *basmati* rice and whose soul was identical with its body. This was apocalypse from afar. To the materialist Philip nothing in the music he was to hear would equal this revelation of the true *nawaabi biryani*. And done without cardamom! He touched a portion with his fork. Not all the guests, he saw, were at ease with this cutlery and some had abandoned it.

The kitchen lay behind closed doors. In a renewed and most inefficient performance, a servant tampered with a door-fastening that could sometimes be made to catch. He succeeded in sticking it fast but at the worst moments, inhibiting the passage of bearers fetching new courses, or returning with the empty plates one after another. A swing door, as in a restaurant, would have speeded things up no end. But there was (Philip perceived) no reason in the world for things to be speeded up. He well saw that he was not in a restaurant. He ate to repletion. He managed the *payasam* and the *badam kheer* (a *payasam* with almonds) but could only watch, defeated, as the jellies and halwas, the apricot dish with whipped cream and the platters with nuts and fruits were borne in and the Khan Bahadur set the example by tasting and relishing all of them.

The guests grew talkative. Some were discussing their estates. Philip's Urdu was improving but he needed all the help he could get: a plain English word strewn in the midst of their exchanges. Here that word was 'blockade'. They were discussing the blockade of Hyderabad by the government of India: to what end, he could not find, or whether the blockade was working. At mid-table, where he sat, companions on both sides were befriending him in English. The talk where he sat was not of blockades and blockade-running (the spectre of Sidney Cotton must be at hand) but of dams and irrigation projects and outlays, investments and improvements. Philip was counted among the investments and improvements, and so he should be. He blundered by supposing there was a dam in Warangal district. "No, no, there is rain in that district. The tanks there are rain-fed. Why should there be a dam?"

"Have you visited Nizamsagar?" someone asked him.

"What is Nizamsagar?"

The diners around Philip were all in the same line of work. They were past, present or prospective Public Works Department engineers and administrators, though none of them resembled what *he* thought of as an engineer. The Khan Bahadur himself was an engineer. It was he who recited the eventful story of Nizamsagar. Yet towering from the end of the table Philip heard a sandpaper voice – the voice of his enemy, the proponent of Urdu in schools – declaiming in that language on a matter of almost tearful urgency.

He hearkened in vain for the chime of a female voice – of either female voice. If he could not have the wife, he would settle for the oldster who bore her in.

The table broke up. The Khan Bahadur stood, and everybody stood. No announcement was made, for nothing could be surer. Tea would be served in the music room. Philip, swivelling in his chair, encountered a gaze meant for him. She must have been as curious as he was. A silk *dupatta* hid her hair, but her gaze was free. It was Philip, too conscious in India of decorum in eye contact, who averted his.

How, under tacit circumstances, did you find the men's toilet? Philip inquired of none other than the Khan Bahadur, whom he rated his ally, since he had known him the longest.

The Khan directed him through several rooms. As he emerged at last from the marbled premises, his path was blocked. He could swear no-one had followed him. And who but a foreigner would choose to stand in front of an erect, cracked-glaze porcelain urinal manufactured in 1888 by W. Plummer of Stoke-on-Trent? Yet his ways were observed. A malign figure awaited him. That adversary to whom he was destined, the man who had challenged him about an Urdu curriculum and was struggling, Philip plainly saw, in the toils of an extravagant emotion, took him by the arm and propelled him, with a suggestion of force, through a suite of rooms to the corridor with all the pictures. Scorning the family gallery, the villain half guided and half hoisted him to confront a solitary portrait hanging in an alcove he had missed. Still without uttering a word he stood his ground, contemplating Philip taking in the picture. It showed a black-bearded warrior in a white turban, white garments and embroidered shoes, gripping with crossed hands, at waist level, a long, curved sword, whose point barely touched the ground. This appeared to be a studio photograph – taken not long ago, for all its archaism of stance and mood.

"*Yeh kaun hai?*" asked Philip in Urdu. Who is this? His wording might have done for a servant or despised individual, but was hopelessly ungracious. To atone, he pored over the image. The majesty, simplicity and oddity of the white-clad figure – to his mind, a contemporary – puzzled and eluded him. This was no Nizam, no boyar administrator, no landlord marooned on his estate. After a long minute his guide, satisfied for some reason, led Philip away.

He expected a tirade, but none followed. This lion on the path forsook him in an ante-room and did not proceed to the music room. There Philip arrived, unconducted and unaccompanied. Except for the three P.W.D. administrators – work-colleagues and boon-companions of the Khan Bahadur – the company of the dinner-table had evaporated. Half the new audience were women, and seated among the women was the Australian wife of the Khan Bahadur. Her curls were so blond as to be red. Her shawl or *dupatta* – edge-embroidered in the same colour – had fallen into two parts and covered no more than her ears and her shoulders, revealing, in front, a long gown, of sober stuff, perhaps not meant to be glimpsed at all. She was moving and shining in a galaxy of women: adolescent girls, some older women, and a small boy or two. Wasn't she the *second* wife? Philip did not even know her name, but now he heard it: Miss Chrissie! Miss Chrissie! – bawled from the male quarter of the room by a few ... drunks, were they? ... whose liberties he resented at once. Where was the Khan Bahadur? Were these women all of his family? Where were the musicians?

There was plenty of revelry without them but it all centred on the Australian wife. Philip was in two minds about her hair colour. Russet? – or cinnabar? No, gingerheaded. One of our Irish. Miss Chrissie did not meet his look and took scant notice of him throughout the programme, which was soon to commence.

An hour later, when Philip's attention had flagged – abandoning its last perching-place, on uncertain ground between the fourth and fifth notes of the infinitesimally self-disclosing *alapana* of the raga – his thoughts turned to Ragini. Stopping his ears to the sound, he stationed his Ragini in a clearing of the Warangal forest. What was she, Ragini? A lover of music? A firebrand revolutionary? She was also some kind of educationist, who inspected his charts and had volunteered to take classes. And wasn't she a student? She was too many things. Was she a fraud, teetering nervously on the outskirts of a revolutionary party? He had never much contemplated where she went, or how she spent her days, her real days, the days when she was real. Leaving Philip, she cycled to the edge of the forest and there, he surmised, she turned tail, scuttling for the hostel where she kept a sister and posed as a medical student. His Ragini faked it all. And Anand was entranced! From the moment Philip brought her to Anand, Ragini was no longer his own and that mysterious setting in the forest to his sorrow and confusion assumed a name. Its name was Palampet.

The *tabla* had entered the performance and the singer's voice began to shake. Covertly, Philip inspected the audience. No-one was yawning, not even the small boys in their ornamental shirts and wool hats, which descended over their ears. The mirrors shone, the wall cabinets were polished and the chandelier lightly swayed. In the midst of her women, the blond Australian wife was listening with her mouth open. Philip admired her, looked away, and admired her again. With all these people around, this was as close as he dared: she'd seemed quite interested at the table, but the women wouldn't have it. Even as he wondered he encountered one vigilant, handsome woman who had adjusted her gauzy veil for a better look, consuming him with her eyes. She spat him out, like an apricot stone. So knowing, yet so contemptuous, was her appraisal that Philip turned bolt upright to 'face the music'. It was at least a little more like music than the hammering in the silverware bazaar. Did his Ragini call *that* music? – or was Anand, with his wounding condescension, becoming just too impertinent to bear?

5

"I don't love him. But I know I'm incapable of love. That's why I married him."

"Is he important?"

"Is he important? I suppose he's important. The family is important. His elder brother ... I don't think Masud is important."

"Masud. Masud is his name."

"It's what I call him."

All the while she spoke Miss Chrissie tightened and re-tightened her buttoned angora wool cardigan around her shoulders. She wore the garment over her *qamiz* and her shawl, as if it alone could keep her warm. Too warm. The windows were closed and the coal braziers smoked a little. Philip might have supposed they were killing him with kindness, stoking or smoking him out of his skin as a courtesy of the house, were it not for the manifest discomfort of his companion. Through living in too cold a house, she was chilled to the bone.

"My auntie here" – Chrissie won an uncertain smile from an angular woman in a stiff brocade gown, who had a sofa to herself in a room stuffed with furniture – "she's a very nice person, but unfortunately she doesn't speak English. We can say what we like. Masud doesn't mind what we say. If he minded what we said, he'd be here. He's in his cups now."

"Cups?"

"His wine cups. Music has that effect on him."

Philip had not observed any effect of music on the Khan Bahadur, who to his mind had not even attended the performance. "So he drinks," he said.

"Sure he drinks."

"Is he a drunk?"

"Not that you'd ever notice. Don't sit close. To my auntie, close is the only thing that matters."

Philip, admiring her flushed cheeks from a distance – to him, she looked warmer than warm – lifted a bare arm and pinched his own flesh. "I can't believe I'm here."

"Be here as often as you like. I'll expect you here."

"My job is at Warangal."

"Now, how far is Warangal?" said Chrissie. "Just look for me where I am and you'll find me. This is my place. I'll be here forever."

"In Hyderabad."

"In these very rooms."

"*You're* confident, to make that prediction."

"I'll make you a further prediction. When I'm old and grey – and I've given him children – you'll find me in this room, reclining on that spot, where *she* sits, if I live so long. Training my beady eye on the young. Guests like you will have come and gone."

"But do you think …" began Philip, astounded at the serenity, as much as at the content, of this bleak forecast. "Do you think it can last? Things won't be like this forever. The Indian Army …"

"The Indian Army. The Indian Army, *that* army?"

"You don't believe they'll come?"

"I'm not sure I know what you're talking about."

Philip collected his thoughts. The temptation was to ignore her response, let it roll right over him. Glide off the topic. He'd have done so. But he was curious. "How can you *not* know what I'm talking about?"

"If you mean what I think you mean, that India will invade and Masud and I will be chased out of the palace, well, it won't happen."

"That *is* what I mean. Why won't it happen?"

"Nobody is talking about that here."

"Perhaps they should be. Perhaps they should be looking to their arrangements."

"Arrangements for what? Arrangements to accede to India? Either we accede to India or we'll all be dead, is that it?"

"I don't want you dead."

"You're as stupid as the others. The Nizam's Army is commanded by General El Edroos. Besides that army, there are irregular forces all over the country. Every jagirdar has his levy. Besides these levies, there are troops commanded in the name of Bahadur Yar Jung, who is dead, who can't move his limbs, but his troops will march for him. Those troops won't be fighting for *us*, for the Khan Bahadur and the likes of his *gori* wife. But I think if you calculate, in the long run – those troops will keep us safe."

Philip was amazed. Miss Chrissie – the *gori* wife – a foreigner like himself. And look at all she knew. All she had taken on herself. "How will those troops keep you safe. Who *are* those troops? Who's Bahadur Yar Jung?"

"Who's Bahadur Yar Jung?" Chrissie repeated contemptuously.

"I believe I know who you mean. With a curved sword? Dresses in white?"

"Never mind his sword. His sword is straight, none of *those* will be fighting with a curved sword. They'll have bullet-firing guns, they'll have uniforms and proper equipment, let me tell you."

"Who are '*those*'? You don't mean the Razakars!"

The incredulity in Philip's voice rivalled her own. It came to her as a surprise. She stared at him. Her eyes blazed, then moistened alarmingly. Her chin wobbled. She seemed, for a moment, about to cry but composed her features in a new attitude of defiance, her small mouth turned downwards.

"What's wrong?" Philip exclaimed. "Have I upset you?"

His kindliness was Philip's saving grace. Another might have pursued the matter, to daunting effect. But Philip's first instinct was to console Chrissie. "Nothing will happen to you. Nothing will happen to your husband. If it comes to that, there's a way out."

"What do I care about a way out?"

"You haven't surrendered your passport, have you? Your husband has pots of money?"

"Yes. Pots of money is what he does have."

"Then migrate to Australia. Both of you. What is it he does? He can set up in business. Accredited Engineer, Public Works Department, the Nizam's Dominions. That's his job reference."

"Will it help?"

"Of course it will help." How soft – and how unerring – was Philip's instinct on that occasion. Chrissie may not have believed him. But she was reconciled at once.

In years to come, Philip would harden his heart. This was a man who would turn his back on the country of his birth, on the woman he said he loved, who would father two daughters, one of whom never forgave him, while the other was dead, all for the sake of Indian achievements. This man would found schools and would pioneer educational reforms in India. Soft as pie at twenty-three, he would become in India an optimist of the hard climb, a grizzled mammoth who insisted on being useful past his sixty-fifth year. At last, with energy to burn and the wisdom of a lifetime to impart, he would find himself a prophet without honour in his own country. But what had he ever done for his own country? His honours were in India. Reclaim them. What was he looking for in Australia? A brand-new career?

"Tell me why you are called Miss Chrissie?" he had said then.

"Because, in Adelaide ... because that was my name as a dancing instructress. They know that here. Here they're all waiting to see me dance."

"And when will you dance for them?"

"Never."

"Then who will you dance for? Perhaps you will never dance again."

"I don't call it dancing what I did. I've seen them dance here. Professional dancers – 'prostitutes', you and I would call them. But they can dance. They can sing, they compose poetry on the spot and they take money. It's a little blurred."

"Does your husband pay them?"

"He pays them to dance, but not for other kinds of favours. He's a moral person. You know I'm a second wife, but I have the same privileges as the first wife – no more, no less. I do respect him. Let's just forget that I'm bored out of my tiny mind here."

6

Philip was displaced. Waiting for Anand in his room, in the famous 'hostel' – so long impenetrable to Philip – he was more of a trespasser in India than ever before. He hovered high above the city, removed from its dangers. All the dangers were in the street below. The city was patrolled by the *kotwal*. Peace-keeping gangs in uniform ensured the wrong people were deterred from roaming the streets.

That left the right people. There were so few of these that the streets were deserted. To scale this height, he had slipped unobserved from a dark street, meeting no-one on the climb. You climbed to the roofs by the stairways of various buildings. At the last step you were silently admitted to a world open to the stars. People moved here and there at this level but extended no safe-conduct to visitors. The sounds of bicycle bells, of street voices in argument and of the occasional voice raised in song penetrated at a remove, debris from the ocean floor.

Anand's room was unlocked. The room had a mattress on the floor, a few thumbed books in Marathi, *Gulliver's Travels*, a towel, and a soap-dish. A curtained recess in the wall hid more objects. There was nowhere to sit, so Philip fetched a chair from the roof. This was roof city. The world at this height consisted of roofs, a succession of flat roofs, at numerous levels, with improvised stairs between the levels, and cabins erected here and there. Anand's room was one of these cabins.

The night wore on; Philip returned his chair and perched out-of-doors, where it was cooler. He trailed his chair to a succession of lookouts. He did not want to be found gazing too long over one prospect.

How beautiful was the night sky! The city was dark but the stars blazed, as they did – he'd been assured – nowhere in India as over the east Deccan plateau. Warangal had its stars. He'd observed them. But here, anxiety spoiled his leisure. Would Anand come? Or had Anand retreated to his district? – 'advanced' to his district, at the behest of Congress – to avoid further censure from Philip about his conduct with Ragini? Philip had no plan to mention Ragini. But what if Anand did so first? Philip would be 'advancing' to his own district in the morning, but did not wish to 'retreat' from Hyderabad without a word to Anand.

All along the roofs, shadowy figures came and went. But on Anand's roof, no-one moved. No-one came looking for him. Where, in this world, were the cooking smells? Were there women? Were there *households* up here? A vagabond figure approached Philip very near, but departed without a word. Then two men appeared. They clambered on their hands and knees from a lower roof, one helping the other. The helper lingered at the edge – as if to stand guard – while his comrade, approaching Philip, addressed him in rapid Urdu.

"I don't understand. I don't know what you're saying."

"I am saying, you are alone here. It's late."

"I'm waiting for somebody. Perhaps you can tell me where my friend is," said Philip, uneasy but encouraged, since the other had replied in English. "Where Anand is. I saw him yesterday."

"Anand? Anand is Hindu?"

"Well, yes …"

"You are Englishman?"

"Well, no … Yes. That's about it," said Philip. This was no time for distinctions. How could he be friendlier? There was something about the voice: it was soft, not hospitable but artless and a trifle plaintive, like the voices of students, students in Australia who were behind in their lessons. A brainwave occurred to him. "Where is your college? I think you are a college student."

"My college is at Osmania."

This college student's helper drew near, protective, as if some defence might be needed. They were as unsure of Philip as he of them.

A light breeze had arisen and a mournful smell, not hard to identify – it was a latrine smell – drifted across the rooftops. This pitiable hostel! – a few poor souls marooned on the heights. A real student place. Acres of space, but no-one cooked at home. In Sydney, the reason no-one cooked was that they'd all troop out for a cheap dinner most nights and get drunk – then storm home at one in the morning. But here, Philip believed, no student got drunk. What did they want with him, these two?

"He says Anand. He is waiting for Anand."

"Ask him how he reached," said the second man, though he, too, had a tongue in his head and spoke English.

Ask me yourself, thought Philip. Reached where? I climbed by these steps, the same as you, unless you flew here, or were born here and have never looked down. But Philip made no such reply. He was reluctant to inquire about Anand, in case they were hostile to Anand. They already had him down as a Hindu.

"Parvaiz – leave him." The helper turned to go. He took Parvaiz by the arm, unbalancing him a little.

Parvaiz stood his ground. "You are also student?"

"I *was* a student. Now I teach school. What's it like at Osmania? Your lessons. Are they really in Urdu? Are your textbooks in Urdu?" Philip had heard, from Hardcastle, about the Urdu experiment. Of all the regions in India, including, of course, those long ruled by the British, it was in Hyderabad – a backward state – that the governors of a university had gone farthest in translating textbooks into a vernacular language. Hardcastle thought this ridiculous, but Philip was inclined to commend it. All kinds of trailblazing experiment, including his own – though *he* taught in English – flourished under the Nizam in the last days.

"Are your textbooks in Urdu?" he inquired again.

"You would like to know?"

"If I ask something, I would like to know."

"My textbooks are in mathematics. One part in mathematics, and one part in Urdu."

"You're a maths student."

It was not about being a maths student. The truth was affirmed at last by Parvaiz' companion, who had spoken so little. "He is blind student."

"Blind." All Philip could supply was an echo.

He stretched out his hand to Parvaiz, in consolation. Inept, but perhaps not ineffectual. Parvaiz did not recoil. Philip's hand remained on his arm.

"You are blind, but you're studying," he said, unable to keep the wonder out of his voice.

The friend chimed in. "By wish of God, he is studying. We are all helping him."

'All'? How many were they 'all' along this charmed corridor of roofs that ran for a city block at least, its forlorn cabins lit by dim globes with a switch-pull at the entrance, for this, after all, was a hostel: here they paid rent. They liked it here. Anand liked it here because it was high and out of the way. Perhaps he thought no-one looking for him could be bothered to climb. The place was ideal, safe and high – though the day would come when many would climb so high. By then Anand would be far away, enlisting on a war front, bugling in the invading Army. But what would it mean for Parvaiz, for a blind Muslim student, on the day they climbed high, searching, whoever 'they' were, for whoever they sought? All might depend on who got to him first.

A fourth person crossed the roof. They had been joined on the roof. Anand at last. No. "Philip?" Who was it? "*You're* here!"

"Sukku? Why shouldn't I be here? Both waiting for him!"

"Not both. If you stay, I should leave." Sukku peered wistfully at the door of Anand's cabin, which stood open to reveal a bulb dangling from a cord. "There will be nowhere to sleep. Aren't there more chairs?"

"Why, why would we sleep here? What's going on?"

"He has become crazy. That is what's going on. You haven't seen him?"

Sukku waited for the students to vanish. But they stayed where they were. "Sukhanandam, a friend of Anand," said Philip, "and this is Parvaiz. And this is ..."

Before the other could reveal his name, Anand appeared. He embraced Philip, Sukku and the roof-residents: not crazy (though out-of-breath) but perhaps more than usually urbane. There *were* no chairs, other than the chair Philip had occupied. But Anand set a forthright example by taking a cloth from his pants pocket, dusting the floor of the rooftop and seating himself there and then.

"He's arrived. This is my friend Anand," said Philip to Parvaiz.

"I will be your friend."

"Yes, we'll be friends. I'll try to visit you again."

As the two departed, Philip and Sukku remained standing: Philip to wave them goodbye and Sukkhu to denote a predicament. Anand inquired cheerfully from ground level, "And how did you find Miss Chrissie?"

" 'Miss' Chrissie, you call her," said Philip coldly.

"Oh, I know about Chrissie."

If Anand knew anything at all about Chrissie, it was from Sukku. Sukku had set up the appointment – if not with the retired dance-instructress, then with her husband. But Sukku himself, for now, was having none of Chrissie. "Anand, you will stay here tonight. I insist on that. There will be no good in rushing off anywhere."

"I intend, I intend most emphatically to stay tonight. This is, after all, my home. Will *you* stay tonight? But you have homes. You have beds. Philip?"

"Yes, I have a bed. I'll be leaving for Warangal in the morning."

"Ah, Warangal. Take care. And if you do see her ..."

"No more of that," rapped Sukku, with more force than usual, and quite unnecessarily, it seemed to Philip. He addressed only Anand. "I've been looking for news. Three daily newspapers in Urdu, but nothing in those. Nothing in Telugu."

"And the *Deccan Chronicle*?"

"It hasn't appeared today. That's uncommon. We are entirely depending on word-of-mouth."

"Word-of-mouth. The truth."

"There may be a Communist Party announcement."

"Posted on trees," said Anand. "What was the name of that forest, Philip, not here in India. In the play *As You Like It*? Love-poems on every tree."

Sukku ploughed on. "Or there may be a Nizam's announcement."

"The Nizam makes no such announcements. He may issue a *farman*: something of interest to his Muslim subjects. As for his Hindu subjects ... his disobedient subjects ... or those just waiting to be informed, there will be nothing from him. I think Laiq Ali will have made an announcement."

"I haven't read it."

"Then a secret announcement. For a secret agreement, a secret announcement. Rosalind, I think, Philip, is my favourite heroine in all stage drama. She hides her feelings. But so, of course, does our Indian Rosalind, our Shakuntala. You know I mean Ragini."

Sukku turned to Philip at last. "The Nizam has lifted the ban on the Communist Party."

"And the ban on Congress?" said Philip, surprised.

"That stays."

"That stays. Then in Warangal ..."

"There will be no more raids by the Nizam against the Communist Party. The Communists will keep all the land they've seized. And they'll seize more. Which leaves," said Sukku, "only one party fighting the Nizam."

"Anand's party."

"One party." Sukku spoke for Anand. "One section of one party. The rest of the Congress Party I am sure will be forming committees, chairing meetings ... praying for the Indian Army to come ... they will be keeping out of harm's way."

Anand had dispensed with his cloth. He reclined at full length. "Nobody will be out of harm's way."

He seemed to Philip – though a trifle exhausted – as much in command of himself as ever.

"What will you do now?" Philip asked him.

"I'll place myself under orders. Swami's orders. I'll proceed to my district. The Razakars are worse there than anywhere else. There are armies of *goondas* running wild in Marathwada. People need protection."

"I was told by Ragini," said Philip with caution, "that she is not exactly a member of the Communist Party. The Andhra Mahasabha ..."

"The Andhra Mahasabha. That's the Communists. The very ones who signed the agreement."

"They've signed an agreement? With the Nizam's Government?"

"So they have, and if you should meet her," said Anand, "if you're fortunate enough to catch up with her, you must offer her from me ... my felicitations. Tell her I expect results. There'll be a People's Soviet covering the whole of Telengana very soon. They have been planning this for weeks."

"You're not dismayed?"

"I'm glad." He sprang to his feet, with the gymnastic alacrity Philip had observed in him more than once, when some decision was overdue. The decision to sleep. The decision to fetch his bed outdoors. His face was calm. "Tell her I'm delighted. Tell her, her Anand has *recovered his wits* and will be proceeding to the Maratha districts as fast as he's ordered."

7

People complained about bus stations but Philip had learned the rules. All the adventure he could wish for he found the next morning, simply by climbing on the bus. Departure station, before the seats were occupied. You dropped in a marker – like so – by the window, and there it would be, lying on the seat when at last you won through. Idle, ignorant fellows – of whom there were enough and to spare in the Nizam's Dominions – would assault others to be first aboard, but none of them would dare to remove the head-towels, store dilly-bags or squares of fabric that were correctly placed. Elbowing entry and carried by the stampede, Philip located the jute bag he had thrown on a window seat.

Beside it, on the corridor side, was an object he recognised.

He sat quietly. Anand's frilled cap. He would have Anand! – not the companion he'd have wished for. Not at this moment in time, thought Philip, foreseeing the heat and exhaustion of a long day. Events in Hyderabad had taken a new turn. It was not this new turn Philip meant, by his 'moment in time', but the moment or personal crisis in his own, simmering narrative. The bus filled up. The driver emerged from the shade and started the motor. If only he had caught the earlier bus. The 7.30! In that case he'd have avoided Anand, and the bus would be half-way to Jangaon before the day turned unpleasant, before the sweat began to pour and his trousers quite stuck to the upholstery. Yet should Anand – who was slow to appear – miss the bus, Philip would make sure to return his cap to him at the first opportunity.

The bus moved into street traffic. A kind of ledge, squarely in the station exit, impeded its passage: a cement slab, which trapped every vehicle. Perhaps it had a function. More likely, no-one had bidden for the authority to remove this slab. The bus was aloft in the sky, like a pinned insect, when Anand, no other, appeared, thumping the bodywork from outside. He was eager to board. But the slender, stooped figure who tumbled down the aisle as if he were blown along was so unlike the real Anand that Philip (thirsting for avoidance) at first doubted it was him. His sorry appearance was the outcome of sleeping on nothing but a pocket cloth on the rooftop. Frail Sukku must have taken the bed.

The bus was stationary. It was still in mid-air. "No, no, let me be," said Anand, for Philip's greeting – to hide his disappointment – was profuse and detaining. Anand wrenched free and sat with his eyes fast shut, chin upturned, like a person in a lighted cinema waiting for the show to start. The bus, to triumphant cries from workmen, jolted free of the obstacle but Anand's posture barely changed. To fend off tedium Philip took a book from his bag – *The Brothers Karamazov*, he was glad of it – and read a few pages. Its chill penetrated his bones. A world removed from the intentions of its arctic author, *The Brothers Karamazov* gamely defied the sun's mid-morning blaze on a Hyderabad bus journey in the month of May. Worlds apart, too, were the friends. One friend was right out of it for the moment. But this was the friend who knew his own mind and was never at a loss while Philip, though knowing his own mind, knew a dissonant organ and was frequently at a loss. With the character Grushenka, a female dynamo had intruded on events in *The Brothers* and he had to close it. How long would it be before Anand started up on Ragini?

Traffic had stalled. The bus driver cut the motor. Somewhere, not far ahead, was a procession.

"Anand, are you some kind of yogi? Don't stir, don't stir. Are you seeking perfection?"

Anand remained as he was. Chanting voices were heard. "If those are your Congress Party workers," said Philip, "protesting the cease-fire – shouldn't you be with them?"

Anand replied without moving, "Nobody will be protesting today."

"Nobody today? Who says so?"

"Philip, I asked you to let me be. This will be a long ride."

"We haven't moved an inch." Philip took the time to ponder Anand's last remark. A long ride. "I know it will be a long ride, but how far are *you* going?"

"All the way. I'll have something to say when we get there. Now I want rest."

"Something to say to whom? If you mean Ragini, you won't find her."

"I'll know where to find her."

Silenced and sadly discomfited by this reply, Philip delved into his bag for some companion besides the Grushenka of Dostoevsky. None was there. He held his peace, consciously vying with Anand who had set himself the same task. The bus bumped for an hour in slow traffic. Bicycles, pedal-rickshaws, pedestrian individuals, pedestrian masses, bullock-carts, small herds of water buffalo, a camel and the road's quantum of sedan cars, many at cross purposes, entangled the way. A cyclist was thrown to the road. Access was then reserved for the emergency vehicle which sounded its siren but made small headway. At last they were in open country. Philip glanced at his rival to see if he was asleep, or feigning sleep. He fetched from his bag a bottle of carbonated water, most elegantly stopped with a marble. Philip sprang the catch and the stopper relented to a fizz of applause. "Drink some."

"Drink that? It's boiling."

"It's not going to get any colder. Where will you find Ragini?"

With these words, Philip surrendered all claim of his own to private knowledge.

Anand considered his reply.

"She bicycles in," said Philip, "but only when she can. There are police everywhere."

"Let her bicycle in," said Anand, "with a police bodyguard, seeing there are police everywhere. The police will escort her. I imagine that was always the case."

"Ragini with the police? Are you kidding?"

"Not kidding." These words were grunted by a man made to register a plea in a court he fails to recognise. He refused to enlarge his statement. But Philip was hankering for enlargement.

"You appear to know where she'll be. You can find her."

"All I mean to do," said Anand, "is to ask her one question. She'll reply – face-to-face – to that question. Let's not talk for now."

"What question?"

"My question to Ragini."

This was going nowhere. To Philip, who had his own question to put to Ragini – there were more than one – such evasiveness, as he saw it, on the part of the front-runner in a desperate race was peculiarly upsetting. He sprang to her defence. "Ragini has done nothing wrong. She's a cog in a wheel. She belongs to a party, the Andhra Mahasabha, which is run from outside the state, from Bezwada I think, and does not usually decide on a new strategy by consulting its members. No more does the Congress. You know that as well as I do."

"What do I know as well as you do?"

"She's not high up."

"She is low, very low in the hierarchy of the Communist Party," said Anand. "Which makes it worse. She could always leave the Party."

"Will you ask her to leave?"

"I could ask her to leave. But that would be to place her under *my* orders," said Anand, with a curious sarcasm and relish. "The deed is done."

"The deed? The deal with the Nizam? What if Ragini knows nothing about it."

"How true, she knows nothing about anything. The complete ignoramus. The perfect willing cadre. You have only to look at her. Such a feeble specimen: how could piddling *Ragini* know what she's doing? To think I'd ever have believed that a woman like that, an *idli*, a rice dumpling without a tongue in her head, would act for the best and speak her mind."

"She always speaks her mind."

"I'd thought so too."

"An *idli* is not a rice dumpling. Stay off her food preferences."

"I see from your words that the melodious Ragini has one champion. She may warble to deceive, she may cast off the vision of free India like a bad dream, but there will always be one *rasika* from Australia to stick up for her.

This woman who always speaks her mind."

"You know she does. She's spoken her mind to you!" Phillip thought: She's told him she loves him, I have no doubt.

"She's spoken what *I* took to be her mind. But I was deceived. Her mind is the workers' and peasants' party. That party is her mind. The workers' and peasants' party, which is how they refer to themselves, these Communists who've achieved so much. They have expelled the landlords, they've restored the peasants' land to the peasants, they've opposed forest logging and clearing, they've fought off the police and they've avenged village women: for every rape a death ... That's how she puts it. It's a tally they keep: she'd like to chalk it up on the school blackboard. Have you shown Ragini your keys to the school? Don't forget the blackboard. Inspect what it says. It won't be in English, it won't be in Urdu, she'll have taken no chances, she'll have chalked it up in plain Telugu bhasa so the pupils will understand: 'Long live the Nizam of Hyderabad.'"

"Oh, I'll hide my keys."

"She'll perform it for your class. She's a one-woman band – did you know that? I've explained, she's very gifted at music."

"And you've heard her sing." Philip would have rendered up his passport – well, almost – in exchange for that windfall. He had small concern with Ragini's beliefs, her views. But he wished that, when she sang, he had listened. He'd simply thought of her music as a kind of talk. They'd talked and talked, and he'd received it as talk. She had given up on him.

"Yes, Philip, I've heard her sing. I've heard her sing Mira Bai. I've heard her sing Purandara Dasa in Telugu. I've heard her sing 'ko-el, ko-el, I am pining for my lover.' Such junk she sings. And this is what I say to her—"

Anand drew breath. He stared wildly, without seeing Philip and without hearing him. At that instant the bus, which had been tearing along, braked and slowed down. With no idea what was out there, Anand leapt to his feet and spun down the aisle. The bus door was open. It could not be closed: to defend that door was just what the driver's assistant was for. That assistant now battled with Anand, more grimly than might have been predicted. Anand careered from his grasp, tumbled at large from the still-moving vehicle, rose, spurned the dust from his body and hurtled like a firecracker – the sort that runs along the ground; Philip knew it well from the Sydney celebrations on Empire Day. His friend scudded like a firecracker into a spinney of trees and was lost among the granite boulders of the landscape.

In Philip's Australia he'd have been let go, but in India the driver's assistant pursued him with a vim worthy of the chase. A passenger had got away!

And so did it prove: the chaser returned empty-handed, and the bus resumed its way, minus that passenger, along the dust road miles from anywhere.

8

The next day was a Monday. At his school, where Philip appeared early, a deputation awaited him. The old gentleman, Sri Srinivasan, who was not of the school but had everything to do with the street, had assembled the families of four boys. Once the headmaster unlocked the door, they crowded inside.

Srinivasan was keen to be their spokesman. But his English was poor. He had with him a caste-fellow, or perhaps just co-worshipper at the Hanuman temple – both dressed in white, their foreheads scored with identical markings, freshly applied – whom he introduced as the school governor. Philip had never set eyes on him. He would certainly have been glad, more than once, to meet the school governor, to be sure in Warangal that there was such a person. This man was no governor. But what harm could he do? At these meetings of stakeholders – shy, incommunicative, but determined to find out, and flatly unwilling to disperse – it was not always their valid representative who would prove of use.

For all his dallying at table and in the Khan's drawing-room, Philip had not altogether wasted his time in Hyderabad. He had learned from Hardcastle that the State Congress Cabinet-in-waiting had approved one aspect of the Nizam's recent policy: his innovations in schools. They would extend the project! Education in English would not lapse in an Indian Hyderabad, but would expand. This was good news, and "pukka" said Hardcastle, laying one finger to the side of his nose as if the Indian epithet bore an occult meaning. Philip had been cheered – and convinced. But how might he convey his conviction to an audience that did not speak his language, and were perhaps not yet willing to contemplate the upheavals to come? In fact they were willing. They had contemplated these upheavals for some time. It was Philip, not they, who shrank from disloyal utterance. It was Philip who had no wish to say of his employer: "After the Nizam goes …"

The school governor was no help, but Philip's best pupil, a boy of eleven, was playing in the street. He confided his news to him. This boy, Subbaiah, surmounted the difficulties in their own tongue.

The families thought well of their teacher. They were proud of their offspring and had each formed the opinion that English in Warangal – thanks to the departure from India of the English themselves! – was bound to soar.

The boys settled down to their lessons. Eleven pupils were in attendance: the biggest class ever. Members of the families were inclined to stay, but Philip did not want them. He was counting on a visit from Ragini.

Small chance of that. Today was the opening of a new term. People were about. Ragini must pedal for miles. Obstacles in her path would abound. Having heard all Anand had to say, Philip was unable to conclude that she or her party – the Andhra Mahasabha, to him – had signed any pact with the Nizam. He no longer trusted Anand in anything and was content for the moment to have him stumbling among the boulders around Bhongir somewhere.

One datum – alone – persuaded him Ragini would visit. That was his hope. Call it his impatience.

Having the boys learn hard plurals was a pleasure for Philip. "Not 'mans' – 'men'," he instructed them. "Now, 'woman'. What do you say when there are two?" They were becoming proficient – even the tiniest boys – at this kind of thing.

Mohan was signalling from behind the class. Philip took no notice. If Mohan thought it was hot – then let him appear with the water-tumblers from the clay *matka*. This servant, with allies from the street, kept up a continual banter in the kitchen. Sometimes Mohan and his crew stood under the fans. But they seldom interrupted the class. A note was passed. Philip brightened as he read. 'Accompany this boy. R.' He frowned. How was he to accompany anyone while the class was in session?

Philip's impatience had worked wonders. A boy stood with Mohan. He dispatched the boy with a note: 'Teaching plurals. Can you come yourself? I'll wait till 4. P.'

Four o'clock. Having sent the class home, Philip was compiling the pupils' register, drafting the new term's expectations of every child. He was pleased with them all. The boy courier appeared, without Ragini. He led the way on foot. Once they left the main street, keeping to a wall of the fort, more police could be found picnicking in the shade. Poor houses. A white Muslim shrine, its green flags downcast in the still-blazing heat. Subbash Leatherworks, where a twenty-year-old tailor, a ten-year old tailor and a nine-year-old tailor were working on the straps of a schoolbag. The sash kept coming off the wheel linking treadle and needle. Philip had time to watch because it was here, in the street, that his boy left him. He was befriended in no time by the three tailors.

"Stephen, is it?" A young woman called from a distance, from a lone step.

She was the image of Ragini.

Philip did not correct her. She led, and he followed. The Subbash Leather-works, he saw – and the same was true of the Diamond Photo Frame Works, Owliya Industries and a line of enterprises – was merely a rented cell in a stained, tumbledown building which might be anything, a seat inconspicuous by its vast extent.

They skirted a grassed yard, with outbuildings. Peering into one of those buildings, searching for his whereabouts, he saw, on a littered floor, a disfigured woman, the soft tissue of her mouth coarsely inflated by some monstrous disease. She lay prone. Philip stood without moving. He looked away, looked again.

Where were they? The notices were in Urdu. His guide had vanished between buildings.

But here, at the next turn, was the hospital entrance. They had approached the entrance through the grounds, from *within* the hospital. People were clustered on the grass. They made no sound. Or something had happened to Philip's hearing, as well as to his eyes.

He was badly shaken. One more sight like that, and he would cower with his fists screwed into his eyes.

Were these patients? Patients' families? Not all were townspeople. Some were villagers. And one was a youth in birdcatcher's attire, with beads, feathered armlets, his spear borne upright for convenience. They stood so silently. Philip watched. He saw they moved, but not a sound reached his ears.

Scurrying, keeping to the path, he heard radio music. A spell was lifted. There, there his guide was, on her step: she paused always on a single step. He followed Ragini's sister – who else could it be? – indoors, upstairs, and down a corridor. She stopped at a door. The door was opened from the inside.

Before he could thank her – or win *her* acknowledgement – the sister had vanished.

A mean hostel room. There was one chair, but Ragini, posted at the door, did not take it. She crossed to the bed. She did not speak. Philip, for his part, remained standing, surveying the room without reflecting that it be-longed to another, who had mistaken his name, had not volunteered her own and would not relish his scrutiny of her clothes and wall-hangings. But he had to survey something. It could not be Ragini. And why could it not be Ragini? Philip had rules. He had been summoned by Ragini. Let Ragini speak. It was for Ragini to survey him.

In fact, she *was* gazing at him in a meaningful way. She would gaze at a twig-broom-seller in a meaningful way if she thought he brought news of Anand. It was all about Anand: this truth had not occurred to him so distinctly till the last moment. He would not meet her eye.

"Nice room," he exclaimed at last.

"Oh, they don't house them well. Rukku was glad to have even this room. She shared for a year – four nurses to a room. But because she's on special duties ..."

"She's a nurse. Isn't she a medical student?"

"In Warangal?"

Up to this moment Philip had half-believed that Ragini herself was somehow, mysteriously, a student in Warangal. She was all things at once.

"What do they cure here?" he said.

"Most things. Nothing you'll ever catch."

No wiles of hers would coax Philip to that chair. Ragini deployed no wiles but continued gazing at him with the mildness and expectancy that had been hers before either of them spoke a word.

His good nature, never far from the surface, delivered him at last from his vigil. "The journey from Hyderabad is getting longer," he said. That was a beginning. What next? He was loath to describe his achievement in the capital – saving the school – because of the known stance on schooling of the Andhra Mahasabha. To the Mahasabha, school lessons in English were a waste. Classes should be in Telugu. Blab more. Perhaps Miss Chrissie was the safest of topics.

"Who did you meet in Hyderabad?" she said.

"I met whoever you'd expect. It was quiet. Sometimes you can't tell whether the town is under curfew, or it's just bad lighting."

"Sometimes you can't tell whether the headmaster travels there for business or pleasure."

Philip crossed to the window. He looked down on a scene of muffled chaos, in a courtyard he'd missed. Patients with disabilities were being sorted into line. "Such a big hospital," he said. "Kind of out of the way. But it has a name."

"The Ghazi Imam Hospital. It's a benefaction."

"It's huge."

"Not huge. The Outpatients is huge. But there are only six beds. And it's grossly underfunded. The State gives nothing."

"But people know it's here. It has an address. I could have found my own way."

"Why send the boy? Is that what you mean?"

"Why send the boy twice? Why these precautions? Why hide away in a hospital? Why can't you come and go at will?"

"I'm unable to come and go at will. There are watchers."

"Watchers. But no longer the police."

"*No longer* the police? Oh, I see what you're getting at."

Philip left his window. He dropped into the chair.

"The Nizam's ban," she said. "Yes, the ban was lifted on the Communist Party. It affects us too. Even the police have heard about it."

"Wasn't it a deal?"

There was no immediate reply from Ragini. Her expression did not change, but Philip could be sure she was composing herself. "Is that what he calls it?" she said at last.

"Is that what who calls it?"

"Is that what he calls it? A 'deal'?"

Better for her if she had named him.

"Anand meant to come with his own message," he said. "I'm afraid he got lost."

"He got lost?"

"But seeing *I'm* here, you can explain it to me instead. The bans have been lifted. The Communist Party is free to organise. Not that you're Communist Party. What do I know? But the Andhra Mahasabha, too, is free to organise."

"Not free. There are rival groups."

"Rival groups. Like the Communist Party. Are those two groups?" he said, quite disowning, in his pique over Anand, the benefit of the doubt he owed Ragini. "Or don't they coincide a little?"

"A great deal," she said. "When have I pretended otherwise?"

"Never – to me. You have never pretended otherwise to me. You have never pretended. You have never consulted. You have never informed me one way or the other. *I'm* not offended about the 'deal'. I'd say everything is above board between you and me."

"Then if that's settled," she said, smiling faintly, "where are things 'below board'?"

"To name names – with Anand."

"Anand is not one for distinctions. To Anand, the Party and the Mahasabha were always the same thing."

"And where's the difference?"

"There is a difference. The Communist Party of India is not interested in the Telugu language. The Party *dalams* are not interested in Telugu epic poetry, in Andhra folk theatre, in the music of South India, or in the kinds of performances you'd have seen on Ugadi … if you'd chosen to come. You'd have seen, if you'd come."

"It's not me you have to persuade," he said. "Who will you fight?"

"Who will I fight? What makes you think I'll fight?"

"Who will you fight? The landlords? The moneylenders? The Forestry Department?"

"You have the right list."

"The Congress? Anand's party?"

"The Congress? I've barely set eyes on the Congress. You tell me when Congress workers have appeared in these districts. Philip," she said, rising from the bed and placing her fine-boned hand on his arm, "you're no Torquemada, do you know that? You're asking me the kindest of questions. You're doing me no service. This is not even practice for me. If ever I'm caught, those who interrogate me will know what to ask. But do *you* know what to ask? You're a mild, beneficent person."

"Who will you fight?" he said. "The Indian Army? How soon did you know? How soon – before May the 4th – did you know the ban would be lifted?"

"How soon did I know? If Anand dreamed up this question, let him ask me himself. Let him come himself. Let him not get lost, let him not send a go-between, with no interest or stake in the matter."

Philip did not *shake* his arm free. Instead, with his free hand, he carefully removed her hand.

She replaced it, repenting a little, clinging a little.

"Anand won't come," he said.

"And why won't he come?" After a short interval Ragini removed her hand of her own accord. "You are no go-between," she admitted. "Ask me what you like."

"No – on this matter, I'm a go-between. I may not have chosen to be, but that's what I am. As for Anand ... even if Anand were to come," he said – he intended harsh words – "he's in no mood for you."

"If Anand thinks I knew in advance, he's wrong. I did not know in advance. That night – when we partied in your room ... I had a long way to go before it was light. I took Anand with me. I did not know then what was in the Nizam's mind or Laiq Ali's mind or what was in the mind of the Party. I swear to you."

"Don't swear to me."

"I *will* swear, I did not mislead Anand. How do you mean he got lost, how can he get lost? I swear, to *you* – Anand well remembers that night. He remembers all I said, and all he said. How did I mislead him? Mislead him by *knowing*? – what did *I* know? I took him some way, I took him where I felt most safe, I took him to Palampet, the old temple ..."

"He told me. And there you sang junk."

"Sang what? I sang what?"

"You sang junk."

"How do you know what I sang? Whose word is 'junk'?"

"It's not my word. I have no opinion, I'm the go-between. Anand trusted me with a message, and just to please Anand I'll convey it in his exact words. Tell her, tell Ragini she's the same as her food, a roly-poly *idli* without a tongue in her head."

Ragini began to laugh. She ceased laughing. "What *is* this? You're malicious. I don't hear Anand in those words, and I don't hear you. You're kindness itself."

"Perhaps we were *all* mistaken in one another."

As Philip spoke those words – not the words about the *idli*, which he could take back, but the words about 'mistaken', the *epitaph* – he felt like the very stone on which this dictum was carved. His features were set in stone, his heart was stone, his voice itself had the gravity of stone as he said what was said, having merely to repeat what was said: "Tell Ragini the police will be on her side. Shut her out of your school, or she'll write up what she thinks on the blackboard. 'Long live the Nizam', that was it. 'Fraternal greetings from Moscow to the Nizam of Hyderabad.'"

" 'Long live the Nizam', how absurd." Ragini was not so far gone as Philip. She still hoped this was some jest of his.

"*I* don't know if you've deceived Anand," he said, "but he thinks you have. He ran off. He despairs of you."

What had he said next? In Gibbes Street, memory baulked at this point. Perhaps what baulked was not memory, but the wish to understand: for from that day on – he was to know her again – Philip no longer believed he had any just claim on Ragini, not as a lover, nor even as a friend, since the words she flung at him were true. He was malicious. That day he became more malicious, and who knows what *she* said in return? He had no clear idea, he did not seem to wish to remember, but whatever it was, a life sentence – sealed orders – had remained on his head. He stumbled from her presence and retreated through the terrible sights of the hospital, of India itself, the India of sights, though he averted his eyes from such sights. He was nothing to Ragini, no longer a go-between. He had not even presented her with Anand's true ultimatum, which was to leave the Party.

Chapter Four.
The Last Candles of the Night

1

Traffic poured day and night along the Princes Highway. In a short alley between the highway and the train station Rockdale Council, for some forgotten purpose, had cemented a body-length wall mirror. Jenny used it as others did. She glanced with disfavour as she passed, not at her face but at the ribbed wool cardigan over her sari, bunched at the hip by grocery parcels. Someone rambling in the opposite direction paused in the mirror. An out-of-house encounter. The housemates, former wife and former husband, did not speak at once but continued to stare, each at the apparition of the other in the out-of-place mirror.

Now's his chance, she thought. He'd paused, just as uneasily, twice in the past two nights at a closed door, the door from the interior of the house to the room where Jenny sat alone. Sometimes her guests stayed late, Nora the latest, since a woman is entitled to dawdle with her own mother. When they'd gone Philip passed through, to the bathroom or the kitchen. But on neither of those two occasions did he pass through. He stopped at the door, and at last retreated to his room. What was ailing him?

"Let me take your shopping."

"I see you have shopping of your own." He did: some kind of fan-radiator, unboxed. It was winter, August already. "Are you cold at night?"

"It's for the house."

Jenny was not yet inclined to return to the house. She'd meant to linger at the cake shop. But she was tired. Years of carrying. She accepted the offer of help, but without embracing the attendant offer, the gift of a companion. Philip crossed busy roads at sight, a practice acquired in India. "No need for that here," she said sharply, as he stepped out. They moved to the traffic crossing. Once across, he proposed, "Let's sit down somewhere."

"Where?" Seventy-seven years old as she was, she seldom sat down at all on these excursions but went and returned in the same arc, laden, far from exultant, but obscurely proud. She knew one place, Ibrahims, where she sometimes bought baklavas. But Philip said, "Time for South Indian coffee."

She stopped dead. "You've been here six months, what do you know of South Indian coffee? It's an Arab suburb."

Jenny had tramped this street many times, but without ever noticing the Bombay Chinese Restaurant near the Bay Street corner.

Such Indian Chinese restaurants, a known quantity, if a rare one, did not serve coffee of any kind. They had never heard of coffee. She trailed into the shop behind him. Philip made no reference to its oddity, the Taoist shrine, the calendar painting of Ganesh and, among the decorations, a dangling papier-mâché image of Santa Claus, stranded between Christmases just as the lone patrons were stranded between the lunch hour and the dinner hour. Philip asked for coffee, but the chubby waitress was not content. She hovered for the meal order. "You always take *gobi* Manchurian."

"I have a guest."

"It's the real thing!" said Jenny of the coffee, poured by the waitress from a height without spilling a drop. "Who would have thought?" In her mind, she'd wandered far from the coffee. Who would have thought, 'a guest'! The guest of a guest, for as long as she sat: since to everyone else she was the host. Philip was the guest. Four times he had returned from India, each time as a guest. He had never stayed longer than a month, but on the first of these visits, a second daughter was conceived. They exchanged glances, for, without either being aware of it, their thoughts were running on the same lines. Philip's turned sombre before hers did. A line of Urdu verse came into his head. His hands, on the table, moved convulsively, then were still. He said, more abruptly than he'd have wished, "What's this hospital business?"

"Why do you ask?"

"I'm a fool for leaving it so long."

"Do you want the true answer? Or do you want the answer I give people?"

"I want the answer you give Nora. And Jim."

"Have you asked Jim?"

"No, I haven't asked Jim. I ask you. I've been working right up to it."

"I know you've been working up to something. So this is it? Well, the answer I give Jim, and give Nora, and Kate and all my friends is: ask me in a year."

"Who'll wait a year?" he said. "You're always at the hospital. It must be for tests – unless you're under treatment already. Will you tell me what it is?"

"Tests is what it is."

"Tests for what?"

"Ask me in a year. Ask Jim, if you think you'll learn more."

"Your health is the important thing. But then," he mused, "there are many important things."

"Like what?"

"I'll come out with what I have, when you come out with what you have."

"No bargains. No secret revelations. Thanks very much, Philip, for bringing me here. I'll remember this for coffee." Though of course she would not stir outside for coffee: she brewed it at home, by decoction, with a stainless steel cylinder, the full set. Who, in South India, would venture out for tiffin she could assemble at home? "I'm surprised the staff here know how to make it."

"I taught them."

"I should have guessed."

It was plain to Jenny that Philip had not found voice for something he meant. He had meant to inquire into her health; she had baulked him in that; he'd inquire elsewhere, but there *was* something more. Something he meant to 'come out with'. He had taken to lurking in the house corridor at night, outside the closed door. One of these nights he'd burst through. Let him. She believed she was ready for him.

With Philip carrying all the shopping they made light work of the short climb up Bryant Street. He really was fit, for a man his age. And with no set exercise, other than walking. She knew that the moment they reached home he'd drop the fan, and be off again. Where? He had work in some places, and play in others, like the 'Bombay' restaurant. She should ask him how his classes were going, his attempts to forge a role for himself. But, as she did with her health, Philip would deny her an answer.

2

One day a week, afternoons, Philip taught lessons in a real schoolroom. His work these days was coaching boys, but for once he coached in a school. The boys in this class were his favourites, the ones he'd begun with: Ashwin, Terry, and a Korean friend of them both, Jo-young. Here they were, spaced around their own schoolroom after hours, enjoying their holiday in the workplace. Terry needed coaching in English. Jo-young, who had plunged from a higher grade, needed coaching in everything: "not because Koreans aren't bright," he assured Philip. This Korean was extremely bright, but a scamp. Thanks to his japes, he failed most subjects in the selective school.

Ashwin stayed on because his father, defying his uncle, had decided he would benefit from Philip. If Ashwin had a weakness at all, it was geometry. But here Terry shone. Philip's tactic was to have Terry teach Ashwin maths and to have Ashwin and Jo-young (who spouted like an orator) bring rules, bite, and extroversion to the Chinese boy's English. As for Jo-young, his problem was morale. So Philip set none-too-easy tasks, which the boy would pass.

Even without Philip, Ashwin might ably have coached Terry and Terry Ashwin. But this solution had occurred to neither of them. Once out of school, with homework still to be done, they played. "None of you are swots, are you?" said Philip, without approval. The boys were uncertain. They no longer knew the word, current in Philip's schooldays. It was Jo-young who said, with a bravado which rather excited the others, "We don't study hard, because we're Australian."

"A little less of the 'Australian', is what I advise."

But how could Philip mean it, when so much of his own time was spent – as these lives would be spent – in fathoming and performing 'Australian'? Philip had not lost the knack. Few he met mistook him for a foreign-born, or corrected his language. His act was sound, sound enough. Mostly Philip saw 'Australian' as an obstacle to his advancement (if only in Australia), and Australians as the last people in the world to profess an interest in what he'd achieved in India. No-one would hire him. That he had learned the hard way. Yet at times, his heart blossomed with the pride and serenity of being with his own kind in his own country, a country of democratic ways which had got things wrong – think only of the ruthless dispossession of the Aborigines – but was getting things right.

When the lesson was finished the boys took off in carnival affray to Petersham station, and Philip watched them go. He would later catch a train himself. But he never joined them. He was indeed a little worried about them, not so much Ashwin, or even Jo-young, but Terry. What was Terry's father thinking, letting him in for this kind of education? Most of the Chinese boys and girls were enrolled in the James An coaching school. They did not hire personal coaches, they went to cram-school. Superior intellects, as some were, were encouraged by their parents to take no chances in a new country, and to cram for exams. Was this so unreasonable? The way Terry was going he would fail to come out top of his class, as he would – in the short run – if he went to cram-school. Philip hoped the father had taken the measure of his son's coach. If he had, all was well.

From a near classroom, Mr Kable's boys spilled out. Mr Kable kept back a class, assembled from the level-nine classes studying Shakespeare.

"*Midsummer Night's Dream*," he called jovially across the way. "The boys don't get fairies."

Philip fell in with him. "My problem was *Othello*. I laughed at Sir Laurence Olivier in the old Savoy Cinema in Bligh Street."

"Your problem was jealousy. What boy understands adult jealousy?"

"My problem was black. The *plastered-on* black. If it was Paul Robeson, I don't think I'd have laughed. Perhaps I'd have laughed. Who knows, with *Othello*."

"*Macbeth* is the play for schoolkids," Kable declared. "They snigger at fairies, but they respect witches. There has to be some dark reason."

The two crossed Parramatta Road by the footbridge and walked through Leichhardt to the Bar Italia. "Did you read Howard's press conference?" said Kable. "Deterrence at sea? There's a Norwegian container ship off Christmas Island, but we won't let it land."

"Why should we?"

"You haven't read the news? It's jam-packed with refugees. The captain made a sea-rescue off a leaking boat. Now Howard wants to turn them round to Indonesia."

Philip was silent. He had read the news. He had no wish to discuss asylum-seekers with Kable. He was – in his eyes – an asylum-seeker himself. Yet no-one remarked on it. His status was benign.

"Something is badly wrong in this country," said Kable, "with the teaching of boys."

"Not enough male teachers?"

"That's part of it. But what man *or* woman would be a teacher, when the profession is so reviled?'

"Do you feel reviled?"

"Not reviled. Just rated below my worth. The nation thinks citizens will sprout by themselves. They'll sprout in the dark, like mushrooms. But boys in the dark ..."

"Sprout like potatoes in a sack."

"They do. All limbs and eyes. Well, things could be worse. One way or another, our boys will sprout. Boys won't sprout behind razor-wire." When Philip said nothing, Kable was surprised. "It doesn't upset you?"

"Jim talks of nothing else."

Kable knew who Jim was. The two had met. Their views on taking refugees were much the same, but they did not get on. They were a study in contrasts. Jim grew furious while Kable, twenty years older, enjoyed irony and talked in riddles. He wore a bristling moustache, flew light aircraft out of Bankstown on weekends, and was a teacher by vocation, consumed by the fate of teachers. He saw them as a dying breed, and some as ghosts, haunting a lost profession. "There will always be teachers," Philip had consoled him once. "Who would replace them?" Kable merely snorted, as if he well knew the answer to that.

They ordered the strong coffee which the old establishment so well provided. "Your three boys," said Kable. "Those are not all you have. What about the others?"

Philip, again, was silent.

"Whoa, Philip. Where am I to tread? You're a minefield today. We'll stay off asylum-seekers, and we'll stay off boys."

"Yes, enough about boys. You're fine, you're an employed teacher. You have pupils laid on. 'Just let me at them' is my motto."

'Just let me at them' had not always been Philip's motto. For the past twelve years he had been free of boys, and had risen to the top, or somewhere near the top, of the education bureaucracy in India. A career mistake.

"You're good with your boys. If ever I met up with a teacher," Kable exclaimed, "who deserved a class more … But you know it's not that. You're seventy-six years old, man. You should thank God aloud for the pupils you have. The three girls in Auburn …"

"In Merrylands." Philip drained his coffee, left Kable, and travelled to Rockdale by two trains, changing at Redfern. There was the Aboriginal flag, fluttering over the sheds not far from the site of Paul Keating's Redfern address. Matters had improved, just a little, for the Aborigines – so Philip was told. But for refugees? – new arrivals? Not all was well. He wished he could show more empathy. Advancing age (could it be?), a narrowing of compass, shrank his vision when it should be expanding in a new country. He did not think much of Kable's advice, which boiled down to three words: count your blessings.

3

Jim was home. Philip dined with his grandson and Jenny. He himself cooked the meal, a lamb and eggplant curry with *basmati* rice. Jenny cooked South Indian, with gluggy rice, but Jim preferred *basmati* and had bonded with his grandfather on this matter. They switched on the television news. Jim had a word or two for the impasse off Christmas Island, but was awaited somewhere and soon went out. Philip retreated to his room. He had no occupation there, apart from his thoughts. Once he looked into the passage. It was late – near eleven – when there came a knock on the door, which was never fully closed.

Jenny stood there. He pulled the door but it jammed halfway. Neither spoke. It was clear to Jenny that she had surprised him, to the point of consternation. He again wrested at the door. It again jammed. Philip recoiled, to bump the bed. But Jenny would not advance into the room.

She led the way down the passage. She switched on a light that was never used. Her bedroom, like Jim's, ran off the room so illuminated – a vacancy they passed through at night in utter darkness. This was the 'middle room', where in his pre-war childhood, in 1938, Philip, his grandparents, his aunt and two uncles had listened on the radio to the Test cricket at Lords. Now nobody lingered there for anything. Only a tract of flowered carpet distinguished this room from the passage. There were a settee and two armchairs, both uncomfortable.

"Is something wrong?" That was Philip.

"You tell me."

"I was in bed …"

He returned to his room for a dressing gown. The nights were cold – not cruelly so, but he brought out a radiator just in case. Jenny was rugged in a gown she would never wear in public, a dun brown unravelling garment which she swore kept her warm like no other. "Let me be the one to ask," she said. "What's the matter?"

"Didn't I ask you first? About your health. But you gave me no answer."

"I appointed a time for an answer."

"Shall I appoint a time?" This would not do. "It's hard finding work in Sydney," he lied. Half-lied. That much was true. It was hard finding work here.

"Do you have to find work?"

"Well … work. When have you acknowledged my work?" he said lightly. "Not now, not then."

" 'Then' was so long ago. If you mean 'acknowledged', then what have we ever acknowledged of each other in all these years?"

"That could change. We'll talk about it."

"With all the breath saved." She did not take her eyes off him. Tread softly with Philip. His grievance about 'work', once unbottled, might pour a long while. She might not know how to stop him.

Philip stopped himself. "A colleague asked me only today," he said, "about work, about teaching. When was I happy, when was I happiest with my teaching, with the whole world. Do you know what I replied?"

"When you founded your own school in Gwalior?"

"I replied: that one year in Delhi."

Jenny took this in. "You blame me for having to leave Delhi, I know that."

"What should it matter to you, Delhi?" he said. "When you blame me for so much more – and you're right to do so."

"I don't blame you. I haven't blamed you for many years."

"I accept that's true. The day you wearied of me – *then* you stopped blaming me."

"Not at all: I wearied of you first. Then I blamed you."

That hushed him. She continued without anger. Her poise, her venture, would be lost if she displayed her emotion. "You could have taught school in Australia. It's a bit late now."

"It had to be in India."

"Do I know why?"

"I've always supposed you knew why."

"Let it be enough for my enlightenment, that I married a teacher."

"You married a man who had taught. I *became* a teacher. What made me a teacher? – that year in Delhi. Warangal was a first step. I began in Warangal, but at the school in Delhi – my joy knew no bounds. I could not get to the school fast enough in the mornings. I could not hurry to my bride fast enough in the evenings. I'd wed my Ragini" – she heard this without expression – "I'd lain all night, all the weekend in her arms. My teaching had wings. The boys listened with rapt faces. All the years I taught, it was never like that first year in Delhi."

"Rapt faces. All those long years."

"I swear it's true."

"You could have lain in her arms here."

I wish I had. The words, though untrue, all but spoke themselves. How his Ragini would have despaired of him, have despaired of them both, had he said that now. Were Philip to profess such a wish, in defiance of the truth, in cold blood and with nothing to be done about it – that wish would have been his last, and Jim would be sleeping again in his old room.

"Well, the years passed," she said, "and I ended up here. I made myself a good life here." She rose from her chair, not to leave, rather to extract from him what he meant, why he lingered so many nights in the passage. For could this be all? – these luckless reminiscences of Delhi?

"When *I* hear you speak of India," she said, "of teaching in India, one thought occurs to me, and it occurred to me a long time ago. And the thought is this. There is no kinder way of putting it. You believed you brought something to India. But India had no need of you. India had teachers enough. India had all kinds of teachers. India had patriots of its own hue. Gandhi was dead, but Vinoba Bhave I think was alive. Maulana Azad was alive.

B.R. Ambedkar was still alive."

"Such names, coming from you. Such names would not have passed her lips, the Ragini of those days."

"Which names would you like? Do you want revolutionaries? Ravi Narayan Reddy was still alive. Sundarayya was alive. Makhdoom Mohiuddin was alive. None of those people from Hyderabad took fright and fled to get married and live in a quiet bungalow in Jangpura Extension in Delhi."

"Is that what I did? Fled?"

"Not you, am I talking about you? *I* fled."

But Philip beamed at her, unscathed. "You can't blot out that year in Delhi. I came to tell you, it was the most magical year of my life."

Still Delhi? He came about Delhi? "First of all, you did not come to me. I came to you. But when you did come – two nights ago – it was not to relive your magical year. It was for some pressing reason. What was that?"

Philip must do better. Some pressing reason: so there was. And yet – shorn of his wiles, his own way of leading up to things – he could not name it. He groped for it. All was cotton-wool. "It had to be in India," he said, as if dreaming, mulish in his repetition. He could go no further.

"You've made that plain. You've made that plain, throughout life, once, twice, any number of times."

"I think I lost something."

"You lost something? You did, we all did, but we live with it. I lost a sister, a person far more material to me than anyone was to you."

"Or I *did* something. My own choices and actions."

"Be sure what you say. Philip Chalk is not repenting of his choices and actions. You may be a sinner, but I know you: you're not one to repent. I don't see you crying over spilt milk, not you. It was something more than that."

She knew what he was thinking: if only she would wait, not come knocking at the door of his bedroom but await *his* knock, on her own door.

"What else in Delhi?" she said.

"Before Delhi. It's hard to describe, it's hard for me to say, Jenny."

"Jenny? You never call me Jenny. You never call me anything. If you're sure you mean *before Delhi*, there is one name we haven't mentioned."

Philip called an end to this vigil. He did so abruptly, rising at those words. He left the room. She followed him. But he was not quite done; turning at his bedroom door, he said in confusion, almost as if she weren't present, "Why do you think this is happening now?"

"What is happening?"

"Remembering it all. Remembering you. Though we live in the same house."

"What are you remembering?"

"I'll sort it out. There was a trigger, it was something Jim said."

Jenny inquired sharply, because it concerned her grandson. "Why, what did Jim say? What have you been laying on Jim?"

"Nothing. It was nothing he said, and it was nothing I said … I said nothing." Philip squeezed her arm, her upper arm, the shoulder blade really, for the first time on this visit, or on any visit, and took himself off. Jenny had the last word: "Then keep on saying nothing."

She meant, where Jim was concerned. She pictured them together. Philip, it appeared, had secrets, he was trailing his coat to Jenny but the words would not come out. How could he go quietly to bed after an interview like that? She turned on all the lights and for the next quarter-hour found herself drifting here and there, in her own house – like a ghost, she thought, not guessing the half of it. She had appeared in his room to Philip in that very guise.

4

There is one name we haven't mentioned. Until she spoke of him – until she dared Philip to speak of him – that name had lain neglected between them, as if they had buried it long ago with their own hands. The grass grew over it.

Had Philip not leapt free when he did, they'd have spoken of Anand. It was what Philip wanted. He knew – didn't he? – what he wanted: but in his time, not hers. Not at her behest. He did not know how seldom or how often Jenny thought of Anand, or what she thought. She must think of him sometimes, when she thought of the places left behind. *What news of Anand, Philip, did you meet with Anand? Where's Anand? Why haven't you mentioned Anand?* Once too often, she'd asked him.

That once, Philip had complied. He'd conveyed Anand's message to Ragini, in Anand's own words. When that was done, he'd had Warangal to himself.

"Glued to each other. The joke's on them." His mutterings came back to him. Mumblings of all those years ago, just a formula that did for a thought, not a thought but a diffuse formation, or *refusal* to form, like a cloud that would not lead to rain, and would not disperse. It hovered round him all that month, the pre-monsoonal month, the worst weather he had known in that distant reach of India. His ill-formed thought *was* the weather. Persons and personages of all kinds in the Nizam's Dominions, high and low, in and out of office, had a great deal to occupy them in May and June of the year of the State's downfall. And Philip had his thought. Yet he continued to teach – and well, too. Those boys did not suffer in the least.

He'd supposed she might visit, undo this mess. The day after, in fear and chagrin at what he'd done, Philip walked his bicycle to the line of the walls to gaze, if only to gaze, at the back entrance to the hospital, the approach he'd taken. He could not find it! Nor could he find the front entrance! The parents of the boys in his class – all Hindus – had never heard of the Ghazi Imam Hospital.

Warangal changed. Bands of men in uniform no longer just stood about. They paraded the streets. Philip heard of shopkeepers beaten, the merchandise of shops overturned. He had not, so far, witnessed these intrusions with his own eyes. A question arose. Which of these bands were Razakars and which were police? Philip favoured Anand's criterion: the Razakars drilled more and were better clothed, while the police were a rabble. But in practice this was misleading. What he did understand was that more and more Razakars had filed in from the surrounding districts and were battening on the town, waiting, some said, for the Indian Army invasion, which they would oppose to the end. Why then, with a border to defend, did they gather in the town? The reason was plain: the Communists were swiftly expanding their base in the countryside. The Razakars were too frightened to remain there. So were the police. Units of the Hyderabad Army might have fought their way there, but were under the Nizam's orders to refrain. Refrain? – they were never seen. Such was the effect of the Nizam's *farman* of May 4, which had so incensed Anand. But the Communists ruled the land – with or without the Nizam's *farman*. Would the Communists themselves, Philip asked Sri Srinivasan – a man who knew Ragini, her comings and goings – would the Communists, like the Razakars, do battle with the Indian Army should it reach the border, should it cross the mighty Godavari and head this way? "The Communists are Hindus," said Srinivasan. "The Razakars are Muslims." That was his answer.

Where was Ragini, in all this? She would no longer be hiding in her sister's room.

Philip asked Bashir, who was a Muslim, about the Ghazi Imam Hospital, and learned there was indeed such a place.

Bashir continued to fetch eggs, onions, chillis and aubergines from the market, to cook two meals daily and – here was a departure – to seek to communicate in English, rather than in Urdu. His English he acquired from

Philip, and from nobody else. So Philip was hearing his own words and phrases shaken up, in jigsaw, and positioned in new combinations. When a notion was expressed which his words and phrases had not prefigured, the effect was strange. Events in a mirror stole a march on the world. This fellow was smart. He would succeed anywhere (though of course, being where he was and when he was, he would succeed nowhere). He sat in a chair – once in the armchair – and Philip forbore to tell him off. Guests would have seen this as imprudent but Philip could not view hierarchy in the Indian manner. His colleagues in the liberal wing of the Nizam's service, Hardcastle and Smart, were similarly free with their tea-bearers and office peons, but merely for form's sake, not to learn anything. Yet much of what Philip did learn he had from Bashir, in an idiolect framed by them both.

Bashir had his projects. He liked to hear of strange customs, comparing them with his own. Funerals, for example: on this one topic he rained a regular inquisition, furthered from one interview to the next. In Australia, what became of the dead? How were they buried? In the grave, which way did they point? How long would they have to wait? To this last question, above all, Philip had no answer. He had never wondered. In all his days, he had never once thought of the problem of the resurrection of the dead.

Bashir was not curious about everything. He knew little of the Communists or the State Congress. When Philip mentioned the Razakars, a circumspect understanding dawned on his face, but he clammed up. Some time later he remarked, "They are getting petrol."

"Who?"

"*Badmash*. They are getting petrol. They don't pay. Ghee, *vanaspati*, cooking oil."

"Why don't they pay?"

The long blockade, imposed by India on the Nizam's Dominions as far back as November, was beginning to bite. Something had happened to offend India and the blockade was tightened. Philip bought a radio in the bazaar. But his purchase was void. Electrical wiring ran to the house, but the current had expired. The print in the Urdu dailies – except for the headlines – was too small for him to read. Bereft in Warangal, Philip had no news of Anand. But what news of Anand could there be? The leaders and office-bearers of his party, along with the hundreds of volunteers and students, were back in gaol. Among them was Swami Ramananda Tirtha, the State Congress President and leading spirit in the resistance. It was only because Anand was obscure that he could come and go, in these Telengana districts, without being recognised. Did he still come and go? Had Anand, after leaping off the bus, straggled home safe and sound? Had he resumed his journey? Had he forgiven Ragini? The way Philip saw it, there was nothing to forgive. If a breach had been widened between Anand and Ragini, the offence was to Ragini and the breach was his doing, Philip's doing. He had blurted his heart out.

Philip closed the school for three days, pleasing nobody. He boarded the Hyderabad bus, encountered only police on the road and sat like the old stager he was through the check-points. The monsoon struck on the journey. He alighted in a pause in the rain. Anand's hut on the hostel roof – he now knew the way – was empty. He ended up late in a windowless room near Nampally station, saved from the elements but terrorised all night long by a blade fan half-moored to the ceiling.

How was he to find Anand in a day? And what was he to say? Must he confess? *Had* Anand reached Warangal? *Had* he spoken to Ragini? And even if Anand knew nothing of Philip's cruel action, wasn't it for Philip to atone, to shower grace on Anand and Ragini? And how would he shower grace? Was he a grace-showering type of person?

The morrow broke clear and fine but the clouds gathered and dumped on him midway between the Osmania University bus shelter and the Arts College. His crowd at Osmania had been moved from the Arabic Department and now occupied Business Studies. The four of them – Sukku included – were poring over the card files from wooden drawers. Hardcastle sprang up. "Philip, how's your book-keeping? We've found treasure. These drawers weren't cleared."

"What's this? Headings and numbers. They're handwritten."

"That's why we need help. We can all read *printed* Urdu."

"Here's a name," said Philip at once. "Mo'in Nawaz Jung."

The four stared, dumbfounded. "Beginner's luck. Now Mo'in Nawaz Jung, who's an important man – what has he been up to?"

One sitting and four standing, they deciphered the page in what was to Philip a lost vigil, painfully prolonged. He stared through the window at the thudding rain.

"We're not, as you might suppose, bringing crooks to justice," Hardcastle explained. "We're hoping to track down our funding. An amount has been set aside, but it's not coming through and we're sure it's being siphoned off somewhere."

"Is my school all right?"

"Well, nothing is all right, but your school ..."

At the word 'school' a blond, boisterous, dripping figure burst into the room, whom the others knew so well they forbore to greet him. "Secunderabad is awash," he cried. "The parade ground at Bolarum is under water.

The rail line is cut at Sitafalmandi ..."

An alarmist. It was the first day of rain. Nothing was 'awash'.

"Sven, this is Philip."

Sven was introduced to Philip, not Philip to Sven. The two eyed each other narrowly, as rivals. For all its best efforts, Educational Reform had succeeded in appointing only two headmasters. These were they, Philip and Sven, the one no older, no more reassuring and no better prepared for his task than the other. Philip relented towards Sven only when he heard of his misfortune: he had been chased from his post.

Sukku told him all about it as they set out in pursuit – not of Anand, a yeti to them, but of someone who might know his whereabouts. "Sven would have battled for his school. He is Viking. Pugnacious fellow."

"He is an excitable fellow."

"Philip, have you heard of Aurangabad? Of what happened there? You, too, would be excitable if you went to Aurangabad. I, too, would be excited, but I would not be making that journey, for cowardice reasons. Razakars have taken over the Marathwada districts. They are harming and teasing people, they are closing down shops and schools and their leader or fuehrer, whom I compare to Hitler, is encouraging these beatings and manhandlings of poor Hindus. You know these Razakars. Last November, they prevented the Nizam. This month, there is a new draft agreement with India. They prevented that! The Nizam will not sign. They intend to fight the Indian Army. They have guns. You are an Australian. You may know how they acquire guns."

"I know. Don't remind me. It's still going on, is it?"

"Some nights at Bidar airfield. He lands at night."

"In Warangal, too, we have these Razakars."

Unless Philip was mistaken, his timid friend snorted aloud at the idea of Razakars in Warangal. "Warangal, Nalgonda ... those are Communist districts."

Perhaps Sven, thought Philip, seeing he is pugnacious, might like to try his hand teaching school in Communist districts. He was sheepishly aware that neither he, nor his school, had suffered the smallest inconvenience. "Where the devil is Anand?" he said. "Where are you taking me?"

Sukku kept his own counsel.

It was Philip's first monsoon, and he was enjoying it. He had, last November, experienced a little rain, attributed to the north-east monsoon. Those winds played havoc on the Andhra coast, on the Bay of Bengal, but bore only lightly inland. Today was the south-west monsoon, the real thing in Hyderabad. It was not raining at present but the lull was amazing, the chaos it revealed. For as long as it rained, folk in the midst of it were blinded, as well as deafened. You could see nothing. But when the rain paused, all that obliterating energy was cast onto a refreshed plane, as spectacle. They had crossed Husain Sagar by the Bund and were proceeding up the long hill towards Abids. The direct route from the university to Abids, by Himayatnagar, had been closed for military manoeuvres. Now here was a military manoeuvre worth watching. A camouflaged lorry, bearing a heavy field gun mounted on the flatbed with its barrel slowly rotating – some fault in the mechanism? – stood hopelessly marooned in the road, in water so deep it covered the tops of the wheels. The current raced past and barefoot boys speeded in the shallows, splashing water at the leviathan. You would think it a captured vehicle. But no, its swarming crew wore the jackets and slanted turbans of the Nizam's Household Troops, deputing for the Hyderabad Army. From the hilltop at Gunfoundry the road poured debris, coloured paper and packets, damp fireworks, discarded garments, light rubble and snapped branches of banyans. Spars and awnings dangled from shops. Cycle-rickshaw drivers with vast loads – Philip and Sukku, crammed in one seat, were among the lightest – dismounted to navigate the road. A kind of hilarity, the upwash and antipodes of all that vehemence from on high, flickered from soul to soul in reprieved snatches of song and applause. Dogs and pigs trotted about. The two passengers and their wading driver, a young man whose vehicle was up to the challenge, hooted and applauded as their cycle mounted the steep grade. Only the soldiers were not laughing.

At Sultan Bazaar euphoria was no less. The cheer and clamour of a rediscovery of the world – not unmingled with loud vexation – engulfed them as they tumbled from their carriage near the Jain temple. Already dank water lapped the step of a doorway. What would the monsoon not accomplish on its second day! Sukku knocked, a voice from inside called something in Telugu and Sukku replied. The door was opened.

"*Ekkad' andi?*" We are two friends, the friends of Anand. Sukku made this plain. Well-wishers to the Indian National Congress and fast friends of Anand.

"Who is this *Angrez?*"

The question was in English. Philip undertook to explain himself. Fearing he would confess to the Nizam's employment, Sukku cut him short and completed the introduction. How charming and rare to find, an Australian.

"Australian? He is gun-runner? Like Sidney Cotton?"

Philip took over from Sukku, being, he supposed, of the two, the dearer to Anand. "I would like to see Anand, if he's here."

"He is not here."

"Then where is he?"

As they left the place, Sukku observed: "Some trouble." He steered Philip to a tea-shop, more a kind of stove-house, where tea was brewed on a kerosene flame and carried in cups by boys all up and down Sultan Bazaar, a flashpoint in this city of distances. They perched on stools on the marble sill of the tea-house, viewing the scene, which was drabber than usual though quite as active. Heavy tarpaulins covered the pyramids of nuts, fruits and coloured spices. "There is trouble," said Sukku. "They don't admit to us. They admit to themselves, but not to us."

"What trouble?" Why wouldn't there be trouble?

"I know where Anand has gone. But I brought you here, so you could see for yourself."

"Why, what did I see?"

"These are rooms of the Hyderabad State Congress."

"So they are. And where is Anand?"

Was Sukku one of those people who hold back information, not for good reason but to make a mystery of themselves, of all that surrounds them and of all they know (which is not much)? Philip hadn't thought so. And indeed the answer came soon enough. "I will tell you where he is. Then I will tell you why he has gone there."

"Where is he?"

"He is somewhere in the Kannada districts. Not his own district."

"And not in Warangal district? Looking for Ragini?"

Sukku, if he knew the name Ragini, failed to show it. "The Congress has factions. There are new faction and old faction. The warlike faction and the wait-and-see faction."

"Nothing 'wait-and-see' about Anand." *Too* 'warlike', in his ire with his lover. By now, surely, the two had made up.

"The 'wait-and-see' faction. And the warlike faction. Their leader is Swami. Swami to this day is President of the Hyderabad State Congress, respected as such by Nehru and the Delhi leaders though he lies in gaol. When I say warlike, I don't mean that Swami enjoys firearms. He is holy man. But he did go two years ago to Suryapet village in Nalgonda, to plead with the Tahsildar and the Army. Procurement of grain was too high. The villagers could not afford the grain levy, and some had refused. They were beaten and killed. There were Communists even in those days in Nalgonda District."

"The Communists beat and killed peasants?"

"First the police beat peasants. Then the army fired, and some were killed. The Communists opposed, and Swami Ramananda Tirtha went to investigate. He wrote his report, published in the *Deccan Chronicle*."

"That's warlike?"

"'Go-and-see' and 'wait-and-see'. They are two factions."

A line of women, Lambadis as they were called, Banjaras or (wrongly) gypsies, had appeared with bailers and were clearing the gutters of water. Such women, in their long skirts and mirrored blouses, stood at building sites all over the Nizam's Dominions, lofting rough stones and bleak cauldrons of mud from hand to hand. They were no respecters of persons and as their horde drew near, the two tea-house patrons, keeping dry, sought to abandon their perch. They took up another, a popular location on high ground under a decrepit balcony whose beams were fused with branches of trees and dangerous-looking electrical wiring. A street bookseller spread his pages out of the weather. Though cramped for room, Philip and Sukku refrained from trampling the printed word; other fugitives were not so nice. The rain might descend at any moment.

"What has all this to do with Anand?"

"His leader is in gaol. All the *satyagrahis* are in gaol. The Party is rudderless, according to Anand."

"But Anand did not offer *satyagraha*."

"That was by command. Anand was saved for another purpose."

Saved for a purpose? To moon over Ragini, wearing out the seat leather on the bus between Hyderabad and Warangal? To be fair to Anand, he was not the one who mooned. He had acted, successfully, being warlike, and thanks to that action, had ceased to moon.

"I tried to counsel him," said Sukku. "His mood is strange. He says good people are in gaol. He must fight by himself. He says there is no time. The Indian Army will invade, who knows when that will be ... it is close ... the Nizam has torn up the agreement ..."

"*What* does he say? *Who* is he going to fight by himself?"

"First, the Razakars. Then, if there is time, the Communists."

"He'll fight them by himself."

"He will fight. He may not be victorious. But, Anand swears, he will do some good."

"He'll fight the Communists."

"Of course. The Swami and his faction," Sukku explained, " they admire the Communists. They would like to defend villagers against the Nizam. But, instead, the Communists have defended. Now Communists are strong. They will have to be stopped."

"By the Indian Army. It can't be by Anand! One man can't do everything."

"He is in strange mood. He will fight."

"How can I reach him?"

5

Philip did not reach Anand. He left Hyderabad the next day. His *own* mood was strange. Sights were as usual, the convulsion in the streets was as usual. Yet nothing, to him, was as usual. Then what was different? He fixed on one sight, a family approaching the lattice portal of a brick-paved enclosure fluttering black flags, green flags, tapestry squares and pinions, and obscure battle standards.

He knew this as an *'ashur-khana*. There was no English word for it. Floats in procession set out from these rallying-places on the Shi'a Muslim festival of 'Ashura, the tenth day of Muharram. Today was no such day and this party of one family – the men in white *dhotis*, the women in starched, sombre garb and the children dressed for an excursion – were having to contest their passage with others who frequented the street. None were onlookers. All were participants. Some begged for alms, some thrust and toiled to make headway while vendors spread their wares on whatever space could be found between puddles and flying feet as the monsoon cloud filled the sky. Nothing to do with a war to come. No-one here had heard of the defence of the realm. A bare-chested mendicant smeared with ash and carrying a *trisul* – Siva himself – accepted coins from donors. All was 'as usual'.

Was it because he knew better, foresaw what was coming, that Philip had so little faith in the usual? Could he be mistaken? It was surely in the power of the usual to protect its own.

If only Anand were on the bus seat beside him! They would travel to Warangal, all misunderstandings – his own and Anand's – cleared out of the way, with Philip, second fiddle, gladly extolling the woman so beloved of Anand. But Anand was not on the bus. This was no bus ride. Philip rode in state. Some visiting scribe, professor of education, or Member of Cabinet, perhaps Laiq Ali himself, for all he could remember of him, wanted to inspect Philip's school and had requisitioned a car, as well as a rifle detachment of one of the innumerable armies of Irregulars to be had in Hyderabad, bundled into lorries before and behind to sweep the road clear of Communists. There were no such encounters on this journey or if there were, Philip had forgotten what happened, what rounds were fired, who was hit, and what his new benefactor thought of his school: all he remembered in Sydney was the long departure, the leaving of Hyderabad. What had been so unsettling about that departure? What were his fears? That he'd never see Hyderabad again? That its memory would be lost? That the city he had begun to know would be so changed, by the next time he viewed it, that life's benediction – 'as usual' – could no longer be pronounced? If those were his thoughts, Philip was overdoing it. He would see Hyderabad again and Hyderabad is there to this day, I.T. and all. A glittering techno-city, the rival of Bangalore. He could visit it this year, 2001, if he were so inclined (he was not).

In market towns on the road were the onlookers he had missed in the capital, people with nothing to do who watched the cavalcade in silence. This *was* unusual. An enforced peace had descended on the road. On vil-lages far from the road, far out of sight, no peace had descended. A new social order was in the making. Godowns and granaries were looted, police *thanas* were burned, men and women fought and were killed, hopes were born, crushed, and born again. Was she out there? Then leave her to it. It was not till they had passed through the roadblocks and were safe within Warangal town, itself transformed by the presence of so many armed groups under diverse commands, that Philip surrendered without warning to a sorrow from nowhere, a rain of inner sand like a rain of tears. It was chickens that set him off. The houses dyed chickens bright colours to tell them apart. A toddler pursued chickens amid the rubbish, and Philip was consumed by a grief unnamed. He mourned, not what he saw nor even what he imagined: he could not have said what he mourned. The car's occupants, to their amazement, heard him bawl outright.

Just as suddenly, the fit was over. Philip composed himself, and was able to point to his own house. He was fond of his locality and vowed then and there to stay on, to work on at his school when the armed men had gone, when the image of Ragini had faded and there was no longer a Hyderabad to grieve for.

6

The car that bore Philip abandoned him some way from his school. The vanguard lorry was halted by police. A policeman wearing braid approached the car. Its occupants, the forgotten dignitary in European clothes and the officials escorting him, stepped onto the road. Only Philip and the driver were left.

Now Philip stood bereft on the road, the one road of Warangal. He was dumped. Vehicle by vehicle, the convoy turned aside. Yet the alley they took led blind, to a Devi temple. That temple was all there was. Unless someone in one of the lorries knew a way out. A way to the airfield. To inspect a crisis. Or perhaps to be bundled out by plane.

"Your school is safe" – a parting assurance. Philip felt safe, but could not be sure the convoy and car were safe. In a suburb of Sydney he had once seen the enormous Small's Chocolate van, which carried a revolving cylinder like a cement mixer, trapped in a side-street. It whirred but could not fly. Should he follow the convoy, perhaps to proffer useless advice as suburban wiseacres had to the chocolate van? His own house, behind him on the road, was a long way.

He looked for a rickshaw. Normally they cycled past in droves, like the peloton on the Tour de France. But none were in sight. His school was the nearest haven. Philip began to walk. It was a Monday. Most of the shops were shuttered down, no surprise at noon. The paramilitary units sparring on all sides wore a rainbow of uniforms: the black shirts were the Razakars, but there were also green Razakars, and Razakars whose turnout was so mean that they could only have failed the famed drill or *qawaid* he heard about. There were squads of police, soldierly platoons and even a mounted formation bearing lances but with gunsticks protruding under their coats. Were all these on the same side? Rival forces for order? Their profusion was troubling, the very icon of disorder. But for now they were harmless. They just stood there. Some of them carried umbrellas: those clouds spelled rain.

Philip, who'd stayed away three days, had fixed Monday as a school holiday. But he approached the school. Somebody might be around.

He fished the key from his pocket. But the bolt was already drawn and the lock broken.

Bystanders flocked to him as he stood before the broken lock with the key in his hand. He pushed the door and they all trooped in. Here was chaos. Kitchen china was shattered on the floor of the schoolroom. The forms, solid teak, were strewn, all legs, in a maze. The wall charts were down. His desk was hacked and something had been scrawled on the blackboard. No, worse: it had been gouged with a knife. A portion of the blacking was off. A beard of splinters protruded like a coarse gesture into the room.

Others helped him right the forms. Violence still reigned, as an afterglow. The tall desks were undamaged and, lifting the top of his desk, he saw his ledgers were intact. The reams of data he kept for his own use, never to be revealed to the pupils, their families or an inspector (inspector there was none), were just as he'd left them. Good glue – the shops kept it – would mend the wall charts. When had this happened?

No-one had seen it happen.

No-one spoke. Where are we, in Sicily? In Palermo? Trumped by the Mafia? The atmosphere in the room was suspenseful, though it held a dozen people. Seconds passed. Then Philip was lustily reminded that he was not in Sicily at all. Everyone had an opinion and voiced it. The Razakars, their youth wing, the Communists, the Indian National Congress, disgruntled police, appalling hoodlums who flourished in contempt of all these: such was the volume and variety of suggestions that Philip would have learned more from the consensus of a cowed silence. He stepped into the street. There, in the midst of a public hearing of even more generous scope and size, which confirmed one thing – the assault had taken place at night, and the schoolroom door had gaped wide all morning until the police closed it – Philip was handed a note. He was handed the note by a person he had never met, though he knew the face. The face belonged to one of the auto-shop apprentices down the street, a youth about his own age who unlike the other workmen wore a spotless pair of overalls, which covered his *dhoti*. Philip had only ever glanced at him, but he had a name for him: Snow White. Snow White pressed the note into Philip's hand and made off. Besieged though he was, Philip unfolded the note there and then. He read at a gulp.

'I authorise this note and its bearer. I visited your house but can't stay. I don't know where I'll be. Come to Hyderabad. Anand.'

Great. Come to Hyderabad. Philip left the school to its wellwishers. He roved the street but the messenger had vanished.

Nothing was easier in Warangal than fitting a new lock to a door. You could not buy postage stamps in Warangal, but every fourth store was a locksmith's. The schoolroom bore its scars well. Philip was proud even of the blackboard. It taught a lesson – as a blackboard should. It imposed a value. Its affliction would recall to the boys what its health should be. Philip was not one to be scared off by *goondas*, though in truth he had never met a *goonda*.

The days passed. The boys returned to the school. There were now only four, but these four appeared every day. The assault on their building was not repeated. The monsoon with its din and its blindfold bore down for a couple of hours each day. Ramazan, too, had come. The boys, all Hindus, carried their own tiffin to school since Mohan had absconded and Omar Din, his replacement, was a Muslim and would not lay out food, or make tea, between dawn and sunset. Philip had discovered, on a pavement bookstall in Hyderabad, a copy, in flyspeck condition, of *Doctor Dolittle*, and acquainted the boys with this text. He found in himself a gift for teaching whimsical events. By the time he got to the pushme-pullyou, they were all behind him.

His calm was wholly on the surface. And the calm of the ancient town, long-drawn-out on the unevenly tarred road between Kazipet station, where the broad-gauge line pointed to Delhi, and the fort and citadel in the east, was disrupted more and more often by harmful events. Philip came only on the wreckage of such events. A cyclist lay in his blood at a crossroads. A truck manned by cheering Razakars had come blundering out of nowhere and put paid to a life. A ruin lay smouldering: the headquarters of the Arya Samaj in the district. Shop window-glass littered the pavements. Gunfire was heard. Yet the threat of personal danger – of the kind that had driven a 'pugnacious' headmaster from Aurangabad – at no time troubled Philip. It was not that he was brave; but his being was consumed by the slow burn of a contrition, a prostration and a misery, so unlike him, that fear itself might have burst on him as the trumpet-sound of a deliverance. He visited Snow White in his workshop and found a Muslim among Muslims, intent on keeping Ramazan, known to Anand, but wanting nothing to do with Philip. A secret Congress worker (Philip surmised), he had no wish to be unmasked and could not comprehend Philip: an appointee of the Nizam, as he saw him. And so Philip was, an appointee: but not an agent. He had neither disowned the Nizam, nor did he own to him. He persisted in this now unsafe job without giving it a second thought. All his thoughts, other than of lessons, were of Anand and Ragini. He thought of them apart, and he thought of them together. While Philip was in Hyderabad – searching for Anand! – Anand was in Warangal – searching for him! Not just for him. Yet he *had* come for Philip. For the two of them: each precious to him, thought Philip, in some unique way.

Philip was heedless of his life but it did not escape him that, pottering around Warangal in the Nizam's service, he was a person of interest. Who were they, who had demolished his schoolroom? Could it have been some 'benign' force, like the Congress? – an enraged Congress activist? He cooked up a ridiculous scenario in which Anand, on Congress business, thumbing his nose at the police, the Razakars, the Hyderabad Army and the Communists – Ragini among them – had travelled from Hyderabad in person to smash the lock, vandalise the room, scrawl a note ... no doubt after Ragini had explained to him what Philip had done! Or it was Ragini herself, consumed by revenge? He'd dismantled her dream of Anand! Or she remembered the wall sheets! She'd been dismayed to find wall sheets in Urdu, but none in Telugu. Her political movement, after all, was not just a Communist Party. It was the nationalist party of a nation. It was the Andhra Mahasabha.

He confided his worst thoughts to Bashir. Bashir's English was improving by leaps and bounds. He well understood that Philip had lost faith in himself. He had mismanaged two friendships, had deceived two friends who loved one another. Bashir knew the word 'love', reserved by him for the Prophet of Islam. If its meaning eluded him in the present context he did not show it, but raised his usual questions, so little to the point that they served Philip as a cordial distraction. Philip had been raised as a Protestant, Bashir now learned: different from a Catholic. Philip had no truck with priests. His relation with God was direct. It was unmediated. Yet Bashir had never seen him pray.

The impression of Philip successfully conveyed to Bashir was of a parasite who misused his friends. Yet Bashir could not view this status as an enduring one. One Thursday, when Philip had time, he would take him to the *dargah*. Philip would become a Muslim, the only solution. He offered his solution, not out of zeal – in order to convert a *firangi* – but simply to help.

Waiting, waiting, it's all in the waiting. From day to day the Indian Army was suspended, as if in the sky, at its occult distance.

Philip took long walks. His steps led him, without misdirection – a second, then a third time – to the Ghazi Imam Hospital. But he dared not walk in. As if Ragini would be hovering in the same room. As if she would receive his amends. What amends could those be? His confession of truth? There was no truth to confess. Anand had indeed uttered those words, every word Philip had ascribed to him. If Anand had since appeared, had unsaid those words, then who was Philip to unsay them?

Philip admitted to his understanding what he had known all along. Ragini belonged to Anand, and Anand in turn was consumed by his longing for Ragini. He had heard this, a thousand times, from Anand. She, of course, being Ragini, said nothing of the kind. With her yen for concealment she did her level best to imply the opposite. And yet, to Philip, she was not a hard person to understand. What he understood was a love story. A love story doomed from the beginning – doomed of its nature, and without his help.

The two were predestined for each other. The new Philip did not shrink from 'predestined'. He embraced the word – as if his hyperbole could save them. But nothing could save them. The perfections they recognised in each other, that had whirled them together, now skied them, lofted them apart. They were agents of good, persons of principle. In Philip's eyes even their principles were the same. But their attachments were different, and they would not abandon these attachments. Each fell in love: yet each abandoned nothing.

Philip had observed it all at close quarters. Ragini followed her own bent, her elective path. Her course was set. To love was grand, but deep, deeper to them both than impulse or longing or esteem, was a force that eluded their observer, what *he* called attachment, their ill-starred attachment ... Philip pronounced this judgment, but with no right to judge: for what did he know of attachment to a cause? What he knew, too well, was attachment to Ragini, attachment to a friend like Anand. Forget for now that he had deceived them both.

The Indian Army would storm down. The Congress, at New Delhi, would dissolve Hyderabad State and rule its districts. Anand was on the right side. The judgment from might was the judgment of right. But tell this to Ragini. In a thousand years, Ragini would not agree. And the argument from might was not Anand's.

At his distance of fifty-three years, it was morning. In the kitchen at Rockdale Philip had risen early, before Jenny. He meant to brew coffee, have it wait, pour it for them both. Shunning the decoction equipment and trusting to a saucepan, he paused over the waning colours of this memory, the memory of days on end which clung now like a wrapper too filmy, too insubstantial to quite discard. What more was there to learn from this memory? Had it more to give? Its dangers – had he defused them? Stared them down? He paused, to gauge one more event – unable to quite junk the wrapper.

7

He was cycling pell-mell. The bike swerved, without his volition, almost toppling him. The school was closed. None of the pupils had shown for days. Police and Razakars, police or Razakars – what was the point, any longer, in the distinction? – loitered in clumps along the one road. None menaced Philip. When he left the road, to follow the broken ramparts of the fort through the maze of alleys that concealed the hospital, he collided with a funeral procession: Muslim mourners, a natural death, the body borne aloft on a charpoy. Some shops and workshops stood open. The rest were shuttered down. But in their workshop near the hospital the three boy tailors, Hindus, still plied their trade.

Philip wheeled through the gate. He looked neither right nor left as he crossed the yard where he had once been panicked by a sight terrible to his eyes, but routine in hospitals. He smelled ammonia, phenol, grey water. Where the crowd – patients and their families – spilled from the grounds onto the waiting-room steps he located a bike rack. He followed a path, mounted stairs at a corner of the building.

Here was the room. The door was closed. He knocked.

"*Enn'ammaa ...*"

Philip pushed the door. Small chance that Ragini would be found in the room. Yet here was her sister, curled on her own bed, sleepily responding at midday to some matron or nurse. She scrambled, near-naked, to an erect posture. This was intrusion. Philip backed into the corridor. She called. "Wait there. I'll come out."

She was five minutes about it but stood before him at last, unsmiling, in her full nurse's uniform. "I'll take you to reception."

They sat in the lobby on facing chairs. Their knees touched. The reception desk was unstaffed but a team of orderlies scanned the multitude at the entrance, noisily barring some, admitting others, escorting them to galleries out of sight. "Stephen, is it?"

"Philip."

"You see, no patients or doctors. I've brought you to a quiet place."

Philip rested his gaze on the commotion.

"Visitors, visitors. Turning away visitors is the all-the-time business of this hospital."

"Where are the patients?"

"Are you a patient? Don't ask for patients, there are many. Too many broken heads."

"I've seen heads broken."

"It will get worse. And here, only six beds. There is no room, even on the floor. Nothing is to be gained in Warangal by taking processions. I am speaking from a Night-Ward perspective. Hindus should keep to their homes."

"I've sent my boys home."

"That was responsible."

"The Indian flag will fly, soon enough," said Philip, perhaps unwisely: this was the sister of a revolutionary he was addressing. But the sister made no reply. Nationalist or Communist, she hid her opinion.

From his back pocket he hauled an envelope. Two smaller envelopes were contained within this long one: the sealed, and the unsealed. Fetched to him by Snow White, on a second occasion, this packet had travelled to Warangal by a means unknown. He passed the sealed envelope to the nurse. "Mission accomplished," he said lightly.

" 'For Ragini'. Is this from you?"

"Not from me."

"*Not* from you," she said, mistrustful, but inquiring no further.

Philip too was silent. To keep a lid on his catch-phrase, 'mission accomplished', was all he could do. The phrase had no sense, but what made it irresistible – for want of sense – was its symbolic value. It betokened the new Philip, discharging the mandate of a friend, with no thought of self. 'Mission impossible' would have been more like it.

"Ragini is not here. She is indisposed," said the sister at last.

"I would like you to take this letter to her."

The sister had not fully accepted the envelope. She glanced at it in her hand. The diagonal flap, though torn, was effectively in place. "Have you opened this? Do you know what is in the letter?"

"I do not know what is in the letter."

She toyed with it, while Philip retained in his own hand the unsealed letter, the one Anand had scrawled for him. Snow White – on his second errand – had had no idea where Anand was. There was no fresh news for Philip in the letter to him. 'Come to Hyderabad.' Why the wild-goose chase? He saw nothing binding him, for now, in Anand's directive – except for one part. 'Take this letter to Ragini.' He fulfilled that part.

But the part was not yet fulfilled. The sister, for the third or fourth time, turned over the envelope, 'For Ragini'. Over and over she turned it. "Did he hand you this?"

"Did 'he' hand it? You know who it's from."

"I can imagine who it's from. Let him come himself."

How alike they were, the two sisters. Philip, to his pain, found between them a luminous resemblance, in looks, in stature, in voice. He could have done with more gaiety in the present case. He responded best in life to a teasing affection, of the kind Ragini displayed, had displayed. Had displayed to him. Even their words were alike. Let him come. Let Anand come himself. Just as well Anand had sealed his message, had had no occasion to speak it aloud. Just as well for Anand that his rival's conduct had improved; he had respected the seal and now heard himself defending Anand to Ragini's sister. "How can he come? He is in danger."

"Why have *you* come?"

The gaze she trained on him was so restful, and at the same time implacable – Ragini's gaze – that Philip, to his bottomless confusion, in a reckless spasm burned with extravagant lust for this sister. He was too far gone to reply that he had come in forbearance. He'd forborne from opening the letter, or composing his own letter. His mission was just. He carried the petition of a true lover. Events may have thrust them apart, but Philip would atone for events. He said none of this and the sister waited, expecting an answer.

So near. Almost Ragini in person. Yet Ragini – forever more – was out of his reach.

And Anand? When Anand came to Warangal – in Philip's absence – how had *he* fared, then, with Ragini? Of course he'd have looked for her. Wasn't this a follow-up letter? Or was this a letter new-framed, to break a long silence?

Wearied by the charge laid on her and irked, no doubt, by Philip who to her eyes was just sitting there, the sister held out the letter. "I can't give it."

"You can't reach her?"

"Ragini is with her father, she's caring for her father. That's where she is now, but where she *will* be, with all that's about to happen …"

"Her father?" When had the free spirit who was Ragini ever owned to a father? What could a father mean to her? It was true, she had mentioned a father, time and time over to be fair, but Philip had never given the appointment a moment's thought. To Philip she had sprung, like Pallas Athena, from no mortal parent.

"One of us must always be with him. One of us must go."

"Her father is ailing!"

"Ragini is there. She's a doctor, or should be. She's the one who can be spared, while I'm the night nurse, mopping up the disasters in Casualty. If Ragini says she can be spared, she can be spared. Spared from whatever she does. You'll know what she does. I won't answer for what she does, but if she sticks to her post, I'll get this to her. If she's where she's meant to be, I'll do that. I can't be more resourceful than that."

Disgorged from his body's reverie, fuddled and chastised, Philip took his bike from the rack and pedalled through the streets so much emptier than usual, pondering the sister's emotion, which baffled him more than her words. Wasn't there bitterness to that emotion? – or simply exasperation with a beloved sister, or perhaps with him? What did the sister think of Ragini? What did she *know* of Ragini, from whom he was so helplessly estranged that the spillover from his despair washed over him in the kitchen in Rockdale with no depletion of its force, secreted – thought dead! – in a forgotten memory. Poised at the gas stove over a struggling brown liquid – he always brewed coffee in this pan – Philip stood aghast at the thought that Ragini was in his house! That idol was there in his house, though not even the house lay in his possession.

8

Ragini was in the house. He heard her step, heard the door from the passage open and close. Both stood on one side of the door, blocked from the sleeping rooms of the house.

"You've never done this before."

"Made coffee? I've often made coffee, but not the way you make it."

"I mean so early."

"Will you drink what I've made?" he said. She stood near, and because she was near, and for no thought-out reason, he lifted his hand, touched her withered cheek. She did not move away, nor did her expression change. Something must follow. He embraced her, one hand gliding to the small of her back. Jenny allowed this to happen, detaching herself at last. "I'm skinny and I'm bony."

"I'm worse."

"Worse? Never mind who's worse. Relate your sad tale – 'before Delhi'. Isn't that what matters?"

Philip was aggrieved. The same topic. This was too fast (he was far from referring to the embrace, which was unprecedented). Allow him at least to present his coffee. He had lost the initiative, and just stood there.

She prompted him. "Remembering, you say."

"All right. I've been remembering you."

"Me."

"Remembering you. And all the rest."

"All the rest. Let me see. Anand. School days. All those bus journeys to Hyderabad. All those mixed timetables, school timetables, bus timetables," she ran on, making light of these and of Anand, hurrying to erase the name she had spoken for the first time. "Do you want to hear what I think? What I think's been troubling you?"

"I'll hear. How can you be right?"

"That it hasn't worked out for you," she said. "It hasn't worked out in Australia, and it never did. Not even at first. We'd been married barely fifteen months, and you brought me here. At my own request, I know, but how long did *you* last? You stayed a few months, you came and you went, four times, but – I know, I know – this time is different. This time it's expected to work out."

"This time I have you," he said.

"You always had me. *That's* not the difference. The difference this time is you've burned your boats. You can't go back to India. That's the difference. Having me in the past made no difference, so why should it now? Having me, now or then, what could that mean? It means nothing. It means nothing at all, that's why I'm so unwilling to hand over. Hand over myself, I mean."

"Whatever has been 'troubling' me," he said, "lies in India. It lies in the past. It's behind us."

"No. It's before us. It's here now. I watch it every day. Disappointment. You know what I watch. You can't go on teach, teach, teaching all your life as if there was no end. It may be because I'm Indian, but a man at the end of his life has much to prepare for, he can't just teach or build houses or watch television or whatever he's been doing all his life to the brink of the grave, the grave that lies in wait for us both."

"There must be a reckoning, is that it?"

"Not a reckoning. *Not* a reckoning. I may go to a Christian church but I'm not a Christian, I do not believe in judgment and reckoning, or redemption either for that matter. I mean there's an appropriate way, at your stage of life, at both our stages."

"You'd like to see me holy up. Become a *sanyasin*."

"There's wisdom in it."

Philip had taken two cups from the sideboard. He poured out the coffee, black. "But you know why I stayed. You know why I stayed on in India."

"That's not the point. I don't reproach you."

"Why did I stay on?"

"I don't reproach you. Don't you reproach me, Philip."

"Why did I stay on? Just to help? There were teachers in India. You yourself pointed that out. I stayed on as a means to an end – and that end took time. You wondered and wondered, but when you asked me the reason, I couldn't tell you. *I'd* thought it was to teach. I was wrong, I've had to learn, and I've learned here. I'll tell you now. It was the two of you."

"The two?"

"The bold and the beautiful. I won't say which is which, I'm not poking fun, there were just no other words to describe you. Both so helplessly devoted to whatever was right, the two causes. And so much in love with each other."

"Stop it now, Philip."

"Where else could I go but India? I had to stay on, to live up to the pair of you."

"This is satire. A satire on yourself."

"Let me say it right."

"A mischievous story. You *had* to stay on, for *my* sake?"

"Not sake. Your example, your two examples. For my own sake. And, why leave it out, for the sake of the boys."

"The schoolboys? Boys of the future? Boys out of sight? Boys you'd never met?"

"I was an ed-ucationist," said Philip, slurring the word, as if he was drunk. He was not drunk but odd, vibrant. Super-fired up. Super-dangerous, slurring his words.

"It's the coffee," said Jenny. "Your own brew." She had taken one mouthful.

"I stayed on in India, because of you. Not for your sake. It was to make something of myself, that I stayed on. That I returned to India, kept returning. *I'd* thought it was to teach."

"And teach you did," said Jenny after a moment.

"I won a place. You'd shown me what it meant, a place, a stake in events, a stake in the comedy of events, which is how events always seem to a bystander. I was that bystander, and I was ashamed. But I had a model. My model was Ragini and Anand. India was where I lost place, and India was where I had to find it. And I did find a place. Of course that was after Delhi, after our golden year together as man and wife. You won't hear of that. And why should you? – it's not what you asked for. It's not what I'm remembering. What I'm remembering is 'before Delhi'."

"Your first job," she said, keeping him in humour, searching now for a way out.

"My first job was in Sydney, at a petrol pump. I'm far from remembering my first job."

"Your second job."

"My second was in the Army Reserve. But, Jenny, what do *you* remember? You closed that chapter. Who was it who searched for Anand? I searched for Anand. I searched, twice, in Hyderabad: one last time, as the Indian Army marched in. Then I searched again. I wonder," he said, "but I've never asked, what was the last you saw of him?"

"Saw of Anand?"

"Or heard of him. There was a letter."

"A letter. Oh, nothing too recent, nothing of late, was there? I really haven't been checking the mail."

Her pleasantry escaped Philip. "In Warangal. Before the Police Action. Your sister was alive. Anand got a letter to me, and another to you, and I handed it to your sister at the hospital."

"You handed it. A letter."

"You know that letter? You received that letter?"

She answered without hesitation. "Yes, I did."

The back door of the house rattled. Before they could account for the disturbance Jim was with them, crossing the table room to the kitchen in a stride or two. His face was set. He barely greeted them. He was through the house, in and out of his own room. He brushed past them to the kitchen tap in an action so unlike him that all they could do was watch as he gulped down a tumbler of water.

He said at last, "You do listen to the news, you two?"

"What news?"

Jim stared at his grandmother. "Last night they put a bill before Parliament. Howard means to bar the courts. He'll go it alone."

"This is about *Tampa*?"

"You bet your life it's about *Tampa*. Where have you been hiding, the pair of you, under what rock?" Although he addressed them both, it appeared not to signify to Jim that the grandparents were in the kitchen in each other's company, sharing a coffee. If the bill about *Tampa* was (as he thought) a significant event, then so was this.

"It's their 'Border Protection Bill'. It's been clear from the start that the *Tampa* will not land refugees, not on Australian soil. Not while Howard is Prime Minister. Who knows how many sick and desperate people are among them? Howard says none. Or, rather, to convey his outlook, it doesn't matter, since they're illegal entrants and the poor, dumb Norwegian sea captain who picked them up, in the belief he was following the naval code, he's a tool of the people smugglers. If he's not, he's a crook in his own right. He entered Australian waters! It's against the law! Or it will be, once Howard makes the law. What law will that be? The government will dictate the law."

"But the Labor Party won't have it," said Jenny serenely.

"Labor opposed the bill. For once they stood up for their principles and opposed something."

"So what's your fuss?" said his grandfather. "The bill was defeated."

"Do you know that?"

"I switched on the radio before bedtime."

Jim eyed him darkly. "So it was," he muttered. Yet in an instant, a charge of optimism coursed through his body. They saw him transformed. "Nice try, Prime Minister. That's as far as it will go! People won't stand for it. We're not villains. We may not like foreigners, but our hearts aren't stone. What are we afraid of? A handful of starved refugees shitting in a bucket."

"What people won't stand for it?" said Philip.

"The Australian people."

Philip's employment that day took him far out into the western suburbs, to the apartment of a Bangladeshi family. A boy facing matriculation, perfect in his manners but perhaps the most reluctant student he had ever met, reported once a week after school for his maths coaching. Philip coached maths, he coached the curriculum. Set theory was new to him, but he mastered it – all for this boy.

The winter dusk set in early, though the days were getting longer. The boy, Muzaffar, was late to arrive and while his mother and sister served

Philip kebabs, the father switched on the television. Philip watched. He was feigning an interest in holiday giveaways when there came a news flash. The *Tampa*, as before, was standing off Christmas Island, an Australian outpost in the Indian Ocean. Troops of the Special Air Service, which had raided the vessel for purposes unknown, were still aboard. It was not the news from the *Tampa*, where nothing had changed, that excited the announcer, who had been repeating his lesson all day. His lesson was the Labor Party. Switchboards at media offices all over Australia were jammed with complaints against the Party for rejecting the Border Protection Bill. There was talk of an election on this very matter. The government, behind in the polls from January, when the state Liberals were routed in Queensland, were predicted to win, by a landslide, unless something new happened. Their prospects had somersaulted in a few days.

Muzaffar's father heard out the bulletin in silence. Philip, too, listened in silence. The family were becoming anxious. Muzaffar stayed away. To Philip's mind, he was simply avoiding the lesson but by the time he left – before his hour was up, so as not to claim payment – he had imbibed from both parents something of the panic of the outsider, the new arrival, when a tried pattern fails. He waited out of sight, down the street, willing the boy to come home but there was no sign of him.

The days passed. Jim made the house in Gibbes Street, Rockdale, his base. He squeezed people into the table room. Jenny sat in on their meetings and Philip, too, put in an appearance, standing in the doorway and once or twice accepting a chair. He heard, as they all did, of the government's restless search for a compliant nation, a taker for nearly four hundred refugees. The *Tampa* was forbidden to approach land; but neither, with all its human cargo, could it be turned round. These days Philip and Jenny were together more than at any other time, watching the television with Jim's friends. But their broken-off conversation was not resumed. For so long as the *Tampa* was about, they could not find a way.

"What will happen?" asked Philip of Kable, in the Bar Italia.

"Why, what does your grandson suppose will happen?"

"He's subject to mood swings. But he's an optimist. I daresay I'm the same. Our faith is in the Australian people."

Kable rocked in his chair. "After all," he said, "it's why you came home."

Philip watched television daily. Besides taking in the news, he was waiting for a glimpse of the asylum-seekers. No-one disputed that they were Afghans; and all Australia had heard of their war-torn country and of the cruelties of the Taliban. Their flight, then, was rational, if far from orderly, and the sight on television of a face or two would at least naturalise their plight. But this never happened. To set them on dry land far away and to turn round the *Tampa*, the Foreign Minister entered into talks with Nauru, a shell of an island hollowed out by phosphate mining until nothing of value was left. Australia paid well, and the 'Pacific solution' was a done deal. To ferry the Afghans to Nauru, a Navy troopship was diverted from its errand to Thailand and the Afghans were conveyed to it by barges from the far side of the *Tampa*, blocked from the cameras. An idea occurred to Jim. He and his gang would release names, photographs and personal details of the asylum-seekers into the public domain, since the tactic of the government was to hide them. This proposal of theirs lasted five minutes. The task was beyond them. They did not know how to go about it, which was hardly surprising, since no information had been divulged and no record existed of the dripping multitudes whom Captain Arne Rinnan had fished from the waters.

Jenny noticed someone missing. "Where is Rhondda in all this?" Philip knew a little, but he had his instructions. He did not breathe a word. As the saga wore on he found Jim's alternations of outlook too much to bear, what-ever the source that fed them: the breach with Rhondda, or the gradual, but plain, repudiation of all his hopes. Jim's temper craved action and where he found action his wits flowered, at rallies, branch meetings of the Labor Party and excursions to the detention camp at Villawood, where cruelties were afoot. But in the house he grew morose and excited, all the more because he insisted on listening to talkback radio. Philip was sorry for his grandson but had never heard anyone anywhere like Alan Jones. He took to staying out of the house.

He had few engagements but where he coached he met with some return, some reward. Philip had never been one to laze. He found, in his boys – and the three girls at Merrylands – a tonic for low spirits. But he was rudder-less. Where boats and refugees were concerned, emotion ran so high on both sides that Philip felt unable to compete. 'Compete' was his own word. The laden troopship, the *Manorah*, chugged towards Nauru but Philip was becalmed. Events raged around him but Philip was exiled from the common scene and it did not seem to matter where he was, in distant Hyderabad or in his own country.

9

He'd waved his goodbye, but the Nizam's Hyderabad was still there! Here he was again. These were the last days, still – absurdly prolonged, though the prospect was always as before: imminent disappearance.

A door in Sultan Bazaar. It was to that very door – Congress headquarters – that Sukku had led him on the first day of the monsoon. Now Philip stood alone. He knocked, on his own authority.

Foolishly relieved – for no-one came to shut the door in his face – Philip knocked a last time, retreated to the midst of the bazaar, returned, and knocked once more. Still no-one came. His relief was foolish because this was his chance. He knew no other way to find Anand.

The afternoon was warm. Mid-September. Almost October, the month cold air began stealing over the city. Nothing like that yet. No sign or omen of any profound change in the weather. No sign or omen of any profound change in the life of the city. Well, there were a few. Streets were emptied. Shopkeepers stayed indoors of their own accord. But at Moazzem Jahi, the fresh produce market, the crowds were enormous. Sultan Bazaar was as vibrant as he had ever found it. Traders from other parts of the city were here in such numbers that buyers and sellers were compacted as one. Prospectors and idlers could make no headway but were swilled along the streets, or eddied unluckily as obstacles. Here in the bazaar were dates, almonds, spices, dyes, toys, fireworks, caps, mirrored tunics, Hindu and Jain holy images, holy pamphlets, Qu'rans offered as a gift, for which you paid nothing, gilt-edged volumes of *hadith*, flowers in abundance, garlands sewn from flowers, rubber-banded bundles of sweets for *prasad* and *tabarruk*, and sporting equipment, bats, balls, shuttlecocks, soccer balls, even the sticks and bails used for *guli-danda,* and kits and implements for games unknown. Squares of shrunken leather in piles, what were those for? He fought his way to a tomb with a high plinth. He stared like a castaway at the furious element from which he'd emerged. Here it all was. His heartfelt, half-sorrowing farewell to Hyderabad had been pledged too soon. How could he have doubted the insouciant power of life 'as usual'?

He set out for the Musi bridge. He had trudged some way when a voice called to him – not, indeed, by name, but in English. A man his own age, inconspicuous in shirt-pant and stitched leather sandals, overtook him at speed then walked ahead so slowly that they almost collided. "Good sir. You know Hyderabad? You are going where?"

"Why do you ask?"

"You are Englishman."

Philip's way was blocked. He had a mind to push past. Strangers, to befriend, were forever hailing him as an Englishman. Today he was ill, too ill to contest the matter. "What do you care, whether I'm an Englishman or not?"

"You knocked our door."

"Hang on, hang on a moment. Have you been following me from the bazaar?"

They moved to the gateway of a wall, under trees. Philip's defiance had grown, but he struggled to conceal it. Vexed and ill, he yielded up his agenda in a few words. "I was looking for Anand."

"Anand?"

"Anand from Marathwada. I know him as Anand."

" 'Swamiji' Anand."

"That's him. He's a follower of the Swami."

"There are two Anands. 'Swamiji' Anand and 'Sardar Patel' Anand."

"I'm sure he's 'Swamiji'."

"The days of his Swamiji are past. This is Sardar's operation."

" 'Operation'?" said Philip. "Where is Anand?"

" 'Swamiji' Anand is at Bidar. He will return with the Army."

"The Indian Army is at Bidar?"

"The Indian army is at Zaheerabad. They have taken Bidar. The Army will be here in the next day, one, two days."

Bidar, a city of renown – Philip had heard it praised for its beauty – was no frontier outpost but stood at hand, in the Kannada district that bore its name. "How do you know?"

"We know this. From Deccan Radio. We listen to Laiq Ali's broadcasts. You speak Urdu? You can do the same."

"Laiq Ali says this? That the Indian Army has broken through!"

"He is pleading."

"And do you have your own sources? Your own wireless?"

"Wireless and codes. As the Army comes near, our reception by leaps and bounds is improving." This informant – who had his own codes, and had tailed Philip – gazed restfully at the scene before him, the near-empty road, cyclists, trees. "All so still."

Philip, too ill to be impressed, smarting, too, at the repudiation of Anand, of his Swami, to whom, without meeting him, Philip had become attached, could think of no reason why a State Congress worker would pursue him all this way with false intelligence. He believed what he heard. The Indians were at Bidar, past Bidar. And Anand would return with the Army.

Unacccountably, his knees shook. As if Anand were at hand, he foresaw his task. He must confess to Anand his deceit, his deception of Ragini in Anand's name. Yes, this – to restore their friendship – at the *cost* of their friendship – was what he must do.

A noble act. Murmuring a farewell, he resumed his plod. The Musi, its greenery, its long, castellated wall and its bridge for wheeled traffic, now came in sight. "You are going? Where?" was the cry again.

"To wait for Anand."

"Not there. Not that way …"

"Which way, then?"

"Do not cross the river." The other caught up with him, seizing him by the arm but withholding his objection, until Philip's silence forced him to make it. "The Army will come."

"Let it come." A fine last phrase, which saw off his pursuer. "Let me be," growled Philip. A dire misanthropy possessed him on those rare occasions when he fell ill. Something he'd taken on the bus. The market stalls were closed and a bus traveller, equipped for the ordeal, had offered him chick-peas from a cardboard box. His gut was fine, but his temples were burning.

Fewer pedestrians than usual were on the bridge footway. People knew something. Philip had his tip-off – the latest! The Army will come. Don't cross the bridge. That is, avoid the Old City. But the thing was to find Anand's hostel, and to wait for him there. It was true, the entire social structure with all its spokes and spars, the Nizam's warped frame, would come toppling down in a cloud of dust, but this had been foretold for so long that by the time it came Philip was insensible, as if the apocalypse was behind him.

To plod boiling distances, count the hours: *this* was the spell he lay under; but till Anand was found, his sense of the occasion was lost. His puddle of fellow-feeling had evaporated. Stepping over beggars and sleeping figures he negotiated the extreme poverty of this majestic quarter of old Hyderabad, with the Purana Shahr, the Muslim or Old City proper, some way up the rise to his left and Osmania Hospital to his right. Such terrible sights huddled in the forecourts of hospitals. He averted his eyes. He came as if by chance on the sagging pile with its staircases and its alleys, the hostel! – which he had never once approached by daylight. He climbed like a missile on radar to Anand's hut. Exploring along the roofs, climbing and descending by iron ladders and handrails, he encountered no-one. They were students, they might be at their lessons. He thought not. No-one was about. They were gone. The building was deserted, a ghost city within the city.

Perhaps it came alive only at night. In the sun's rays (though the sun was declining) the ensemble of huts, lean-tos and makeshift homes, with buckets and everyday utensils lying about in the open, looked private, woebegone and unfairly exposed. He peered down a staircase to the level below. There was movement. Someone he knew. The blind boy, Parvaiz, was about to climb the stairs. "Wait!" Philip rattled down to him. "Where are they? What's become of people?"

Parvaiz knew his voice. "This is my friend."

He did not sound wholly delighted, but those were his words.

"Yes. It's me, Philip. I've come back."

A room opened on the landing at Parvaiz's level. It held a table, bedding, and a picture, tacked to the wall, of a garlanded holy man. Parvaiz felt with both hands for the table and transferred his weight. He leaned there. Philip followed suit. The bare boards creaked. They stood awkwardly. "Hindu boys have fled," said Parvaiz matter-of-factly.

"Fled? *Hindu* boys?" On this day of days?

"Razakars came."

"Will they be back?"

"This is Sunil's room."

Nothing was smashed or overturned but as Philip looked round him he saw signs of a too-hurried departure. A portable cooking-range was unlit, but the odour of splashed kerosene filled the room. Matches with large phosphorescent heads, like tear-drops, were scattered here and there and a flour-bag stood open. Trodden clods of flour smudged the boards.

Sleep called to him. On the point of collapse, Philip eyed the rolled coverlet and mattress. But an hour later, when he had helped Parvaiz up the stairs to his billet and had feasted on cold rice and *dhal*, his malaise began to lift. Some verve was restored. He was in a mood to listen. A party of the Ittehad, as Parvaiz referred to them, had appeared, yesterday morning, on these roofs, requisitioned the building, beaten up one of the lodgers, and departed as suddenly as they arrived. They had not returned. Were they expected? Parvaiz did not know what was expected. "And all the others fled – but you. Why did they leave you behind?"

"Where would I go?"

"You can't be the only Muslim in the entire hostel!"

Parvaiz said he was. Philip was not sure he believed him. He had not got the hang of Parvaiz. Why this calm? – this bottomless self-sufficiency, in one so blind? "But your helper? The boy who helps you with your studies? Why didn't he take you with him?"

"They beat Sunil."

"Sunil was the one who was beaten? Why was he beaten? – because he was a Hindu?"

"Because he was close – nearest boy."

Parvaiz clammed up. He would say no more, but of his own accord he took Philip's hand, glad at the reappearance of this friend, who had come for him: he quite passed over the Anand connection. Philip was touched. Fresh sympathies bubbled to the surface. It suited him well to be yarning on a rooftop, sociable and content, with no duties till Anand came, while the angry elements swarmed and stung in the city below to a tempo of a changing of the guard.

Parvaiz, he learned, was not so blind that he forbore poring over his books in the direct sunlight for an hour every morning. All he needed was someone to guide him to the page in the maths textbook. He could do the sums in his head. He had been credited with a pass in most subjects. "Your family must be proud of you." But Parvaiz would not talk family, he valued his friends. He had never been without at least one. Philip's return, at a desolate hour, was proof of that.

"If your friends are Hindus, they'll be here soon. There'll be no more Ittehad-ul Muslimeen to torment them. The Indian Army is drawing close."

"We will chase them back," said Parvaiz. "Those duffers of Indians."

Philip was not sure he had heard aright. "The Indian Army," he repeated. "They've taken Bidar and Zaheerabad. The west front has collapsed. East and north-east, I'm not sure. I think I might have got out of Warangal just in time."

What did it mean, return with the Army? Would Anand march in? Would he march up to Philip, having learned of his actions? Or must Philip confess to him from scratch?

Why even confess? Why make his mean act known? Was it Methodist conscience, an accident of upbringing, that would not let him rest? Was it simply that Ragini – herself – was no longer to be hoped for? She had spurned him, and – thanks alone to him – had spurned Anand. She had disposed of two friends – all thanks to the perfidy of one.

And Anand, did Anand pine for her? Or had he cut her from his life? *What* had he put in his letter?

Philip might not have left Warangal even when he did, as late as he did, but for Bashir's disappearance. The airport was bombed and the market ran out of ghee and *vanaspati*. All this might have been endured, with the help of Bashir. But Bashir left. Without warning, he returned to his village.

"It's getting dark," Philip said. "Don't you have a lantern?"

"Electric light." The blind boy scrambled to his feet, tugged at a cord and a single globe, which dangled from the roof of his hut, sprang into effect. It made things darker, not brighter. Parvaiz remained standing. So reposeful was Philip that he simply waited for his companion to sit down. At last he realised that this would not happen.

"Are you off somewhere?"

Parvaiz made his way, unaided, to the head of the stairs.

"I'll come. What's the rush? We'll go down. What do you want, something in Sunil's room?"

Parvaiz made no answer. There were three flights to street level. Philip accompanied him, holding his arm every step of the way, warning of the street and its dangers, but without response from Parvaiz who – it seemed – was abandoning him.

Obstinate little bugger. "Are you clearing out? What is it? – the Indian
Army?"

Parvaiz replied, but his voice was so muted that Philip caught only one
word: "Safe."

"Safe? You'll be safer upstairs, where no-one can reach you ..." Philip
broke off, trapped in an absurdity of his own making.

The world downstairs had changed. There was excitement in the air,
a drumming and wailing, the stutter and report of motors and squeal of
brakes in the patches of sombre light, the rain – how could there be rain?
Not rain, but the slanting lines of debris, fine and windborne like the rain,
in the headlamps of cars – how could there be so many cars? There were
not so many cars in Hyderabad. When he'd crossed this road by day it
was empty. All the gilded youth of Marredpally must be out in their cars,
honking for sheer delight. He saved Parvaiz from an accident ... *Now* where
was he heading?

I'll go with him so far and no further, he's blind, for God's sake, thought
Philip. He can't be on his own. They marched some way, in the bleak yellow
light of the few streetlights that functioned – most were out – and a few car
headlamps. He'd been wrong about the number of cars. But cycles, cycles
in droves: it was cyclists who were making this racket. Bands of boys had
commandeered cycle-rickshaws. Pity the poor pedallers, their craft over-
loaded and the din of ridiculous pea-whistles and banged iron trays in
their ears. And of course, being India, buffaloes, laden wagons and errant
pigs and dogs could not keep out of it. Had the Army arrived? Were there
elephants? – *that* would be the Hyderabad Army, which revered elephants.
Perhaps the fag end of a procession, one last anachronism, as the soldiers
departed for the last battle of all.

It *was* a kind of a procession but there was no real proceeding, just the
uproar, and the milling of bodies. Who was guiding whom? Parvaiz led him
round a corner. The sturdy fellow showed no sign of reposing on Philip's
arm but his feet scurried; he was alarmed. Now the way led uphill. A granite
arch was in sight, spanning the road, and beyond that arch, Charminar.
Had the shops on both sides been lit, the splendour of a civil triumph would
have been in no doubt. But the quarter was shut down. These shopkeepers
had stayed home. They were Muslims. Their business was in perfumes,
jewellery, and sumptuous cloths, garments and ornaments for the courts
and *havelis*. The rejoicing (for rejoicing it was) erupted to the occasional soar
of fireworks along the darkened street.

"Where's the 'safe' here? Won't you turn back?" Parvaiz had tired, he
began to stumble. A rickshaw, empty, came freewheeling towards them in
a charmed space. Philip saw his chance. He hailed it. The two crawled in.

"Now. Give him an address. Tell him where you want to be."

Parvaiz offered no directive that Philip could hear but the driver heard. The going was steep and the crowd, though directionless, thicker than before. Uphill, close to Charminar, in a roped and cleared circle, some troupe was performing. Expectant boys lit fireworks. In the slow crush Philip inspected their store: nothing much, more sparklers than anything, just a few sky-rockets. The performers – or was this his imagination? – wore the Indian national colours, saffron, white and green. There were no flags. Much joy, more confusion, and nothing properly organised. He confided to Parvaiz, "Nothing's happened – yet." He squeezed his arm. "Where did you say we were going?"

At Charminar, the crowd thinned out. The travellers wheeled around the grand monument. At the Mecca Masjid, the hour had dawned for the *Isha'* prayer. The forecourt was lit but no-one stood about. Along the now level street – the street where Anand once defied him to peel music from discord – the rickshaw sped to the inhabited heart of the Old City. Philip peered one way and the other. All was new to him, lanterns, windows, walls lettered to the glory of God, and men – no women – gathered in twos and threes at the heads of alleys. The rickshaw stopped. Fare time! Philip, affluent to a fault, tried to pay but Parvaiz would have none of it. Besides, Philip's note was too large. He watched in a kind of stupefaction as Parvaiz counted from his pocket, by the feel of the coins, what seemed to him an infinitesimally small amount. He burned to reward the driver, if only for appearing when he was needed.

"Well," he quipped, "you *are* safe: nobody will be rolling you for your cash." Parvaiz laughed too, as if the joke were a wink of light on this blackest of nights. He did not know where to go. Philip watched, in suspense, then in amazement as Parvaiz, approaching the nearest house, ran the palm of his hand along the mud wall to the door-frame. The doors here were of wood, deep-set. He traced the pattern of the wood, without knocking. Then he moved to the next house. Three houses were catechised in this way. Then Philip's view of him was blocked. He shouted for Parvaiz as bearded figures bore down on him, inquisitive and relentless, like the beau monde on a curio in an art museum.

Not a hand was laid on him. So much for 'bearded figures'. Philip as curio was neglected, but not let fall: the men's attention switched to Parvaiz, and solely from their interdynamics – of their language he understood not a word – Philip learned that his ward was a perfect stranger to all of them. Yet they took him in. The pattern of rushed speech slowed and was perforated by oaths of assurance. Then all was quiet. Philip called, louder than before, to Parvaiz who in the spirit of welcome was being urged, even hustled, from the street.

Parvaiz heard, tried to turn, but to no avail.

Philip was alone. Yet he had his escort: a powerful, square-bearded older man and a youth, younger than himself. What would they do with him?

They too appeared to wonder. Houses were thrown open, interiors shone by lantern-light. Children had advanced from doorways into the street and were watching, not playing; their silence, more than anything, communicated to Philip the nature of the problem he posed. The two set off; he was ordered to follow. They walked this street, and many another. At last they led him behind a high wall into a courtyard, flanked by buildings. Philip trod close. He glimpsed in a lit room what he took at first for the cardboard boxes, piled one on top of the other, of an accountancy office. A wireless was playing: Deccan Radio. A man in a pale frock-coat buttoned to the throat, with grey in his beard and a narrow, urgent face, looked up from a spread map on a table. He saw Philip. Betraying no displeasure, he advanced on the three of them. The yard was lined – no mistake! – with armed bodyguards. His escort and the greybeard conversed. Philip picked up the English word, 'headmaster'. Parvaiz had accounted for what he was.

Philip was in no way afraid but a short time after – as he lay on a charpoy in a darkened room, in a building to himself – he tried to guess where he was. No key had been turned, not in his hearing, but there were guards all round. And think what he'd seen: row after row of vertical wooden compartments. Not guns, but the racks for them. And boxes of ammunition. How could he doubt it? Was he a prisoner, or free to go? Not that he was anxious to go. For where would he go? He was weak, fuzzy-headed. He felt himself dozing off. What if he should sleep all night, at the headquarters of defiance, surrounded by weapons or, at least, by the compartments for weapons, and be wakened at last to a new world, by the Indian Army!

10

He was roused, none too gently. He was shaken awake. He knew – a half-century on, in the house in Rockdale – that he was hauled from sleep. He knew his surprise, not at rough hands but at the eruption into light. What light? There was no light. Two guards, perhaps three, set him on his feet and walked him to the gate in pitch darkness. One of them spoke to him, a few words. *Lara'i ho ja'egi.* There will be fighting. For his own good, they sent him on his way.

How long had he slept? Four hours? Five? He had no wristwatch. A pocket compass, if its face could be seen, would have proved more useful as he stumbled without bearings, colliding with walls of houses in the black alleys. Dogs barked. A rooster crowed, that showed promise. Here was a graveyard! Wasn't it a site they'd crossed, that same night? All graveyards are alike but here, much as he remembered, was a goat dozing on a slab with its forefeet tucked. But all goats are alike. Had there been a moon? Philip was one of those people, even in India, who fail to notice the moon, its phases or its very existence. The moon had either set, or was napping. A spell of darkness, of ultra-darkness, had descended on the night itself, sealing his eyes.

He emerged from his labyrinth. On a bare road the perspective was lightening. The way was downhill. A shrouded figure, with rifle, slumbered at a housefront. A pavilion jutted high from a wall, against the reddening sky: the *naubat* pavilion. Kettledrums, oboes. The world of grand domain. If he came out on Chowk Maidan Khan he could recover his bearings and retrace his steps to the hostel. There Anand would appear with the Army. Not *with* the Army, but by grace of the Army.

On open ground, his illness forgotten, Philip made his way to the river, to an unfamiliar bank with no bridge in sight. When the victorious Army bore down, led by its commander – unless they reserved him for a motorcade – it might well cross by the Purana Pul and march, beneath Charminar, to the Ittehad-ul Muslimeen fortress: by fortress, he meant the place where he'd slept. He surmised that for Shahalibuda or Lal Darwaza – resonant names, Muslim places – at least a column might be spared. Not likely. The Army in its triumph would proceed to barracks. Secunderabad and Bolarum would see the parade – before nightfall, by his prediction. But why predict? Philip knew only what he'd been told. In a welcome reprise of last evening a cycle-rickshaw, the same one, or as near as mattered – for like goats in a cemetery, all rickshaws are alike – came wheeling along the embankment and Philip stopped it with a bizarre command in Urdu: *idhar udhar chala ja'o*, 'ride around'.

They crossed the Musi by a weird bridge. People 'as usual' were about. In a bazaar, early buyers prowled the merchandise. Sweepers prodded the litter, tides of it: flower garlands, extinct double-bungers, and Indian paper flags on sticks which the sweepers dumped with the rest, for a new age of patriotism had not yet dawned in Hyderabad. As the light improved, he viewed the mean handiwork of a pitiable defiance: a pasted proclamation of Laiq Ali, whose dandified features graced his message, and hand-chalked graffiti on every wall and smooth surface the chalk could reach. *Nizam ki daulat zindabad. Fauj-i Hindustan mordabad.*

Nothing to be seen. Professions of faith abounded, but nothing had happened. Even in this world of appearances, the sphere of bright spectacle and grand array, where it should have triumphed, the *Nizam ki daulat* had not put up much of a fight.

Philip hadn't the patience for the entire circuit, by the lake – Hussain Sagar – to Secunderabad and round by the university, where as late as yesterday, no-one could be found. He dismounted at Abids. He bought tea and *puris*, a breakfast not only for himself but for the rickshaw-walla. Seated alone, he stared mutely through the grille of the café at the street, at the dialogue of a frock-coated Muslim scholar with two small boys. Would today bring defeat, a crushing defeat? Or, rather, the news of a defeat that had happened already? Which of the armies would appear first, the retreating army, or the advancing army with the Nizam's tanks in tow, the twenty-five–pounder guns captured and trailed with the rearguard?

Could Philip be wrong? Could his Congress informant be wrong, and the deafening but somehow directionless gaiety of the night before be a vast mistake? News travels, and, ahead of the news, a zone of no-news, of elation or despair with no substance, like the haze that surrounds a flaring match. People waited. Some knew – they were resigned. He imagined Miss Chrissie and her Nawab would be the last to know.

Should he ride and tell them? He remembered the portrait in the *haveli*, the stance of the redoubtable *ghazi* with the curved sword. When the dust of transition had settled, Philip must inquire. Try to get her out. In the house in Gibbes Street, far removed in time and space, he well knew that he had never inquired. He had gleaned no more knowledge of Miss Chrissie, of her fate and whereabouts, than he had of Parvaiz. He had tried to follow up Parvaiz. For himself, deliverance was sure: Philip had known even fifty years ago that he stood in no danger and would see no violence, none on a grand scale. In Hyderabad and Australia, in those two places, worlds apart, nothing would ever be decided by violence for Philip.

In the early morning café he tried, in thought, to confer this immunity of his on Anand. Anand was to catch no stray bullet. With a tremor of pain he glimpsed, in both places at once – in Hyderabad, and in Sydney, where outcomes were known – the immeasurable difference in kind between himself and Anand. *Ragini preferred Anand*. The depth of his folly, his rivalry with Anand, the oddity of the offering he presented in his love for Ragini – it all swept over him in a gust. That gust had him pay his bill and again walk the streets.

So alike, Anand and Ragini. They embraced their likeness – yet they missed it. Yearning for each other, they yearned for something that outsoared them and outsoared any other. Anand called it India. And Ragini, a just social order. Philip saw that there was, indeed, a difference, but he was right to enrol them in the same cause. 'May the 4th' – the Nizam's deal with the Communist Party – was, to Philip, so much eyewash. They would rise above that! It was for Ragini to leave the Party, and for Anand to seek her out, not with *a letter* but in presence, in person. Those two should be fighting side by side on the same front and if, through blind circumstance, they were not, it was for Philip to restore them as one. Philip, it was true, had thrust them apart, but would undo his vile work. Their being was their being in one another, the 'mutual flame' (he had once read *The Phoenix and the Turtle*, but without quite discerning the outcome for those two birds). Climbing at a stiff pace by Gunfoundry to the crest of the road then the long slope that would carry him down by the lake, he brooded on wretchedness and disproportion, on passion and estrangement and his own wretchedness.

Where did he suppose he was heading? – to view the parade? Better wait in the hostel. He would not find Anand in the street, whooping from a gun carriage like a soldier. And when he found him – to mend their relation – what was there to mend? What did Anand know? What *should* he know? Why should Philip weigh him down with the thankless story of his mischief, his deception of Ragini? – since Ragini and Anand (left to themselves) were perfectly capable of making a bonfire of their miraculous good luck in one another, with no help from Philip. Rather than repent his own villainy as he tramped by the lake, he mulled over his loss, his insignificance and envy in the glow of that bonfire, the senseless conflagration by which the two people he loved the most worked their destruction of one another, and all for want of compromise, rejoicing like goblins in the hectic illumination of their doom and defeat.

Part Two :

Jenny

Chapter Five. The Blackstone Dancers

1

When Nora was a girl she sang in the Rockdale Philharmonic Choir. The old Rockdale choir was absorbed into the Sydney Philharmonic and there Nora sang with the sopranos till her marriage, and with the contraltos after the breakup of her marriage.

In the Christmas *Messiah* and other big events Nora had a part, but the rest of the time she roved, as she put it, from one suburban choir to another. The lesser the occasion, the more her mother Jenny enjoyed, not so much the singing, but the reception afterwards. Fans, locals and hobnobbers regaled these singers. So it was that Jenny, her daughter and her granddaughter travelled to Cronulla, Campsie and other near places and encountered new faces, as well as old ones from the Sydney-wide cohort of second-string mixed-choir professionals.

"Isn't your husband back, Jenny? We never see him."

"What is he, Indian?" asked a bystander.

Jenny failed to hear, but from the responses of those round her the mistake became known: this person (who had wandered away) supposed on the evidence of her sari that Jenny, an Australian, had married a despot from India who made her wear one.

In the car, as Nora fetched her home – it was a long drive from Toongabbie – this event was picked over. "It's the *bindi*, *amma*. You must wear it as if you believed in it."

"I do believe in it."

"But how can that *woman*," Nora exclaimed, "have mistaken you for an Australian? You're nothing like one. Your looks are different, your body carriage is different, your voice has a lilt in it."

"What's a lilt? An Indian accent?"

"Your voice is musical."

"I don't think that woman was a singer," Vinta protested, "or, *avva*, she'd have known from your voice. She's tone-deaf, that's what she is."

"Right *and* wrong!" cried Nora, in derision and triumph. "That woman is Lesley Chown, she was a noted performer who sang the *Pie Jesu* in the *Faure Requiem* from high in the rafters, they suspended her in the rafters like an angel. That was in Wollongong. She can't get work now, but she does call herself a singer."

"*I* don't call her a singer," said loyal Vinta.

At Gibbes Street Philip was abed. Jenny consulted, not the three-quarter-length mirror in her bedroom but the specked bathroom mirror in which was reflected, not only her appearance, but the light-bulb. Her store-bought *bindi* was in place. She wore it, it seemed to her, with her usual assurance. Untroubled by a bystander's error she was curious, all the same, to inspect what was Indian, and what was Australian about her.

2

He's near. He's back. He's kept to his room for weeks, rising late, going out for breakfast. Now there's no end to him. He's up by seven. He makes me coffee. He wants to talk. I don't know what it is, what he wants.

3

To her daughter, Jenny's voice was musical. But Nora meant her spoken voice. When she and Tilly were small, they'd have heard Jenny singing. Jenny recovered her voice for the children, but had lost it again by the time of the grandchildren. Instead, she told them stories. Siva and his household. Krishna and Kamsa, his maternal uncle.

Without taking her eyes from the mirror – as if the experiment bore watching, rather than listening – she tried her voice.

Rama nannu brovara
Rama nannu brovara
Rama nannu brovara
Rama nannu brovara
Ra-ama nannu bro-ovara

Too bad. It ran on, it unspooled all right, until she sang too loud, attempted something with that voice of hers.

Was this the song? The one I sang first for Anand? No, something by

Purandara Dasa. He knew no Hindi (those were the days! – before you were obliged to know Hindi). He spoke only Marathi and English, but he wanted some *thumri* in Urdu. I told him, I only sing Telugu. I'll sing Marathi, if you want, but you'll have to teach me.

Nearby was the temple. Blackstone female figures in dancers' poses, bearing the enormous weight of the roof. They leaned nearer when I sang. To believe Anand, the roof swayed.

How did we get there? I had ridden to Palampet before, but always by the back way. Or I'd caught the bus from Mulug. We had one bicycle. I can't think how it was done. By a chain of safe villages. The map was once in my head, but try as I may, I can't restore it. Safe villages, police outposts, dusk-to-dawn calculations. If one of those 'safe village' cadres had caught sight of Anand ...

I had never appeared with one man, never.

Rukku was the same. Rukmini and I puzzled people: both in our twenties, unmarried and unspoken for. Neither of us loitered at home, but I had it easier. I was the medical student in Madras, out of sight. My sister was the nurse, but in Warangal. She was the elder, the one who'd dreamed of a medical training; she pleaded with our father and, kind man, he relented. When it became my turn he'd relented further. I went one better. I spent up our revenues in distant Madras and returned, after less than two years, not as a doctor but as a hand-on-heart revolutionary. While Rukku toiled in the wards, I matured a new plan for the estate. A father like ours was not one to arrange marriages for his daughters but he *was* a landlord, a moneylender, as all the landlords were in our district. And we were his heirs. Very patiently, I explained my scheme to Rukku.

4

It was past midnight when Jenny came home. She had the house to herself until Philip emerged from his room in his dressing-gown, venturing into the street for some reason. He took the usual route, through the back door and along the side passage, by the fence, where a ghost walked: Mrs Conrick's magpie. That magpie died in 1940, but Jenny knew all about it.

Philip returned. He was surprised to find her at the mirror, inspecting her looks, to all appearances. He made no reference to her song. "There's a car in the street. Lights on. I think it's ..."

"Jim, probably. It's a Wednesday."

"Not Jim."

The door stood part-open. It was pushed, very lightly. Whoever it was knocked, more a scratch, but did not appear round the side of the door. Philip, forewarned, answered the appeal.

"Rhondda. It's you. Come inside."

An octopus, limb by limb, could not have approached with more stealth. The girl slid in. She stood before them in the blaze of her beauty, shocked and repentant. Jenny took fright. "What have you done?"

Her only thought was of Jim. "Has there been an accident? Has something happened?" Rhondda looked about to fall but would not take a seat until Philip, inexpert in his haste, rammed one behind her, collapsing her at the knees.

"It's nothing like you think."

"Well. I'm glad," said Jenny. She blamed Rhondda for her fright. She was not so impressionable as Philip who, looking around for something medicinal, and finding no brandy, was testing the seal on a prized bottle of Cointreau Jenny kept for her guests. "I'll make tea. Don't go forcing that down her throat."

The flame-haired young woman, whose malady showed in her abjection – there were no sobs or sniffles – pleaded with her hosts. "Let me wait for him. I won't keep *you* up. I'll wait in his room. If he's not here in an hour …"

"Jim could be any time."

"I'll leave, then."

"No, wait all you like." That was Philip.

Jenny thought she guessed what this was about. "You see him every day. He talks and talks, but it's all the same thing. You can get no sense out of him. Am I right?"

"None of that is right."

"He makes sense?"

"I think he's gone off me. I don't think, I know. Not that he says so. We spent a whole day at Villawood, signalling to the refugees in the camp, dodging the security guards. He climbed the wire fence. He wanted to know about the escapes. But that was old news, the escapes had nothing to do with *Tampa*. Jim didn't care about them a week ago."

"I'm sure he cared," said Jenny coldly.

"Yes, he did. But he didn't go haring off to Villawood to see for himself."

"Villawood is where they'll end up, the asylum-seekers."

"It's not where they'll end up. Not the *Tampa* ones. They won't be taken in in Australia. They're going to Nauru."

Jenny was contradicted. She found this sharp. But she hid her annoyance. She did not disapprove of Rhondda, if Rhondda was what Jim wanted. But if Rhondda was *not* what Jim wanted … She began to make tea. "Don't take it so personally," she called from the kitchen range. "Even when *I* talk to Jim … all I hear from him these days is Afghanistan, refugees, Hazara, naval blockade, the Migration Act. It's all that matters to him."

"But you don't sleep with him."

Jenny could not believe her ears.

"You don't have sex. When Jim comes, you and he talk. You're his grand-mother, for God's sake."

Rhondda's voice had edge. Slumped in her chair, she looked a dejected figure – but boxed above her weight in words. Jenny said merely, "You think to sleep with somebody is so important?"

Rhondda took her measure. She eyed Jenny thoughtfully for a moment. "I know what he's like. I have to know what he's like, not that it helps. I can't have a grandmother idea of him. He's not unique. He's not the only one who feels things. I'm upset, so are many others, by the way we've turned on the boat people. But no-one can keep up with Jim. He's consumed by it. I'd tramp out to Villawood every day of the week if it meant not losing him, but I can't eat, drink, breathe, sleep refugees. I do think of other things. We both have exams to pass. I'm sure our nation will recover. People aren't monsters, they'll see the light. But Jim has no confidence in people. He goes trumpeting his faith in Australia, but he thinks one wrong deed will damn us forever, if it's not contested. All right, contest it! – but there's so little he can do. What use can he be? Climbing the fence at Villawood. He's not a lawyer. Jim is an architect, he builds things. He's built nothing yet, that's true, but you must have seen his drawings. So neat. So much attention to detail, but here – it becomes a vice. All into the mix, up, down, round and round, like confetti in a whirlpool. He sits, he leaps up, he dozes in his chair, he wakes, he's off to the Trades Hall or the Public Library. And he's so ideological. Is this Jim? Is it really his nature? Do *you* recognise him? How did he get like this?"

Philip, too, wanted to hoe in but Jenny held up her hand. "Are these all one question?"

Believing she'd said too much, Rhondda was silent. Minutes passed while Jenny let the tea brew then poured it for three. Rhondda sat bolt upright, took what was handed to her and, for some time, persisted in her silence, as they all did. Her question – one question, or many – was not repeated, and went unanswered.

5

Jenny put away the tea things, and departed for her room. Philip sat with Rhondda. Let him sit, thought Jenny. He thinks her questions are for him

– let him answer them.

Jim might yet appear, it's a weekday. The girl must be desperate. "Do *you* recognise him?" I should. He takes after me. But I can't say I recognise him, not under her description.

She's incautious, she has a loose tongue. She's caught in an unhappy bind, she's baffled and she's lost, but convinced she knows Jim better than anyone else. After all, she's slept with him. She lists his traits. Some of those are news to me. My father had every reason, but not even he called me 'ideological'. Not even Rukku thought of putting it that way.

Jim takes after me. Not after his mother, not after his father wherever *he* may be, and not after Philip, I'm sure the least 'ideological' person I've met in my life.

Jim says he's drawn to Philip because when he was twenty-three, the same age as Jim, Philip set off, he did something entirely new. Jim doesn't know it, but the model for him is his grandmother. *I* was twenty-three. I, too, thought of one thing and nothing else. I rode roughshod over both my father, my sister. When I stopped to draw breath, our land was gone. Vanished in a wink. I never looked back, though others did. It was said a year later that we'd favoured our own tenants in the distribution, without conferring with the Party. But where was the Party in those days? Poor Anand, you've heard all this. I confessed it all to Anand, he knows it. We kept one field to ourselves, how were we to live?

My sister was the one to decide. And to listen: it was she, not our father, who heard me out, and identified my thoughts as her own. Now our statuses were reversed. Had I been Rukku – watching my baby sister ride in with the vanguard, shooting from the hip – I'd have wanted to know why Ragini wasn't at her lessons. Because I was the pet, in our family. While Rukku bent her back, slaving at Ghazi Imam in the night wards, I was to study hard and become a doctor. I was meant to study skills in Madras, not grand ideals in Bezwada.

Rukku wrote to Madras but the letter took its time. It reached me in Bezwada. I opened it on the steps of the *sangam*. Two comrades were with me. I ran down the steps. We seized bicycles from the racks. We set off for home. My father's illness drove everything from my mind: my own safety, the safety of others, my faith and energy in my new calling. We crossed, by night, from British India. His condition had improved and once I saw that, I had no wish to leave or to be anywhere else. Yet my peace could last only for so long as my tongue was tied.

I had two persons to convince and it would not be easy. Had I been Rukku, I'd have wheeled on this upstart and held her to account for the lost term's fees at Stanley College. I'd have not let her speak. Until *that* cost was cleared, had she the right? I'd have asked what she supposed her words meant – to 'stamp out the evil of forced labour' – when that evil, and others like it, had paid for her studies.

Rukku did nothing of the kind. That afternoon or the next, when much had been said but there was more to say, she accompanied me on foot to Narayanapet, the nearest village. I carried with me for the first time – she'd have to get used to it – the brand-new medical box and the sterile equipment to cleanse, wipe and inject. Rukku snapped branches to clear a path. The ditches were confusing. The field boundaries ran haywire. The soil was banded: dark between seedlings in the ricefields, red where the village trees were planted, but white and wan, mere sand, the colour of neglect, in tracts where no water trickled and no crops were ever sown. Bedrock to the surface took much of this land out of cultivation.

In sight of houses, I supposed the tilled fields belonged to the village. But Rukku reminded me: all this was our family property. When had *I* ever thought about property? I'd drawn on it without knowing. I'd known so little. I'd played there as a girl. My playmates were children from this village, two girls in particular. And there was one, Yashoda! – I failed to glimpse her but Rukku had kept up the acquaintance and called to her in a line of women stooped at their work in the ricefield. Yashoda straightened her back, waved, but would not approach. Abandoning me on the path, my sister ran to the village to locate the foreman, or someone who'd answer in his place. I stood in the afternoon sun, with the kit dangling from one arm and my free hand shading my eyes as I scanned the landscape for its low jungli hills, its belts of sand, rocky drifts and glints of water in unlikely places.

The women trailed in from the field. The work foreman, not a villager but a kind of bailiff, showed deference but was slow to leave our side, curious to see what we would do with his weeding party. We trooped to a grove of trees in the compound at the heart of the village. We could not single out Yashoda. They all came.

Rukku said grandly, "Sister has travelled from Madras" – a cause for reunion. It was I who had asked for the reunion, but she made it her project.

Neela appeared from one of the houses. She stood at a distance from the work-gang: I noticed it, but Rukku did not. "Now sit all round. What is this?" She herself had not quite fathomed my kitbox, gleaming wood and a brass clasp.

Yashoda piped up: "A *saz*." She mistook my coffer for a musical instrument.

The month was December, a year, to the day, before I met him, before I met Anand. I sat, withdrawn, while Rukku made all the running in the

Telugu of that village. My language had dried up. I volunteered nothing. I had no call to intervene, no right, with the passing of the years, to my old companionships with Neela and Yashoda. My first real task, but I baulked. I lost nerve. The more I floundered, the vaster my impatience. I'd grown up in this countryside, climbed its trees, raced its paths, I'd played and quarrelled on this very spot, I'd looked without seeing. All the revolutionary measures I planned were at least half a century overdue but only now did I turn to them, now was the time for them: the time, not of our intentions but the time of history, which builds of its own accord. Hyderabad of the landlords was about to implode. These women must know. Did they sense what might come?

The women, wondering at my plight, listened to all the news Rukku could tell. Neela shot me one of her glances: she meant it as a claim, to distinguish her acquaintance with me from that of others. I looked away but my heart gave a bound and my lively disposition was restored, not at once – I had nothing to propose, not today. The wrong day. Even the medical box made no impression, on people with all kinds of ailments. They expected music, but the box wouldn't play. One of the women asked what it would sell for, all that equipment. This got them onto costs and debts. Rukku was alarmed, and chastised them, when she heard of the repayments: some of them repaid half the loan, in half-yearly instalments, without closing on the debt. "Rao *pandit* should give loans," said Yashoda. "His rates would be lower." Rukku ignored the plea – Rao *pandit* was our father – but then it was repeated. "The *doras*, big farmers, should make loans, not the Marwaris." This was so misguided that I broke in at once: "Are *dora* rates lower than the Marwaris'? I'm not sure they are. And if you owe money to a *dora*, he will want your land as collateral and seize the land." They all chimed in at that. What I said was so mistaken: the landlord – who, unlike the Marwari, lived in or by the village – knew the smallholders by name and would never foreclose on their land, but would recline on his bed and draw down the instalments at ruinous cost till the last day of Kali Yuga.

The families of all these women were smallholder families whose shrunken plots, dwarfed more and more by the holdings of landlords like our father, could not support them and drove them out onto the estates as day-labourers.

"Rao *pandit* does not give loans," said Neela, addressing the women but with her eye on me, "because he sees our misery. Loans make it worse."

"He paid for Lalita's marriage," said Yashoda. "That was because she ..."

"Because she what?" said Rukku.

"Because she was poor, like the rest of us."

On that magnanimous note, we left off. Neither Rukku nor I inquired further. We knew our place, as kindly daughters of a landlord by no means so rapacious as the rest. We would not give the women the chance to affirm or to deny that common verdict.

"Ragini," said Neela slyly, "can you climb that wall?"

She meant the granary wall. "Last time, there was a tree," I said.

"The tree's been cut down."

The wall was sheer. It defined one side of the compound. Two sides of the pleasant, red-earth compound opened on the rest of the village, and a fourth on the rice-fields, the *rabi*, which were green in this winter season. Along that fourth side ran the irrigation ditch from the tank, which watered three villages. There was scant water at the best of times. But once, six or seven years before, when the July monsoon really came, I'd 'surfed' the ditch for a mile. Well, not a mile. And I'd had to clamber out and plunge in again, many times. These women remembered. A few of them, then children, had joined the fun for part of the way. And Neela, Yashoda, those children, and reproving oldsters, when the men were in the fields at plough-time, had watched me climb the granary wall.

My sister grabbed my wrist. She would not let go. I broke her hold with what I hoped was a comic gesture, one to be forgiven. I crossed the square, skirting the well. Our well was near-dry and the granary, too, counted for little, but outside it (not inside) was the floor where the paddy would be spread and sorted. That wall, made of clay-bricks plastered over – the gaps gave affordance to the climber – contained a low door, whose jambs would help me at a low height. Above, it soared thirty feet. To repeat my achievement of years ago I would need to climb high onto the roof, whose iron eaves jutted a little. I kicked off my chappals, hitched my sari to the waist – in a style unfamiliar to those discouraged as grown women from racing and climbing – and, bare-legged, I scaled the wall. It took a while and raised panic in the rest, but not in me. Thanks to the deterioration of brick and plaster, I found it much easier than the first time.

6

I think Anand had the measure of me before I did. Before I knew who I was or what I was up to, I believe Anand knew. I was not an insightful person. I did not explain myself: I 'declared'. To Anand, so he said, I was transparent. He says he saw through me and I, of course, was flattered enough by what he saw.

But at first, he misunderstood. He leapt to judgment. He had me so wrong. When you are to love someone – you don't know that yet, but it will happen – what will be the *costs* of a dazzling first entrance? I swept him off his feet – before either of us was aware of a thing. The notion of an Anand was far from my mind as I crawled from my hiding place under a bus seat and, because I knew Philip, scrambled – unobserved – into a seat behind him. My second ambush of the day.

My second in one day. I'd seized my chance. When the others fled into the bush, I emerged from it. The police lorry was untended. The road was deserted. The bus was empty. An assistant to the driver, tinkering with a wheel, saw me brush thorns and spider-web from my clothes. Near enough to count the scratches, he watched me board. I was never sure of him, and till we reached Bhongir – a safe town by dark – I was on a knife-edge. It didn't show. I wowed those boys – Philip was uncomfortable – and a week later, next time I caught Philip at his school, a message awaited me. On a torn page in uneven block letters, that companion of his favoured me with an assignation. On successive afternoons of one week, he would station himself 'near the gate of the fort' (he little knew Warangal fort). There I should come. I obeyed. I appeared. Not at once, but on the second day.

Approaching from the hospital, I climbed the west rampart of the fort (no gate, no wall) and crossed the little world from one end to the other. Such a beautiful place, indestructible. Nothing fort-like about it. Wherever there was grass, goatherds had colonised the space with their huts and animals. You'd expect the numbers to overflow but, I don't know why, perhaps through the interdiction of some god or some goddess (not the police!) most of the land was ungrazed. The ramparts snaked here and there, not really defining the layout. As sure as you climbed them, you faced jungle on both sides, but if you kept to rock and grass, the way was not long. The ruins of a great temple lay about. As I neared the complex of buildings at the east gate, I saw any number of boys who might be Anand – but in twos and threes. My admirer would come alone.

Suppose he failed to recognise me! I might not prove quite so electrifying a figure as he'd beheld on the bus. My wow factor might have evaporated.

Anand was not there. I returned on the third day.

He was nowhere near any gate. I turned back, towards the 'Am-I Diwan, which was built by Muhammad bin Tughluq in the mid-fourteenth century as an emblem of Muslim capture of the Hindu fort. As I passed that tower of shade a voice called: "Ragini". A man in a Western ironed shirt and pants but with his hair slicked and rather long, as a villager would wear it, approached at a sauntering pace from the monument.

Apology was in his voice, but not in his eyes. "I'm sorry, I missed two days. I *could not get away.* Have you come every day?"

"And if I had, would I tell you?"

That levelled everything. *I* had been turning up for days, while the author of the appointment contrived – his face did not show it, but I knew it – to appear at this late hour. *He* led the way to that vaulted enclosure, the 'Am-I Diwan, which he made his own. "Ragini, do you live near? How did you reach this place?"

Before I could reply he saved me the trouble. He explained who he was and all he stood for, with rather more detail than I asked. The Congress Party ruled India, but was banned in Hyderabad. This Anand, Maratha-born, from Sholapur in India, was stationed as a party volunteer, not in that north-west corner of the Nizam's Dominions where his language was spoken, but somewhere in the Kannada districts. There he moved warily from place to place. A price was on his head. He used the English phrase (we spoke English) with the ghost of a smile. Treasuring the ghost, not the smile, I formed an opinion but held my tongue.

He lived, now, in Hyderabad city, where nothing was known of him and the Congress Party kept him hidden. A third beat of his was these north-eastern districts, the Telengana districts. He'd travelled here before, for the party, but on the present occasion – he did not make it clear – he had other reasons. So here he was. I found my voice. "Why are you telling me all this?"

"Telling you … ?"

"You talk a lot. Why confide in me? Why trust me? Is it something that shines in my face?"

I'd offered him the chance – he should take it! – to declare how I figured in his scheme of things.

Yet Anand was perplexed. And of course if he'd paid even the lightest compliment, I'd have perplexed him further. He'd have played into my hands. He little knew of me what *I'd* find to say.

"Ragini …"

"Yes. Anand." I waited. But nothing followed. He was leaning on the pier of an arch, while I stood erect. He gazed at me, full on, with an imploring expression, helpless to reply with anything but a set speech. Lounging and dumbfounded at the same time, he watched me in a suspense of his own making.

Anand had the loveliest features, the finest, most sensuous line of mouth and, for all his confusion, the clearest eyes I had ever beheld. I returned his gaze without pity, fearing even then that he might swallow me up.

"Can't you talk about anything," I said, "but your own self?"

Not then, he couldn't. I forget how we got out of this, but a short time later, as if set down by love in an enamelled field, we were wading through the spider-web, grassed-over shafts and wells and untidy brambles of this landscape of India, the neglected compound. It was then I showed him the gate immmemorial, the steps and platform to which the last raja of the Kakatiyas ascended to tumultuous acclaim while the going was good, and from which he was led away by Tughluq the conqueror in the year of his downfall. "A Hindu place," I said – for Anand knew Golconda near Hyderabad. To him, all forts were Muslim. I was to find later that although he was Maratha born and bred and his close mentor in the Congress was a swami who carried the Gita wherever he went, he held as a tenet of faith that Muslims, too, were as Indian as anyone else. Much of the glory of the nation was owed to them.

I scraped earth and grass from a fallen column that portrayed the *hamsa* – neither goose nor swan – as an emblem of those lost kings.

"Is there somewhere in Warangal," he said, "where they serve tiffin?"

I found such a place and, over the teacups, I again caught myself poring over his face, neck and hands with a kind of rapture, a rapture so heavily disguised that its object took fright. Anand that day was an effigy of himself. He walked, sipped tea, barely spoke, now his self-narration was over. He failed to smile, was supremely still. It no more occurred to him to make a light remark of his feelings than it did to pay court, or acknowledge me as the object of his quest.

"Where did you meet Philip?" I said. "Was it in Hyderabad?"

"Some place there. At the Qutb Shahi tombs. He was sightseeing."

"Both sightseeing." Or why go to the Qutb Shahi tombs?

"I liked the fellow at once."

"I liked the fellow," I said. "Not at once." Let him ask. Now the name was out, we were both on tenterhooks: Anand supposing some tie between us, I impatient to be told just how much Philip, with his jigsaw knowledge, had blabbed about me. Very little, I was to find.

Anand clammed up. He'd come a long way to find me and began with a rush but once he'd clammed up – it was my *bel esprit* that did it – I could get nothing out of him. All he would reveal was his affection for Philip.

I learned very little that day, but I was quick to act on what I did learn. When Anand revealed where he was staying – with K.A. Sharma of the Andhra Mahasabha – I saw what I must do. The Andhra Mahasabha was my own party. Before K.A. Sharma, of its rival faction, its pro-Congress faction, could cement in Anand the impression Sharma held of me, I must speak for myself.

7

After leaving Anand I walked to the hospital and retrieved my bike. At that hour, police units were bunched along the main street and at the few cross-roads out of town. It would be easy – till nightfall – to avoid the police. The threat they posed lay all in their sudden descent on the villages.

I rode perched high, open to the view, along a crumbled ridge between paddy fields. In those days I let myself be seen, not out of bravado, but to help define what was normal. Soon low *jangal* swallowed the fields. At every blocked end new trails appeared and I could criss-cross the land in this manner, like the knight on a chessboard, dismounting and wheeling, doubling and veering in fastnesses lost to sight. When night fell, this ruse no longer worked. Police might be anywhere.

I sang as I rode. The Telugu *kritis* and *kirtanas* I'd learned from my father, from the musicians that came to our house, were my treasured companions on lone excursions. I was, on those rides, a kind of bird. The day I met Anand – for I don't count the bus trip, though he did – melody and words bore me so far aloft I crashed the bike. Its front wheel buckled and the lamp was smashed. I tramped three miles, leaning to support the wheel. At nightfall I reached the house, the house with four sons in a woebegone village, a village without land or trees. The sons went out as labourers to distant villages, sleeping away when they had to. Their widowed mother, convinced she'd lose them, greeted my comings and goings with a crooked smile. But tonight the boys were all home: they rallied round me, fed me on the spot, wrested the useless wheel in vain, and we set out again on foot. After three days in Warangal, without their guidance, how would I have known where the comrades would be?

Four boys who did everything together but toiled apart, pursuing work where they found it. They took me as a sister, while the mother viewed me as a kind of Yellamma, the baleful goddess, whose eruption into their lives spelled a danger she was powerless to prevent. Because I chose not to move with the *dalams*, I was always having to find them, to draw on intermediaries to that purpose. I would bind myself to their cause with a bold action – then hover, unwilling to plunge, at the brink of the stream. My actions, though few and far between since we surrendered our land, were a little larger than life, as if to notify my presence among them. I won great credit for the ambush. We ambushed a bus, merely to harangue the passengers. The police arrived, Venkat was shot but got away, and I carried the news to Bhongir by lurking in the *jangal* and boarding the bus. I hardly showed my face. Yet I was hailed for my composure – not by the leaders; but everyone heard of it. The boys carried me to the base like a warrior on a shield, though I was not puffed, nor lame, and the busted bike, in those days, was the worst thing that happened to me.

The day I most remember, with Anand, is the long day at Palampet, the last day. But *this* day of days, the first day, the day we met, the day I crashed the bike, has kept all its perfume. Perfume of expectation. I can't scrub it from my skin nor have I tried. So long as I rode, the pedals moved under me of their own accord. The kingfishers and the wood-pigeons, the kites and eagles, the plop of small fishes in the ricefields, the songs I sang, my attachment to father and sister, my involvement with the hopes and trials of others, my gift of our land, my own worth, my pride in myself for not concealing from Anand who I was, all these aspects and appearances fused in a moment of gladness I have never forgotten and could never have contrived for myself. The temptation was to stay behind in Warangal, see him the next day. Instead I located my escort, the woman's sons, and travelled beyond police lines.

We approached the base without fanfare, but with small precaution; for our scouts knew where the patrols were and watched the police, more than the police watched us. When you are in hiding, to cook meat, so much as a chicken, is suicidal. But tonight, a feast was in the making. Kartik and Murli made for the pans. I ate no meat, never had. I stood in the bare earth clearing sketched by the fires, like the swept floor before an altar. Everyone shouting, no-one listening. The dispute was an old one, perpetual in those days: how to raise manpower, where to deploy it and what to defend, for the liberated areas, as they were called, those tracts where the landlords were driven away (but schemed to return), had expanded faster than we'd dreamed, far beyond our capacity to defend them. Hanumant Rao, the Communist – and fellow Brahmin – whom I'd known in Bezwada but had not expected to find in our country, drew near me without a word of greeting. He took my arm (the boys never touched me) and led me to the outermost fire. We stood where I couldn't see his face, but he saw mine. "We are proud of you, Ragini. You've achieved a lot. You've achieved too much. How are we to keep an eye on those out-of-the-way places?"

"They're not out-of-the way to me."

"You can't reach them."

"My father is there."

"Is it long since you saw your father?"

"It's been fifty-two days," I said. I enlarged my voice, betrayed by its shrivelled timbre. "Fifty-two days. I was told that by December ..."

"By December? By now? You suppose we can smuggle you there?"

"It shouldn't be hard," I faltered. "I can go myself, there is no need to smuggle me into my own village. The people know me."

"They know you. Are you sure they'll welcome you?"

"I'm sure."

"We can't risk encounters at present. We need all the manpower we can spare for Nalgonda district."

"I don't want encounters. I can go myself, or my sister can go. She's a nurse in Warangal. All we want from you is permission."

"I wonder you hadn't thought of that," he said, "when you struck out so boldly, you and your sister who's a nurse and all the beauties of the district. Now you need *our* permission. We're all one movement, not a hotchpotch. We are not a *kumbh mela* of rival movements."

"What's rival about me?"

"Nothing about you. Hear what I say. You don't have permission." His tolerance with me at an end, he handed me back into the fire circle. It seemed he'd been spirited from Bezwada to shine his candle of dismay onto the nature of things, to divine my fell purpose: to be with my father, to console him once more for the woes I'd visited on his head. The police, now, were quartered on our lands. Following the first arrests, there had been no more, but my father, still landlord of these fields (by the police reckoning), was effectively a prisoner in his own house. When the police broke camp for longer than one night, our *dalams* swept in, restored justice and order, instructed the villages on how to store grain (whether or not there was a crop to be harvested) and drilled them in the use of firearms. All this was bewildering for the villagers. Yet, because of the presence of the landlord, the police spared them reprisals. The police viewed their short stays as an occupation. We allowed them to think so.

Rukku, on her leave days, had visited my father at will. I, too, paid my visits, during police absences, when our *dalams* watched the fields. Now that alternation, of night and day, dark wing and bright wing of the month, had been suspended. It was not that the police had prevailed but that our fighters had withdrawn. They could not be everywhere. Rukku herself was turned away by the police. To set eyes on my father, I would need to be carried there by the *dalams*. I told Rao I'd go myself, but we both knew I'd be captured or shot if I approached my own village. My blissful impunity as I rode from place to place, shining my face here and there, was a bitter verdict on the folly of striking out alone, on the danger to others of my haste, errancy and zeal for action. In that region of Telengana in December the Nizam's forces (like our own) were overstretched and their intelligence was poor – far worse than ours. But before the rice was harvested, before

procurement quotas were set, the Communist Party would decide whether
to fight for my village – on a terrain it never sought.

8

Anand, you'd heard about me. Philip told you little (of the little he knew),
but K.A. Sharma was far from silent. You can't have disbelieved all he said.
Yet you always took my word. You'd mistaken me first for an upper-caste
Hindu woman of good family, travelling alone for some reason. How right
you were. K.A. Sharma, of the 'Congress' Mahasabha, made short work of
that first impression but you paid him no heed, you had to be told by me.
I told you at once. I told you that afternoon in the tiffin-house. The Andhra
Mahasabha had split, and the wing I belonged to was now affiliated with
the Communist Party. If that makes me a Communist, I said, what do I
care? If their message is land to the peasants, not just in their Communist
villages but in all the villages, I'll gladly call myself a Communist. If they
practise what they preach, I'll preach Communism. The decision is theirs,
not mine.

"What stops them from practising what they preach?"

"What stops them? You mean, in our village? We're a little too far from
their base, that stops them. There's another thing. They like to be first."

"To control things."

"Not only to control things. They like to be first. They like to be first on
the scene."

Anand met Rukku. Her room was our only sure meeting-place. She
distrusted him. She kept reappearing. She heard, in snatches, as I spoke to
Anand, what I was, what I took myself to be, a nursling of the Warangal
region, the daughter of a grand house. A student who'd abandoned her
studies, a songstress and shadow puppeteer (I had a wardrobe of puppets) who
was of no particular use to anyone but would rally for a cause, would fight for
Andhra Sabha. And yet I was miserable. I missed my father. Neither Rukku
(so long as she worked) nor I could approach him. At times, I repented of
what I'd done. Only when the police were driven out would the lands we'd
owned, the lands we'd transferred to our tenants (the word I used), fall at last
into the safe hands of the Mahasabha, not the 'Congress' Mahasabha but the
true Mahasabha, which acknowledged no commandment in Urdu or Hindi
but gloried in the Telugu language. I did not say 'Communist' again. Hanumant Rao was a Communist and had once been my teacher, but I'd stolen a
march on him. I did not boast of this success to Anand.

I said to Anand: "Now the British have left, I suppose you think of your India as a free nation."

9

Philip appeared in the morning, as he often did, but Jenny, encountering him too early, shooed him from the house. "The others will arrive. If Nora puts up with you you can stay, but it might not be so pleasant for you."

"She's thawed a bit."

"She's thawed not a whit. You know that."

"But it's you who's afraid of me."

Jenny was slipping a cake from a cake-tin with a greased knife. She laid down knife and tin. She crossed to the sink, washed her hands, dried them. Her mind began to race, then went blank. The nothing she was left with might have served, given time, as a deterrent, but Philip would allow no time.

"I have to speak out," he said. "We were getting nowhere. You have to know what I've uncovered. You may not want to know, but I think, once I've shown you … Of course, it may make matters worse. I'm resigned to that."

"I'm afraid of you, am I?"

"I'm a little afraid of myself."

"Why should that be? And why should *I* be afraid? "

"You suspect I'll lay it all on you."

"Lay what?"

"You think you can guess. You think you know, but how can you know? You don't even know you appeared in my room. In May, you stepped into my room, without knocking, without a word of greeting, looking as you used to look. Like in the schoolroom at Warangal."

"Young and beautiful," she said, "was I?"

"Jenny, don't taunt me. I've misfired once."

"Philip, talk sense, and you won't misfire. I will not be told you stayed on in India because of me. Or Anand – why bring him into it?"

"Everything concerns Anand."

"There's nothing you can tell me about Anand. Now listen here, Philip, I know only too well what you've 'uncovered', and I do know why. If you want to 'uncover' so much, write your memoirs. I won't have you uncovering in my house."

"Walk into the street, then."

"Is that a challenge? Then tell me. Tell me at once. Tell me what you've found." But Philip would not proceed, in such circumstances, with a knife at his throat, and it was Jenny who resumed. "*I'll* tell what you've found. You've found your home, you've found where you live. India is behind you. It's time the prodigal was forgiven. Say that's not it."

"That's not it."

"Time is running out and, after all, I have to thank you for very little. For rescuing me once. For a mission of rescue. For a proposal of marriage. For seeing what was wrong. For bringing me to Australia, which as it's turned out is a kind of blessing. For deserting me here."

"I deserted you here, but that's not it. That's not where I'd begin."

"Oh, begin in Delhi. Begin with marrying me in the first place. Forget what went first. Forget Hyderabad. Have done with Hyderabad, and with Anand, he has nothing to do with it. Begin in Delhi, then you'll have something to forgive *me* for."

"I have nothing to forgive you for."

"Oh, spare me, Philip. Spare me your denial. Spare me your denial, just tell me your hurts and your disappointments and we'll both forgive. We'll forgive each other. Your forgiveness, I'll accept that. If you think we can begin again, wipe the slate clean, well of course that won't happen. It can't happen, it won't happen, I don't even know if it's what you want, and here comes your daughter, your only remaining daughter with all her brood. Out the door, make a clean getaway. They've come to plan for the esteidfodd."

"What esteidfodd?" said Philip, but it was too late for that. The side gate had clicked. As Jenny was tuned to hear, a crowd of people arriving together had forged along the side path and were rounding the house to the door with no advance notice until the gate clicked.

10

Vinta hared into the room. "*Avva*, have you heard what they say? It's lies, all lies. As if people would drown their children!" Her small, bright-eyed face, pigtails awry, trailing ribbons like a kite, was electrified on greeting her *avva*. Nora's sharp glance warned Jenny, before it took in Philip: this girl can run amok. Jenny steered her to the varnished-wood cabinet, built in the workshed by Philip's grandfather, and still smelling of the sugared confections of the 1890s.

Try Monte Carlos. Try the piano. Why must the mother – *and* the grandmother – always damp the girl down? It was Philip, whispering a promise, who led Vinta out the door and up the diagonal path to the locked shed.

God knows what he had in there but it worked and when they reappeared, after a few minutes, the girl was quiet. The family group was quiet. Esteid-fodd was the last thing on their minds.

"Sit, Philip," said Nora, the permission so novel that he obeyed. But his daughter – having disposed of him – paid him no attention. Vinta wandered to the piano. She struck a chord. She ran an arpeggio. Jim was silent. "There are four letters, and a number," said Nora to Jenny. "That's how they grade them. S-I-E-V. Suspected Illegal Entry Vessel number 4, SIEV 4."

"It sank at once? Or did the Navy board first?"

"I don't know when and how it sank," said Nora, looking to Jim for guidance but Jim was in a world of his own. "They towed it, I think. A little piece of Afghanistan."

"Philip has been to Afghanistan. When was that, Philip?"

"Not quite Afghanistan," said Philip, addressing the three of them by turn. "In December, 1980, I visited Pakistan. The Afghan camps in Chitral."

"Refugees," Jenny exclaimed. "Even in those days."

Jim spoke out of nowhere. "And weren't those refugees just the kind," he said, retreating to nowhere once his sentence was out, "weren't they just the kind to throw their own children into the sea?"

"Why, is that what they've done?"

Nora froze him with a look. It was Jenny who said, "Mr Howard called an election three days ago. Now this happens."

"Oh, I see. Do I?"

"Think terror. Think 9/11."

The events of the 11th of September, 2001 – when hijackers flew passenger airplanes into the World Trade Centre in New York and the Pentagon – was still fresh news, fresher by the day.

Philip looked blank. His daughter shot him such a glance that he climbed to his feet: he was due at the Blacktown City Council in any case. His slim valise, with marked papers inside, was at the ready. "Where do you think you're going?" said Jim – his distance from the rest of them shrinking swiftly, and alarmingly, as if he'd been catapulted into their midst.

"To an appointment. I'm late."

"I think your appointment is with us."

Philip gaped at him. He had never been addressed in this way by his grandson.

"So now we have all four together," said Jim, without remarking his sister who had crept back into the room, "here's an opportunity too good to miss. What can Philip tell us? Whatever did this patriarch do to enrage his daughter, to place himself so far in the wrong that nothing we can ever do

will bring him back, while the woman he shamed, the offended person" –
his eyes barely rested on Jenny – "does not seem to be offended at all. Pissed
off, no doubt. Anyone would be, with a husband who'd visited her three
times in fifty years …"

Philip stood his ground. Nora's indignation would save him. But Nora
said nothing. It seemed even she was curious. Jim's hide was stupendous.
And so was his neglect of his cause. Shouldn't he be spouting SIEV 4?
To build on the hysteria over *Tampa*, refreshed by the catastrophe in New
York, an election had been called, injustice was afoot, one more calumny (it
appeared) was heaped on the Afghans, and Jim, Philip knew, had given up
looking to the Australians for fairness in such an emergency. He despaired
of his countrymen. Helplessness, disillusion, maturing grief: all these were
wrapped and fired as one missile but it was pointed at *him* – such an odd
direction.

"I would like my grandfather to confess," said Jim, "what he did to my
mother. We know what she thinks, let's hear from him what he thinks."

Philip said, without glancing at Nora, "I know I neglected her as a child."

"You had two children. Aunt Tilly – you neglected her as well?"

"I neglected Tilly. But Tilly was different. She sought me out. Tilly came
to India."

"Tilly came to India. And she died there."

"You know she died there. And why are you peering at me like that,"
said Philip, at last returning fire, "with your head on one side? You're not a
bower-bird. I'm not a shred of blue paper."

Jenny broke in. "Let *me* play Twenty Questions. My first is to Jim. Jim,
is this a game, to you? Don't you have work? What does it matter to you
what Philip did or anyone did? Live your life. You have a girl of your own,
where is she?"

"No, let him speak," said Philip.

"I'll let him speak. But he won't be the only one to ask questions."

"Let him ask. Let him throw the book. If Jim wants me to atone, I'll
atone."

"No, no, 'atone' is just what nobody wants you to do."

"It's the last thing *I* want of him," said Nora, "since I'm the one who's
supposed to sit quietly without complaining."

All looked to Jim, but Jim was spent. His fount had dried up. Rather than
avert his gaze he had directed it inward and his posture for now resembled
that of a spiritual master, one lost in silent prayer. Too restless to sustain
that posture, he climbed to his feet, but relapsed into his chair with nothing
to say.

"My second question is to Philip," said Jenny. "Shouldn't you be catching your train?"

"I'll stay."

No-one knew why Philip chose to stay, the only one of them all who had paid work that morning and was expected elsewhere. But his presence helped. Philip had survived, and question-time was over. There was, all the same, a hollowness to the occasion. Guests sat where they had perched, instead of spacing themselves round the table. Jenny had not served tea. The jar of Monte Carlos made a poor hub, though Vinta, who had spurned the treat before, helped herself to two of them. Talk was struck but, like a weakling match, did not take. The usual phosphorescence was missing. The air was damp. Something to do with 'children overboard'.

"Philip, be on your way," said Jenny at last. "Enjoy your students. In November we'll be heading to Newcastle and I mean you to come. I mean you, Philip, to come. We'll make the arrangements, and you'll fall in with them. Either you're a part of this family, or you're on your own." She squeezed past Philip to the stove. Jim murmured a kind of reproach, most likely of himself, and Jenny retraced her steps, inconveniencing Philip a second time.

"Did you all hear? In November we're all going to the esteidfodd. A new beginning. Philip has arrived, he's shown he's excellent at beginnings and I want the rest of us to be. As for you, Jim, the world won't end and you know it. Save something for November."

11

He doesn't know what to do, where to look. I've seen this in him. When he was a child, if his mother or I let him down, he took it to heart, took it as his own shame. Because we were dear to him. But, of course, with an ordinary person, Jim more than stood up for himself.

He's active: he scales wire fences, tours with his walkie-talkie, grabs the loud-hailer, argues with police, though the police are not to blame. On talk-back radio they barred him, but still he phoned in. He wrote to the *Sydney Morning Herald*. Two letters were published. His faith in 'the people', in sound reason, sound institutions, he pitted against evil intentions. Howard had whisked *Tampa* out of the hat before the Americans caught on. Our leader had vision. He went for the jugular from the first. Jim matched him word for deed but once the Twin Towers were levelled and the 'War against Terror' was proclaimed in earnest, in Australia the hostility broke out like a flame newly fanned. Its direction took him by surprise. He watched it redound on the outcast few in the detention centres. To Australians as Jim had conceived of them, the truth mattered. The lies of government were transparent. Terror and *Tampa* had nothing to do with each other. But for want of a forum it was hard to make this distinction, to remind Australians of their birthright. Jim and those like him fell back on their small (and piti-able) circles of the disbelieving. They continued to speak out but sounded hoarse and righteous in their own ears and Jim lost voice. I say he lost heart, I don't care how many fences he's climbed.

He's aimless and lost. I can't heal him. Even at close quarters I lean towards him across an enormous gulf, half a century. It's 1950. I am in Delhi.

Under the orange, green and white marquees of the India Coffee House, Philip adjusts his chair. He's caught me searching for faces. He's followed my gaze. The bearer reappears with our order, two cups, plonked down. There's nothing to be done with these cups, no sugar, no stirring, but I push his towards him. Neither of us smokes, fidgets, or bites our nails. You would imagine that, spared these distractions, we'd have seen further into one another. But I'm not looking, and Philip has cultivated his own form of blindness. That once, at the India Coffee House, my husband found words. "He's not out there," he said.

"Why, have you looked?"

"But you've looked."

"Why wouldn't he be in Delhi?"

It's not in Philip to reproach me. It's his métier to console me: by looks, small favours, the kinds of things he says making love. It's plain to him that because we make love, because at those times he's a witness to my elation, I'll emerge from my grief. But it's always lovemaking we emerge from, not grief.

Philip met Rukku. He refers to her death as if he'd witnessed it with his own eyes. You'd think his loss was as real as mine. It's a sorrow to him that he never met my father. He's been told I nursed him, though not as my sister nursed him, a maid-of-all-work who could ill afford the time. Philip well knew, or had been told, what I did with my time. When he was headmaster at Warangal, before the Police Action, I'd visit him at his school. I told him then. He learned how we'd donated our land. He had so many versions of me but that's what I was, I told him: a revolutionary. He only half believed me, and he was right. Part-timer was all I was, before the Police Action, before the deaths of my father and my sister. Then I went full-time. Seated at an iron table at the India Coffee House in Delhi, in March, 1950, Philip would grant me, if I wanted it, the standing I'd claimed, the privilege I'd declared before I had earned the right. 'Revolutionary' at last. Yet here, too, Philip has his version, that I bolted in despair, fled those two deaths, fled and enlisted out of despair, and if I stayed on in the *jangal* it was in search of my own death.

If that's true, why am I alive? Why did I return? There are comrades still out there. The fight goes on. He'll allow me to mourn two deaths, the two that are dead, my sister and my father, but there's one death he doesn't perceive. I call it a death, the slow death of the revolution. I carried my cache of bandages and sterile equipment along the Godavari, all through the rainy season, and then I turned back. I saved my life. If Philip is right about despair, why did I quit before the cause I fought for was wholly beaten down? What does Philip know of despair? I would never wish on Jim, or on any other, the blackness of heart, the sheer want of energy and light, of a glimmer of the sense of life's meaning, that I carried with me, gutted and empty, back to Warangal town from the forests of the Godavari. There Philip found me, found me in Warangal and bore me as his wife to Delhi. Anand was God knows where but Philip was there, there for me, and I married him. He coaxed me from grief, from despair. At times it must seem that I'm dead, encased in deadness from top to toe. But to him, the worst is behind us. I'm his, he's mine. He doesn't speak of Anand but, on this one occasion, he caught me looking for him.

"Why wouldn't he be in Delhi?"

I last looked for Anand – fifty-one years had passed – the day they all accompanied me to the hospital, the day in August. That's August, 2001. The month of *Tampa*, though we hadn't yet heard of *Tampa*. I wanted news of my tests. They put off the news, they ordered a fresh series of tests and referred me to my G.P. Nora had the car and Philip appeared. He climbed in. She ordered him from the car. Jim went with him. From the front seat, beside Nora, disheartened and not speaking a word, I watched the pavements. So many Indians these days. Sri Lankan Tamils, Turks, Vietnamese. I was sorting South Asians from the rest, idly at first. Then I glimpsed someone I thought was Anand and I let out a cry; Nora heard it. The man I'd identified, taller than I remembered him, walked with a woman wearing a *chador*. He could not have been twenty-five years old. I was trawling for young men! This was no longer delusion, it was a vice.

Why wouldn't he have been in Delhi? If Anand was freed, wouldn't he have come looking for me? I was sure at the time. I think so now. Yet how would he find I was in Delhi? Who would he ask? My sister was dead. Nobody was left.

He would inquire at the school. He would inquire for Philip and, to this day, I suppose he did.

But whether he inquired or not, the trail was lost. Where Anand was concerned, not even Philip knew which gaol he was in. Philip did his best, but it seemed Anand had become a state secret. A state secret he remained and, so long as Sardar Patel was Home Minister, it was foolish to suppose that any word would leak out about Anand, his whereabouts, or when he'd be released. Philip spoke to Qazi Abdulghaffar, the former editor of *Payam*, the Hyderabad Urdu paper, whom Anand sought out after the Police Action. This Qazi was a man to be trusted, a veteran opponent of the Nizam's state and of the Razakars. He'd set his own inquiry under way. But now that inquiry was completed – with Patel's rebuke ringing in his ears – he would not say a word, not to Philip, not about Anand. And why would he be freed so soon? What fantasy was this?

Once he learned whose wife I was ... Yet in India, I did not think ahead. What Anand would learn, how he might respond, just what his response might bring about, none of this concerned me. I simply supposed he would find me.

12

We abandoned our vigil, my vigil. We stood in Connaught Place near the striped tents of the India Coffee House till an auto pulled over to take us home. Home, in those days, was a single-bedroom unit in Jangpura Extension, far from Philip's school, which was in Okhla. Everywhere was far from Okhla.

While Philip taught boys, or travelled to and from his school, I sat for hours at the fragile wooden stand which doubled as the kitchen table, and watched the furniture of the room, its chair, the coin-fed electricity meter, the celluloid lampshade with the cottage scene, as the sun mounted each item turn by turn, painted them with its beam, and deserted them. I recall every detail of this solar procession. Yet what went through my mind I can't say. The day he caught me searching for Anand, Philip was meditative on the ride home. Once home, he occupied my seat. I retreated to the bedroom, a room that, on Philip's workdays, I avoided all day. Soon he followed. He touched my ear, then (still with his fingers) my lips, not quite in his usual way but with a reverence, some deep emotion. I responded, not with emotion but with something else, something less, or more: there was no time to wonder at it. He began to undress me but I stood up. I removed my own clothes. Though an Indian woman, I declined to wait. Timeless resources of coquetry and deferment were encoded in my body, but Philip was never to learn of them.

What Philip was to learn of me was more than I recognised of myself and *that* I surrendered in abundance, too churned to set limits and with no care to, since the woman whose body I disposed of was no-one I knew. The woman I knew, the Ragini of those days, I was glad to have left behind for as long as it took. Her return was slow and as she reclaimed my body in the wideawake interval after lovemaking a troubled emotion surfaced that *was* an emotion, a grief I no longer call a grief. It was to expand in my life. A part of it was simply the knowledge that once, once only in the very little time we'd had, had I made love to Anand. That once was soon over and was nothing like this.

The place in all Warangal district where I'd taken Anand was hard to reach. I returned, weeks later, without him. Then it was harder still to reach. Philip had appeared at the hospital with some garbled message from Anand. He made no sense. The moment he was gone, I raced for the bus-stand. There were obstacles on the road: but what deterred me was my sheer ignorance of Hyderabad, no city of mine. Even if Anand was in Hyderabad, where would I look for him? At Congress main office? – a cloak-and-dagger address if there ever was one. So I took off in the opposite direction! I reached Palampet by bike, though it cost me a day. The temple was deserted. Not even the *pujari* was present. Anand of course was not there, he would hardly be waiting for me there, so why go?

Night had fallen. The hut where we'd stayed was locked. I knew a way in, but I had not come all this way to rest. Keeping to the broken line of a path, as I had with Anand, I approached the temple. I scrambled to the dais and stood with the Nandi. There was a moon, but I could barely make out the dancers, whom we'd seen move. They were there but they were stone, encased in their dark habit which forbade them to move.

Now Philip, in Delhi, beside me on the bed, began to stir, while I lay motionless, imbibing the reticence of those dancers. Philip crossed to the window, to pull the curtain. He had a good body in those days, the bearing of an athlete though he thought nothing of it. I knew he'd played games, was good at them, but I never watched. He made so little of himself. I wish he'd made more of himself and I'd watched, when there was something to watch.

13

Here he comes again. Philip lived in the house, he appeared when he chose. Among the pots and pans, that's where he caught her.

"There's more to say."

"I'll hear you. But tell me about Jim. You still talk with Jim."

"Not much. Not so much as before."

"How is his Afghan?" she said.

Philip was perplexed. "His Afghan? You mean the language? There's Pashto, and there's Dari, that's Persian."

"The one his Hazaras speak."

"The Hazaras speak Dari. Jim was learning Dari, but now I'm not sure. I don't see much of him."

"I thought you might help him. Help them. Help them learn English; it's one step towards their getting a job."

"There are ESL programmes."

"Not in the detention camps."

"There are jobs?" said Philip. "In the detention camps?"

The mid-morning light reached their corner through a frosted-glass window. The glint she caught in his eye owed nothing to that light. "I'll hear you," she said, "but I want you to promise me something."

"You want me to arrange English lessons."

"You know why I ask."

He nodded. Only to get the topic out of the way, but a promise was a promise. It would do Philip good to have something, perhaps anything, to bring to his grandson. How she'd envied their long walks together. She tried not to say, but did: "Is he a good listener? As good as he was? Or are you looking for a new listener?"

"I'm looking for an old one."

"With an old story. I don't have Jim's patience with Hyderabad."

"Let me begin."

This time she let him.

"The strangest part is the beginning. The part you won't like is the first part, the fact that you were sent."

"I was sent."

"You were not the agent. If you *were* the agent, if you'd come to my room here of your own accord – *I'd* be listening. You'd be telling *me*."

"What am I, in this scenario? The ghost of a twenty-year-old woman?"

"Ragini was older than twenty. Ragini was my age."

"Ragini was sent. Ragini may have come to your room. But *I* wasn't sent!" she exclaimed, with an energy that surprised him.

That surprise shook both. The hazard of a giant false step, that might sunder them forever. The hazard lay not in talk of ghosts, of ghosts being sent, or looming of their own accord, but in persons and names: the conundrum of two-in-one, of Ragini and Jenny in the same being. Philip stood outside the conundrum. Philip was Philip. But Jenny was more than Jenny. If Jenny was Ragini, what if there was no way back? What if the thread was snapped? – then there was no way to Ragini, or not for Jenny. Jenny was less than Jenny.

Was this what she feared, that all reminiscence on his part would divide her in two?

"I would like to know this," she said. "When you dreamed her up, and I was in the house ... what became of me? What had she to do with me?"

"Did I say I dreamed her up?"

"No, of course not. She came. She was sent." Both were speaking of Ragini as if she were a distinct being, alive to Philip, entombed in Jenny. "She led you to Anand, I suppose."

"Not at once," he said.

"And what did you uncover between you?" 'Uncover' was his word. "What is this, Philip? You're stalking me with this."

Philip took so long to reply that she feared she'd prompted him beyond recall, as she had when she'd ventured down the corridor and stood at his door, pre-empting his bidding. Be docile, be dutiful. One more time. Wait for him to speak.

"Before you met Anand," he mused – she could not yet tell whether this was his revelation, or a kind of preamble – "all you had was me. I had you both, you in Warangal, Anand in Hyderabad. There were two of you, two in two places. That's how it might have stayed. But the Congress ordered him to Telengana."

"The Congress? I say his Swami. His Swami sent him."

"The Congress, his Swami ... There is one thing we know about Anand," he said, meeting her gaze. "He worked for the Congress, and he dreamed of a united India. That's what makes what happened to him so hard to bear."

She averted her eyes; she did not want him meeting them every time Anand's name was mentioned.

"But that's over with. Why go into all that?" he exclaimed, with sudden resolution, like a man shrugging off the past, though it was to the past he turned. The past he shrugged off was wholly Anand's. A past of his own awaited Philip, and Jenny, had she been looking, would have seen him wilt as it met him too soon. He'd meant to edge up, but his own clear-the-decks gesture pitchforked him into the midst of it. Still nothing showed in his voice. He said, steady-as-she-goes, "Do you remember a date, May the Fourth?"

"May the Fourth when?"

"1948. The Nizam lifted the ban on the Communist Party. I was in Hyderabad with Anand."

"I last saw Anand … before then. Before that date."

"I returned from Hyderabad. You wanted to meet me. You sent a boy to the school. I came to you."

"To the hospital. So you did."

Philip stood now on the verge of confession, his eyes bright. "So you remember."

"I remember. How could I forget? All the bollocks you talked about Anand."

"Bollocks?" he said, put out. "That doesn't sound like your word."

"I reach for a word, and there it is. *You* may not recall, but you stamped and roared like a troll, and I was as bad. Why remember that day, of all the days of our lives?"

"You were as bad?" Braced to spill all, he was not braced for an offender as bad as he. He'd reviewed her taunts: all were justified.

"I thought I was as bad. I thought so then. I have no idea what I think now. I've never wondered about it" – though she had. But try explaining her next action to Philip! The instant he left, she'd set off for Hyderabad in quest of Anand, and the road being hard, had propelled herself, with no less danger, to the loneliest place on earth. Philip knew nothing of the temple, the blackstone dancers.

Philip was deterred. She had scoffed at his misdeeds and called him a troll, which was to let him off lightly. She had discounted his fault, made light of his ruinous intervention: 'bollocks', she said, men's balls, a word she never used. His confession had not worn on as he'd imagined it.

"With one deed," he affirmed, chopping with one hand, "I destroyed two friendships."

A person so spoken to under normal circumstances, whether by reflex or (more likely) out of real curiosity, would surely have inquired: "Which deed was that?"

She was silent, emphatic in her silence, and because he beheld in her her foreboding of every word that would come out of his mouth, Philip knew mere hyperbole would not be enough.

"Tell me one thing," said Jenny at last, "about Anand. Not about how splendid we were, and how you forgot about us for fifty years. Is he alive still?"

"You think I know!"

"I don't think you know, but I want you to declare. Dead or alive?" She held up a warning finger. "No counter-questions."

"He'd be our age."

"You think Anand is alive."

"He'd have come to me if he was alive. I was sure he'd track me down, though I hadn't tracked *him* down! They shifted him from gaol to gaol, it was like the British all over again ..."

"So he's dead, you say."

"You must listen to what I do say. I'm lamenting that I didn't find Anand. I searched hard, but not hard enough."

"And there was I," she said, "lost on the Godavari – while you searched hard. You had no-one to ask, no way in to Congress ..."

"By the time I had my line to Congress, the case was closed. I had no claim – I'd worked for the Nizam! My best chance was right at the beginning, at the Police Action. I waited in Hyderabad. I heard he'd be riding in with the Indian Army. Of course, we know now, he was detained. He was detained by the Army, from the moment he opened his mouth."

"Then they freed him."

"The Congress in Hyderabad freed him. They freed him from the Army, at once. He'd committed no crime. But after five days, he went to *Payam* with his story. That was his mistake. Nobody but *Payam* wanted to hear about reprisals, attacks on Muslims. Who'd want to hear things like that? Nobody does. Nobody does hear," he said, meaning by that that there was no chronicle at all of Anand and the events he witnessed. "Nothing in the newspapers, nothing in the court records."

"Nothing left at Bidar."

"I went to Bidar. It was all tidied up. They gaoled him, and when he was released, he may have signed something. Some undertaking. Who knows? I never saw him again."

"But you heard of him."

"Sailed for Canada. That's all I heard."

"And there he's alive."

"I don't know where he's alive," said Philip, "or whether he sailed for Canada, but somewhere he's alive." He'd answered her question, he'd 'declared' that Anand was alive.

Jenny was left to her thoughts while Philip, having more to say, enlarged on his own. She tuned in at a certain point. Up to that point, her thoughts ran on one plane. Philip had been as helpless as she but it was Philip, not she, who had searched for Anand. *She* made no search. Why, why had she made no search? There had been a reason. It went without saying. What, she now tried to recall, went without saying? Something that went without saying hove within reach, but eluded words; her hand went to the pit of her stomach. Lost days, lost weeks on the Godavari. She had been in no place to search for Anand, or even to inquire about him. But when she returned … Philip searched for Anand, but Ragini did not. She waited. In pique? In anger? She continued to wait. As if it were her due, she waited for Anand to appear. She waited in Delhi, she waited in a suburb of Sydney. Even now, at the mention of Canada, her heart gave a bound: the two nations, Canada and Australia, were versions of one another. If Anand departed for one, why not for the other? Her heart gave its bound. Her thoughts sped on as before, in their one direction.

A note in Philip's voice stayed her. He was searching for a word. A word *she* was asked to find; then he found it. "*Lakshan.* The Hindi word. I think it means sign. Something radiant. I only had to look at you. You only had to look at each other, but you looked and saw something else, you looked through each other or beyond each other. You didn't see it."

Jenny said, abruptly, "I don't want this."

"You refused to look. But *I* looked – I don't know how long, or how often. Perhaps once was enough."

"Once was enough for what?" she said, in derision.

"Once was enough – to bind me to India for the rest of my life. All that long absence I imposed on your life – it was all on your account, yours and Anand's."

Jenny could not find words for this. *You 'imposed' an absence. You did? I'm so glad I noticed.*

"Because India was where I went missing. It's taken me fifty years, to know this for what it was. Looking at you both … It didn't seem to matter to you whether you lived or died, there was something in India more important to you than your own lives, or so it seemed to me. I had nothing like that. I'd lost all regard for myself. Even when we married, I rated myself so low I no longer aspired to you. But I aspired to your stake."

"To my stake."

"Yours and Anand's. I call that 'stake', something that if you lose it you lose yourself. If you lose it, and find yourself again, that's a different self. I don't say a worse one. The two of you lost one another, renounced one another. Anand broke with you. You never looked for him. You turned your back on India. Perhaps you had to. Perhaps there was nothing else for you. You renounced your stake. But how could I turn my back? How could I renounce it? Renounce what I'd never had? I had to find it."

The gradient of his speech began to climb. Now the words soared. Their cadence was afire. Philip was launching an assault. He had never spoken out like this. "You trashed all you had. What you two did was squander it, all you had. You multiplied the difference between you. There *was* no difference. Not an atom of difference but you had to invent one. You each had to mean one thing, Anand who stood for the nation ..." He glimpsed her expression. His voice lost pitch. "Anand who jumped off the bus, and you with your secrets, your Andhra Sabha or Communist Party or whatever it was" – he paused, for Jenny to intrude. She refrained. "You saw so much. You saw what was bigger than yourselves ..." He was backing down. "Things I've missed seeing all my life ..."

"And what did we miss? Each other."

He could hardly improve on his own thought.

"How little you know." But Jenny had no wish to inform him of all he didn't know, nor could she recognise in herself the symbolic being – a kind of monster – that Philip made of her, and of Anand, two monstrous beings, each fitted with a *lakshan*, like Karna in the Mahabharata, among whose wondrous signs was a breastplate that glowed, and could not be tugged from his body. To step into India – as Philip did – and to invoke in live people dread heroes with their radiant signs and their zeal for superhuman achievements – even if, like Karna, they sided, all unknowing, with evil, and died a mortal death – was to propound a muddle, like a true foreigner: for neither she, Jenny, nor the ageless Ragini had been blessed with such a sign, nor did they crave one. "Why does it disturb you so much?"

"I've said enough."

"No, there's more. I'll get to the bottom of this. You stayed on in India," she said, "in your schoolrooms and boardrooms and government offices ... Something to do with us two ..."

"I harmed you both."

"No, it's not that you harmed us both. How could you harm? A harmless person."

He didn't like that.

"You stayed on in India," she said, "apparently to make up for something, something you'd missed but you saw it in me and Anand ... At the same time, you're convinced you harmed us! It seems you've done good, you've never proved to me any harm you've done ..."

Her tone displeased him. *How little you know.* Was this a taunt, or her statement of a matter of fact? There was something to be known, but *she* held back. "He wrote you a letter," Philip said.

"A letter? He did? Anand did?"

"You received that letter."

"The one that came by you ..." Jenny took stock. "I received it. Yes, all in good time."

"What was in it?"

"Rukku had to die first," she said.

He relented, barely. His silence held the hope, quite plain, that she might still tell him what was in the letter he'd handed to Rukku, the message from Anand she admitted she'd received at last.

"You, Philip, harmed nobody," she said. "You were there when I came in from the Godavari. You were there for me when nobody else was. I depended on you as I've depended on nobody all these years. It's a shame, if it's true, that you had to spend a lifetime in India – living up to us both!"

"I harmed Anand too," he repeated.

"And I say, you harmed nobody."

"I harmed Anand too. If I hadn't spoken as I did – to you – I know you'd have looked for him. You'd have found him."

His eyes never left her face. What more did he want? Still to make amends? – or was he just curious? Curious and unsettling. For a year of marriage he had her under his gaze. He knew nothing about her then, and now he wanted to know every last detail, right down to Anand's letter. The past was reborn in Philip. The past was alive in Philip, there's much he wanted, but she didn't see it as her task to help him.

14

There *had* been a letter, Anand's letter. His bold scrawl stood out on the envelope. She found it among Rukku's effects.

In June, 1948, when their father died, both daughters were in attendance. He died on Ragini's watch, at daybreak. Rukku must soon return to the hospital: she could not be spared, though she'd nursed him at intervals through the weeks. In the weeks when Rukku nursed their father, Ragini – who might have been spared – had been unable to approach house or village. But now, after May the 4th, the village was safe. The sisters spent long hours together in their father's company. This time it was Ragini who kept house, while Rukku came and went.

The three saw eye to eye. They were not much alike but had been bred alike, raising one another. The daughters raised the father while Rukku raised Ragini. R.R. Venkat Rama Rao, their father, had lived all his life in the zamindar household where he was born. He had quarrelled with his brothers, or the other way round, and he was, besides, the only Brahmin landlord in the district. He was a musician, and that, said his brothers' wives, was all he was. He seldom travelled far but gifted performers, among them

the *veena* maestro K. Lakshman and his company, appeared from time to
time in the village and were quartered not in the outhouses but in the house
itself. Rao *pandit*, as he was called for some reason – he was not a *pandit*,
and taught nobody but his daughters – sang self-accompanied from dawn to
dusk, till the dead of night, his voice as native to the house as a rival sound,
the tinkling of the dried-grass chicks, or blinds, when a breeze touched
door or window. He sang from the *tambura*, refusing to keep a harmonium in the house. He refused many things. All those conveniences he did
without he neglected on principle. He well knew what was wanted: for one
thing, the grooming of alliances so his daughters could marry. First Rukku
sang, and Ragini listened. Then Rukku fell silent, while Ragini found her
voice. Ragini believed she remembered her mother, who died at her birth,
while Rukku, three years old at the time, acknowledged no memory and
no mother. That was how Rukku was, an unwavering, one-thing-at-a-time
person, governed by her will. Who would have thought it would be Ragini
who fell in with the Party, and gave away their lands?

Waylaid by her dead sister's image, Jenny wondered how the step was
taken. Was she – Jim's girlfriend used the word – was she 'ideological'? She'd
read Marx in Bezwada. Ragini was no stranger to Marx, that was sure. But
nothing in Marx had meant so much to her or to her sister as the Telugu
songs and verses they had from their father, and the open-air performances
of the Mahabharata they'd watched with Neela and Yashoda and the entire
village when the troupes came to Narayanapet. As for the gift or *dan*, the
distribution of lands, it was carried to perfection in that village, where the
cultivators were already small owners, beholden to her father. There were
none of the layered claims and complex determinations that bewildered the
Communist organisers in the villages that became their heartland, where
the cruellest landlords-turned-moneylenders were paraded and shot. The
transfers at Narayanapet were effected at a public meeting, where the landlord presided. Their father's bailiff witnessed the deeds, which were stored
in the teak *almirah* in his bedroom till after his death.

Then his brothers appeared, to ferret them out. To the brothers' eyes at
first nothing had changed. The same labourers worked the fields. To learn
they now owned them you would have had to inspect the accounts. In time
they did. But the week Rao *pandit* died, between the walk to the cremation
ground and their return with the ashes, his brothers saw nothing to alarm
them. The police were gone, the *dalams* had withdrawn from the rough
ground outlying the fields. Only a few sentries, on bicycles, appeared now
and then. There was nothing to give fright, nothing to signify the dawn of
a new era.

Ragini's vigil was far from over. The brothers were on the warpath; but her sister was at hand, and the countryside at peace. How could there have been such peace? – her father was dead. He died in the lull of events. He died in a quiet month of the revolution. Was this all that was meant by revolution? – some traded consent or understanding with the people of her father's village, where she'd played as a girl? Some version of domestic peace? She sat on the high verandah of the bungalow, her father's voice hushed but a breeze chattering in the door blinds. Soon Rukku would push them aside and emerge from the interior of the house.

The moment was framed. You could frame it in a word. Grief and peace. A sister in the house, the peace of the fields, of the revolution, of all she had known of revolution. The peace would end. Her grief – and all it held of peace – would be changed into something stark and blind. But that moment endured, with the grace of an illusion. An illusion was what the past was, but was not all it was. What Jenny remembered was unforgotten. It did not have to be retrieved, but was a part of her. Memory was long, and what was long, a long instant, became a part of the person. That was the difference between herself and Philip. She continued to inhabit the long instant that, when it was imagined, when something restored it to consciousness, came as no surprise. Past and present were enfolded in the same instant. Long memory embraced the peace of the fields. It embraced her dead sister, occupied in the house, yet to emerge. The long memory, not of a presence but of the imminence of a presence.

The letter ... Anand's last message. It had no place in the long instant that enfolded Anand. Jenny recoiled, not from the letter but from the emptied bed in the hospital, from Rukku's possessions in a heap and the letter propped against them as if it were from Rukku to her, when all her sister had done was keep it for her.

Some hand had arranged it.

I'll return for it. Was that what she'd thought? Jenny, with caution now – she was at risk; there were no enfolding instants – threaded the fissure of events. She stumbled the minefield of hazards and outcomes. On a day her father was dead and her sister still alive, the middle brother Vikram, or more likely his wife Sita and their son Jaideep, called in the *patwari* and the heads of the cultivator families – to them, 'the tenants' – and asked them to explain the layout of the granary floor, the proceeds of sale and how these were divided. That morning Rukku was to leave for the hospital. She had the keys. She carried the signed and sealed documents from the *almirah*. In the struggle with Jaideep that followed, the deeds were torn. They were only half valid; the signatures and the thumbprints were all there but the attestation was wrong. A lawyer from Warangal, not the Nizam's empowered official, had witnessed the agreement without filing a copy in the *daftar* at Hyderabad. In a few weeks from now there would be no Nizam, no *daftar* and no official. But in soon-to-be India, something would have to be lodged at a records office. Rukku snatched back the papers and carried them away with her. She cycled to a bus-stop, Jaideep wrangling with her the whole time. Ragini kept to the background and in the days that followed, as Jaideep pored for hours over the accounts with the *patwari*, who kept his own records, she sought out her old contacts in the Communist Party.

Jaideep trailed her to the village. He went where she went, intruding on a shed where a woman was ailing. In the house, he and his father and his uncle sorted through her medicine-box, which no longer held vaccines but was good still for splints and scratches. So shaming was their contempt that one morning, under their eyes, Ragini assembled the children of Narayan-apet for eye-tests. She meant to take four of them to Ghazi Imam, the hospital, with Yashoda and Yashoda's husband, who was unfit for work. Near the bus-stop, two comrades cycled in: Kartik, and a middle-ranking leader. The Indian Army, they said, had reached Hyderabad, marching in, not this way, but from the west.

Soldiers and artillery would turn this way. Once Hyderabad was secured, they would turn this way. But in the time left the Communist Party, if she asked, would empower six men to expel the brothers. After that, they were unsure: the *sangam* did not want pitched battles. They would not under-take to defend a village so far from their base. Ragini must decide. She was weighing alternatives, standing with Yashoda, the children and the two Party emissaries, when the bus arrived. One passenger alighted.

He stared at her, with respect and fear. Jenny froze at the memory, but her lost self, counting children and moving to her decision, was barely curious. She had no premonition but the messenger, barefoot in the grey cotton uniform of a hospital orderly, that grade of workmen who slopped floors and lifted people from their beds, knew her at a glance. The likeness. It was his choked emotion, before hers, that burst forth at last.

When Ragini was told that her sister was dead, she fled to the house, as if her father were there. She wheeled at the flower gardens. Jaideep's mother saw her collide, as she ran back, with the advancing messenger. It was Yashoda's husband who rode with Ragini to the hospital, stood in the lobby, and was forgotten for hours as she came and went through corridors and exits, first to the police *thana*, then to the magistrate's bungalow, and at last to the temple. Her sister's cremation took place at Narayanapet with the hospital staff, some patients' families and the entire village in attendance.

Her ashes, like her father's ashes, and at Ragini's insistence, were poured in an urn in the house courtyard and there they lay. Till the thirteenth-day *puja* Ragini shuttled between the house, where house management slipped from her grasp, and a room in Warangal. The school was closed and she did not look for Philip. She did not hope for Anand. She did not retrieve Anand's letter. In the emptiness of her days the Nizam's police and auxiliaries and the rag-tag militias were replaced in the streets by columns of soldiers without the change registering to her. India to her was born in a vacuum so complete – nothing crumbled, for to her eye, it had crumbled already – that when air was let in and she had the space and leisure to breathe, the new nation swam in a haze that might have been the weather, the topsoil whirled from Marathwada when the monsoon failed: it did not seem real. Days passed before she learned for sure that, a short distance from her home and village, there was, still, a region of the state of Hyderabad that was held by the Sangam, that was not yet India.

Rukku was killed in a scuffle of no importance. Ideals of the nation had nothing to do with it, nor did the prospect of freedom in a neglected place. She died in Warangal on the 17th of September, the date of the entry of Indian troops into the city of Hyderabad. Not a patient but a crazed family member broke into a ward. Rukku was standing by a new-fangled mounted drip mechanism which appeared to the madman to leash his brother's son to the bed. With the cudgel he leaned on in his village, he struck the nurse before she could take a step. Her body was laid out on a charpoy. When Ragini saw her, her hair had been cut away at the temple, exposing the single wound. The sisterly resemblance was breathtaking, even to Ragini, who touched Rukku's lips with dazed fingers. She carried off an image of the dead woman, intimate and fearful, that was her own image.

At times when Ragini glanced in a mirror, her sister would appear. But at last this ceased to happen.

Nor did Jenny, now, pine for the dead. Only in a proper rite, conducted by a son or grandson, can anything be done for the dead. Something can be done for the living. There are those too, dead or alive, of whose circumstances nothing can be known or will ever be known. But besides these, there are the living and their case comes first.

15

It was to her grandson she turned, in her mind and only in her mind: for he was not in the house. She saw less of Jim these days. Sightings of Jim were rare since 9/11, a black-letter day in America: a day that might have turned out so differently, for Australia at least. There were more events than one on that day. Earlier that day, while Americans were still abed, a Federal Court judge in Melbourne had delivered his ruling on a case mounted by *pro bono* lawyers. The asylum-seekers from the *Tampa* (now on HMAS *Manoora*) must be brought to the mainland. Their detention was unlawful. News of this finding was quickly overshadowed, and to Jenny came late. But Jim would have heard of it at once, before the catastrophe in New York. She'd pictured the sunburst, the elation, as he and others discussed Justice North's finding. A small window, soon closed. Raised in a backwater, she knew and she had relished small windows. The Telengana uprising, the largest mobilisation of peasants and landless labourers as such in the history of India! – an event in a backwater, the glimpse of a limitless expanse through a small window. A dashed wave. Was this how to talk to Jim, in the shadow of the Twin Towers, to mock the naivety of his hopes by telling of a lost revolution in a distant place? Was this her counsel? Was this how she'd console him?

One day in that October she returned from the shops and Jim was there. He had books and spreadsheets on the table, but far from poring over these he was seated, legs crossed, on the flat of a chair, as if he'd turned world-renouncer. Jenny dropped her parcels and all but ran to her bedroom. She was shaken by his pose. She was shaken by the toil, the taskwork she foresaw for Jim. By the time she emerged, Jim had taken up her shopping and was trying to sort it onto the shelves in the kitchen. He had the refrigerator open. The alarm was bleating. "I scared you," he said.

"Why were you sitting that way? Is it your back?"

"Nothing wrong with my back."

"You look pale."

"Well, pale ..." Jim spread his arms, then let them fall.

"How terrible it was in New York," she said. "People fell from buildings. And it's bad here too. The shock there has made things worse, for the asylum-seekers it can only get worse."

"You're right about that, *avva*. Where does this lettuce go, there's a crisper, isn't there?"

"Leave everything where it is. We must talk. I'm afraid, don't you see?" She edged him from the kitchen. "I'm afraid for you."

"For me? I should be the last thing."

"I know very well, you should be the last thing. I know you're not afraid for yourself, but I am. I should care first for the state of the world, but that's not how I am. I care first for you."

"I know you do."

"You know I care. But you don't know it all. You know love, but you don't know resemblance. I resemble you so much."

"We're kin."

"We're alike. Kin or no kin."

She could not tell how receptive he was to that idea. She looked away. Her eyes were on the whistle-y-bob, the furred wire contraption riding from the beam of the door that gave onto the interior passage. Her eyes were on the dark of that passage from which (she thought of it too late) Philip might emerge. Time was when Jim and his grandmother had the house to themselves.

"Take care," she said. "I'm about to warn you."

"Then look at me, *avva*, while you warn me."

She looked. On the same chair – his chair of penance – Jim lounged, obedient and amused. For so long as she made it about him, he would stay amused. She'd be unable to reach him. Their trust, familiarity, long acquaintance were nothing to her purpose, but were simply the furniture of the house. To reach him she had somehow to derail him, to dismay or alarm him, before she could gladden and advise him. What Jenny did next was to alarm herself. Flailing in her thoughts, she touched a chord within reach. "You know I had a sister."

"A sister. You mean my Aunt Tilly. A daughter."

"A sister. I had a sister, did you know that?"

He did not know that. For reasons once plain, now lost, she had never told her grandchildren. She believed even Nora had forgotten.

"My sister Rukmini. She died, a long time ago. A pointless, needless death."

"In India?"

"In India. Not quite India. She was killed in Warangal, on the last day of the old Hyderabad state."

Jim knew Warangal. "Where Philip taught school."

"Yes, Philip taught school. It was in Warangal that I first met Philip."

"In Delhi, you told me."

"I don't recall that I ever told you."

Jenny was faltering in her mission. Now she owed words to the dead, with an obligation to speak of Rukku from which she could not retreat. So it was just as well at that moment that the door from the backyard was pushed, and Rhondda stepped in.

To Jenny her bearing had quite changed. She was nothing like the waif who had slid, like protoplasm, around the same door the last time she'd called. Jenny was transfixed by her beauty, so different in kind from the Indian beauty. So bleached, so blond. Auburn, Jim called it, a kind of red, freckles all over her but somehow combining, not colliding, in the damask gift of her complexion. Rhondda moved a chair, scraping it on the wood floor. Last time, she'd been noiseless.

"My grandmother has news of Philip," Jim said, addressing the girl but with his eyes on Jenny. "She met Philip long before I knew, in the town of Warangal. Warangal in Hyderabad."

"The Nizam's Dominions," said Rhondda politely. She had not been invited to sit, so she stood.

"It was there they met. Philip has told me about his school, God knows, all those schools, but nothing about … I'm beginning to see. Now I'm beginning to see. There was a Ragini," he said, as if in an aside to a witness. It was not clear to Rhondda which part she was to play, to acknowledge words addressed to her, or to defer to Jenny. Jenny saw her dilemma before she did. She drew out a chair.

"We'll all sit. You hear this too, Rhondda. It's news to Jim, why shouldn't you hear the same news? I'm not the grandmother Jim supposed, or the one he wants. I'm a person far more like him – or I *was* such a person – than Jim would like to hear, and the reason he now has to hear is this, there are risks to being such a person. I stopped being such a person. That's why he was never told, but I'm telling him now. I know what he's like, he's like me, like *I was*. I'm afraid the likeness will devour him."

"No, here is what devours me," said Jim. "Why all this now? Why the state secret? Why was I never told? Was my mother told? Who else has been keeping things from me?"

"You were never told," said Jenny, "because we live in Australia. Australia is Australia. What's in India stays in India. And until I see the good of it here …"

"But we live in the world. 'It's all one world.' How's that, *avva*, for a principle?"

"I know that principle. I've ignored that principle."

"Then what's changed? Tell me what's changed."

"What's changed is this. I see my experience can be of use."

"Of use. You once had a sister. You met Philip …"

"Philip is so far from the case," said Jenny, speaking slowly, for she meant to leave him in no doubt, "so far from the case that I don't know what good it would do to discuss Philip. Philip grew up here, in this house. Philip was an orphan in Hyderabad. But at least he saw public events, he'll have acquainted you with those, surely."

"Public events? Events in Hyderabad? You were a nationalist! You fought the Nizam!"

"The nation was not my calling," she said.

"Your calling? I know you studied medicine in India, you did tell me this."

"Medicine was not my calling. My sister loved medicine, it was her calling. It was Rukku who shone but I was the one who went to medical college. And there I met people from Andhra, people who did not study medicine and it was people from Andhra I followed. I followed where they led. I had to be shown. I did not have to be shown the Nizam, I was the Nizam's subject. I did not have to be told of oppression. But I did have to be shown what could be done about it. I'd grown up playing with the village girls. My father was a landlord. My sister and I had a service ethic, we wanted to be 'just', and we wanted to be of use. There were female doctors, in India, even in those days, even in Hyderabad. What there was in Hyderabad ..." she waited on Jim to complete the thought. "Philip must have told you about our movement, the great movement, the Telengana revolution."

"What were you? – a revolutionary?"

"You don't believe it?"

"This is all very new, *avva*."

"Isn't it something to remark?" she said. "It's something to declare – that I was a part, a small part, of the Telengana revolution, that mammoth undertaking, that failed, and so many people went down with it. I tell you because I was a part of it."

"Why now?" he said.

And Rhondda added, "What's that to Jim?"

"I have never put to sea. I have never been on a ship," said Jenny, "but I've watched in the movies, the bombed ships in wartime newsreels. You swim to escape, but if you're anywhere near that ship, you will be sucked down."

"You're comparing great things with small," said Jim. "A revolution in India with a scuffle here over small boats. I'm safe. I'm an onlooker. The danger is to others, and not to me."

"There is a danger to you."

"No, *avva*," said Jim. He deserted his chair, rounded the table to his grandmother and took her hand. He placed it against his cheek, as much for his comfort as for hers.

"Don't become too attached," she said. "Fight for the boat people, all you can, but don't think you can change the country. It's a task beyond you. I don't want you to despair. I've watched you despair."

"The ones who are entitled to despair," he said, "are shivering on the boats."

"I can't reach them. But I can reach you."

"And what do you advise me to do," he said, "now you've reached me?"

"I don't advise. I do know things will get worse, the boats will keep coming because there is nothing we can do about them at this end. Desperate people won't be stopped. And because people here won't understand, won't understand that desperation, nothing will be done to help them, and if I know you, you'll turn against your own people. You'll want them to rise to the occasion, but very few will rise to the occasion. Don't expect too much of Australians. Australians are misled. Bad leaders. Talk-back radio. It's so easy to mislead people in a democracy. I see all this, Jim, because we're alike, we're people who believe in a cause – I once did – and when our cause is defeated – and yours will be …"

"What do you suggest I do, *avva*?"

"*I* made a clean break," she said.

"What's that, a clean break?"

"I turned back. I went out to fight, to fight, not to die, but I turned back. I'm not proud of it."

"Then if *you're* not proud … You'll want me to be proud of my life …"

"Are you proud, like this? – able to do nothing?"

Their faces were close together, their voices unraised. "You were a turn-coat?" said Jim – a fierce word, but he imparted a mildness. "How long did you fight?"

"How long was I in the forest? The entire rainy season," she said, "and a while before that. Less than a year. Less than half a year."

It seemed a long time to Jim.

"I was not a 'turncoat'," she said. "I did not change sides. I gave in. Two years passed. Then I came to Australia."

"And where do you suggest *I* go?"

She made no reply.

"I quite believe you had a sister," said Jim. "I can believe you were a revolutionary. But *I'm* not a revolutionary. I've never fought. I've watched. I've cheered and jeered. I'm an onlooker."

"That's true of everyone," said Rhondda, suddenly and unexpectedly.

To deal herself in, in this colloquy between grandmother and grandson, she'd have had to wrench hand from cheek: it was amazing to her, how they kept a close posture while wrangling over points of likeness – Rhondda saw no likeness. Jim, to her, was like no-one else and to make this plain she asserted what was true of everyone. "No-one, that I've ever met, is a

heroic person. No-one has laid down their life. We're all 'onlookers'. Jim
is the same as all the rest, but the difference with Jim is not Jim, it's what's
passing away, and will never be the same." To Jenny's ears, Rhondda's voice
had a choke in it. Jenny could not gauge her emotion, but she was stating
Jim's case. What moved Rhondda was not so much Jim's case, as Jim. "The
people have changed, the country he grew up in has changed, and all in one
moment, in one act of panic, through one craven, cowardly deed, people like
Jim find themselves responsible: that's what *Tampa* means to him. And you
say" – wheeling on Jenny – "he should make a clean break! He should join
the 'silent majority', and leave the asylum-seekers to their fate. I take that to
be your advice!"

"I gave no advice. I know what it's like to hear advice."

"You're all advice. Nothing but advice. Don't throw yourself away, don't
pledge your precious self to anything too hard, for fear of despair – what is
that, if it's not advice?"

She found them peering at her, a reactionary old woman. The girl's
enmity amazed her: but this was no time for amazement, nor for urging
a likeness which was not perhaps the likeness she imagined. Jim's face was
close to hers and drew closer, as at last he awaited what directive she had
to give. But true to her word – and perhaps Rhondda's jealous inspection
had something to do with it – she offered him no directive. She believed
the misdeed of *Tampa* might not be reversed. The legacy of a people, to
Jenny an instinctive generosity, well alive under Whitlam and Fraser, had
been lost in the turmoil of events and its expulsion was final. A birthright
of the Australians – and Jenny, too, counted herself as an Australian – was
squandered and lost. Why shouldn't all we have be lost?

16

Jenny dug for words, for a message – not advice – that both could receive. She
commended Philip's example to Jim. Philip had approached her in the house.
He had a lot on his mind. Here was a man who'd known success in life,
but who believed he had suffered a check. What others call 'retirement age'
Philip had experienced as a personal assault, launched with malice by the
Indian state, his employer at the time. The blow had taken years to descend,
but to Philip had instant force. He returned to Australia with the expectations of a twenty-three-year-old, his age when he left. The work he found
here – mostly unpaid – was far lowlier than he thought he deserved. Yet
for all that – Jenny affirmed – Philip knuckled down. He was disappointed

but he took to his work. It was work worth doing and perhaps no-one was better equipped than Philip for such work. Thus, for all her reluctance to advise, Jenny imparted a lesson: do what you can. On Jim, who was himself twenty-three years old, the lesson was wasted. Why, he wanted to know, had Philip, who after all lived in the house, gone 'approaching' Jenny in the first place? Had he something to confess? Had he something to make up for?

"Yes, I would say he had."

"He had."

"He believed he'd acknowledged something. He tried to convince me. He blamed others, blamed me, and he blamed himself. All in one whirl. It may be true."

"What may be true?"

"It was not clear to me. It was not clear to him, I think. All kinds of things, rolled together. Reasons for staying on in India, for spending his whole life in India. I thought we both knew why he stayed. I'd known for years. I thought *I'd* turned him away."

"Well, had you?"

"Yes. I had, yes. That was my belief. When Philip and I came to Australia – we'd been married a year – it was all my doing. I had to leave India. I'd lost all I'd believed in in India, or I thought I had. I was adrift. While Philip, all he wanted to do, poor fellow, was teach in his school, teach and teach. I'd thought he could teach anywhere."

"But he couldn't? He couldn't teach anywhere?" said Jim. He spoke lightly, but this was, to him, a searching question. And Jenny did not answer his question.

"I had never let him close, as a wife. I was not kind to Philip. I thought that, in Australia, I'd make up to him here. So when Philip brought me to Australia, then returned to India, I was sure I'd failed. I thought *I'd* turned him away. But that's not what it was, it's not what *he* says it was."

"What was it?" said Jim, who, in all those years, had never asked. The motive to ask had only appeared to him with Philip.

"I think why he came to me at last," said Jenny, "I think he came to share, just to share his thoughts. His thoughts and his memories. He wanted to speak them out loud. It was not even confirmation he was after, I think, just exchange."

"Exchange of thoughts."

"Thoughts, places. I'm the only one who knows some of these things."

"It must be good to exchange," said Rhondda, aspiring to make peace. She much preferred Philip to Jenny.

Jenny departed for the kitchen. The two sat on while, a short way away, recollection brimmed in Jenny. She had said too much, or too little; affronted

Jim, or perhaps only Rhondda was affronted. Never far away, the thought
of Anand, who had not been mentioned, accosted her in a new guise. This
Anand was Philip's Anand, his notion of Anand, twinned with his notion
of herself. Deflated but excited, she strove to view herself, to view Anand, as
Philip saw them both. He saw them as ideal. Jenny meant to take the same
view. She meant to stand both outside and inside: to be herself, yet also to
be what she observed. The task proved beyond her. The Ragini she now
became, into whose being she swam, but without ocular perspective, was
not Anand's lover, nor was it the Ragini she sought.

The Ragini she became was alone in a setting. She hurried. The setting
embraced her blind at close quarters: a sodden path, mud underfoot, walled
on both sides by the shelving brambly tree of the Deccan half-*jangal*, whose
thorns are unsoftened by rain. It was the rainy season. Ragini, scratched and
sore, barefoot since she had lost one chappal and discarded the other, her
clothes plastered to her body and her shoulder aching because she carried the
medicine-box, useless and empty, was hastening through a rift that seemed
endless. The scene changed. Here she was in Warangal town, where there
were police about – screened by the rain. Here she was again, at last in a
genuine refuge, a hiding-place. She'd removed her wet clothes. A hospital
smock had been supplied. She sneezed at intervals. The room, whitewashed
clean, blank and clean like the immensity of a life snatched from destruction,
a life not yet dreamed of but assured, a life without events, was no wider than
a cupboard, and a cupboard it was, a deep wall-cupboard storing mops, pails
and carbolic soaps and liquids. There was a cot, dragged from somewhere in
the hospital, but no fan. To reach a lavatory she must cross the wards. But her
panic, as much as her exhaustion, pasted her to this room.

Now Philip, how did he turn up? How did she find him? Did she
even look for him? How can she have imagined he'd be there? – Philip in
Warangal, teaching in the same school, which had not been closed, but
enlarged! Philip was the boss but now he had someone to boss: a graduate
teacher, teaching in Hindi.

She did not look for him at the school. And when she ran into him, she
did not ask at once about Anand. Anand then had not been reborn in her.
In her twenty-nine weeks in the forest – not the Deccan half-*jangal* but the
deep, true forest bordering the Godavari and its streams where the villagers
snared birds and traded wildflowers – her life's round had fretted away in
Ragini an entire climate of thought, of thought as hope: not that she didn't
hope. She hoped for what she worked for. But she ceased to hope on her
own account, or to believe. In the sense in which hope and belief are the
same thing, Ragini did away with Anand because her sister was dead, her
father was dead, and her father's brothers, armed with the power of the

law, had descended on the people of her village, discounted their arrangements and ejected Ragini from her place. In a kind of free-fall she became what she had long played at being, a revolutionary. When she returned to India (Warangal now was in India!) not all of her returned at once. With what there was, what there was of her, she encountered Philip, who stood neither for hope nor loss. She eyed him – who saw whom first? – then felt, to her confusion, a surge of gladness that ran through her entire body. She embraced him dearly.

Her old friend was elated, confiding, larger than life. He, too, made no mention of Anand. "You should leave Warangal. I have an idea. Go to Delhi. The Communist Party is not banned in Delhi. Anywhere but here, you'll be safe."

"And if I go to Delhi, who will I find in Delhi?"

He said nothing then. She was to learn in time that Philip had applied to Delhi, to the schools there. His own, substantial piece of luck, to be restored to his old school in Warangal, to him was a portent and nothing more. He yearned to be closer to the action in a new nation. He was of no mind to teach school in Australia.

His gaze took her in – the savage weals on her arms, the glass bangles, the nondescript cotton sari – and returned to her face. She read in it his old admiration, but also his concern. Concern for what? For her complexion? The youthful hue had been swabbed from her face and arms by the sunless ordeal, the dump of the rains. Then the sun, when it blazed, seared her skin with its emblem, its dire brand. "You know I ran off," she said.

"Ran off?" He guessed, of course, that she had thrown in her lot with the Communists. But he did not know why, the chain of events.

"I deserted my post. Now I'm here."

People were watching. They must have looked queer, a white man and some kind of mendicant. Philip wanted them both to move away, move on.

Something went unsaid. Some elemental fact that, let slip, would have warned him, beyond her direct power to warn. Would have deterred him for life. She was to tell him, in meetings yet to come, of her sister's death. They would sift through so much. But wasn't there something she might have said, one fact more that would have scared him off? If she'd painted herself in a truer light?

She left it out. Some detail, no more than a detail, a wobble not a detail, that should have inflected every detail. Some datum she left out, for fear of appearing in her true light, presumptuous and not even brave. The daughter of a musical landlord who stooped from her height, some kind of a Savitri or Rani Rudrama Devi, who had to be the one to bring revolution to her home village. Hastening to the forest with her medicine-box, with quinine, peni-

cillin ointment and sterile equipment from the hospital: a healing person.
Her stock lasted four days. Her stock ran out, she kept watch amidst the
trees but never learned to handle a rifle and there were none to spare. Just
another mouth to feed. She taught them songs. Taught whom? Why, the
children of course, the boys first, the lively Koya boys who knew no *bhajans*
but had songs of their own, songs with few notes, songs with many words,
play songs, songs to the forest, songs to their prey, to animals and birds,
songs to trees; Ragini learned theirs, and their mothers and sisters, the men
too, listened to hers. They felt, or they showed, no scorn for Sri Annam-
acharya and Purandara Dasa. The patrol fighters, even the organisers on
their brief tours, would listen to Brahmin songs, for Ragini sang well and
there were days on end, days without end, to while away, she told Philip. It
was no part of her conduct with Philip, nor would it have helped, to count
deaths, malarial deaths, deaths in battle, deaths from when the grass-hut
villages were set on fire; or to lead him through the long hours of vigil, the
tedious hours of shifting camp, of dismantling houses and building houses,
the short hours of onslaught and confused alarm. She left *this* out. But she
left out more than this. She deceived him somehow. Philip gazed and gazed
at Ragini, with his new concern, and with something, a reverence, that was
new in him. It continued to grow no matter what she told him. It must have
been the way she told him. She'd deserted her post, she'd failed a test, she'd
abandoned an ideal, not through disenchantment, but through funk, sheer
failure of nerve. She confessed to all this; what was it, then, that she failed
to confess? At that meeting in Warangal, Ragini stumbled, paused often
to let him in. She did not want it to be just one way. He told her very little
about himself, reluctant to speak; and yet, she saw plainly, he was anxious to
speak. At last he did. "Ragini. You should know something …"

"Is it Anand?"

She knew. Yet all she knew was one thing, that Philip meant Anand. For
some time Philip did not reply – as if to mean Anand was enough.

"Is he dead?"

"No, no, he's not dead, how can he be dead? He's safe. He's fallen into
the wrong hands."

"What hands?" she said.

"He's a prisoner. I haven't been able to get to him."

She pictured at once – Jenny retained the picture, retained all these years
while his real circumstances she never pictured – a bleak cement house,
unpainted, on the limitless blacksoil plain she thought of as Marathwada,
the Marathi-speaking portion of the Nizam's Dominions. Outside the hut
stood black-bearded Razakars in identical poses, their rifle-butts aloft. All
around were the cotton-plants, dun and misshapen and not in flower. She

knew this image was mistaken. The Razakars were gone. But whose, in free India, were 'the wrong hands'? There were no Communists in Marathwada.

"I can't find where he is," Philip said. "I've been searching for a year now."

A year. It was August, '49. In September last year, Philip told her, Anand left Hyderabad for the old Muslim capital of Bidar, to cheer in the Indian Army. He had letters of appointment from the State Congress. He set out alone and arrived in good time, while a lorryload of State Congress workers from a rival faction, with better documents, were stopped at Zaheerabad by police. All these travellers were in on a secret, an open secret. Yet Laiq Ali, who planned the defence, the Nizam and his advisers and the Commander of the Hyderabad Army, General El Edroos, had all forgotten about the road, the new-built road, which snaked in on Bidar from the south-west. The Indian Army knew of that road. It carried their tanks along the line of advance. Even Philip had been told of that road – by no less than the Chief Engineer, a guest of the Khan Bahadur at his dinner party. When Anand reached Bidar (so Philip guessed) the town was undefended. Anand would have found no soldiers, not so much as a garrison. No radio operators, no explosives experts, nothing but a supply depot in a yard though every man, woman and child in Bidar (Philip permitted himself this thought) knew the Indian Army was coming and which way it was coming. A jubilant crowd, Anand among them, streamed out of the town along the new road.

Here Philip, whose tale this was, was unable to proceed. The Army rolled in – rolled out – of Bidar, but Anand stayed. The Army rolled on, but in its wake, in the wake of the army ... Philip expressly said 'in its wake', though whether the Army had left town, or only the main body had left, he didn't know. Or where Anand 'stayed'. But since it was Anand, not the Indian Army, he was explaining to Ragini, he abandoned his order of narration and came out with the worst. Men with stakes and knives toured the bazaar, clamouring for donations and looting shops. There were deaths in Bidar, many deaths. How did Philip know? He knew because he'd followed it up, searching from pillar to post for news of Anand. And not only in Bidar – and not only when the Army passed through, or in its wake – but in Yadagir, in Gulbarga, in Aurangabad, in towns and villages where there were Muslims, hundreds, perhaps thousands, died in hand-to-hand killings, at the mercy of local *goondas*, emboldened by the sight or rumour of a victorious Indian Army. These were revenge killings. The Razakars had fumed in these villages, lording it over Hindus. But a full year since August '47, when India was divided, a year since the slaughter in the Punjab, since Muslims, Sikhs and Hindus collided as they fled both ways over the new border with Pakistan, a counterpart drama, on a much smaller scale, was enacted in Hyderabad state. Anand was in Bidar. He saw what he saw, appalled, and wrote what he saw. Philip knew he wrote it down. He took what he wrote to the State Congress at Sultan Bazaar. He handed it at last to the editorial offices of *Payam*, a defunct journal, closed down two years before by the Nizam's Government. There it tallied with other documents. For Anand was not the only witness. He was not the only Congress witness. Such testimony as his reached the *Payam* offices from many places in the Kannada- and Marathi-speaking districts. The editor was a Muslim who, because of his opposition to the Nizam, was trusted by Nehru in Delhi.

"Now Anand is in gaol? Or worse?"

"I don't know about worse. He's in gaol somewhere."

"Have you seen what he wrote?"

"Not with my own eyes."

"With whose eyes, then?" said Ragini. But this was her one rebuke to Philip.

'*I'll* look for him.' To spare Philip, who had done his best, she did not speak these words. Did she look for him? She must have – like Philip, without finding him. Philip wrote to Nehru and he had a reply, from a secretary of one of the offices, who revealed nothing – in a letter with a letterhead, approved, though not countersigned, by Nehru. How Philip treasured that correspondence, his first of many.

Did she look for him? She must have – from that moment on. From the time she met Philip. But where did she begin? She began right there. Something flashed into her mind then. Distractedly, she stared around Philip, to his right and left, plotting her escape. She fixed a new date and meeting place, and rushed to the hospital.

Were Rukku's things still there? Hadn't they been kept in a locker? – of course not. She had brought them home, to her home, her home in those days. She had sorted them, counted them herself, last October, before she took flight. She had slipped them through a near-lifeless hand, implements, clothing, jewellery. An envelope. Wasn't there his letter somewhere?

17

She stood in the kitchen of her house. Her grandson and Rhondda, who had been conversing in their usual voices, had gone quiet, as if they too were listening for something unheard, some prompt or light sound that travelled an enormous distance, that of her lifetime. There was something musical about remembering, the quest to remember. Jenny remembered. Time was furled. One time was furled within another, and another within that. You could smooth them out, but could never be sure you had come to the last furl. Her encounter in Warangal with Philip hid the time it took – days! – to find the courage, to embrace the necessity, to hoard her strength for the ride home to retrieve the letter. There her father's brothers, their wives and sons, were in residence. Nearby were the women, the women of the village, Neela and Yashoda and the others whose families had trusted her advice, had accepted her gift, had entered into the spirit of an enterprise that became their enterprise, commended by her spirit. Did she hope to avoid them? Did she think it was possible to avoid that meeting? She had abandoned them and their village. She had plunged into that cul-de-sac, the forest, at a time when others were emerging from it. What would she say to them, or they to her? Were it not for Anand's letter, would she have come this way again?

Why had she not taken up the letter while there was time? – while it lay on a table by the bed, by her sister's dead body? Or looked for it after. Why had she not looked for it after? – that one artifact of his she had, the one thing left to her? In her confusion … Jenny did not blame her confusion. She knew of more than her confusion. She knew her injustice, her wrong to Anand, the work of her confusion but a wrong that outlasted her confusion and perished only when her being ran dead, when the energies of her heart died. In Australia, these energies were reborn. With Philip or without him, she made a new being of herself. But there in India, for months on end, with all the ferocity of injustice, she had blamed Anand as she blamed her sister and her father for their desertion, the crudity of their absence. What could he have done, what did she imagine he could have done? Anand was with Congress. How could he have sided with Ragini? She had not even expected him to change, to renounce his party. Yet his place was at her side. Anand had forfeited his place. Was this what she'd believed? Was this what explained her neglect, her refusal to search for him while there was time?

She found no letter. It was lost – and Anand with his letter. Ragini gave up on the letter, but did not know yet that Anand was lost. Or was it Jenny who did not know, even now, that Anand was lost? Words of reproach, words of love – such words there must have been, scrawled by his hand, but she was not to read them. There were no last words. There was no verdict of peace, no *requiescat*: words to be pronounced when an action has ended, when a life has been rounded.

India was achieved. A nation was born and a revolution was at an end. She'd have known this sooner but, blinded by grief, she had fled, not so much to fight as to testify! – with the diehards. When in time her own life came to mean more to her than her grief, she'd forsaken that quest and those companions. Then what of Anand? His faith was in India. India came to be! – and through that fruition the faith of an activist, of a Congress worker, was tested in the fire, was transformed into the faith of a witness. Since his faith meant more to him than his life, he'd surrendered his life. Jenny sought no other verdict. If *her* cause had prevailed, her ideal would have been tested in the same way. She did not know what she'd have done, but she knew that whatever had become of Anand, his fate was willed, he was not its plaything. Nor did she believe he was dead. Anand was Anand and in no mean corner of her being, he existed for her.

18

April, 1948.

"Are these all the songs you know?"

"All I'll sing now."

"*Bhakti* songs. To a god."

"There is a god here," she said.

The temple – the platform, and the columns of the entrance hall – were becoming visible. Day was breaking. The interior, to which she pointed, was still in darkness – was forever in darkness. "*I* don't see anyone," he said.

She leaned and kissed him on the mouth. A rebuke, to begin with, her kiss altered with the light. It muddled their place and orientation and released them on soft ground facing down the path, away from the temple. She pulled free, adjusting the loosened flap of her sari. "I left my *choli* in the hut."

Anand glimpsed her bared breast. "I'll go for it."

When he returned, dangling the garment, Ragini had climbed to the platform and stood before a frieze, fingering an outline. "Village girls. You see. This is a stick-dance."

"Someone is following," he said.

The two had broken into the hut, the easiest of tasks even as the moon sank. But with dawn, the *chowkidar* had arrived. Ragini turned to gaze. The path was empty. "He's making tea," Anand said.

"Then he'll come."

A bent figure appeared, not with tea-things but with the offerings for *prasadam*, the half-coconuts, flower petals and sugar sweets. He strayed from the path, placing them under a bush somewhere. "What's he up to?" Anand said.

"This is half his job. He doubles as the *pujari*."

"You know him?"

"I know the job. I don't know this *pujari*."

"The *pujari* makes tea?"

"The *chowkidar* makes tea. The *pujari* makes prayer, but here, in this faraway place, they are the same person."

"Who am I to know?" said Anand humbly. "When have I done this?"

"You've never done this? Never prayed in a temple?"

"In our family ..."

She stared in wonder. "Even Philip has done this."

The *chowkidar* had returned to the hut. She led the way. "The most beautiful carvings are over here." She avoided the uplifted stone flags, rifts in the floor which she said were the work of Aurangzeb.

"Aurangzeb? He's blamed for everything."

"He'll be blamed for much more, you'll find out, now the Muslims have Pakistan." The sandstone columns had turned pink in the morning light. Cornices, wall-brackets, even the ceilings were intricately carved in black granite, the roof's stout beams lofted from below by the slender fingers of the dancers leaning from the columns. Ragini struck a dance pose; Anand took notice and she abandoned it at once. "My namesake is here."

"A dancer? This one with the snakes?"

"She's Nagini. Mine is Ragini. The one in high heels."

Anand compared the lithe shapes, one flesh, one stone. "So this is why you brought me," he said. "To show me her."

"I'd forgotten. I've just remembered."

"You're a very unusual Communist."

"What's 'usual'?" she said, then, after a pause, "None of them are usual. The ones I've met."

"I've heard them talk. I've met Communists. They're sworn to a party line, they watch what they say. But you don't watch what you say."

"I say very little," she said, "that's of consequence."

"Then tell me this. One thing of consequence." He saw her eyes flash, ready with her answer before the question was put. "What are you, Ragini? You appear from nowhere. You hide behind bus seats, you vanish and you reappear. You sing like a bird. You dance."

"You're too kind. I don't dance. I strike poses."

"Let me finish. You're the queen of the night, you shed perfume like that flower of the night. You're radiant like the dawn. In that hut you made love to me like Urvasi herself, one of the *apsaras* who steals away – I can't believe you won't steal away."

"They all steal away," she said. "But I'm not one of those, not an *apsara*, not even a bona fide bus passenger ... What am I? Is that what you want to know, Anand?"

"It would be of some help," he said, "to know."

She laughed, well-satisfied, with the state of affairs, with his confession of wonder. But a while later as they sat, legs folded under them, at an edge of the platform, she relented, or was moved to declare herself at last. "It's true what you say. I'm unusual for a Communist, if that's what I am. But I'm far more usual, far less remarkable as a person, just an upper-caste person, than many of the Communists I've met, or you've met. I wasn't driven to it, for one thing. I'm simply an upper-caste person, like the ones you've met. I've had a gentle upbringing. I chose this life."

"Chose what?"

"This life. If I'd grown up in Madras, I'd sing for a profession, I'd attend all the concerts in the music season. That would be my choice. But here, where I am, I'm a revolutionary on my days off. I gave away lands, that's my one noteworthy act. The Communists don't thank me, and in the eyes of the villagers, so long as my father is alive the lands are his. We've transferred title, but the villagers are hardly aware of it. They're stuck with those lands. The Indian Army will come down, and unless they grow wings, where will they go? They'll fight, or they'll lose them."

"And where will you go?"

"Oh, I can go anywhere. If I respect myself – *if* I respect myself – I'll stay and I'll fight."

"Fight whom?"

"These days, it's the Nizam."

"And you'll continue to fight," he said, "when India is one nation?"

"Oh, don't say 'continue' to fight, I haven't fought yet. Did you think I'd fought? I've ferried intelligence here and there, it's all I do. You say, when India is one nation."

"That is what I say."

"What about the small nations? All those small nations: Telugu desham is not the only one."

"Then what's missing? I see you have a nation already." Anand spoke lightly: it seemed, to her, too lightly, as if he discounted her words. But she refrained from adding to them.

"There will be one India," he said at last, "and these 'nations' will remain what they are, small nations, and part of one India. Your Telugu will still be spoken. We'll see to that."

"And the villagers will keep their lands, will you see to that? Or will the landlords ride back?"

"If the landlords ride back ..." said Anand. He stayed with the thought, but did not complete the sentence.

The *chowkidar* fetched a table and two chairs. He placed them on that part of the lawn the sun reached. A white (though stained) tablecloth, milk tea in a pot, cups with saucers, a vegetable cutlet apiece on white plates. Anand and Ragini, shivering a little, their garments still clammy with the dew in which they'd lain for too long after leaving the hut, sat opposite one another in sight of the *mandapam* where the bull Nandi crouched in everlasting worship. They forgot to wonder how Anand would return to Hyderabad. Ragini feasted her eyes; he was looking away, perhaps wrestling with his last, unspoken thought, with the landlords. Then, conscious of her look, he returned it; she expected some teasing remark, and perhaps this was what it was. "India will come," he said. Still expectant, she gave him every chance to continue, but no words followed. Anand took her hand. They gazed at one another, a long moment.

Glossary of Indian Names

Ambedkar, B.R.   eminent Dalit leader in Congress, principal
                             draftsman of the Constitution of India

Aurangzeb   the sixth Mughal emperor (r. 1658-1707),
                             titled also 'Alamgir' ('world-seizer') who
                             carried the empire to its farthest extent from
                             Delhi, far south into the Deccan

Azad, Maulana Abul Kalam eminent Muslim leader in Congress

Bahadur Yar Jung   Muslim supremacist figure in Hyderabad of
                             the 1930s

Banjara   an itinerant people or tribe, nowadays often
                             employed on construction sites; also Lambadi

Congress Party   the Indian National Congress, the party of
                             Gandhi and Nehru which guided the freedom
                             movement

El Edroos, Syed Ahmed   commander-in-chief of the Hyderabad Army
                             in 1948

Ittehad   Ittehad-ul Muslimeen: Muslim political
                             movement of Hyderabad

Kakatiya   the Hindu dynasty that ruled Warangal and
                             much of South India in medieval times

Kayastha   a learned caste from north India, below
                             Brahmans, which partly migrated to the south

Laiq Ali   last Prime Minister of Hyderabad State under
                             the Nizam's rule

Lambadi   *see* Banjara

Makhdoom Mohiuddin   an Urdu poet of Hyderabad

Mira Bai   16th-century princess of Chitoor, cherished
                             for her devotional songs to Krishna

Mo'in Nawaz Jung   Finance Minister and External Affairs
                             Minister in the Nizam's Government

Patel, Vallabhbhai   known as 'Sardar' (leader): a Congress
                             politican, authorised to secure the accession
                             of the princely states (such as Hyderabad) to
                             India

'Prince of Renouncers'	a translation of 'Tyagaraja', the composer of renowned devotional songs in Telugu (18th century)
Purandara Dasa	16th-century composer of renowned devotional songs in Telugu
Rani Rudrama Devi	a famed queen of the Kakatiya (q.v.) dynasty at Warangal (13th century)
Ravi Narayan Reddy	a landholder and Communist of Telengana who distributed his family lands to peasants early in the revolution
Razakars	Muslim storm-troopers in the last days of Hyderabad state
Razvi, Kasim	prominent figure in the Ittehad-ul Muslimeen (q.v.)
Savitri	in the epic Mahabharata, a wife whose devotion to her husband overcomes death
Shakuntala	heroine of Kalidasa's Sanskrit drama (4th or 5th century CE)
Sri Sri	a Telugu poet of revolution
Sundarayya	a notable Communist, participant in the Telengana revolution
Swami Ramananda Tirtha	chief office-holder of the Hyderabad State Congress and figurehead of the *satyagraha* movement in Hyderabad, often in gaol
Urvasi	an *apsara* (q.v.), heroine of an episode of the Rig Veda (1st millennium BCE) and of the Mahabharata, and also of a play by Kalidasa; an immortal being who is loved by Pururavas, a mortal man
Vinoba Bhave	a figure of great spiritual status (comparable to though lesser than Gandhi) who persuaded some landholders in the Telengana region to part with their lands at the end of the revolution, so initiating the 'Bhoodan' movement
Yellamma	a South Indian goddess, viewed as powerful and intimidating

Glossary of Indian Words

Indian words used are from Arabic, Hindi, Persian, Telugu and Urdu languages. Reference to language of origin is supplied only for Telugu words.

alapana	in South Indian (Karnatik) classical music, the opening, unmeasured portion
almirah	a wardrobe
amma	(Telugu) mother
ammalu	(Telugu) plural of *amma* (q.v.); used respectfully for women and girls
Angrez	English people
apsara	a graceful and immortal female being
ashram	a refuge; hermitage of a guru
'ashur-khana	a place where the floats and pennants for the Muslim Shi'a procession of 'Ashura (q.v.) are stored
'Ashura	10th day of the month of Muharram
avva	(Telugu) grandmother
badam kheer	a fabled milk sweet with almonds
badmash	ruffian
baghi	rebel
basmati	a North Indian rice variety of superior fragrance and texture
begum	honorific title for Muslim women of rank
bhajan	popular devotional singing among Hindus
bhakti	in Hindu observance, devotional religion entailing personal devotion to a god or goddess
bindi	an auspicious mark on the forehead
biryani	a famed Hyderabadi dish with rice, spices and meat as the base
chador	a headscarf
chakra	a wheel; the emperor Ashoka's sovereign emblem, displayed on the Indian flag
chappals	open-toed leather footwear; sandals
charpoy	a jute-string bed

cheruvu	(Telugu) a water tank or local dam
choli	a woman's tightly fitting upper garment
chowkidar	a watchman
churidar	a tight-fitting trouser garment
daftar	a record office; a bundle of documents
dalam	a band, file, armed column
dan	gift
darbar	a royal court; the term is also used for a major Sufi shrine
dargah	a Muslim Sufi shrine
dhal	a dish of cooked lentils, mildly spiced
dhoti	a sarong-like garment for the lower body worn by men
dora	(Telugu) landholder
dupatta	a shoulder-scarf
farman	an administrative pronouncement
firangi	foreigner; European ('Frank')
ghazi	a warrior of the Muslim frontier
gobi	cauliflower
godown	store, warehouse
goonda	ruffian
gori	fair-haired, fair-skinned; a foreigner
guli-danda	a children's game, played with two sticks, or with stick and bail
halwa	dense, sweet confection made of semolina and honey
hamsa	a mythical bird, not exactly a swan
haveli	an imposing residence; a palace
idli	a South Indian food for breakfast or tiffin, made of rice and black gram flour, fermented and ground separately and steamed together
Isha' prayer	Muslim night-time daily prayer
jagirdar	a landholder under a political settlement
jangal	wilderness (not necessarily with trees)
jumhuriyat	democracy

kamarband	a wide sash worn at the waist
khatib	a preacher who recites the *khutba* (sermon) in the Friday mosque noon-service
kili	a parrot
kirtana, kriti	two different kinds of devotional song elaborated in South Indian classical music
kolam	an auspicious ornamental pattern on the street in front of South Indian houses, renewed daily by women of the home
kotwal	a villager with a state (police) function
kriti	*see* kirtana
kumbh mela	a mass Hindu pilgrimage of faith in which Hindus gather to bathe in a sacred river
lakshan	a signifying mark
lathi	a truncheon or rod
mahasabha	assembly
mandapam	a pavilion; a consecrated structure
mandi	a market
masala	a spice mix
matka	a clay pot
maktab	a school
Muharram	Muslim Shi'a month of mourning
naubat	a trumpet; a sounding of the trumpet
naubat pavilion	an eminence at the gateway of aristocratic houses, for ceremonial drumming at entrances and exits
nawaabi	princely, noble
nawab	honorific title for a man of distinction or rank
pajama	a distinctive long-trousered garment
pan	a complex recreational preparation of betel leaf, chewed and spat out
pandit	a learned or authoritative Hindu, often a Brahmin
paratha	a delicious layered bread interleaved with ghee and baked on a griddle
patwari	a revenue official, resident in the village

payasam	a sweet dish, made from milk and vermicelli or rice
pottu	(Telugu, Tamil) *see* bindi
prasad, prasadam	in a Hindu temple, the part of an offering, or its equivalent, returned to a worshipper and charged with the power of the god or goddess
puja	Hindu ritual of worship
pujari	the Brahmin officiant in a Hindu temple
puri	a common, specialised variety of bread, different from naan or chapati
qamiz	a tunic-like upper garment, part of an ensemble
qawaid	a drill
rabi	a seasonal rice crop
raga	in Indian classical music systems, the distinctive mode or scale, and pertaining elements
raja	a king, ruler
Ramazan	Muslim month of fasting
rasika	a devotee of an aesthetic performance or mode, from the Sanskrit word for 'taste'
rawza-khan	one who prays over the dead
rukhsat	leave (n.), act of departing
sambar	a staple, highly seasoned vegetarian liquid dish with a lentil base, accompanying South Indian meals
sangam	an association or institution, literally 'meeting place'
sanyasin	a Hindu ascetic withdrawn from society
sarangi	a North Indian musical instrument, older than the violin in India
satyagraha	the policy of non-violent resistance spearheaded by Gandhi in the freedom movement
saz	a musical instrument
shahnai	a plangent instrument sounding like the oboe
suprabhatam	a dawn hymn in Sanskrit chanted to awaken the god
tabarruk	in a Sufi shrine, sweets or a gift, considered blessed and carried away by a worshipper
tabla	in North Indian classical music, the pair of tuned drums

tamasha	amusement, a show
tambura	an instrument accompanying vocals in classical music (North and South Indian)
Telugu bhasa	the Telugu language
Telugu desham	the Telugu country
thali	a plate containing a meal, typically vegetarian
thana	a police station
thumri	in North Indian music, a piece in classical style for the female voice with an explicit emotional content, made especially famous in the 20th century by some fabled singers, including Begum Akhtar
trisul	a significant, three-pointed emblem, borne on occasion by Siva or by some forms of the goddess
Ugadi	first day of the New Year in the Telugu country
vakil	a lawyer, scribe or court official
vanakili	a wild parrot
vanaspati	a staple vegetable oil
varanda	a shaded external portion of a house (in English, *verandah*)
veena	a classical musical instrument of South India, resembling the sitar but older, and deeper in tone
zamindar	a landholder

Author's Note on Places, People and Events

In this novel distances are not always realistic. It would take more than a night to travel from Warangal to Palampet on one bicycle, as Ragini and Anand do. But in all other respects I have tried to keep to the proper chronology and geography of public events, both in Australia in 2001 – events I lived through – and in Hyderabad.

I was first in Hyderabad state – formerly the Nizam's Dominions – on fieldwork for a Ph.D. from the Australian National University in 1965 and 1966. I have revisited the city and region ever since. In the 1960s and '70s I spoke often with people there who recalled local events at the time of Indian independence, events referred to in this novel.

No speaking character in the novel is based on any person in India or Australia, alive or dead. The story is imaginary. There were, so far as I know, no volunteer 'headmasters' from overseas in the rural districts.

About the Author

IAN BEDFORD is a Sydney-based writer who has lived and travelled in India, Pakistan, Iran and south Central Asia. He has worked for many years in the Anthropology Department at Macquarie University. *The Last Candles of the Night* is his fourth published novel.

Also by Ian Bedford:

The Shell of the Old (Rigby, 1981)

A View from the Bund (Rain Bazaar Press, 1990)

The Resemblance (Rain Bazar Press, 2008)

www.ingramcontent.com/pod-product-compliance
Lightning Source LLC
Chambersburg PA
CBHW020601030726
47497CB00007B/2045